THE
SILENT
WIFE

ALSO BY ANDY MASLEN

See the Dead Birds Fly

Playing the Devil's Music

Gabriel Wolfe Thrillers:

Trigger Point

Reversal of Fortune

Blind Impact

Condor

First Casualty

Fury

Rattlesnake

Minefield

No Further

Torpedo

Three Kingdoms

Ivory Nation

Crooked Shadow

Brass Vows

Seven Seconds

Peacemaker

Other Fiction:

Blood Loss – A Vampire Story

Purity Kills

You're Always With Me

Green-Eyed Mobster

THE SILENT WIFE

A DETECTIVE KAT BALLANTYNE THRILLER

ANDY MASLEN

This is a work of fiction. Names, characters, organizations, places, events, and incidents are either products of the author's imagination or are used fictitiously. Any resemblance to actual persons, living or dead, or actual events is purely coincidental.

Text copyright © 2024, Andy Maslen
All rights reserved.

No part of this book may be reproduced, or stored in a retrieval system, or transmitted in any form or by any means, electronic, mechanical, photocopying, recording, or otherwise, without express written permission of the publisher.

Published by Thomas & Mercer, Seattle

www.apub.com

Amazon, the Amazon logo, and Thomas & Mercer are trademarks of Amazon.com, Inc., or its affiliates.

ISBN-13: 9781662511264
eISBN: 9781662511271

Cover photography and design by Dom Forbes

Printed in the United States of America

In memory of Marge Kelly.

Chapter One

Women who taught four-year-olds to read didn't strangle their best friends.

But as Laura Paxton stared at Alanna's body, she had to concede that it was possible.

The police would be here soon. She'd confess. They'd arrest her. And then she'd spend the rest of her life behind bars.

From teaching assistant to convicted killer in one easy step. What would they tell the children? She laughed crazily, a cracked sound in the hard-surfaced hallway. That was hardly the biggest problem facing her right now, was it?

Dry-eyed despite the horror, she hauled herself up the cream-carpeted stairs. She felt distanced from reality. As if someone else was manipulating her sluggish limbs. Laura the murderous glove-puppet.

Her vision had telescoped to a small circle surrounded by black in which silver sparks danced like fireflies.

She found what she was looking for in the master bedroom. On Alanna's dressing table. A forest-green velvet bag with a twisted gold-silk drawstring, from which make-up spilled onto the polished oak top. Now the tears came, leaking slyly from the corners of her eyes, as if unwilling to make too much of a fuss.

She picked up and discarded several eyebrow pencils and eye-liners, careful to squeeze each between her trembling fingers.

The first lipstick she picked up was a pale pink. Not enough contrast. She dropped it to the carpet where it almost disappeared into the soft white tufts. The second was better. A bright crimson.

She nodded to herself. Swallowed a clot of tears and mucus that had gathered at the back of her throat and which was making it hard to breathe.

Navigating her way out of the bedroom, she stumbled over a pair of heels Alanna must have kicked off the previous night. She bent to inspect the label. Jimmy Choo. Gorgeous. Navy suede, three inches at least.

Keeping one hand on the wall, she walked on stiff legs to the top of the stairs. For a second, she imagined how easy – how *simple* – it would be to close her eyes and lean forward, until her centre of gravity shifted enough to take her toppling and tumbling to join Alanna at the bottom.

No. A plan was a plan.

She descended carefully, gripping the banister.

Breathing slowly, and pleased to discover that the sparkles in her eyes had almost gone – so she could control this, at least – she knelt beside her friend's dead body.

Alanna had been truly beautiful. Yes, she'd had work done. Her nose was maybe a little too thin and uptilted to look entirely natural. And her lips were plumped beyond any level Mother Nature might have bestowed on a woman, even on her most generous days. But none of that took away from the fact that Alanna's face had always radiated true inner beauty. She was kind. She was loving. And, to Laura, she had been that rarity of rarities. A really, utterly, wonderfully good friend.

Until the affair. That's what she would tell the police.

What she would tell Kat.

Laura lifted her dead friend's right eyelid. Then the left. The whites of her eyes, already curdled-looking, were spotted with tiny red flowers like distant fireworks. There was a name for it. She couldn't remember.

Will would know. But Will wasn't here. He'd gone to work.

She gripped the loose ends of the tie again. It was wound so tightly around Alanna's neck it had dug deep into the soft flesh under her jaw.

And she pulled it tighter still.

Her tears dripped on to Alanna's T-shirt, turning the coral cotton a deeper shade. Like really good-quality salmon fillets. The sockeye kind Will loved her to fry with a little butter and fresh dill. Not that awful flabby, fatty, farmed stuff. She shook her head violently. Why was she thinking of fish? She had work to do.

Laura dragged her fists outwards until the ends of the tie flopped free to lie on each side of Alanna's neck. The bruising, a livid purple, was spreading beyond the twisted rope of fabric.

Petechiae! That was it.

Not these bruises. They were called *contusions.* Petechiae were the ones that had flowered on Alanna's corneas when she was gasping for breath.

Laura nodded decisively. Little joints popped inside her neck.

She opened the lipstick and placed the lid on the hall floor. Big, square tiles; white granite with silver flakes in them that twinkled in the purple-white light from the halogen downlighters.

Holding the silver barrel in her left hand, she twisted the base to propel the waxy crimson bullet out of its hidey-hole.

Then she stretched out her right hand. In crude capitals she scraped a word across Alanna's Botoxed forehead.

C . . .

Finished, she raised the blunt chisel tip to her own mouth and gently rubbed it over her own lips.

She placed the lipstick on Alanna's chest.

Raising Alanna's hand in hers, she admired the perfect manicure. Long nails, beautifully shaped and tipped in sparkling green polish.

She sighed. So tidy. Unlike her own, bitten to the quick.

Chapter Two

Two days earlier

She woke at 3.00 a.m., a shouted accusation echoing in her sleep-addled brain.

You're dirty, DS Ballantyne.

The voice belonged to Kat's perpetually smirking boss, DI Stuart Carver.

He'd slapped the charge on her at a surprise meeting to which he'd invited a stone-faced DI from 3C-ACU, the Three Counties Anti-Corruption Unit. Their unofficial motto, *Banging up dirty cops in Hertfordshire, Bedfordshire and Buckinghamshire.* Hated and feared in equal measure.

Kat tried to think of something else.

Next week's meals. Her current caseload. The names of her sixth-form classmates, arranged in reverse alphabetical order.

But it was no good. Every time she let her mind stray from whatever narrow path she'd set it on, it circled back, like a crow to fresh roadkill, to that dreadful, hated word.

Even though she was innocent, she felt stained to her core by Carve-up's accusation. The fact it had been made by possibly the dirtiest cop in Jubilee Place police station, if not the whole of Middlehampton, had ground the muck in deeper.

She'd told Van the previous evening. He'd been shocked, then indignant, then angry.

'You're being set up!'

Reassured that he, at least, believed her, she'd consumed a bottle of wine with dinner, plus a gin and tonic afterwards. The alcohol had knocked her out, but now she lay awake and hyper-alert. Stomach roiling, skin clammy, on the verge of a full-blown panic attack.

After lying awake for an hour, trying and failing to calm herself with breathing exercises, she slid from the bed. Leaving Van snoring, she went downstairs to make tea. Her year-old cairn terrier Smokey raised his head for a few seconds and looked at her as if winking. A puppyhood seizure had left his right eyelid droopy.

'Far too early, Smokes, go back to sleep.'

As the dog snuffled in his sleep, she clutched the mug of tea until it burned her palms. She released it with a hiss.

This was bad. *Beyond* bad. This was catastrophic.

Her career as a homicide detective was about to go up in smoke. Hell, she could even end up facing criminal charges. *Unless* she could explain the fifty grand that had appeared in her current account out of nowhere.

Despite the time, she considered calling Liv. Her best friend would drop everything and come tearing over from Wales full of fire and fury, eager to ream out whoever was gunning for Kat.

But their complicated relationship gave her pause.

Liv had disappeared just after her eighteenth birthday, presumed murdered by a serial killer. Only, that had turned out to be a false alarm. Believing the manager of the children's home she'd just left was the killer, Liv had faked her own death and fled to a commune in the Welsh countryside. When the murders had restarted after a fifteen-year gap, Liv had come back to Middlehampton. She'd appeared like a ghost in the street, waiting for Kat to notice her.

They were rebuilding their relationship, but it was definitely a work in progress. Involving Liv might cause more problems.

Kat stood, suddenly, rousing Smokey a second time. No. This was not going to happen. She was a detective. So she'd *detect* it. She had no choice.

And she knew exactly where she'd start. Because there was one man she knew who had that kind of cash. One man who had all kinds of connections in the town, from politicians to police officers. One man whose devious mind made Machiavelli look like a kids' TV presenter.

Anger and fear churned up her insides.

Was Colin Morton – Middlehampton's biggest property developer, and her own father – really trying to get her kicked off the force by cooking up a corruption sting? Why the hell would he do that?

He was in thick with Carve-up. They played golf together regularly, and she, among others, suspected he was the source of much of Carve-up's disposable income. It would explain the swaggering DI's extensive collection of designer suits. And the flashy red Alfa Romeo he'd bought just weeks after his divorce came through.

She and her dad had reached a tacit if uneasy agreement that just about maintained the peace. Provided he got involved in nothing worse than financial irregularities connected with his property firm, she could – more or less in good conscience – leave him alone, her job being homicide investigations. But then, during her last case, she'd discovered that the first victim had been her half-sister. Now, expecting her to leave her father alone was like asking a child not to pick a scab.

Having her suspended, possibly busted back to DC or sent somewhere she could do him no harm, would be the nuclear option. But men like Colin Morton weren't afraid to slam a soft palm down on the big red button. Especially when their fortunes were at stake.

She'd kept her side of the unholy bargain easily, since a discreet enquiry had led her to understand that while he was on Fraud's radar, so far there was nothing concrete they could hit him with.

Kat had suggested a paving slab. The fraud officer's answering laugh had been genuine, if world-weary.

So what had changed? Had her dad grown fearful she'd start passing information on to her colleagues in the fraud squad? Or look into her half-sister's childhood and his role in it? Or was there something else? Something worse?

Chapter Three

As Kat walked Smokey round the farm that bordered their village on the outskirts of Middlehampton, she tried to stay calm. She didn't want to worry Riley, who'd volunteered to come out with her and the dog.

Her anxiety mounted. What if he found out anyway? What if that bastard Carve-up told him? She wouldn't put it past him.

Even though the accusation wasn't true, Riley would never see her the same way again. Never fully trust her. And just as he was entering adolescence, too. It would drive a wedge between them she might never be able to remove.

'What's the matter, Mum?'

Riley, just thirteen and wise beyond his years, was looking at her with concern on his smooth-skinned face. No trace of stubble yet, even though his voice had been swooping and diving recently like a skylark over the fields.

Kat swallowed. 'Oh, it's nothing, sweetheart. Just a work thing.'

'A case, you mean?'

'Not a case. A personnel thing.'

'But what? Tell me.'

Then he did something that surprised her. He reached out his right hand and took her left. With a soft tug, he brought her to a halt. While Smokey roamed in the hedgerow, sniffing

9

out other dogs' 'pee-mails', Kat found herself standing face to face with her son.

'Honestly, darling, it's nothing.' She looked away, to the horizon. Rooks flapping untidily in the trees. She touched her throat, suddenly feeling hot. 'It's just . . . it's just something I need to sort out at work. A misunderstanding, that's all.'

He scowled. The emotional weather changing like a summer storm.

'I'm not a baby, Mum. I always know when you're lying. You won't look me in the eye and your neck blushes.'

Damn! Caught out by a teenage forensic psychologist.

'I might be in a bit of trouble. But I didn't do anything wrong, OK? I want you to know that.'

He stuck his fists on his hips.

'What *kind* of trouble?'

'Riley, I—'

'Just tell me, OK? You have to.' He touched her again – this time on the shoulder, and she thought she might cry with the tenderness of the gesture. 'It's like what you always say to me. "Whatever you've done, I'll always love you."'

Tears pricking her eyes, she met Riley's questioning gaze.

Should she tell him or not? How would he react to the news she was being investigated by Anti-Corruption? Would he lose his faith in her? Would he retreat from her, placing all his emotions in trust with his dad?

She remembered the pain as she'd brought him out of her body. The tears and then the joy as that puckered red face with its shock of black hair had come into focus. He was her son. Maybe she owed him the truth.

She inhaled. Held on to the memory of that first moment in his life, when she'd been the centre of his entire universe. Spoke on the out-breath, pulling back from a full confession as her lips parted.

'It's a money thing.'

He frowned. 'Like what?'

'Like someone sent a lot of money to my bank account and now my idiot boss—'

'Carve-up or Ma-Linda?'

Kat grinned, out of nerves as much as anything else. She'd shared her bosses' nicknames with Riley earlier in the year, and now he delighted in using them whenever he got the chance.

'Carve-up. He's saying I've got it from someone I shouldn't have. If I can't find out where it came from, I'm going to be in trouble.'

Riley's eyes widened and his voice dripped with contempt.

'He's accusing you of corruption? You're like the best cop in the whole of Middlehampton. Probably England.'

Kat smiled at Riley's blind faith in her. If he trusted her, maybe others would, too. She would fight this thing. Fight it and win. The knot of tension in her stomach began to unwind. She was *not* a dirty cop. And she was going to prove it. Not just to her son but to everyone.

'Where did you learn about corruption?' she asked.

Riley rolled his eyes, only a five on a scale that ran all the way to a million.

'Er, hello? The internet? Plus, I don't know if you've heard the news recently, but corruption is like destroying the public's faith in the police. Especially in the Met.'

Kat laughed. 'You sound like some late-night discussion programme.'

Frowning, Riley swept his floppy fringe back from his forehead. 'I heard it on this podcast.'

Kat's heart sank. It could only be one. She'd gone to school with its host, Ethan Metcalfe. He'd had a crush on her back then – strictly one-way. And he'd recently started acting decidedly weirdly around her. A borderline stalker.

'Which one was that? Maybe I've heard of it.'

'*Home Counties Homicide.* The guy who hosts it is a bit of a loser, but he did this whole episode about the Met and how bad they are. We did it in PSHE.'

Personal, social, health and economic education. That was the full name. From Riley's sporadic reports, it covered everything from sex and relationships to volunteering and voting. Interesting that whoever was running the lessons now took in law and order. Mind you, with the number of Met officers going up before the courts for sexual assault, sharing crime scene photos and God knew what else, maybe it wasn't such a bad idea. Still, Kat felt a residual need to defend her colleagues. The good ones, at least.

'Fair enough. There are some bad men working as police officers.'

Riley's lower jaw dropped. '*Some?*'

'OK, quite a few. But that doesn't mean every police officer is bad. In my station, Tom and Leah are good. Craig. Molly. Darcy. Linda, obviously. They're fantastic cops.'

Riley looked at her, askance. 'Yeah, but what about Carve-up? Is *he* good?'

'Carve-up is a special case.'

'Told you.' He paused to throw a stick for Smokey, who raced off, yelping with joy as it whirled high overhead and into the drying barley. 'Grandpa's rich. I bet he sent it to you. He probably wanted to surprise you.'

Kat nodded. Said nothing. Maybe Grandpa wanted to do a lot more than that.

♦ ♦ ♦

Leaving Riley curled up on a garden swing seat reading a comic book, with Smokey nestled against his side on a folded blanket, Kat called her parents' house. While she listened to the phone ring, Van came into the kitchen and hefted two carrier bags of groceries on to the table.

She smiled up at him and accepted the hungry kiss he bestowed on her lips. Something had got into him recently. Maybe it was their recent argument about a female client of his with whom Kat had mistakenly thought he was having an affair. Slapping his roaming hands away, she sat straighter as her mother picked up the phone.

'Morton residence.'

Why did she do it? Sarah Morton née Crabbe came from solid working-class Middlehampton stock and had grown up on a council estate. But ever since Kat had been old enough to notice such things, her mother had had these affectations she presumably thought gave her a more sophisticated air.

She referred to her husband as 'Daddy' when talking to her three children.

She also called the loo the 'little girls' room', which made Kat shudder.

And called having people round for dinner 'a little supper party'.

'Hi, Mum. Is Dad there?'

'Oh, hello, Kat darling. How are you?'

I'm facing a corruption charge I'm starting to think Dad might have cooked up with my bent boss.

'Fine, Mum. Is he?'

'And Ivan?'

Kat sighed. 'Yep, good. Riley is, too. And Smokey.'

'No need to snap, darling. You may not have heard, but some daughters manage to have perfectly civilised conversations with their mothers. Diana, for example. Did you know she's opening a new office in Milton Keynes?'

'I didn't. Who knew there were so many dodgy businesses in the Home Counties that needed accountants?'

'Oh, Kat, for goodness' sake! Diana's business is perfectly above board. She even does Daddy's accounts.'

Kat bit back the obvious rejoinder. *Exactly!* Then shivered as an unwelcome thought crossed her mind. What if Diana was involved, too? After all, who would know better than a company's accountant how to move money around without leaving a trail?

She made a mental note to call Diana later. She'd need to tread carefully, though. Diana could be prickly about her clients.

'Look, I really need to talk to Dad.'

'Well, he's playing golf at the moment. But he promised me he'd be back for lunch. Why don't you join us? Bring Van and Riley, too. It's been simply ages since we all got together. Do say yes. We'll have a dining room picnic. Riley would love that, wouldn't he? I remember Nathan—'

'Yes! OK, Mum, yes. We'd love to. What time?'

Having agreed to arrive at 'one sharp', Kat went to find her boys and give them the good news.

Riley was delighted. Kat experienced a pang of guilt. Her mum might be a faux-ditsy society girl these days, but she did love her grandson and she was right about the picnic.

For all his sins, her dad genuinely loved Riley too. They enjoyed a whole set of grandpa-grandson jokes, games and silly routines that not just she, but also Van, was excluded from. It was one of the reasons she strove to keep things on a civil footing with her dad.

Whatever her feelings about him, she didn't want to deny Riley a relationship with his grandpa.

Van, on the other hand, was resigned. Colin would, as usual, try to talk him into investing in one of his developments. Having neither the spare cash nor the inclination, Van would then have to spend most of the visit fending off his father-in-law's offers of financial assistance.

At 12.40 p.m. they set off, Smokey snug in the loadspace of Van's Skoda estate, Riley already speculating about what sort of cake his grandma might provide.

Kat's stomach had shrunk to the size of a golf ball.

Chapter Four

Despite Kat's misgivings, the lunch was going well.

Colin Morton had – so far – managed not to pitch his latest venture to Van, who was talking to his father-in-law animatedly about Middlehampton FC.

Sarah Morton had dressed for the occasion in a floral-print Liberty tea dress. She was pressing Riley to have ever-greater slices of Black Forest gateau, which he was hoovering up, eyes sugar-drugged, as if Kat didn't feed him.

Kat nibbled at a tiny triangular cucumber sandwich and gamely swooped a couple of carrot sticks through a bowl of hummus. But her anxiety about confronting her father had clamped handcuffs round her appetite.

Sarah Morton was too busy chattering about Diana's new office to notice her younger daughter's nervousness.

'Of course, it means children will be off the agenda for another year, but she and Eamonn still have plenty of time. I just hope they don't leave it too long. One rather loves the thought of another grandchild. There's Nathan, obviously, but he's far too young, although he does have a new girlfriend. Her name's Kristeena.' She sniffed. 'With a K and two Es. Apparently.'

Just as Kat thought she might scream with frustration, her dad got to his feet and headed indoors. Kat excused herself, leaving her mum tutting before summoning Van to join her with a coquettishly crooked finger.

She'd thought her dad had been heading for the downstairs cloakroom, but he was crossing the vast drawing room in the direction of his study. Perfect.

'Dad! Wait.'

He turned, a flash of irritation on his smooth-shaven and tanned face hastily replaced with a smile. It didn't fool Kat.

'What is it, Kitty-Kat?'

'Can I have a word? In private?'

'I was just going to make a couple of calls, but they can wait. Join me?'

She followed him in, inhaling the clubroom scent of cigar smoke, her dad's Aramis aftershave, and expensive Italian leather. He closed the door behind her. For a second, she felt a twinge of fear. As if she'd been trapped with someone very dangerous.

Half expecting him to turn a key in the lock, she smiled with relief as he simply rounded his desk to sit in the swivel chair, its swollen and pleated oxblood upholstery reminding her unpleasantly of human flesh. She chided herself for letting her imagination run away with her.

He interlaced his fingers. A thin blade of sunlight sliced through the dusty air and caught the fat signet ring on his right hand. The slab of garnet grooved with his initials glowed like blood. A mafia don couldn't have emanated a more complete image of power.

Kat swallowed. How should she start? Her dad showed no inclination to help her out. He simply sat facing her, waiting. He'd make a pretty good interviewer, she thought.

Oh, God. What if she was wrong? What if it was nothing to do with him? After all, she had no evidence. Just a 3.00 a.m. nightmare and its bastard offspring – unfounded suspicion. She swerved the question she'd been about to ask him, fearful she'd torpedo their delicate truce and undo all the work she'd put in smoothing the path for Riley and his grandpa.

'How's business?' she asked, heart pounding, shoving all her suspicions behind a hastily built dam in her head.

He shrugged minutely. 'Oh, you know. Good, could be better. The usual.'

Bribed any council officials recently? That was one for the imaginary conversation. The one where she told him what she really thought about his business methods.

'Much spare cash kicking around in the account?'

His neatly groomed salt-and-pepper eyebrows drew together by several millimetres.

'I don't follow.'

It was no good. The dam wouldn't hold. 'Did you sent fifty grand to my bank account, Dad?' she blurted. 'Because Stuart Carver thinks I'm on the take and you're the only person I know with that kind of money.' Her pulse was thumping in her ears and her palms were slippery with sweat. 'Are you trying to get me booted off the force because of your affair with Tasha Starling? Because that would make me more likely to tell Mum, not less.'

He recoiled physically, unclasping his hands and slapping them on to the bottle-green leather insert in front of him. His eyes snapped open, flashing clear white around the irises. His reaction produced an unusual reaction in her. Trust.

'Kat, I swear to you, wherever this money came from, it wasn't from me. We've had our little arguments about ethics. But that's just father-daughter stuff. I know that. You don't mean anything by it.' He leaned forward, across the desk. The look in his eyes was beseeching. She strained to detect even a sliver of deception. Found none. 'I know you won't believe this, but I am – Mum and I both are, I mean – genuinely proud of you. Catching murderers? Well, it was never something we imagined you'd do after that jaunt you took around the world. But you're good at it, Kat. Bloody good.'

Making this speech seemed to have exhausted him. He slumped against the meaty backrest and dragged a pink silk pocket square from his blazer. He wiped his forehead, inspected the scrap of fabric and stuffed it back into the display pocket.

Kat wasn't done yet. And she hadn't missed his glib reference to 'father-daughter stuff'. But this wasn't the time to get into her true feelings about his relationships with the people who pulled the levers of power in Middlehampton. Or the former business partners on whom he'd fathered children.

'It came from a Swiss bank account. I don't suppose you have one of those, do you?'

He shook his head. But there! She caught it. The slip she'd known would come if she pushed hard enough.

His eyes flicked over to a painting of huntsmen in red jackets, a pack of beagles racing ahead. Behind the all-too-predictable artwork was a safe. She'd discovered it as a teenager when she'd sneaked into her father's office looking for booze.

Somewhere beyond the painted and varnished canvas and the thick steel-plate door it concealed would lie a notebook, or a set of documents, or a phone. Something that held the secrets to Morton Land's convoluted finances.

His eyes were back on Kat's now. But she could see it. The insight stretched between them like a single strand of silk pulled loose from his sweat-dampened pocket square. He was lying. She knew it. And he knew she knew.

'I didn't send the money, Kat. You have to believe me.'

She glared at him, but the heat was leaving her. She felt nauseous suddenly, as her stomach unclenched.

Even if he did have a Swiss bank account, what did that prove? If a DC like her fast-track bagman, Tom Gray, came to her with a theory like that, she'd tear them a new one. All in the cause of continuous professional development, obviously.

'You swear you didn't transfer fifty thousand pounds from a Swiss bank to my account, Dad?'

He smiled. Relieved he'd gained the upper hand, it looked like. Maybe she was being harsh. She had just accused him of trying to sabotage her career, after all.

He placed his right hand over his heart. 'On my grandchild's life.' He sighed loudly. 'Look, Kat, I'm sorry you're in trouble at work, but you have to believe me, I don't know where that money came from. Quite honestly, if I did have a spare fifty K knocking around, I'd use it for the deal I'm working on. I could do with a slightly softer cushion, if you know what I mean.'

Kat didn't. Not precisely. The inner workings of her dad's business, of the property business in general, fell way outside her field of expertise. Not to mention her interest.

But there was someone Kat knew for whom complex financial structures were as seductive as the juiciest of homicides. She'd call her first thing on Monday morning.

Chapter Five

Kat was first in at work on Monday morning. Before anyone else arrived, she called a forensic accountant she'd worked with a couple of times while on rotation with the fraud squad.

After speaking to Iris, who agreed immediately to help – *It might be rather fun* – Kat leaned back, eyes closed, enjoying the sensation of relief. Someone was on her side. Yes, Van and Riley had her back emotionally, but Iris was a professional. If anyone could pull her chestnuts out of the fire, Iris could.

The man responsible for shoving them into the flames in the first place sauntered over to her desk. Kat couldn't decide which was blaring the loudest, Carve-up's latest aftershave or the fuchsia lining of his suit jacket.

'Morning, DS Ballantyne. Who was that, an outplacement consultant?' His smirk widened. 'Seriously though, I need to see you in my office.'

She followed him through MCU, her colleagues offering her looks of, variously, sympathy, amusement and, in one case, open contempt. Her cheeks heated up. *Dirty cop.* You might as well wander down Middlehampton High Street on a Saturday night wearing a sign reading *I'm a paedo*.

'What is it, Stu?' she asked, not bothering to take the seat he waved at.

'You're off the Hartsbury murder.'

'What? Why? I was duty DS when the call came in.'

'You were also not under investigation by 3C-ACU at the time.'

Kat folded her arms, knowing it was a defensive posture. Damning her own instinctive response. 'Yeah, well, whose fault is that? And you still haven't told me how you knew about the money in my account.'

Carve-up tapped the side of his nose. 'Never you mind. Let's just say, despite being a senior manager at this station, DS Ballantyne, I do still retain a modicum of investigative skill.'

Kat glared at him. 'Modicum' was about right. Carve-up had mastered the techniques of greasy-pole climbing so effectively it was a miracle the stains didn't show on his suit trousers.

One of these techniques was never to shine too brightly as an investigator. The brass were reluctant to promote the best thief-takers. They preferred to leave them in place where they could improve the 'metrics': Kat's most hated word in all of policing.

'If I'm not on the Hartsbury murder, what do you want me to do instead? Filing?'

Carve-up's patronising smile widened still further. 'Don't be silly, DS Ballantyne. You're a valuable resource. Just. Why not take a look at a couple of cold cases? You know, blow on the embers a little. See if anything catches light.'

Kat visualised Carve-up shrieking in the centre of an inferno.

He frowned. 'Something funny?'

Kat shook her head. 'Cold cases. Fine. Thanks, Stu.'

She turned on her heel and left.

Carve-up had a parting shot ready. 'That means desk duty, Kitty-Kat. The only time you set foot outside the station is when you go home or under supervision of a senior officer. Mind you, now you're a rich woman, you'll probably be thinking of taking early retirement, won't you?'

Unbelievable. He was mocking her. He knew more than he was letting on. After all, he'd got wind of the mystery money before she had. Someone must have tipped him off. But if not her dad, then who?

Fighting down the urge to confront him over his involvement, she kept walking.

'Close the door behind you.'

She left it wide open.

Halfway across MCU, Kat's mobile rang. It was Annie Brewster, DCI Linda Ockenden's secretary. Kat was wanted in the boss's office immediately.

Kat desperately wanted to visit the ladies; her guts had turned to water. But in the current situation, she felt keeping the Head of Crime waiting would be less than wise, to put it mildly.

With Carve-up's insults echoing in her head, she made her way to Linda's office.

Linda didn't smile when Kat sat in the visitors' chair.

'What the f—' Linda began, then compressed her lips tight enough to groove vertical lines through the plum-red lipstick. She stared at Kat over a pair of reading glasses. 'What happened, Kat?'

'Honestly, Ma—' Kat stopped herself, as the Head of Crime had done a moment earlier. 'Linda, I have no idea where it came from. But I'm investigating. I'll have an answer for you in a week.'

Linda's finely curved eyebrows elevated. '*You're* investigating. Oh, well, that's a relief. You see, *I* thought it was only 3C-AC-bloody-U who were crawling all over the finances of one of my team.'

Kat felt close to tears. It was so unfair. She'd never taken so much as a free drink in her eleven years as a cop. How could Linda imagine, even for a second, that she'd suddenly flip-flop and take a fifty-K bung?'

'I'm not dirty!' she squawked, her cracking voice sounding, to her own ears at least, uncomfortably like Riley's.

Linda patted the air. 'Of course you're not, you silly mare! Someone's obviously got it in for you and I think we both know which designer-suited copper is *el primo* suspect, don't we?'

Kat's lips pursed. 'St—'

Linda held up a hand. 'No! Don't say it! There will not be a conversation in this office where a senior detective is named aloud as being involved in a conspiracy to have another sacked.'

'Sorry, Linda, but if you think I'm clean, why *am* I here?'

Linda's finely plucked eyebrows arched. 'Jesus, Kat, do I have to spell it out for you? One of my officers is facing a serious disciplinary investigation by Anti-Corruption. That's a massive deal. Did you think I'd just pat you on the head and tell you not to worry? That it was probably all a big mistake by your bank? This is serious, Kat. Whether you're as dirty as the smokers' alley behind the station or as pure as the driven snow, I have to follow protocols. So, here's what's going to happen. One, you're on desk duty. I believe DI Carver has already told you as much, yes?'

'Yes.'

'Two, you've got a week to produce a reasonable account of the money. Three, if you can't, I'll be placing you on administrative leave while 3C-ACU do their thing.' Linda sighed, her chest rising and falling. 'Kat, you know this isn't looking good for you. If you can't satisfy their investigators, you'll be facing criminal charges as well as disciplinary proceedings. Do I need to spell out the consequences?'

'No, ma'am,' Kat whispered, visualising the inside of a cell and her name splashed over the front page of the Middlehampton *Echo*. Oh, Jesus, the looks on Van's and Riley's faces.

Linda's expression softened.

'Good. Because I have spent a considerable amount of my goodwill with the Undertaker keeping your career out of a coffin.'

Kat swallowed down a lump in her throat the size of an avocado stone. For Linda to have gone to bat for her with Detective Superintendent David Deerfield showed so much faith, she felt a momentary pang of doubt that she'd be able to repay it. She squashed the thought down. Iris would come good. Carve-up would be exposed and, hopefully, disciplined himself. And Kat would be back on active cases.

Once Linda had dismissed her, Kat made her way back to her desk. Now that she'd engaged Iris, she realised she ought to be consulting other professionals who might be able to help her. The first person she called was eating his lunch nearby. Perfect.

She logged out of her PC and headed for the stairs. Carve-up had told her to stay inside the station, but surely a body was allowed a breath of fresh air?

Chapter Six

Three hundred yards from Jubilee Place lay a tiny park, squashed in between a backstreet, the offices of a firm of solicitors and the loading bays for a parade of shops.

Few people knew of its existence. Fewer still stopped there. Probably because of the rank-smelling winos who congregated in its leafy environs to chat, drink and catcall the odd passing female.

Kat walked straight to the park. *Could* she lose her job? Just because she couldn't explain the money didn't mean it was illegally obtained, did it? She groaned quietly. Because legalistic niceties like that didn't matter, did they? Linda had made the consequences vividly clear.

Christ! This was bad.

She felt sick.

Thankfully, when she arrived, the winos were absent, though the smell of their super-strength lager persisted.

The lawyer she'd called, a criminal defence solicitor, was sitting on a mossy bench, reading some papers.

She and Ben Short had met in interview rooms over the years. He'd always struck her as someone who played fair. Although the nature of his job meant he was always representing people Kat and her colleagues believed to be guilty, he seemed to avoid the kind of sharply dressed clients who had their briefs on speed dial.

She joined him on the bench and sighed loudly, dropping her head down over her knees. He turned to her, placing the papers in his briefcase.

'What's up, Kat? Why the cloak-and-dagger stuff?'

She snatched a breath, butterflies flittering around in her belly. 'I need some advice.'

He grinned. 'Welcome to my conference room.'

She tried to reciprocate the smile, but her nerves got the better of her and the expression got caught behind her teeth.

'This is a bit awkward. But I need to ask you about police corruption.'

'Anyone I know?'

'Confidentially?'

He put his hand over his heart. 'Always.'

'Well, then. Confidentially, it's me.'

If he was shocked, he didn't show it. Maybe he was too used to dealing with the worst of people to be surprised.

'Go on.'

She inhaled deeply. Rattled off the facts on the out-breath.

'Right.'

He sounded doubtful. Not suspicious. Not yet. But definitely doubtful.

'I'm not dirty!' she blurted. 'But I can't explain it. I've got someone looking into it, but I only have a week before I get the book thrown at me and I need to know what my options are.'

'We'll proceed from the fact that you are innocent.' He paused. 'As indeed are all my clients when I agree to represent them.'

The two law enforcement professionals shared a wry smile. Both knew the opposite was often the case.

Ben continued. 'For the charge of bribery to be proven, the money in your account *on its own* is not enough. It's not a crime to have an anonymous benefactor, however unusual it may be. The

Crown must show that the source was a person who had something to gain from paying the officer. An organised crime group, for example.'

'A transaction, basically.'

'Basically.'

A sudden surge of optimism seized Kat. Her spirits lifted like a hot-air balloon getting a burst of burning gas.

'But I know for a fact I haven't taken money from *anyone*, OCG or otherwise.'

Ben shrugged. 'That's the good news, then. You're innocent, and without any evidence to the contrary, the Crown would fail. In fact it might not even get to court, given the lack of evidence of wrongdoing on your part.'

Kat frowned. The balloon carrying her hopes drifted into a bank of cold air and started sinking.

'There's bad news?'

'Well, obviously. We've just talked about a criminal prosecution. The burden of proof in police disciplinary proceedings is at the civil level.'

'On the balance of probabilities.'

He nodded. 'The panel might decide, for all kinds of reasons – not least the fear of bad publicity – to make an example out of you. That's a big hit right there. Your reputation's flushed. And if it *did* go to court, you're going to be reported in the media as an officer fired for corruption now facing bribery charges. By the time you're acquitted, the damage has been done.'

The tears that Kat had been holding back since Iris had called overspilled now. 'Oh God, Ben. I'm so sorry,' she said as snot and salt water clotted her throat.

'Don't be,' he said, producing a handkerchief from his display pocket. 'You've been dealt a crap hand. I'm not surprised it's getting to you.'

She took the handkerchief and blew her nose. Rather than handing it back she pocketed it. 'I'll wash it and bring it back to you.'

He smiled easily. 'Keep it. I've loads more. My wife thinks they make me look sharp in court.'

'What shall I do, Ben?'

'In my professional opinion, nothing right now. You said you've got someone investigating. A forensic accountant?'

'Yes.'

'That's your best bet for now. Let them do their job.'

'But I can't do nothing! Suppose she can't find anything?'

Ben looked genuinely troubled. 'If you want legal representation, I'd be happy to help.'

Kat nodded. Resigned. She'd been half hoping Ben would inform her of some devastating legal strategy she could employ to make everything go away. Some hope!

She rose from the damp wooden slats, brushing moss from her bottom.

'Thanks, Ben. In the nicest possible way, I hope I don't see you soon.'

He smiled. 'I'm here most lunchtimes with my sandwich if you need to chat.'

'Winos don't bother you?'

He shrugged. 'We're all God's creatures. Besides, they might need me one day.'

'Please tell me you're joking.'

He favoured her with an inscrutable smile.

Chapter Seven

Back at her desk, Kat propped her chin in her hands. Noticing Carve-up looking in her direction, she snapped her head back up and loaded a cold-case search screen.

She was going to teach him what a *real* investigator did with their time.

Tom sidled up to her desk, glancing over his shoulder at Carve-up.

'Hey, Tomski. You've heard, I take it?'

He answered stiffly, no sympathetic smile. 'I have, actually.'

'That's it?'

'What do you want me to say, Kat?'

'Well, "Sorry you're being fitted up, guv," would be a start.'

'That's not what Stuart says.'

Kat's stomach rolled over. No use of Carve-up's station-wide nickname? Had Tom switched his allegiance so quickly?

'You don't seriously think I'm dirty, do you, Tomski?'

He squared his shoulders. Sniffed, prissily. 'I think I'd prefer you call me Tom.'

'OK, *Tom*. Well, the fact is, I am no more a dirty cop than you are. Linda's given me time to prove it. Until then, I'm innocent of everything "Stuart"' – air quotes – 'is saying about me. And I'd thank you to treat me accordingly.'

The muscles in her chest were as tight as one of those bloody bulletproof vests designed in the days when the cops wearing them didn't have breasts. Why the hell were they squaring off like this? Each standing on their dignity, as if the one who could build the taller plinth would win this stupid argument?

'Look, Tom, I get it. You're my bagman, and now I'm tainted. You're on the fast track and you're worried your association with me could damage your prospects. But can't you even give me the benefit of the doubt?'

Tom relaxed his posture a little. Put his weight on one hip. He unfolded his arms. It was going to be all right.

'Maybe you are. But Stuart has ordered me to steer clear. I'm reporting directly to him while you're under investigation. I'm sorry, Kat.'

She stared at his back as he retreated to his desk and made a great play of staring intently at his monitor. This couldn't be happening. One by one, the people she'd thought she could trust were turning away from her.

Fine. Then it was down to her to survive. She'd done it once, when she'd thought Liv had been murdered by a serial killer. She could do it again.

Chapter Eight

Kat's phone rang, making her jump. One of the girls from her netball team. No sense in letting it go to voicemail. It wasn't as if she had anything pressing to deal with.

'Hey, Laura. How are you?' Kat asked, trying to smile her way into a better mood. 'Good match last week, wasn't it? That goal you—'

'She's dead, Kat. I killed her.' Laura's voice cracked. 'I strangled her and now she's right here. Dead.'

Kat straightened in her chair. Friends called to arrange drinks or discuss netball games, not confess to murder.

'Hold on, Laura. I'm not sure I got that. Can you repeat it?'

'I've just killed a woman. I mean I've murdered her. Her name is Alanna Michie, and she lives at 17 Chamberlayne Avenue in Northbridge. Can you come, please?'

Kat's pulse was bumping in her throat. But her brain clicked over into the calm, detail-oriented mode that always accompanied a death-call. Emotions could wait. Something about the dead woman's name was scratching a fingernail over a soft, sensitive part of her brain, but she couldn't place it.

'Laura, I need to ask you one question, all right? And you have to answer me completely and utterly truthfully. Is this some kind of a prank? A wind-up?'

She hoped it was. In bad taste, sure. But even poorly thought-out jokes did no lasting damage. But something in her friend's tone of voice was sending a strident signal that said this was no laughing matter. And in all honesty? Laura wasn't the pranking kind.

'I strangled her with a tie, Kat. And I've' – she snatched a breath that hissed in Kat's ear – 'interfered with the body.'

Kat's imagination leapt into high gear, picturing the worst one human being could do to another. Other crime scenes, autopsy photos, textbook images with cold, dispassionate captions.

'Listen to me, Laura. I want you to stay there. Do not leave. Do not touch anything. Else,' she added. She checked Carve-up's office door. Closed, as usual. Tom was bent over his keyboard, bashing out a report for his new boss, no doubt. 'I'll be there in fifteen minutes, tops,' she murmured.

She got to her feet and sauntered towards DC Leah Hooper's desk. Her former bagwoman looked up and smiled. 'Everything all right?'

'Oh, you know, tippy-top. Just the odd corruption charge hanging over me and Tom giving me the evils, but I've had worse.'

'I believe in you, mate. You'll beat it.'

Relief washed over Kat. 'Thanks, Leah. Look, Carve-up's enforcing my own personal lockdown but there's something I really need to do outside. Can you cover for me if he asks where I am? Say you think I went down to the Exhibits Room.'

Leah grinned. 'Of course. He'd never risk grubbing up his suit down there.'

Kat shrugged. 'If he does, I'll just tell him I was consulting CID. You won't get any blowback.'

Leah snorted. 'From that arsehole? I'd like to see him try.'

Kat smiled. So there were people at Jubilee Place she could trust after all.

She sauntered from Leah's desk towards the kitchen. As soon as she was out of sight of Tom's desk and Carve-up's office, she marched along the corridor and took the back stairs three at a time, down to the car park.

In her own car, she sped out on to Union Street. Without blues and twos it was hard going, but she hustled through the traffic, trying to figure out what the hell her friend had done.

No way would Kat arrest her – or anyone – on the basis of a confession alone. Once a murder had been reported in the press, the phones lit up with cranks and wannabes, attention-seekers and sad losers calling to confess. But they never got the details right and frequently were already known to the police.

This was different. Laura was reporting the murder as well as confessing to it. If there was a dead body then she was the only one who knew about it.

Could Laura Paxton, a sweet-natured woman with a petite build, really have strangled another woman to death? It didn't seem possible.

Kat pictured their last match. Laura had been animated on-court, as usual. Laughing and bantering with the other girls. And in the pub afterwards, though quieter, she'd been enjoying herself. Laughing at Jess Beckett's salty jokes and buying a round of wines like she always did.

Murderers like a wine and a laugh, too, a tiny voice whispered nastily.

Chapter Nine

The lime trees lining Chamberlayne Avenue cast dappled shadows over the wide tarmac roadway, which was devoid of parked cars. These were large houses, with spacious driveways, oak-framed carports, and in some cases, gravelled turning circles.

A homemade sign proclaimed inside a large red circle, *20 is Plenty*. Kat slowed from forty, hitting the brakes hard enough to set the ABS brakes juddering as she swung left into the curving paved drive of number 17.

The front door was open. Not wide, so a casual thief might notice. Just a crack. A sign meant for Kat. She pushed through and gasped.

Sitting cross-legged on the brilliant white tiled floor was her netball teammate and friend Laura Paxton. Eyes red, cheeks wet.

Lying in front of her, arms and legs spread like a dropped marionette, was a woman in her late twenties or early thirties. She was quite obviously dead. Her tongue was blackened, and swollen so much that it protruded from her mouth.

The phrase Laura had used earlier blared like a klaxon. *I've interfered with the body.*

Laura had scrawled the word 'COW' across the dead woman's forehead in what looked like thick, clotted blood. Kat glanced at the black and silver lipstick Laura was clutching.

'Hi, Kat.'

The greeting was so mundane, so everyday, that Kat simply responded in kind.

'Hi, Laura. Could you come towards me, please? Very carefully. I'd like you to sit on the stairs for me. I need to make a couple of calls and then I want to talk to you. Would that be all right?'

She'd instinctively adopted the soft, sympathetic tone she'd more usually use with vomit-and tear-streaked teenagers sitting drunk and miserable in their own mess on a kerb late on a Friday night. Or maybe someone in obvious psychological distress, brandishing a screwdriver in the Bramalls, the town's permanent market.

Because what else could this be but the result of someone undergoing some kind of mental breakdown? Women like Laura didn't go around murdering people. Especially not by strangulation, which took a lot of force and determination.

Laura got to her feet and stepped gingerly over the dead woman's right arm. She sidled past Kat and seated herself on the second-to-last stair, her small hands folded in her lap.

Keeping an eye on her, Kat pulled on a pair of purple nitrile gloves. She turned and pushed the front door closed. Then she approached the body.

Dead was dead. Work homicide long enough – e.g., a few weeks – and you got to know the signs. Corpses only sat bolt upright, gasping and making everybody jump, on the telly. And Alanna Michie was dead.

Nevertheless, Kat squatted by the head and pushed two fingers into the soft place under the jaw. Beneath the tightly cinched tie that was obviously the murder weapon.

No pulse.

Just to be sure, she bent her head and placed her right cheek close to the nostrils. Pretty nose, she thought incongruously. She did not feel the cool whisper of air that would indicate a remaining trace of life.

It wasn't up to her to certify death. She needed a doctor for that.

But now there was no possibility of reviving Alanna Michie, she called Jack Beale, the forensic pathologist based at Middlehampton General Hospital.

'Kat, what have you got for me? Or are you calling to ask me out for coffee?'

Flirting again? Really? The guy was impossible.

'Coffee's probably going to come in a paper cup. Unless you bring a flask. I have a dead body. Suspicious circumstances.'

'At Jubilee Place?' Jack sounded doubtful.

'No. In Northbridge.'

'Oh. I thought you were suspended from active duty.'

Great. So the rumour mill was already churning at full speed. And as someone intimately involved in the work of the police in Middlehampton, of course Jack bloody Beale would have heard the news.

'I am, but there are special circumstances. The suspect called me on my personal mobile.'

'Well, that's your business, Kat. The dead are mine. I'll be there as soon as I can.'

Next, Jubilee Place. And a call that was going to land her in more hot water with the brass. Not just Carve-up, either. Linda would have a fit. Couldn't be helped. Not when she was sharing an upscale hallway with a corpse, and a friend who'd just confessed to murder.

No sense dragging Tom out, not when Carve-up so obviously had plans for him. But she did need Darcy Clements, the forensic coordinator. And a couple of marked cars so patrol officers could set up the crime scene cordon.

With the team on its way, Kat forced down all thoughts of the bollocking waiting for her. She pulled a plastic evidence bag from her pocket and stretched out her gloved hand.

'Can you drop the lipstick in there for me, Laura, please?'

Laura complied robotically, slowly extending her arm and opening her finger and thumb. Ragged scratches scored the delicate pale skin on the insides of her forearms. She turned her head.

'The cap's over there. On the floor by Alanna. Shall I get it for you?'

'No, that's OK. You sit tight. I'll get it.'

With cap and lipstick separately bagged, labelled and sealed, Kat crouched in front of Laura again.

'What happened, Laura?'

'You mean, the details?'

'Yes. Why don't you tell me what happened, right from the beginning?'

Kat fished out a notebook from her jacket pocket and turned to a clean page.

'I think – thought – Alanna was having an affair with Will. My husband?'

Kat nodded.

'I came round to have it out with her. I accused her but she denied it. She laughed in my face. Said I was imagining things. Called me a sad loser. I lost my temper. I saw the tie and I strangled her with it. Then, when I was sure she was dead, I went upstairs, into the bedroom, and I got one of her lipsticks. I came downstairs again and I wrote that on her forehead. Then I called you.'

Kat frowned. It made perfect sense, grammatically. But no sense, realistically. Laura was five foot three and couldn't be a pound over eight stone dripping wet. Alanna looked to be closer to five-eight or five-nine. While not fat, she had an athletic build that spoke of sessions with a personal trainer, or at least a set of gym equipment.

It took several minutes to strangle someone. You had to apply a great deal of force through that time. And the victim didn't just go limp straight away. They struggled, fought back, kicked, scratched and bit. Yet apart from a small bruise on Laura's forehead, and the scratches to her forearms, she was unmarked.

'Tell me again how you strangled her, Laura.'

Laura nodded, sat a little straighter, like a schoolgirl being asked to recite a poem set for homework.

'I pushed her first and she tripped and fell. I heard a noise. I think she hit her head against the floor. Then I saw the tie. It was on a coat hook by the front door. I wrapped it round her neck, and I pulled it tight and I just, you know, kept on pulling until she was dead.'

Kat made a quick note. Something to ask Jack to check for. Blunt force trauma to the back of the head.

'How did you get the bruise on *your* head?'

Laura reached up distractedly and touched the purple bruise above her right eye. Frowned. From pain? Puzzlement?

'She hit me. I think. I'm not sure. It's all a bit of a blur.'

'And the scratches on your arms?'

'That was Alanna, too. You know, when she tried to fight back.'

Kat shook her head. Sexual jealousy was a powerful motive for murder. But this just felt wrong. Or did it? Was she trying to make excuses for Laura because she was a friend? Because the effect of being subjected to a baseless accusation herself was colouring her judgement?

She knew perfectly well what she ought to do. She'd had it drummed into her at police college, and by her mentor DI Molly Steadman, too.

Follow the evidence.

A confession taken over the phone, given by someone unable to confirm a detail the police had deliberately withheld to screen out cranks? That was no kind of evidence at all. Except maybe of the caller's poor mental health, fragile ego or perverse sense of fun.

A confession given freely at a crime scene, by a person holding an implement they'd used to produce an artefact on the corpse? With wounds inflicted by the victim? It was, to use a technical policing term, a slam dunk.

She had no other option. And not for the first time in her police career she wondered how much you ever truly knew somebody else.

Speaking quietly but clearly, she recited the official caution and arrested Laura Paxton for the murder of Alanna Michie.

From beyond the front door, she heard the crunch of tyres on gravel. The cavalry had arrived.

With a sinking feeling in her belly, she went outside to look.

Leading the convoy, a scarlet Alfa Romeo screeched to a halt behind her own car. And out stepped Carve-up. Eyes ablaze with anger – but also triumph.

Kat swallowed hard to stop herself vomiting. Everything was about to get very messy.

Chapter Ten

Carve-up strode up to Kat until his face was just a few inches from hers.

'Get the hell away from my crime scene. I'll deal with you later.'

He pushed past her, jarring her shoulder, and disappeared inside, already barking orders.

Kat walked off, watching the proceedings from the other side of the street, not ready to go yet.

Shortly after the uniforms began stringing crime scene tape across the entrance and exit to the Michies' drive, Jack Beale spoke from behind Kat, making her jump.

'Morning,' he said. 'Everything OK?'

She shrugged. 'You mean apart from a friend calling me confessing to a murder and my boss reaming me out for attending a crime scene while confined to barracks?'

'That bad, eh?'

'Just go and do your stuff, Jack. But could you maybe let me know what you find before you go?'

He smiled and nodded, dislodging a wayward lock of deep brown hair which he left hanging across his eye. He was good-looking, and he knew it. But right now, Jack Beale's charms were as effective on her as a Band-Aid on a stab wound.

Alone, and without a role to play – *for now*, she told herself – she worried about the other huge problem in her life. That damned money.

Even though her dad had flat-out denied it, she couldn't think of anyone else who would want to discredit her by making an anonymous deposit into her current account. Did he even *have* her details? Of course! On each of his children's eighteenth birthdays, he'd announced that from now on their presents would be in cash, paid electronically.

The gifts had dried up as they moved into jobs and a measure of financial security, but she assumed he still had their details on his payments list. Kat had never changed her bank account, even though you were supposed to shop around for better deals every couple of years. Yeah, right! Who had time for that?

She called Diana. Wanting to know if Dad still sent *her* money. Desperate for a straw, however spindly, to grab.

'Hello, Kat. This is a surprise. What do you want?'

'Can't I call my big sister without needing something?'

Diana sniffed. 'You can. You just never do. Anyway, how are you?'

'I'm fine. You?'

'Yes, good, thank you. The new office is doing well. And Eamonn's just got a promotion. We're thinking of moving, actually. Buying somewhere bigger. In a better neighbourhood.'

Was there anywhere better than Diana and Eamonn's gated community in Burleigh? Kat visualised the entrance to their quiet little development of executive homes. They even had a private security guard in a brick hutch behind the tall wrought-iron gates in black and gold.

'That's great,' she said. 'What's Eamonn's new job?'

'Director of UHNWI Client Relations. The bank's expanding into the Far East. Eamonn's going to be spending a lot of time in China.'

Kat wrinkled her nose, puzzled by the acronym. 'Sorry, Di, U-H-what?'

'Ultra-High-Net-Worth Individuals. People with at least thirty million dollars in assets, basically. More in China than any other country except the US. And it's the fastest-growing global market. It's a very important job. They begged Eamonn to take it. Gave him a fifty per cent pay rise, too. We're very pleased.'

Kat could hear her sister purring. And, despite being perfectly happy with her lot, she felt a twinge of envy as she imagined, or tried to, what a double-income, no-kids family would be like. All that cash and nobody but the two of you to spend it on.

She shook her head. But that was the point, wasn't it? Were Diana and Eamonn going to go through life buying more expensive cars, art, jewellery and holidays? Just amassing more *stuff*? What was the point?

Somehow she couldn't see either of them engaging in philanthropy as a hobby. Eamonn was a perfectly nice bloke, but he seemed in thrall to Diana, who definitely beat him hands down in the ambition stakes.

'I'm pleased for you, Di. It sounds very exciting. So, look, I was wondering —'

'Here it comes,' Diana crowed. 'I *knew* you'd rung me for a reason.'

'At least I do ring you.'

And there it was. That old animosity that had always threaded its way through their relationship flaring into life again. They got on well enough in a distant, Christmas-cards-and-family-get-togethers manner. But there was something between them that always got in the way of a loving relationship. Like cogs that, instead of meshing, clashed their teeth together as they spun, striking off sharp metal fragments that stung and burned.

'Oh, stop being so sanctimonious, Katherine.' Diana always used Kat's full name when she was gearing up for a row. 'Just because you're a police officer, you think you've got this moral superiority baked in. Well, Eamonn and I pay your wages, don't forget that.'

'Believe me, I'm grateful, Di. But it sounds like you'll be able to afford it, what with Eamonn's *exciting* new promotion.'

'Jealous, are we?'

'Not at all. I like having my husband home, not ten thousand miles away wining and dining Chinese billionaires. I mean, do you even *know* where they got their money? China's hardly a beacon of human rights, is it?'

'What, and the police here are? I don't know if you follow the news, little sister, but there are girls being strip-searched while they're on their periods. People dying in police custody. Cops sharing photos of murder scenes on WhatsApp.' Diana's voice had risen to a peak of high-pitched indignation. 'Jesus, you're a fine one to talk about human rights. Do you know how many cases of sexual assault by Metropolitan Police officers are currently being investigated? No? Well, let me enlighten you, then. Sixteen hundred!'

Kat took a deep breath.

'Look, Di, I'm sorry. I didn't mean to start an argument. Can I just ask you a question, then I'll leave you in peace.' She nearly added *to plan your house move*, but stopped herself in time. 'Please?'

'Fine,' Diana said with a drawn-out sigh. 'But make it quick, I'm preparing sushi. It's Eamonn's favourite.'

'Does Dad still send you money? On your birthday?'

'Don't be silly! I'm thirty-nine. I run my own business.'

'But he's still got your account details from when he used to?'

'Yes. Why? Is this about you being investigated for corruption?'

'I'm trying to figure out who sent me the money. I can't think of anyone apart from Dad who's got that sort of cash *and* my account details.'

'Well, if you're asking me to go through his books, I can give you my answer right now. Not. Going. To. Happen. There is such a thing as client confidentiality, you know.'

'I had heard, Di. And with the kind of clients you cultivate, that's probably a very good thing.' A five-second pause followed this outburst. Kat knew she'd blown it. 'Di, I'm sorry. I shouldn't have said that.'

'I'm going now, Katherine. But before I return to my sake uramaki, I need to point out three things to you. One, Beijing is *five* thousand miles away, not ten. Two, the kind of clients I culti-vate, which include Morton Land, are legal, regulated and entirely properly run corporations. Which is more than can be said of some of the people you seem to delight in cosying up to. And three, you always were a snotty little cow, and I am sad to see nothing's changed.'

The line went dead.

Kat sighed. Why was it every time she spoke to Diana, they reverted to the roles they'd played since childhood? Arguing, trad-ing verbal blows, scoring points?

Jack emerged from the front door and, after checking the coast was clear, crossed the road to join Kat in the shadow cast by a spreading beech tree.

'Rigor mortis has set in. So she's been dead for at least two hours. You might want to check when the suspect says she killed her. Just to get the timeline straight for the CPS. I found a contu-sion on the back of the skull. I'll know more after the post-mortem, but at first sight, it's consistent with a fall on to a tiled floor.'

Normally, Kat would be, if not rejoicing, then feeling qui-etly satisfied. To catch and solve a homicide inside an hour had to be some sort of record. Yet all she felt was a bewildering sense of dislocation. After her two previous cases, which had involved horrifying levels of brutality and cruelty, this seemed so prosaic by comparison. One woman killed another out of sexual jealousy and then, seized by remorse, confessed all.

And the name of the victim. Where had she heard it before? She closed her eyes.

Michie.

A case file from her days in general CID swam into focus behind her eyelids. Drug importation. The suspect. One Callum Michie. A member – at one remove – of the Strutt crime family. A nephew, they had discovered, of Frank Strutt, acting boss of the organisation and eldest son of paterfamilias Anthony Joseph Strutt.

Was Alanna Michie married to Callum Michie? It was too early to say. The surname wasn't the most common, but neither was it a rarity.

It wouldn't take Kat long to find out.

Chapter Eleven

Back at Jubilee Place, Kat avoided Carve-up by heading to the custody suite.

On duty was Sergeant Julia Myles, a handsome Black woman in her forties with a commanding air and a set of steely eyes that worked like death rays on even the surliest villains.

'Hi, Kat, come to ask about your latest collar?'

'How did she seem to you?'

'Meek and mild. And relieved. I've seen it before.' Julia shook her head. 'They do it in a fit of anger and then, all passion spent, they're just glad to let other people take over.'

Kat liked listening to Julia talk. It was the way she dropped such lovely poetic phrases into what would otherwise be the bureaucratic cop-speak of custody sergeants everywhere.

'"All passion spent"?'

'A novel by Vita Sackville-West. We're reading it in my book club. It's very good. It's about a titled lady who decides to escape from her family's expectations and please herself. Pretty feminist for its day.' Julia rolled her eyes. 'Which you did not come here to discuss. Although it looks like you're pleasing yourself at the moment.'

'You mean going over the wall to make the arrest?'

Julia smiled, then lowered her voice. 'Listen, Kat, between you and me? I wouldn't trust Carve-up further than I could throw that

47

bright red dick-substitute he leaves in the car park every morning. So . . . Laura Paxton. Did you know her hubby's a DC over at Hampton Lane? One of Cherryville's finest.'

'I did not. He's been informed?'

'Seeing as he's job, I made an exception and called him myself. He's on his way over now.'

'How did he sound?'

Julia put a finger to her chin and gazed up at the grubby ceiling tiles with their unfathomable brown stains.

'Hmm, how *did* DC Paxton take the news of his wife's arrest for murder?' She returned her gaze to Kat. 'I think it's fair to say he was not expecting my call.'

'Did Laura ask for a lawyer?'

'Nope. She very much did *not* ask for a lawyer. In fact, I would go so far as to say that she showed a pretty determined intention *not* to have any legal counsel whatsoever. Kept saying, "I did it, so what good is a lawyer?"'

Kat pulled on her earlobe, a mannerism she'd developed in her teens and which returned when things puzzled her.

'Which cell is she in?'

'Number six. It's the least smelly.'

Kat smiled. 'Thanks, Julia.'

Let in by a custody officer, Kat stood with her back to the door while Laura regarded her peaceably from the narrow blue mattress.

'The custody sergeant tells me you've refused a lawyer. Is that right?'

Laura shrugged her narrow shoulders. Touched the bruise on her forehead. Her forearms were bandaged.

'I did it. I don't need a lawyer.'

Kat nodded. 'I see where you're coming from. But the thing is, murder is a serious offence.' She paused. God, she sounded like she was addressing a small child. It was something about Laura's passivity that led her to talk down to her. She squatted so they were eye to eye. Maybe this would help. Tried again. 'In view of the heinous nature of the offence you've confessed to, Laura, I really do think it would be a good idea to have a lawyer present when we interview you.'

'I can't afford a lawyer.'

'If you don't have the money, we can provide one for you. But Will's on his way in. Maybe you and he could discuss it.'

Laura's eyes widened. 'Will? No! He's the reason I killed her. They were having an affair. I don't want to see him.'

There was so much Kat wanted to ask her friend. But now she'd been arrested, the rules applied. Everything would have to wait until she was in an interview room, with the recorder running and the official caution recited again.

'Would you at least consent to having a duty solicitor attend?'

Laura shook her head violently, setting her lank hair swinging. 'I told you! There's no point. I. Am. Guilty.'

Kat had no choice but to leave her friend in her cell, repeating her last three words like a mantra.

Now Carve-up had muscled in, there was no way Kat would be allowed near Laura in an official capacity. So her next task was to find out who'd be leading the investigation. Surely Carve-up wouldn't take it. He was always so smug about being senior management and not having the time to do 'the dirty work' – no irony intended, she assumed.

Kat arrived in MCU just in time to see Tom leaving Carve-up's office and – *Oh my God* – actually shaking hands with the man.

Tom was smiling broadly as he sat behind his desk.

'Carve-up give you a hand-job, Tomski?' Leah called over, a broad grin on her face.

'Haha! Very funny. No, in fact he appointed me lead investigator on the Michie murder.'

Tom didn't get any further. Carve-up leaned around the door jamb of his office.

'DS Ballantyne. In here. Now.'

Once Kat was sitting, the door closed behind her, Carve-up smiled at her.

'You've done it now, DS Ballantyne. You disobeyed a direct order. I'd start putting my CV together if I was you.'

She jutted her chin out. 'Exigent circumstances, DI Carver. I'm still a police constable serving the King. I received a call from a woman I knew personally, confessing to a murder. I felt in the moment I had no choice but to intervene immediately, in case she harmed herself. As soon as the scene was secure and I was convinced she presented no danger to the public or herself, I called it in.'

'That's a very pretty speech. Maybe type it up and give a copy to your lawyer. Now you listen to me, Kitty-Kat,' he grated. 'I know that for some inexplicable reason Linda seems to have some sort of faith in you, but I don't. However, in the interests of not causing Linda any more work, I'm not going to write you up. But I give you fair warning. If I catch you disobeying me again, I won't just throw the book at you. I'll throw the whole bloody bookcase as well. Are we clear?'

'Crystal.'

'Get out.'

Kat emerged from his office into the hubbub of MCU. Her heart was racing and she was clenching her fists so tight her fingerbones hurt.

Tom was talking animatedly to Leah. 'I mean, obviously it's a bit of a slam dunk. Just pink-ribboning it for the CPS, but still.

My first murder case and it's already solved. Suspect in custody, confessing like a sinner at the pearly gates. It's going to look great on my record.'

Kat was distressed to hear Carve-up's phrases tripping so readily off her bagman's tongue.

'You're sure about that, are you, Tom,' she said, joining them.

He folded his arms. 'You aren't?'

'Doesn't it smell just the tiniest bit fishy to you?'

'No. I spoke to Dr Beale. The injuries to the victim are consistent with a violent attack and death by strangulation with a ligature, all as Laura Paxton stated.'

'She's petite, though. The victim was strong-looking. Much taller than her assailant, too. How could Laura Paxton have overcome her like that?'

'Why are you even asking? You're not her defence lawyer. And anyway, it's not your case, it's mine. You shouldn't even have been out there.'

'Come on, Tom, you can't have finished all the Kool-Aid Carve-up poured for you in there.' She jutted her chin towards his office door. 'Where's your curiosity? Where're your instincts? What's your gut telling you?'

Tom straightened in his chair.

'I don't need to listen to my gut or my instincts, Kat. I need to look at the evidence and obey the orders of a DI who just appointed me lead investigator. And they're all saying the same thing. She did it. End of. Now, if you'll excuse me, I have to start writing up my policy book. Item one, the wife of a junior member of the Strutt family has just been murdered.'

Kat's stomach tightened like a fist. A dead Strutt would mean big trouble. Was Tom really up for handling that level of grief?

'You're sure?'

He nodded. 'CSIs found an electricity bill in the kitchen. Addressed to Callum Michie. Who, in case you didn't know, is Frank Strutt's nephew.'

Realising she had nothing to gain, Kat left him to his furious typing and returned to her own desk. If Laura had murdered Callum Michie's wife, then she was in more danger than she realised. A prison cell wouldn't be a safe place for her. Not with the kind of reach and connections the Strutts had.

Her desk phone rang.

'It's Polly on reception, Kat. I've got a DC Paxton down here, from Hampton Lane. Poor thing's in a bit of a state, actually. Apparently, his wife's been arrested? He asked for the lead investigator.'

A dilemma. After exchanging cross words with Tom, what did she do now? Go alone and alienate him further – and further enrage Carve-up? Or tell him, and risk him blundering into a sensitive interview without enough training?

Seeing a way out of her dilemma, Kat went over to Tom's desk.

'What is it now?' he asked in a clipped voice.

Well, that wasn't a great start. Was he really buying Carve-up's version of events? She'd thought she could rely on Tom to have her back.

Kat squatted by his right hip.

'You're right, Tom. We – I mean *you* should follow the evidence.'

'Oh. Well, good. Thanks. I didn't mean to argue with you, Kat. It's just that Stuart—'

'Never mind Stuart. I get it. He's calling the shots and of course you can't go against his orders. This isn't about that. Laura's husband is downstairs. He's just been informed she's being held on suspicion of murder. He's a copper like us, and he asked for the lead investigator. Now' – she held up a hand as he began to object

52

– 'obviously that's you, but I thought, given I've dealt with lots of these situations before, maybe you'd want me to tag along? Just to stop him kicking off. It can't hurt.'

Tom frowned. She could see him weighing up the options, just as she had done a minute earlier. Which way would he jump?

He seemed to come to a decision, nodding his head and pushing himself to his feet.

'Yes, please. But I lead.'

'Yes, guv,' she deadpanned.

Maybe she'd read him wrong after all. He wasn't completely Carve-up's boy.

Chapter Twelve

Kat led Will Paxton into the interview room they used for grieving next of kin and friendly witnesses. She sat next to Tom and across from Will, on an L-shaped sofa.

With his side-parted sandy hair, freckle-spattered face and pale blue eyes, Will Paxton looked more like a primary-school admin clerk than a detective. His tie was at half-mast and she spotted a splodge of what might have been coffee on his lapel.

He collapsed into an armchair and leaned forward, hands clasped between his knees, fingers working against each other.

He looked stunned. As he had every right to be. Eyes flitting between her and Tom like nervous sparrows in a cat-filled garden. Kat tried to imagine how Van would look if Julia Myles called to tell him Kat had confessed to murdering Jess Beckett. Not good. She was certain of it.

'I don't understand. What the hell happened?' Will asked. Then immediately answered himself. 'It's a mistake. It has to be. Laura's had some issues.' He gulped. His Adam's apple jumped in his throat. It looked alive to Kat. 'You know, with her, um, mental health. This could be a cry for help.'

Tom gaped. His eyes widened. But he said nothing. He'd been seized by panic. Kat saw it and shot him the tiniest glance of reassurance. *I've got this.*

Patiently Kat explained. Sticking to the facts. No sense in joining Laura's distraught husband in speculation about Laura's motives.

'The trouble is, Will, she's confessed. And I found her at the crime scene. She'd written on the victim's body with a lipstick. We have to follow protocol.'

Will's eyes widened at the mention of the lipstick. How awful to be told that not only had his wife confessed to a murder, but had apparently – as Laura herself had put it – 'interfered with the body'.

'This is insane. Have you *met* Laura?'

'I actually know her, Will. We're friends. We play on the same netball team.'

'Well then! You have to see it. She's not a murderer. And as for this business with lipstick or whatever. I mean, it's obviously . . . obviously . . .'

He put his head in his hands and sobbed loudly. Kat pushed the box of tissues closer. He snatched out a couple, after tearing the first, and screwed them into his eyes. Finally, after loudly clearing his throat, he spoke in a low voice. He sounded like someone had told him his dog had died, he'd got prostate cancer and his house was being repossessed by the bank. All at once.

'She's going to need a lawyer. A good one. I'm not having one of the duty solicitors anywhere near her. I'll have to remortgage the house. But that's fine. Yes. I can talk to the bank. They'll listen. It's all they ever do now, isn't it? In their ads. Bleating on about how they're there to help. Well, they better bloody well help now.'

The gabbling speech wasn't for Kat's benefit. It was for Will's. Faced with devastating news, he was trying to impose order on a disordered situation. She'd seen it before. Grieving parents talking about games consoles, spouses about gardening club dues, all because anything was better than facing the hideous truth. Life, as they knew it, was over.

'Will, about the lawyer. Laura's been refusing even a duty solicitor. She keeps saying she's guilty so what would be the point.'

'I need to see her, then. Talk to her. Explain the seriousness of the situation. Like I said, she's not always well. She doesn't understand what she's doing. Not always.'

Kat swallowed down her anxiety. Because if he was blindsided about his wife's confession, her motive was going to hit him like a train.

'There's something else, Will. I'm afraid it's going to be painful to hear but I need to tell you. She says she killed this woman because she believed – believes – that you and the victim were having an affair. She told me she doesn't want to see you.'

Will rocked backwards as if she'd just given him a smack with a baton. His eyes popped wide open.

'She *what*? Oh, God,' he groaned, 'this is going from bad to worse. An affair? What's the dead woman's name?'

'Alanna Michie. Does that mean anything to you?'

Will frowned. Scrubbed the wadded-up tissues against his eyes again.

'Wait, Alanna Michie? As in Callum Michie's missus?'

'The very same.'

Will swore violently. He jumped up from the armchair as if scalded and strode over to the window. Looked down at the car park before beginning to pace from one side of the room to the other, hands chopping the air.

'You know who he is, right? Callum Michie? He's a gangster. Part of the Strutt family. His uncle's Frank Strutt. Jesus, this can't be happening.'

Remaining seated, even though his restlessness was making her twitchy, Kat spoke softly. 'Will, come and sit down, yes? I am not going to judge you' – well, she would, because what copper in their right mind, or even their completely and totally *wrong* mind,

56

would enter into an extramarital affair with the wife of any member of the Strutt family? Let alone one of its rising stars? – 'but is there any truth to Laura's accusation?'

He looked at her, startled, as if she'd asked him whether he was keeping a dragon in his garden shed. 'Of course there isn't any truth in it! I *love* her! Laura, I mean. Oh my God, what am I going to do?'

'Look, right now, there's nothing much you can do. She seemed pretty determined not to speak to you. I'll have another word with her. I'll try and get her to see sense and agree to a lawyer. And maybe once she's had a night to calm down, she'll want to see you.'

Will shook his head again. 'No, no, no. You can't keep her in overnight. It'll kill her. She hates confined spaces.'

Part of Kat – the small, uncharitable, overworked-copper part – wanted to say that if Laura didn't like confined spaces, maybe she shouldn't have committed murder. But she shoved the thought away as unworthy. It was just that, if it had been any other suspect, she'd be fully on board with Stuart Carver's approach. Take the win.

'She's on a murder charge, Will. You know as well as I do what that means.'

After Will had left, Kat took a mug of coffee over to Tom at his desk.

'Thanks for including me,' she said, placing the coffee by his elbow. 'You didn't have to do that. Don't worry, I won't tell Carve-up.'

He looked stricken. 'I froze in there, Kat. I totally lost it. How am I going to run a real homicide investigation if I can't even run one that's basically already closed?'

'You'll be fine. Look, it's hard, talking to witnesses like Will. Anyone would struggle. Chalk it down to experience and move on.'

'But how will I *get* experience if I bollocks it up every time like just now?'

Poor Tom. Even if he was temporarily Carve-up's bagman, she still felt for him. Because he'd pinpointed the central issue for all fast-track officers.

How *could* they be expected to come in cold, from university or business, and cope with the messy, complex, emotion-drenched world of homicide? Criminals and victims. Violence. Calls for revenge. And the absolute bloody bucketloads of grief, confusion and anger when one human being murdered another?

It was why seasoned cops, like Kat, who'd seen it all a thousand times before they ever wore plainclothes to work, felt graduate-entry officers needed to earn their spurs. Or as Molly had once colourfully put it, 'get some blood on their shirts'.

She saw a way to help Tom and also stay involved in the case. It was risky, but it had to be worth a try.

'Listen, Tom, you need to contact Callum Michie. Give him the bad news. But the thing is, if you thought Will Paxton's reaction was hard to deal with, imagine how Callum's going to take it. He's going to go ballistic. He'll be taking out a contract on Laura while we're still talking to him.'

Tom's eyes widened. 'Oh, Jesus, I hadn't thought of that. What do I do?'

'We went to see his uncle, remember?'

'Frank Strutt. How could I forget? He treated me like a kid.'

'That's Frank being Frank. Well, I think we need to approach him first. He can help us stop Callum going into full-on vigilante mode.'

'Won't he want the same as Callum? Alanna was married to his nephew, after all.'

'Frank's a businessman. What he wants more than anything else is to be left alone to run his operation. Having his nephew going around like John Wick would be bad for business. I think he'll work with us.' She paused. 'As long as he thinks we're pulling out all the stops.'

Tom thought for a moment, eyes locked on the acoustic tiles on the ceiling as if he might find the answer written there in flip-chart marker.

'OK, yes. Talk to Frank.'

'I can talk to Callum with you, too, if you want. You're leading obviously, and you're writing up the policy book. So anything I discover, you take credit for. I'll just be your unofficial bagwoman, OK? A little bit of role reversal while I sort out this bloody money thing.' She glanced at Carve-up's office door. 'Probably best to let Stuart think you're handling it on your own.'

Maybe it was the stress of an impending confrontation with two members of the Strutt family, but Tom nodded eagerly.

'Yes. Thanks, Kat. And . . .'

'What?'

'Maybe you'd better go back to calling me Tomski. I prefer it.'

She smiled. 'Sure thing.' A beat. 'Guv.'

Dreading the consequences of the next few minutes, Kat called the pub Frank Strutt used as a base of operations. Tom looked on, his mouth a grim line, the muscles around his eyes tight.

'Hope and Anchor,' a young woman said.

'Is Frank in? Tell him it's Kat Ballantyne.'

'I'll just go and see. Hold on a minute.'

Kat listened. Heard high heels clicking. Tried to get her heart to slow down by focusing on her breathing. Only managed to become anxiously aware of how rapidly she was sucking in air.

Frank's gravelly voice rolled down the line. 'Morning, Kat. What's up?'

'I need to speak to Callum Michie. Have you got his number?'

'Speak to him about what?'

Canny Frank. Cautious Frank. Maybe Kat and he did have a relationship of sorts. One built on mutual respect and an awareness that there were rules to be followed in a place like Middlehampton. Boundaries that nobody wanted crossing. But Frank was still a gangster. And Kat was still a cop.

'It's a personal matter.'

'What kind of personal?'

The worst kind! she wanted to scream.

'The kind where I really need to speak to him, and I hope you're going to let me have his mobile number.'

'You're not going to tell me, are you?'

'You'll find out soon enough, Frank. And when you do, I want you to promise to come and see me first.'

'What's that supposed to mean?'

'The number?'

'Hold on.'

He recited a number, which Kat tapped into her phone, then she thanked him and rang off.

Ten seconds later, she listened as Callum Michie's phone began ringing.

Chapter Thirteen

Callum Michie's voice – as well as sounding like he might pull a gun were they face to face – was distorted. Hands-free.

'Who is this?'

'My name is Detective Sergeant Katherine Ballantyne. Am I speaking to Callum Michie?'

'Who gave you my number?'

That was easy, and at least it would allay his suspicions.

'Frank Strutt. He's a—' She hesitated. Yes, what was Frank to Kat? Not a friend. A contact? Sounded too much like they'd met at a networking event in the Guildhall. An acquaintance? 'We know each other,' she decided was sufficiently neutral yet informative.

'I'm Callum. What's this all about?'

'Mr Michie, can I ask you where you are?'

'I'm in my car. On the A41.'

'Could I ask you to come directly to Jubilee Place police station, please.'

'You could *ask* me, DS Ballantyne. But it wouldn't make any difference. I'm going home.'

'Mr Michie, I'm afraid you can't do that. Your home is currently a crime scene. I need you to come to Jubilee Place straight away.'

'A crime scene. What's happened? We been broken into or something? Christ! I'll kill them if they've nicked anything. Is Alanna all right?'

Kat desperately wanted to do this in person. Giving a man the news that his wife was dead over a bad mobile connection while he was driving was just about the worst option. It might even lead to a second death. She made one more effort.

'Come in and let me explain. I'll be waiting for you.'

'Just tell me.'

His voice had dropped into a lower register and she heard it beneath the content. The tone that said he'd probably already worked it out. Did it go with the territory? Or was it simply the reaction of a husband listening to a detective refusing to confirm whether his wife was alive?

'Pull over,' she said.

'Oh, God. Hold on.'

Kat waited, listening as Callum Michie piloted whatever expensive vehicle he was driving to a halt.

'I'm in a bus stop. And if you say anything, I bloody well will come down there . . . and it won't be for a pleasant chat about illegal stopping on the King's highway.'

Kat drew a deep, steadying breath. 'Callum, I'm afraid Alanna is dead. She was murdered this morning. We have a person in custody. I am so, so sorry for your loss.'

The silence stretched out like an unspooling motorway on a night drive. No other sounds. No distractions. Just the wide-open tarmac lit by yellow-white headlights, stretching away into the dark. Into the unknown. Into grief.

A loud airhorn parped. Callum screamed an expletive. Kat caught the faint clatter of a high-mileage, large-capacity diesel engine. Some of the town's buses had been converted to electric. This was obviously not one of them.

'I'll be there in ten.'

The line went dead.

Chapter Fourteen

Before Callum Michie arrived at the station, Kat went to see Darcy Clements to get an update on the initial forensics from the Michies' house.

She found Darcy hunched over her computer, deep grooves marring her usually smooth forehead as she stared at the screen.

'Hey Darce, why the long face? As the bartender said to the horse.'

Darcy looked up, grinned. 'Probs stick to coppering if I were you. I think that stand-up career's looking shaky.'

'I know it's too early for lab reports, but I was wondering whether you'd got any initial thoughts about the crime scene at Chamberlayne Avenue.'

Darcy nodded, and pushed her hair out of her eyes. 'I thought Carve-up had you on cold cases, not red-hot ones,' she said with a sly grin. 'Do you want to pull up a chair?'

Once they were seated almost knee to knee in Darcy's cramped workspace, Darcy pointed at the screen.

'That's what's bothering me. I was just reviewing the exhibits we gathered at the scene.'

'Not much to go on?'

'Kat, there's *nothing* to go on. It's weird. I mean, not *nothing*-nothing. We've got Laura Paxton's prints on the lipstick, the rest of Alanna's make-up, the banisters, the front door. All the stuff you'd expect. Looks like there was saliva on the lippy, too. Might be hers. The tie had a red stain. It's red wine. We retrieved skin cells from under the victim's fingernails. They'll likely belong to Laura although Stuart's told me to hold off on testing for now. He says her confession and presence at the crime scene's enough for a conviction.'

Kat shook her head. Carve-up was wrong. She knew why he didn't want any DNA testing yet. His beloved metrics. If he could save a few thousand quid this month, it would make his financial report look better. Her next confrontation with Carve-up would have to wait.

'Sorry, Darce, but what *do* you mean, then? About it looking off?'

'I'm just not seeing a typical crime scene where there's been a violent assault. You know what I'm talking about, Kat.'

'They're messy, chaotic. Two women struggling while one strangles the other? There'd be scuffmarks, maybe on the walls where Alanna kicked out. Blood, if one of them got rammed against a sharp corner. More in the way of bruising on the victim. Broken mirrors or those little china trinkets on the hall table. Pictures knocked askew or on to the floor.'

Darcy nodded. 'I just don't see the attack happening the way Laura described it. It's like Alanna just stood there offering minimal resistance while Laura killed her.'

Kat nodded. Darcy was right. It *was* odd. Maybe they'd learn more once Jack had conducted his post-mortem.

Polly called Kat just as she was leaving Forensics. Callum Michie had arrived at the station.

For the second time that morning, she found herself sitting beside Tom in the friendly interview room across from a devastated husband. That made one from each side of the line that divided Middlehampton into the law-keepers and the law-breakers. Only, this time, despite his occupation, the law-breaker was innocent of everything except crumbling under stress.

Tears streamed down his face, and they kept flowing despite the tissues he kept yanking from the flower-printed box.

'What happened?' he choked out.

Kat looked at Tom.

His lips parted with a click. 'I'm afraid she was strangled, Mr Michie. And she hit her head, but it wasn't a fatal blow.'

'You said you've got someone in custody?'

Kat nodded. 'A woman. She called me in person and confessed. I arrested her myself.'

His head cranked up from its droop between his shoulders and he eyed her with surprise. 'A woman? Who is she?'

'We aren't at liberty to disclose that information,' Tom said.

In his nervousness he'd fallen back on bureaucratic language that Kat knew would inflame Callum.

Callum thrust his whole upper body forward, pinning Tom with a white-hot glare. 'You know who I am, right? You know I can find out ten minutes after I leave here. So just save yourself the grief and tell me her name.'

Kat weighed up their options. He was right. What choice did they have? And maybe by telling him and breaking a small rule – correction, another rule – she could save trouble down the line. Because, as sure as a bus would need the stop he'd so recently occupied, trouble was most definitely coming.

'Her name is Laura Paxton.'

'How did she know Alanna? I mean, what possible motive could this Paxton woman have for' – he swallowed convulsively – 'for murdering my wife?'

Tom shot Kat a nervous look before replying. 'She says she believed Alanna was having an affair with her husband. Do you think there could be any truth in that?'

Christ! She was out on a tightrope now, swinging and swaying hundreds of metres above a raging torrent. No harness, no safety line. The wind was getting up. The line was swaying.

And Kat Ballantyne was losing her balance.

She was under investigation on a potential corruption charge. And now she'd inserted herself into a live murder investigation, disobeying her line manager's orders for the second time.

But she had no choice. Being a homicide cop wasn't her job. It was who she was.

In that dreadful moment when teenaged Kat was told that her best friend had been murdered, something had changed inside her. Kat had become someone who just couldn't stand by while one person lost their life to another.

Whether the victim was her friend – or the perpetrator was – she had to see justice done. But now all of that was being taken away from her. Unless she could stay out of trouble with Carve-up and get out from under the 3C-ACU investigation.

No pressure, then.

Chapter Fifteen

Callum Michie rocked back in his chair.

His face pulled over to one side as if he'd been fish-hooked in the corner of his mouth.

'You *what?*'

Kat looked him in the eye. Important not to back away from an unpleasant line of enquiry. That's what the lecturers had said at police college.

Easy for them to say. They weren't sitting knee to knee with a known member of an organised crime group who'd just been asked if his murdered wife had made him a cuckold.

'I'm not saying she was, Callum,' Kat said, feeling, but thankfully not hearing, the tremor in her vocal cords. 'I am just telling you what the suspect told me, as the reason for her action.'

'Me and Alanna, we were soulmates. Maybe that sounds old-fashioned to you. Or like some of the crap you read on Instagram. But it's true. So, in answer to your question, no, she wasn't having an affair. I'd bet my life on it.' He paused, dropped his voice to a threatening growl. 'Or yours.'

Kat wanted to wipe away the beads of sweat popping up along her hairline, itching like bugs. She resisted the impulse.

'Like I said, then, we have someone in custody. We will be interviewing her today. Would you like me to appoint a family liaison officer to help you?'

'An FLO? Are you joking? No I don't want a f—' He heaved in a breath. 'A family liaison officer.' He leaned forward and pointed a nicotine-stained index finger at her. Then at Tom. 'But I'll tell you this for free, DS Ballantyne. And you, DC Gray. I'll be doing a little family liaison of my own later on. This Paxton bitch's going to pay for what she done.'

'Look, Callum, please think about what you're doing,' Kat said. 'I know you're hurting. I know. But don't let your grief carry you into any actions you might regret later. Let us – let *me* – deal with it. I'll keep you informed myself if you don't want an FLO.'

He shook his head. 'When can I see her?'

'As soon as the pathologist has completed his post-mortem. Again, I'll call you.'

He stood. Straightened his lapels.

'Make sure you do.'

He left her and Tom sitting on the royal-blue sofa with its stained upholstery.

Tom reached out to straighten the box of tissues.

His hand was shaking.

'Christ, Kat! What are we going to do?'

She patted his shoulder. 'You're going to investigate. And I'm going to help you.'

Chapter Sixteen

Despite Carve-up's injunctions to stay away from the case, Kat *needed* to speak to Laura Paxton. Because, despite the physical evidence recovered at the scene, her doubts about Laura's guilt were multiplying like the rabbits on Bowman's Common. And that meant the real killer was still out there. Maybe even selecting another victim. She couldn't let that happen.

Never mind Darcy's misgivings about the crime scene; Kat's gut said Laura wasn't guilty. The MO was wrong. The stats were against it.

Thinking about her dad, she found it easy to discount a cheating husband's protestations of innocence. But for the allegedly *cheated-upon* to dismiss the idea so completely, as Callum Michie had, was another massive red flag.

She called Jack Beale, aware she was breaking the rules. Again.

'I need to know cause of death.'

'And hello to you, too, Kat.'

'Please, Jack.'

Jack switched from flirtatious to formal in a single breath. 'COD is strangulation by ligature.'

'How much force does it take to actually strangle a person to death? Could a woman do it?'

'Interesting question. It takes four pounds of pressure on the jugular vein for ten seconds to close it off. On the carotid, it's eleven pounds. On the trachea, which appears to have happened here, it jumps substantially. Triples, in fact, to thirty-three. A woman *could* manage it, if she were sufficiently determined. But it's not just about her strength, it's about her persistence.'

'How long she'd have to apply it, you mean.'

'I do. Release the pressure immediately and ordinarily the victim regains consciousness within ten seconds.'

'How long to cause death?'

'Brain death occurs in four to five minutes. It's a long time to maintain that level of pressure, even with a passive victim.'

'What else did you turn up?'

'The victim also suffered blunt force trauma to the back of her head. Specifically, the centre of the occipital bone. I found another largish bruise over her solar plexus: ten by seven centimetres. Judging by shape, and the distinctive lighter and darker areas, it most probably occurred as the result of a punch. A hard punch. She'd have been incapacitated. Struggling to breathe. Might have made her more pliant.'

Kat glanced down at her own hand, which she bunched into a fist. Frowned.

'Hold on a second, Jack.'

Taking a ruler from her desk drawer, she measured knuckle to knuckle, across and down the striking surface.

'I just measured my fist, it's only seven by five. I'm a bit bigger than Laura Paxton, too. That's odd, right?'

'You'd need to measure *her* fist, obviously, but yes, at first glance, the bruise does appear to be caused by either a man's fist or that of a tall and well-built woman. What's the suspect's height?'

Kat shrugged. 'Five-three? Five-four tops?'

70

'This isn't definitive. Bruises aren't potato prints. They're subject to all kinds of variables, from blood flow and density of blood vessels to presence of cancer or liver disease. But, all things being equal, or *ceteris paribus* to use the technical term, I'd have to say that the likelihood is that this injury was caused by an assailant other than your suspect.'

Kat nodded to herself. Whatever had occurred in that bright, shiny hallway in the house on Chamberlayne Avenue, she was increasingly convinced that someone other than Laura Paxton was responsible.

'Would the blow to the back of her head have been enough to knock her out?' she asked.

'It's possible. Head injuries are unpredictable. You can lose consciousness after a glancing blow on a door jamb, or walk away after someone smacks you with a hammer. It depends on bone density, distribution of blood vessels beneath the skull, all sorts of things.'

'But in your opinion, is it likely?'

'It's *possible*. But in my *opinion*, had she lost consciousness, it would have been momentary. Less than a minute.'

'Thanks, Jack. I know you could get into trouble for telling me all this.'

'Oh, I doubt that,' he said airily. 'DI Carver may rule the roost at Jubilee Place. But at MGH, he's just another know-nothing plod.'

There it was again. That casual arrogance. Even though she hated Carve-up's guts, something about the way Jack dismissed him rankled. A conversation for another day.

'Well, I appreciate it anyway.'

Everything Jack had told her confirmed her own take on the murder. Try as she might, she simply could not visualise an attack taking place the way Laura Paxton had described it that would also fit the post-mortem facts.

She needed to pay another visit to the cells.

Chapter Seventeen

Kat sat beside Laura on the narrow, moulded-plastic shelf that served as both bed and chair in the tiny square cell.

She took her friend's hands in her own. Looked her straight in the eye.

'The pathologist found a bruise on Alanna's stomach. Just below her breastbone. Do you know how it got there?'

Laura blinked. Frowned. The information had come as a surprise. Then she nodded.

'I punched her.'

'I see.' Kat held out a transparent plastic ruler. 'Would you let me measure your hand, please, Laura?'

'Why?'

'It's just routine. Can you make a fist for me?'

Laura blinked twice, then slowly folded her fingers. Kat could already see her fist was too small. But she took the measurements anyway. Six-point-five by four-point-five centimetres.

Sure, now, that she was not sitting next to a murderer, she pocketed both ruler and notebook.

'Laura, I don't think you killed Alanna Michie. I think someone else did. And now they're putting pressure on you to confess. I'm right, aren't I?'

Laura dropped her gaze and shook her head. 'I did it.'

'You just told me you punched her. But the bruise is way too big. There's no way you could have made it.'

'The pathologist must have made a mistake.'

'I don't think he did. I think if anyone's making a mistake it's you, Laura. You're throwing your life away. I'd just like to understand why. If someone's threatening you, we can protect you.'

Then Laura did something that surprised Kat. Eyes flashing with sudden fire, she glared at her. It was the first sign of animation from her since Kat had moved her away from Alanna's corpse. 'I want a lawyer.'

'Good. I think that's a sensible idea. I know Will was keen to find you a good solicitor.'

'No! I don't want anything from Will. He's the reason I'm in here. Just get me one of the cheap ones. You know, legal aid.'

Kat nodded. It was a step in the right direction, and she could hardly force a suspect to appoint a lawyer not of her own choosing.

She left Laura in her cell and went to update Tom and share some thoughts on how he might question Laura.

Chapter Eighteen

Kat took a seat beside and slightly behind Tom. They'd agreed she'd sit in on the interview with Laura, but Tom would ask the questions. He'd be on surer ground now he wasn't facing an outraged-slash-grieving gangster.

As long as Carve-up didn't decide to observe, she'd be fine.

Laura's brief was a young, flustered and quite obviously ill-prepared duty solicitor. He was still reading the sketchy case file, eyes flicking left and right, as Tom re-cautioned Laura, introduced both himself and Kat to the recorder and then opened his own copy of the file.

Tom cleared his throat. 'Laura, you claim you strangled Alanna Michie because you believed she was having an affair with your husband, is that right?'

'Yes. That's why I killed her.'

The solicitor hastily scribbled a note.

'Can you tell me what led you to believe they were involved?'

Laura's eyes flicked to the ceiling. Then locked back on to Tom's. 'It was nothing specific. Just a woman's intuition, you know?'

Tom smiled. Nodded. Kat, silent, was sure now that she was listening to lies.

'Why now?'

Laura frowned. 'What do you mean?'

'I'm just wondering why you picked this particular morning. I mean, I get that you had this intuition. But unless it just flashed into your head when you woke up today, why did you wait until now?'

'I don't know. It got too much. I decided to go round there and kill her and I did. Why are you asking me all these questions?'

'At the time of your arrest, when you called DS Ballantyne, you said you'd intended only to have it out with Alanna, but things escalated. Now you say you went there *intending* to kill her. Which is it, Laura?'

'The second one.'

Tom spent a few seconds studying one of the crime scene photos. Alanna lay sprawled on the hall floor.

'Was the tie on the floor?'

'No.' Laura looked down at her hands, started picking at a shred of loose skin on the inner edge of her left index finger. The nail was already rimmed with a dark brown line of dried blood. 'It was on a coat hook.'

'So you hit Alanna, and then you turned and spotted the tie?'

'Yes.'

Tom frowned. 'Sorry, Laura, I'm just trying to visualise the sequence of events here. You pushed her and then, what, looked around for something to strangle her with?'

'My client has already answered that question, DC Gray,' the young solicitor said in a quavering voice.

Kat looked at him. Noticed the way his shirt collar stood out from his neck. And the arrow-straight crease peeping out from inside the jacket. Had he taken it straight out of a packet that morning? It was almost enough to make her feel sorry for him. But in truth, the only person she felt sorry for right now was the woman beside him.

'It's fine,' Laura said to him. She turned to Kat. 'I just saw it. I thought it would do. And it did. Because, as I have already said multiple times, I killed her with it.'

'Yes, I see that,' Tom said, maintaining his reasonable tone. 'You spotted the tie, thought "That'll do," and then bish-bash-bosh, she's dead, you're a murderer, and you called DS Ballantyne to confess? Is that about it?'

'DC Gray, I hardly think that sort of language is appropriate,' the young lawyer piped up.

'Oh, please shut up, won't you?' Laura snapped. 'You're only here because they're trying to put words into my mouth.'

He coloured, staring furiously down at his notepad. Now Kat did feel a flicker of sympathy for him.

'Look, Laura, here's what I'm struggling with.' Tom leaned over the table, just a little. Narrowing the emotional gap between them as much as the physical. Kat was impressed. 'You say you went there to kill her, but you didn't take a weapon with you. Why was that? I mean, what if there hadn't been a tie on the coat rack?'

Laura tightened her lips. Tore a tiny strip of skin free from the side of her fingernail. Bright, fresh blood beaded. She raised her finger to her lips and sucked. 'No comment.'

Tom turned to Kat. A pre-arranged signal. They'd agreed that at the first 'No comment' he'd pass the baton to Kat.

She leaned forward and smiled at Laura.

'We play netball together from time to time, don't we?'

Laura frowned. 'Yes. Why are you asking me that?'

'We get changed together at the leisure centre or wherever we're playing, don't we?'

'Yes. Obviously.'

'Obviously,' Kat agreed. 'You're petite. A size eight, right?'

'Six, mostly.'

'Six? God, I wish I was.' She didn't. She liked her body. 'What size do you reckon Alanna was?'

'I really have no idea.'

'No, me neither. But according to the pathologist, she was nine stone six and just under five foot nine tall. Combined with her measurements, that made her a ten to twelve, depending on the retailer. And she was fit, too.'

'Where are you going with this, Detective Sergeant?' This time the solicitor had asked a half-decent question.

'She was bigger than you. Probably stronger. Did she fight back, Laura?'

'She knocked herself out when she fell.'

'I see. When her head hit the tiles.'

'Yes.'

'After you punched her in the gut?'

'Yes.'

'How long was she unconscious for?'

Laura shrugged. Sucked more blood from her finger. The repeated action disturbed Kat. As if her friend were trying to drink herself dry.

'She didn't wake up. That's all I can tell you.'

'Laura, how would you react if I told you that in the opinion of the pathologist, Alanna would most likely not have been unconscious for more than a minute?'

'It doesn't matter. She was dead anyway.'

'Before the minute was up, you mean?'

'Yes.'

'So is that how long you strangled her for?'

'Yes.'

'A minute. Or thereabouts.'

'Yes.'

Kat made a note. Looked up and smiled at Laura. 'Thanks for clarifying. It's a weird thing, strangulation. I suppose most of us are lucky enough that we only see it on the telly or at the pictures. You know, some badass locks his hands or a rope around the bad guy's neck and boom! He's dead. Have you ever seen a film like that?'

Laura shrugged. 'Maybe. I don't remember.'

Kat nodded. 'I have. They're not really my cup of tea but my boys enjoy them. Here's the thing, though, Laura. And it's been puzzling me as you've been talking to Tom. In fact, ever since you called me to tell me what you'd done. You see, again according to the pathologist, it takes around four to five minutes to kill someone by strangling them. Yet you say you only applied force to Alanna's neck for one minute. Maybe even a bit less. How do you explain that?'

Laura eyeballed Kat. Her lips twitched. She was chewing them on the inside. The blood had stopped beading on her fingertip, but at some point she'd smeared a little on to the tabletop. She looked down and wiped at it with her cuff.

'Maybe it was longer. I was suffering from, what's the word? Heightened emotion.'

'Of course. I understand. You were murdering your friend because you thought she'd been sleeping with your husband behind your back. So maybe it was four minutes? Five?'

'It could have been. Yes.'

'But then Alanna would have regained consciousness, wouldn't she? And started fighting back. And like we've agreed, she was bigger and stronger than you. Yet there's barely a mark on you.'

Laura touched the bruise on her forehead. And pointed at the bandages on her forearms. Winced. Theatrically, Kat thought.

'I got these, didn't I?'

'Yeah, but come on, Laura, are you telling me that against a petite attacker, Alanna only managed to catch you a minor blow

78

to the forehead and give you a couple of scratches? Where are the rest? The bitemarks on your hands, the bruises from where she tried to yank your arms away? The marks on your shins where she back-heeled you? Alanna was fighting for her life, yet it looks like little more than a nasty spat on the netball court.'

Laura glanced sideways. 'No comment.'

Kat hadn't expected her to say anything else.

'So far, Laura, you've told us a story about how, without any evidence except for your woman's intuition, you believed Alanna Michie was having an affair with your husband. That being the case, you decided, completely premeditatedly, to visit her at her house, and murder her. Now I want to tell *you* a story. A different interpretation of events. I think Alanna was already dead when you found her. I think a man murdered her, because strangulation is almost always a method chosen by male killers, especially if the victim is female. It's the strength differential, you see. Now, that raises the question, why would you, totally innocent of the crime, voluntarily confess?'

'I did it! I told you!'

Kat held up her hand. 'Let me finish, please. I think someone forced you to confess. Maybe they threatened to get to Will because of his work. Or they were blackmailing you over a secret you couldn't bear Will or your family and friends to know about. It must have been a terrible threat to make you prefer a life sentence to the truth.

'Because, Laura, and I am speaking as a friend here, as well as a police officer, nothing you've told us in this interview makes any sense. You intended to commit murder, yet you didn't take a weapon. You immobilised a woman physically bigger than you, but not for long enough to kill her by strangling. And in order to do that, your hand miraculously grew in size. Even the method you chose bucks against the statistics. And that's not just here in the UK. In America and other countries, too. I looked it up. How am I doing?'

During the later part of this speech, Laura had resumed picking at her fingers. Two more now sported tiny scarlet lacerations where she'd pulled skin away from the nail. Now she looked straight at Kat.

'Have you checked the lipstick? The tie? My fingerprints and my DNA are all over them. My skin cells are under Alanna's fingernails. I murdered her. I confess. I'm guilty.' She turned to her solicitor, who appeared shell-shocked. 'Do I have to answer any more questions?'

Perhaps relieved at being finally asked for advice, he sat straighter. 'No. You can assert your right not to speak if you don't want to.'

'I'm doing that, then. I would like to go back to my cell now, please.'

Kat sighed. Looked sideways at Tom. He closed his file.

She'd interviewed a lot of people who protested their innocence when she knew they were guilty. But this was the first time she'd interviewed someone who protested their guilt when she knew they were innocent. Of course, knowing someone was innocent was fine if you were authorised to do something about it. But Kat and authorisation were on a break right now.

She'd have to find another way to get to the truth. One that didn't bring her into conflict with Carve-up. Or expose Tom any more than he already was. It was bad enough she was defying the DI and working the case unofficially. But now she was dragging Tom into the mire with her.

Chapter Nineteen

Kat and Tom went to the canteen after leaving Laura to be escorted back to the cells.

'Now do you see, Tomski?' Kat asked, after returning with two mugs of tea.

'I see a woman found *with* a murder victim. A woman whose DNA is, according to her, *on* the murder victim – and the murder weapon. And a woman who confessed on the phone *from* the crime scene. What am I missing?'

Kat tugged her earlobes. Why couldn't Tom see what was right in front of him?

'Her story is full of holes. She's the wrong build. Her fist is the wrong size. She kept flip-flopping about whether she went there intending to kill Alanna. And then there's what Jack told me. If Alanna was unconscious at all, it would have been for less than a minute. She would have woken up and fought back. Hard. Yet there's no signs of that level of struggle.'

'Maybe he's wrong. Maybe Alanna was out cold for longer.'

'But Laura said she only strangled her for a minute.'

'She changed her mind.'

'Only after I pointed out it needed longer to actually kill someone.'

'But the evidence all points to Laura. The CPS are going to love it. We've got means, motive and opportunity. DNA, confession, everything.'

'So let's talk about motive, then?'

Tom huffed out a breath. 'Fine. She thought Alanna was having an affair with her husband. Sexual jealousy is one of the commonest motives for murder.'

'Yes! Of course it is. Don't you think I know that? But for a start, it's much more usually a jealous husband who kills his wife. Possibly the lover as well if he's got the opportunity. And strangling? Really? How many female murderers have ever strangled their victim?'

'I don't know.'

Kat shook her head. 'Well, no, I don't either. But it's got to be vanishingly small, right? We know when it comes to homicides of adults committed by females, the usual methods are poisoning, drugs, drowning and asphyxiation. If it's an intimate partner they might use an improvised weapon if one is at hand. A kitchen knife. A hammer. But strangling? No. That's really brutal. It's violent. It's intimate. And it takes a lot of strength and determination.'

'So, basically, you're saying it had to be a man. Isn't that, I don't know' – he cocked his head – 'a little bit sexist?'

'Tomski, seriously, this isn't a time for jokes.'

'Fine, but even if strangulation is used by men ninety-nine-point-nine per cent of the time, she could still be the outlier, couldn't she? She could even be the first.'

Kat sighed. Because Tom, while irritating, was also correct. And they did, still, have no evidence pointing in any other direction than straight at Laura Paxton. She leant closer to her bagman. Her *fast-track* bagman. Who was suddenly reporting in to a DI instead of a DS.

'Listen, Tomski. I get it. I really do. This is a golden opportunity for you to show what you learned at uni and impress the brass.' Tom opened his mouth, no doubt to protest that this wasn't about him having a degree. She cut him off with a raised hand, and she lowered her voice. 'But one of these days you're going to have to decide where your loyalties lie. Right now, I know what it looks like on the outside. I'm in receipt of a massive wodge of cash I can't explain, and Carve-up's sitting pretty in his Ar-bloody-mani suit and his nice plush office and it looks obvious which way to jump. But he's the dirty one. And one of these days, he will involve you in things you really don't want to be involved in.'

Tom's head had started shaking like the arm of a metronome. And his expression wasn't encouraging. He was upset. No, more than upset. He was pissed off.

'You have no right to talk to me like that! It's emotional blackmail, and it's really, *really* unprofessional. Stuart is giving me orders now. What do you want me to do? Ignore them? Punch him in the nose like you did?' Now it was his turn to speak in an urgent whisper. 'Which, in case you'd forgotten, I witnessed *and* lied to Linda about.'

Kat sat back. Tom's words had struck home like a slap. 'I'm sorry, mate. You're right. That was totally out of order. I apologise.'

'Apology accepted,' Tom said with a strained smile. 'So, do you know where the money came from?'

'I wish I did. It's driving me mad. But I swear to you, Tomski, it's not what it looks like.'

Tom looked uncomfortable. It wasn't hard to see why. She'd just used the same pathetic excuse as the most unimaginative villains.

A man holding a bloody knife over the corpse of a woman.
It's not what it looks like.
A dealer caught with a cling-wrapped kilo of coke.
It's not what it looks like.

Well, what the hell did it look like, then? Of *course* Tom would be sceptical. He had every right to be. And not only was Kat interfering in his investigation and risking screwing it up, she wasn't even focusing fully. Because that damned money was like a siren, wailing away in between her ears all the time.

As Tom outlined his next steps, which all led to Laura Paxton's conviction for murder, Kat was only half listening. Whether or not Laura was guilty, there were ominous storm clouds gathering over Kat's own future. What if Iris couldn't find out anything in time? Or ever?

Not only would Kat be suspended, as Linda had warned. Every moment she stayed involved in Laura's case, every unauthorised action she took, could be jeopardising a successful outcome. *Whoever* was guilty.

But Tom didn't have the experience to get to the bottom of Laura's bogus confession. And he didn't have the motivation, either. Only Kat stood between Laura and a conviction for a murder she didn't commit.

She had to keep working on it. Just, out of Carve-up's crosshairs.

Chapter Twenty

At 6:00 p.m. Kat called Van.

'Hi, darling. You on your way home?' he asked.

'Yes. Can you cook, though? I have to keep working tonight. Might have to come back in or go see some people.'

'Of course.'

'Riley home?'

'Yep. Good news.'

'What?'

'He got an A-star today.'

'What in?'

'Scowling, grunting, rolling his eyes and slamming his bedroom door. Apparently they want to put him forward for the county trials.'

Kat snorted with laughter. A merciful shaft of humour piercing the darkness that enveloped her like a poisonous fog. Yes, Riley was well and truly, and deeply, into the stage of adolescence where, to put it kindly, he couldn't see the point of adults.

'What was it this time?'

'Guess.'

'Oh, I don't know, did you ask him how school was today? Say hello in a totally lame way?'

'Worse. I asked him if he'd like fish fingers for tea.'

Kat smiled. 'Let me guess.' She adopted a tone of voice composed of equal parts derision, sarcasm and contempt. '"Do you think I'm a *baby?*"'

'His exact words.'

'Well, I'd *love* fish fingers, especially if they're in a white-bread sandwich with lots of mayonnaise and ketchup and oven chips.'

'Weirdo.'

'*You're* a weirdo.'

'Yeah, but you love me.'

'I haven't got much choice, have I?' A beat. 'Weirdo.'

Smiling, she pocketed her phone. Only to drag it straight out again to check for a text from Iris. Nothing. Of course there was nothing.

'So what's happened to keep you chained to the copshop?' Van asked once the meal was over. He frowned. 'Is it the money?'

Kat tried to ignore the klaxon blaring in her head. *Yes! Yes, of course it's the bloody money!*

'Do you remember me talking about Laura Paxton? She plays wing attack for the Malbec Mafia.'

Van furrowed his brow. It was unconvincing.

'Not exactly.'

'Doesn't matter,' Kat said, wiping a blob of pink-tinged mayo from the table and sucking it off her finger. 'She called me this morning and confessed to murdering one of her friends.'

'Christ! Why? How?'

Kat sketched in such details as she could.

Van shook his head. 'That sounds weird. It is weird, right? I mean, not like your peculiar taste in fish-finger-sandwich condiments. *Properly* weird.'

'She didn't do it. I'm convinced of it. She's covering for someone. I think she's being coerced somehow to take the fall, but I don't think she's going to break. She's too frightened of what they'll do.'

'But you're going to find the real killer.'

'That's the trouble. Officially I'm not allowed anywhere near the case. Carve-up's put Tom in charge.'

'Isn't he a bit young?'

'Exactly! And all he's interested in is wrapping things up neat and tidy for the CPS. So I have to try. But I've only got a week.'

'Because you need to clear your name with internal affairs.'

'They're called the Three Counties Anti-Corruption Unit officially, but yes.'

'And you're sure it wasn't your dad playing silly buggers?'

'He was adamant when I asked him on Saturday. Got quite shirty with me, actually.'

Van rounded the table and crouched beside her chair. Put an arm around her waist.

'I've seen the way you've looked since Carve-up accused you last Friday. I hate just sitting here watching you struggling. There must be something I can do.' Van grimaced. 'God, that arsehole needs someone to talk some sense into him. That or beat the truth out of him.'

'Whoa, there, cowboy. I don't think getting threatened by an IT consultant, even a very buff one like you, is going to knock Carve-up off his perch.'

'Well, what, then?'

'I just have to keep looking for clues in my own life. Although for the life of me I can't think of anyone who'd have that kind of money and want me off the force.'

'You'll be all right, won't you, darling? I mean this friend of yours, Iris. She *will* get to the bottom of it, won't she?'

'I hope so.' Sudden tears pricked at the backs of Kat's eyes. 'Van, what if she doesn't? I can't lose this job. I love it. It's what I do! From the moment I thought Liv had been murdered, I've had this need deep inside me. It's why I joined the police after we got back from Thailand. It's what I've worked for every day since.'

'Hey, hey. Iris will have a massive whiteboard with all these shell companies and offshore trusts and arrows all over it. Ninety-three computer screens all flashing up tables of bank accounts in red and green numbers.'

'Nitwit, that's *Mission: Impossible 2*!'

'That *could* be how she does it.'

She shuffled her bottom round so she could hug him back. Spoke into the crook of his shoulder.

'You'd still love me if they booted me out, wouldn't you?'

'Hey! Nobody's booting you out. You're the best detective at Jubilee Place. I think this is all going to turn out to be some awful practical joke. Or, I don't know, have you got any distant relatives, or a forgotten godparent who might have left you some money?'

Kat sniffed back her tears and smiled down into her husband's face.

'We already discussed that, and no, I haven't.'

'Ah, but you don't *know* that, do you? That's the whole *point* of long-lost rich relatives. They're *lost*.'

Kat smiled. 'I need to go. I want to talk to Laura's husband again. If he really *was* having an affair with the victim, I need to winkle it out of him. But if he's not, he's a DC, so he might have an insight into who might be putting the screws on Laura. Maybe it's someone he put away.'

Van straightened. Pulled her to him and kissed the top of her head.

'Go carefully, yes? Accusing him of having an affair is unlikely to go down well. Not to mention pissing off Carve-up if he finds out you're still working the case.'

Kat made a 'Well, duh!' face: slack-jawed, rolled-eyes. 'Thanks for that piercing insight into investigative strategy, Van.'

'Oh, it looks like Riley wasn't the only one to get an A-star for sarkiness.'

Grinning, she kissed him, hard. 'I love you.'

'Will you be late?'

'I'll text you, but hopefully not.'

◆　◆　◆

Driving her own car again – no record in the pool car log – Kat arrived outside Will and Laura Paxton's house: a Victorian terrace on Palmerston Street in Cherryville. Plenty of cops lived in the neighbourhood as it was so convenient for the station. Window boxes burgeoned with crimson geraniums that reminded Kat of holidays in Spain.

Will led her into the kitchen. He looked dreadful. Sallow skin, listless movements, a droop to his mouth. Shock did that to a person.

'What the hell happened today, Kat?' he asked with his back to her as he made two coffees. 'Has she had some kind of breakdown, do you think?'

'That's a bit over my pay grade, Will. And, for the record? I'm really sorry you're having to deal with this.'

He handed her a mug of coffee and waved a slack hand for her to take a chair. She sat facing him.

'Listen, Will, you're job, OK? You know the score. I have to ask all kinds of questions.' Kat took a quick sip of her coffee. Winced as the scalding liquid burned the tip of her tongue, so it felt dry and furry. 'What I'm about to ask you, it's going to sound intrusive, but it's just routine. I don't mean anything by it.'

'This is about me having an affair with Alanna, isn't it? I already told you. I'm not. Wasn't, I mean. Christ! Why would Laura say that? Did she give you any reason? Had she found something?'

'Was there anything *to* find?'

'No!' His voice had risen to a panicked squawk. 'Sorry, no. I don't think I ever met Alanna Michie. Except on the pages of intelligence reports. Hang on. Wait here.'

He pulled out his phone, and showed her a text chat between him and Laura. It was flirtatious, bantering, spiked with the sort of private jokes husbands and wives only shared if they trusted each other. Then joint selfies on his Facebook wall; Instagram, too. None of it was *evidence* of a happy marriage, but it went a long way to paint a picture of one.

Kat nodded. 'Thanks, Will. For not going for me.' She smiled, hoping she could build a rapport with him. 'If it's any comfort, I don't believe her. I also don't believe she did it.'

Will's eyes, half closed a second ago, popped fully open. 'You don't? Why? What's your theory?'

'I'm not exactly sure at the moment. But I'm wondering whether someone is pressuring Laura.'

'Forcing her to take the fall for something they did? Yes.' He nodded, scratched the back of his head furiously, as if trying to dislodge something clinging there with clawed feet. 'Yes, that would work.' He slammed an open palm down on the table, making the coffee mugs stutter and slop. 'And I know who.'

'You've got a name?'

He shook his head. 'Not a name, but an idea. There's a gang in London been sniffing round Middlehampton. Looking to expand their territory northwards. Too much pressure in the Smoke from foreign outfits. The Strutts have been targeted. Maybe Alanna was killed as a warning.'

'Why pick Laura to take the fall? Why pick *anyone*?'

'I'm running the team monitoring the London mob. Maybe they're planning to put pressure on me somehow. It's two birds with one stone. They hit the Strutts and distract me at the same time.'

'What's the name of this London lot?'

'It's another family business. Run by the mother. Heather Parsons. Sounds like a fifties housewife, acts like Scarface.'

'Thanks, Will. This is excellent.'

He was frowning, drawing circles in the spilt coffee on the pine tabletop.

'You should get the tie analysed. It'll have the murderer's epithelials all over it. Unless he wore gloves. Maybe DNA if we're lucky.' He looked up at her, face twisted with a guilty expression. 'Which, obviously, you know, being a homicide DS. Sorry, it's just been such a bloody awful day.'

Kat smiled sympathetically. 'It's fine. The problem is, in all likelihood we've already got Laura's skin cells under Alanna's fingernails. She said she used the tie, so if I try and persuade the brass to give me more money for testing, it's probably only going to confirm her story.'

Will tipped his head back and swallowed the rest of his coffee. He stood abruptly, scraping his chair back on the stone floor tiles.

'I need a proper drink.'

He fetched a bottle of supermarket own-label Scotch from a cupboard and grabbed a tumbler from the dishwasher – clean, Kat was pleased to see – and sloshed an inch or so into the bottom. He tipped the neck towards her, eyebrows raised. She shook her head.

'Better not. I'm driving.'

He nodded then sank half the whisky in a single pull. Stared at the remainder, swilled it round in the glass, then finished it. Reached for the bottle and poured another measure, bigger than the first.

Kat was torn. Even though he was hurting, drowning his problems in Scotch wasn't going to solve anything. She felt she should say something, but it wasn't her place. She didn't know him at all. He wasn't a mate from Jubilee Place she could touch on the arm and ask how he was feeling. Suggest maybe an early night would do him more good than getting stinking drunk.

Still, the sight of him, lost and alone at his own kitchen table while his wife was locked away in a cell . . . well, maybe she'd be reaching for the bottle if their positions were reversed.

'I'll get to the bottom of this, Will,' she said, hoping word hadn't leaked from Jubilee Place to Hampton Hill that she shouldn't even be working the case.

Kat returned to Jubilee Place and spent the night alternating between the case and the mystery fifty grand. At 9.45 p.m., she called one of her snouts. They were supposed to call them Covert Human Intelligence Sources – pronounced *chiz*. Nobody did.

The voice on the line was blurry, sleepy. 'Yeah. Who's 'is?'

'It's Kat, Isaac. Can you talk?'

Isaac Handy was a low-level drug dealer. He hung around at the edge of Middlehampton's criminal fraternity like an untucked shirt tail, and could be relied upon to have heard the latest gossip on the streets. She pictured him wreathed in weed smoke in a cramped and squalid bedsit.

'Oh, hi, Kat. Sorry. I was, uh, reading.'

'Oh, really? What?'

'*Treasure Island.*'

'You never fail to surprise me, Isaac.'

'Did you want something, then? Or were you calling to ask me if I wanted to join your book club?'

'Funny.'

'For a drug dealer,' he said in a hurt tone of voice.

'For anyone. Look . . .'

Now what? She'd rung him without a concrete idea of what she was going to ask. Obviously she couldn't mention the money.

'What?'

'I've had a threat,' she improvised. 'And, I just wondered whether you'd heard anything about someone with a grudge against me. An old score to settle. Anything like that?'

'You're a copper.' She could almost see the shrug. 'It goes with the territory.'

'I mean more than the usual bellyaching. Someone with a proper axe to grind. Someone who might want to screw with my career.'

'The only man I know who's been mouthing off about you is Callum Michie.'

She didn't tell Isaac that since the money had arrived before Alanna's murder, she'd discounted Callum. Instead, she thanked him and asked him to keep his ears open.

'Enjoy your book.'

'Aargh, Jim-lad,' he rasped in what he presumably thought was a piratical accent.

The rest of the night yielded little of any value, and she eventually drove home at 10.15 p.m., eyes watering from staring at a computer screen for too long, head pounding from too much coffee and not enough fresh air.

No ideas about the fifty K and no new leads on Alanna Michie's murder.

And the ACU hyenas were circling closer.

Chapter Twenty-One

Kat had got in early again. Waking at 3.30 a.m. made going into work seem like the least worst option.

She'd spent the time rereading all the case notes on Alanna's murder, trying to see if anything at all pointed to the real killer. But she'd come up with nothing. Just background on the Parsons gang. Yes, they had violent men – and women – on their books, but she couldn't connect anything to Alanna or Laura. Beyond what Will had shared – probably unwisely, given her pariah status – she had nothing.

At 9.01 a.m., she texted Iris, only to get a bland, two-word answer.

Nothing yet

She bit her lip. Tried to ignore the anxiety tightening her stomach and making her feel like she needed to rush to the loo. She just couldn't sit there doing nothing and rely on Iris. Good as she was, Iris had other things to do besides trying to exonerate Kat.

She'd been avoiding calling Liv so far, fearful that her friend would do more harm than good. But the longer this went on, the worse Kat felt it would turn out. She needed her friend.

More than anyone, Liv would trust Kat and fight her corner till she either put the other guy down or died trying.

'Hey, Thelma, what's up?' Liv dropped straight back into their teenaged nicknames for each other. Kat was Thelma and Liv was Louise. They'd watched the film so often they had every line of dialogue down. Even Brad Pitt's.

'Do you fancy coming to stay for a couple of days? I could really do with a friend right now.'

'Of course! Is anything the matter?'

Kat headed out to the stairwell before explaining about the money and the tightrope she was walking between helping Tom out and getting suspended properly. Before she'd even finished, Liv was chivvying her off the line: '—so's I can throw some knickers and a washbag in my rucksack. I'll be there as soon as I can. I just need to put some petrol in the car and buy some Red Bulls and Haribo.'

'There's no rush. I'm at work. I just—'

'I'm leaving now, Thelma. Hang tough.'

And then she was gone. Kat smiled. Since her reappearance in Kat's life, Kat had been struggling with accepting her friend was alive but suddenly sixteen years older. A woman, as opposed to the teenaged girl she'd been the last time Kat had seen her. But it felt good. And each time they spoke, a little less awkward. If there was anyone she wanted in her corner fighting against Carve-up and whoever he was in league with, it was Liv Arnold.

Kat's phone rang. She glanced at the screen and then stabbed the green icon. 'Hello, Frank. Is this a social call?'

'We need to talk.'

He didn't need to elaborate. They shared a common interest. Namely, identifying the real killer of Alanna Michie.

'Where?' Not when. That would be now.

'Do you like fish, Kat?'

'A bit early for eating, isn't it?'

'I fancy visiting the aquarium. They've got some new specimens. Apparently, there's an octopus that can open screw-top jars.'

The line went dead.

Kat glanced up guiltily. But she was alone.

Chapter Twenty-Two

Kat could see why Frank had chosen the Sealife Centre.

Small-time villains like Isaac Handy liked to pick out-of-the-way open places. Abandoned factories. Public parks. The towpath. But there, you stuck out like an undertaker at a white wedding. It only needed one passing boater, druggie or strolling off-duty copper and you were made. Entered into a mental log or official notebook.

But here, in the semi-darkness, where crowds of people offered camouflage while focusing anywhere except on their fellow gawpers, you could be truly anonymous.

The morning crowd consisted of sugar-jazzed children, their harassed-looking minders, and gaggles of school students bearing clipboards with photocopied questionnaires.

Kat approached the tall glass tank holding 'Ollie the Octopus, our Newest (and Cleverest!) Resident'.

The octopus was nowhere to be seen. Perhaps not surprisingly, he had thus managed to drive away all but one visitor. Clever creature.

The remaining observer wore a dark suit, impossible to tell the colour in the gloom. And an equally unremarkable dark shirt beneath it. Only his bulk, that of a heavyweight boxer, lent him anything that might be termed noteworthy. Although here again, his sombre outfit disguised just how much muscle Frank Strutt was packing.

Kat stood next to him, staring at her own reflection in the thick glass.

'Amazing creatures,' Frank murmured. 'Did you know, scientists now believe they're conscious? Soon you won't be able to order a plateful when you go on holiday. Shame, really. I love a bit of polpi in umido. Ever had it, Kat?'

'Nope.'

'Stewed octopus in white wine and tomatoes. Comes from Puglia. Me and Sue had a holiday down there a few years back.'

Knowing that Frank hadn't brought her here to lecture here on the tourist delights of southern Italy, Kat forced herself to wait. He'd make his point soon enough.

'I like calamari, myself,' she said.

'Yeah, but octopus is the authentic taste of Italy. Did you know they have three hearts?'

'Italians?'

Frank's left eye twitched. He didn't smile. 'Octopus. Two for the limbs, one exclusively for the organs. It says so right there on that very informative sign.' He inclined his blocky head towards a softly lit board. 'Funny thing is, their arms can think for themselves. So the head might be occupied by one thing, but an arm might have gone off trying to solve some problem or other, without checking in with the brain.'

Ah. Now she saw where he was going with this tale of aquatic miracles. Callum was hot for revenge; Frank wanted a less fiery approach.

'So, even if most of the tentacles are behaving themselves,' she said, adopting Frank's fishy metaphor, 'one might decide to act on its own initiative.'

'Exactly. Now, in the case of my own fish tank, as you can imagine, young Callum wants to avenge Alanna's death.'

'You're not so keen, I take it.'

'Oh, don't get me wrong. I want to see that justice is done. I just don't think—' Frank waited until a couple of slouching late teens paused at the octopus tank, tapped on the glass a couple of times and then left, expressing their doubts about Ollie's intellectual gifts. 'I don't think remaking *Assault on Precinct 13* at Jubilee Place is necessarily going to serve anybody's interests. Even Callum's. Though the poor sod's too cut up over Alanna to think straight.'

'What are you saying, Frank?'

'I want to know what you're doing about it. You don't think this Paxton woman did it?'

He'd phrased it as a question, but they both knew it was a statement.

She shook her head. 'Her story's thinner than a Rizla paper.'

'Right. So who *did* do it, then?'

'That's what I'm trying to find out. Tell me, is there any truth in the rumour that a London family business called the Parsons is after a slice of your business in Middlehampton?'

Frank was far too seasoned in this particular game to ask her how she'd come by that titbit. Instead, he just nodded. 'I'm handling it.'

'Any bad blood between Callum and one of theirs? Or directly with Alanna?'

He shrugged his massive shoulders. 'If there was, neither of them told me.'

'But it's a possibility.'

'It's a possibility. But before you go haring off to the Smoke in search of a "gangland rival" as the *Echo* would probably put it, know this. I've met Heather Parsons a couple of times. Not that we're involved in anything we shouldn't be. But whatever we *are* doing, it's going to be solved through jaw-jaw, not war-war, understand? It's not Heather's crew.'

'Does Callum have any personal enemies? Or did Alanna?'

Frank rotated his head slowly, as if it were carried on smoothly greased bearings.

'That's a serious question, is it?'

'Apart from the obvious. Any family feuds bubbling under? People he's got into a ruck with? People he owes money to, or who owe it to him?'

'Nothing I'm aware of, which as you know, means a lot more than it would coming from someone else.'

Kat nodded. 'Could you look into it?'

'What, I'm your bagman now? What about young Tom? Surely he could put that degree in criminology to good use on some proper detective work.'

'That's a bit tricky right now. We're under some tough management directives.'

Should she explain why? Let Frank in on the shame that clung to her like sewage after some ill-advised wild swimming in the Gade? In fact, what had Van asked her? Who else might have the kind of cash that had turned up in her bank account? Well, Frank Strutt certainly did. But they'd always had a relationship based on mutual respect. She could hardly ask him outright, could she? *Could* she?

Frank cut across her thoughts.

'That doesn't sound good, Kat. I need results on this.'

'What, you're my DI now?'

He favoured her with a searching look. 'Touché. Listen, I'll have a chat with the lad. A *diplomatic* chat. The way he is at the moment, he's likely to make an octopus arm look like the model of obedience. But I mean it, Kat. I can hold him on the leash for a week, tops, then it's open season on Laura Paxton.'

She nodded and left him staring into the tank. Part of her wished she could join Ollie hiding underneath his bucket behind an inch of toughened glass.

But unlike him, she had to face her predators head-on.

Chapter Twenty-Three

Kat laid one of the crime scene photos inside an open cold-case file. If Carve-up should leave his office, she'd have time to close it and maintain the lie that she was doing as she was told.

Alanna Michie looked peaceful. If you ignored the swollen and discoloured tongue, and the livid contusion and laceration at her throat where the tie had been cinched so tightly for five minutes or more.

But it was the word inscribed on her forehead in lipstick she now knew was Rouge Dior that drew Kat's attention.

COW

It seemed too mild. OK, maybe it was about right for a bit of girls' banter, and sadly all too common when a man was abusing a woman. But would a woman so rage-filled over an affair that she'd committed murder really choose that particular insult? Kat didn't think so.

'Leah, can I borrow you for a sec?'

Leah wandered over. Bent close to murmur in Kat's ear, 'Carve-up'd have me on his hit list if he saw me talking to his number-one villain.' She looked over at his closed office door. 'Arsehole.'

God, it felt good to know she still had allies – and friends – at Jubilee Place. That was the trouble with mud. Once flung, it always stuck. The thought of Carve-up beyond that rectangle of cheap plain wood made her nauseous. How had it got to this state of affairs? That he had the power to end her career? And why had his usual antagonism and petty slights escalated to a full-blown attempt to get her kicked off the force? She swallowed hard and dragged in a deep breath. She had to wrestle her attention back to the case.

'Look at the photo and tell me what you see,' she said.

Leah pulled a chair over and scrutinised the image.

'Dead woman. Strangled, obviously. The word "cow" written on her forehead in red lipstick. It's odd though, isn't it? I mean, if I thought my husband had been sleeping with another woman, and I was so angry I strangled her to death, well, I'd probably write something a little bit saltier than that.'

Kat widened her eyes, smiling. She wasn't clutching at straws after all. 'Exactly! I mean, you'd probably write, I don't know—'

Leah supplied a possibility. The nuclear option of insults you could aim at a woman. Perhaps overloud. A few nearby cops looked over, eyebrows raised.

Kat nodded. Offered a fractionally milder alternative.

In this way, they ran through an exhaustive list, ending up with relatively new usages gleaned from other female cops including 'sket', 'slosh', 'jezzy' and 'scabical'.

'Too long,' was Leah's verdict on this final suggestion.

Tom came over, brow furrowed. Today he was kitted out in what Kat thought of as his FTM outfit. She and Leah had coined the acronym, which stood for Fast Track Modesty. Basically unshowy, but still expensive. Grey linen jacket. Soft white shirt. Black designer jeans and a pair of gently distressed but obviously high-end black leather ankle boots.

'I've never heard such a stream of un-PC language. And from two female officers, as well,' he said, half smiling, as if hoping he'd be allowed to join in. *Fat chance, mate*, Kat thought. *This is Girls' Club.*

'Leah and I are discussing why a woman mad enough to strangle a sexual rival would half-arse it on the insult.'

He looked unhappy. 'You're still trying to clear Laura Paxton.'

'I *have* to. She's innocent,' Kat hissed. She jabbed a finger at the photo. 'So?'

He shrugged. 'Easier to write in lippy?'

Kat and Leah both aimed an eyebrows-raised look his way.

'In what, Tomski?' Leah said.

'Sorry. Lipstick.'

'Loads of other words are just as easy,' Kat said.

'Maybe she was in a hurry. Only three letters. I mean, yes, "Ho" only has two but I don't see a woman like Laura Paxton using it.'

Kat shook her head. 'She didn't flee the scene, though. Called me and just waited till I arrived.'

Tom slid his hands into his jean pockets. 'I give up, then. Probably shouldn't have tried to help, what with me being a member of the oppressor class.'

'There he is!' Leah crowed. 'Poor old Tomski, middle-class white man, last of the true minorities!'

'My mum and dad ran pubs, whereas I believe yours are both doctors, Leah.'

Tom was smiling, but Kat could see it was costing him. Lots of sensitivities in Tom's background.

'Look, none of us is exactly a candidate for diversity champion are we, so let's keep focused on this murder,' she said. 'You want to know what I think? Laura *did* write it. Her prints are on the lipstick and I'm sure when the lab results come back, it'll be her saliva on the tip. But when it came to it, out of all the words you might expect her to use, she soft-pedalled because she couldn't bring herself to use anything stronger. This was her friend lying dead in front of her, remember. And if I'm right, a friend she'd discovered already dead.'

Tom frowned. 'Why do it at all, then?'

'Maybe whoever put her up to it said something like, "Do something to the body that connects it directly to you." Maybe they told her to use a knife but she couldn't bear it. She came up with the lipstick instead.'

Leah had been nodding as Kat explained her theory.

'That works. As a narrative, I mean. Trouble is, from an evidentiary point of view it's nowhere near enough. You said so yourself. Laura wrote it.'

Kat sighed. 'I know. She's being clever.'

Later that day, Jack emailed Kat a copy of his full post-mortem report.

As she read, one particular fact leapt off the screen.

Alanna had had consensual sex in the forty-eight hours before her death. Jack had found a condom lubricant in her vagina. He'd also found semen, which he'd sent to Forensics. Clearly the condom had split. Bad news for the man she'd slept with. Good news for Kat.

She showed Tom the email. He nodded eagerly.

'I know. Callum Michie has a criminal record, so his DNA is on the database.'

'Yes, and so is Will Paxton's. Just like yours and mine.'

'Darcy's sent two samples to the lab. I couldn't push for a fast turnaround because Stuart's barely given me any budget.'

'But you need to ask now, Tomski. We need to know who Alanna slept with in the two days before she was murdered. If it's Will, then Laura's story checks out. She's probably guilty after all. If it's Callum's, that leaves her version of events looking shakier still. She's almost certainly innocent—'

Tom interrupted. For once, she didn't mind. If he was on board with her theory, it was a big step towards restoring trust between them. Maybe he'd even start to believe her about the money.

'But if it's another man, we've got a new lead. And if his DNA is on file, we can pull him in.'

'We need to talk to Carve-up,' Kat said, her stomach sinking at the prospect.

'Maybe I should go in alone.'

'No, Tomski. I don't want any blowback coming your way. He told me to stay in the station, and as far as he knows that's exactly what I've done. I'll just say I'm helping you out with the paperwork. He'll love that.'

For the second time in two days, Kat prepared for an unpleasant conversation with her line manager. Because what if she was wrong? What if Carve-up truly lost it? After all, he'd warned her off once already and now here she was, barging her way back into the case. Supposing he tried to speed up the 3C-ACU investigation? Got them started this week instead of next?

With nothing back from Iris, only bad news from the solicitor Ben Short and no new ideas of her own beyond a half-formed suspicion about Frank Strutt, she was leaving herself wide open to an instant suspension.

She swallowed down another crippling wave of nausea.

What else could she do but head into the oncoming storm?

Chapter Twenty-Four

Kat watched Carve-up's lip curl as Tom explained her theory – acting as if it was his own – and asked for a same-day DNA turnaround on the semen sample.

'And this is your idea, is it, Tom?' he asked, eyeing Kat.

'Yes. I mean' – his head rotated a couple of degrees towards Kat before he snapped it square again – 'I was asking Kat for her opinion and she—'

'And she just told you to come into my office and go completely against my orders on how you were to run this case? That about it, Tom? Jesus, I expected better from you. A graduate. A fast-track candidate for DS within the year. What the hell were you thinking? You do know she's under investigation?'

'Don't blame Tom, please, Stuart,' Kat said, hating the pleading tone in her voice. 'You're right. I did suggest we look into it. But can't you see how this changes things?'

Carve-up held both hands up like a man trying to keep a drunken attacker at bay. Then pointed a finger at her.

'No! I *forbid* you to speak. You want me to authorise you to spend money I don't have just so you can pursue some mythical "third man" when Laura bloody Paxton's already confessed? I mean, literally, do you have *any* idea, even a *scintilla* of an idea, of the kind of financial pressures I am operating under here? I can't even authorise a ham sandwich and a Starbucks if some poor sod's had to drive to London.'

His colour had risen alarmingly. It was almost as if he cared about the job. But of course he didn't. He was, to use one of his own favourite words, 'grandstanding'. Just putting on a show, possibly for his own amusement or, given how loud he was shouting, for the entertainment of those beyond the partition wall.

'Look, Stuart, I get it, really I do,' she said. 'And I know how important it is that we produce decent' – she swallowed down her revulsion – 'metrics each month. But if Alanna Michie had sex with a man who wasn't either her husband or Will Paxton, then we have a new potential suspect. Please! You *have* to see it.'

As the last sentence left her mouth, Kat knew she'd blown it. Carve-up had nodded as she'd uttered the hated word 'metrics'. She'd seen the thought flitting through his mind as clearly as if it had been drawn in the air above his head by a celestial cartoonist: *Huh. Maybe DS Ballantyne gets it after all.*

He shook his head. Ran his fingers over the lapels of his suit jacket.

'I'll tell you what I *have* to see, DS Ballantyne. You, at your desk, reviewing cold cases. As I believe I instructed you to do. And Tom. From you I need to see results. Not just cases closed. Not just nominals in the cells. Not just arrests of suspects conducted according to bloody' – he gritted his teeth then spat out the word – 'PACE. I mean *financial* results. No cost overruns. No wastage. Efficiencies at every stage of every investigation. Christ! You have no idea how hard my job is.'

Had this wild-eyed outburst come from anyone else, Kat would have been sympathetic. But Carve-up also seemed to think his job included a whole range of activities whose sole purpose was to diminish her in some way.

Leaking details of her investigations. Belittling her in team briefings. And worst of all, knowing in advance that someone had sent her fifty grand from a Swiss bank account. Oh, yes. And the small matter of almost certainly being in her dad's pocket.

She couldn't take any more. She stood up, thanked him and made to leave.

'Where are you going, DS Ballantyne? It better not be to see Linda.'

She stopped. Turned back to him. 'I'm not prepared to see a woman sent down for a murder she didn't commit. If you bothered to read the files you'd see that there are all kinds of problems with the evidence. Yes, *some* of it points to Laura, but her confession's a fantasy. And there's no way she could have killed Alanna the way she says she did. She's being coerced. I know it.'

His eyes bugged out of his face. 'But she *did* do it! I even watched her videotaped confession. What is *wrong* with you?'

Kat stalked across the few feet of carpet and slammed her palms down on his document-strewn desk, making Carve-up rear back in his sumptuously padded chair. In her side vision, she caught Tom's startled expression.

'I'll tell you what's *wrong* with me, Stu. I'm trying to do my job. My *real* job. And all I get from you is sarcasm, obstruction and abuse. I don't know exactly why you took against me when I joined MCU, and to tell you the truth, I no longer care. But I am *not*' – she slammed her fist down again – 'going to sit on my arse and allow a miscarriage of justice to happen on my watch because of some . . . some . . . *metric*!'

Breathing so rapidly she experienced a sudden flash of vertigo, Kat steadied herself before marching out of MCU, ignoring the questioning glances, and straight for Linda's office.

There, she laid out her theory. And the inconsistencies Jack Beale had highlighted concerning Laura's size and the dimensions of her fist.

'So I'm asking you to authorise Tom to get a twenty-four-hour turnaround on the DNA.'

Linda's knock-back was all the more devastating for being delivered in a reasonable, quiet and sympathetic tone of voice.

'I'm sorry, Kat, but I agree with Stuart. And, by the way, going over his head is not a good look for an officer in your current position. You've got a suspect in custody who confessed from the scene, and who is forensically linked to the body. The DNA will go off to the lab but no rush jobs. The latest cuts are biting deeper than an attack dog. I know you think Stuart's a borderline bean-counter these days, but we just can't afford to spend money we don't have on cases we've already won.'

'But we *haven't* won it, Linda! That's my point. Either Laura's being forced to confess or she's covering for someone.'

'I gave you some time, Kat. Bring me some evidence. Some *hard* evidence. Not just circumstantial based on discrepancies between her fist and a bruise on the victim.'

'That's what I'm *trying* to do. If the DNA comes back negative for either Callum Michie or Will Paxton, then we have a third man. An unidentified intimate partner of a murdered woman. Now, what does that sound like?'

Linda's lips tightened and Kat saw the flash of irritation. Just a little too late.

'It sounds like a DS who's forgotten how to listen to her DI, which, given who he is, I can forgive. But also her DCI, which, given that it's me, I can't. All I'm hearing from you is a lot of ifs. Here's one from me. *If* you're suspicious about Laura Paxton's confession, go and wear out some shoe leather talking to people who know her – and Alanna Michie. Find something that points to another suspect and then maybe we'll talk money. Yes?'

Kat knew when she was beaten. And she respected Linda too much to want to provoke her any further.

'Yes, Ma-Linda.'

Kat left her superior's office knowing she was going to wade deeper out into the water. Far from shore. Far from anything that would help her apart from her own dogged determination to see justice done.

Although Linda had just told her to go and wear out some shoe leather. That sounded like a direct order from a superior officer *not* to stay inside the station.

Chapter Twenty-Five

Fearing what she'd say, or do, if she saw Carve-up again that day, Kat headed out. A curving stretch of riverbank passed within a few yards of the rear of the station.

'I'm basically still on site,' she murmured.

She checked her phone. Nothing from Iris. Bit her lip. Carried on walking.

Finding a quiet stretch of water, Kat played out a scene in her head. Alanna refusing Will Paxton a post-coital cuddle. Sitting up in bed, contrition twisting her features.

I can't do this any more. I've been so disloyal. I'm going to tell Callum.

Will, mouth open, horrified.

You're what? No way. He's a gangster. He'll kill me!

Alanna, jaw set, eyes flashing.

Don't talk about my husband that way. You don't even know him.

The argument escalating. Insults hurled. Him strangling her with his tie.

Kat felt her spirits lift, just for a second. But then reality intruded. And she didn't even need Carve-up to state the obvious for her. *And then he'd force his own wife to confess to the murder he'd just committed. Right.*

A pair of swans glided by, their necks elegant S-shapes.

'Do *you* know who it was?' she asked the lead bird, which had turned its head towards her.

'Kat!'

She started, almost losing her balance and toppling into the water.

Turning around, she groaned. Ethan Metcalfe was making his way towards her, threading between knots of people enjoying the sunshine.

A few months back, Liv had reminded Kat of the nickname she'd bestowed on Ethan – Mutt-calf – for the way he 'slobbered after you'. Kat had come to believe that Ethan hadn't entirely given up. He wasn't stalking her. Not exactly. But for someone she neither liked nor had any reason to encounter socially, he cropped up with surprising regularity.

Recently he'd taken to confronting her in the streets – once, memorably, during a stake-out – demanding to know why she didn't make use of him as some sort of freelance investigator. The more she knocked him back, the more determined he became.

Ethan arrived in front of her, puffing. His soft, pallid torso distended a black Led Zeppelin T-shirt. It bore an unsettling image of what appeared to be naked blonde children on a psychedelic stone causeway.

He pushed his gold-rimmed glasses higher on his nose.

'I'm doing an item on the Alanna Michie case. I'd love to interview you. Could you come to my studio?'

Kat narrowed her eyes. 'How the hell did you find out about that, Ethan? It only happened yesterday.'

He looked left and right, a move straight off an am-dram clichés-to-avoid sheet. Then leaned closer, gusting tobacco-laden breath into her face.

'A journalist never reveals his sources. But if it'll persuade you to chat on air – well, it's a member of a certain well-known

Middlehampton family. Maybe "notorious" would be a better word. I'll leave you to join the dots,' he added, winking.

'Was it Callum Michie?' she asked.

Ethan visibly brought his features under control and said, 'I couldn't possibly comment.' He might as well have held up a sign with a massive 'YES' printed on it in neon capitals.

What could Callum have to gain from talking to Ethan? The person he wanted was currently locked up tight in a cell. Maybe he was hoping that by muddying the waters he'd get Laura released on bail. Where she'd be easy prey.

Nothing Ethan broadcast to his handful of listeners could possibly affect that. Or could it? Was his reach bigger than she thought? *Be a detective, Kat. Ask!*

'Just how many people listen to your podcast anyway?'

He grinned, revealing teeth clotted at the gumlines with some indefinable greyish substance she thought might be porridge.

'As of 7.03 a.m. today' – he prodded his glasses higher on his nose – 'twenty-three thousand, six hundred and nineteen.'

Kat strove to keep her face neutral. She had no idea what was considered good for a podcast. Didn't listen to them herself. But Ethan was reaching an audience equal to almost a tenth of the population of Middlehampton. Who knew which influential people might be listening?

'Impressive,' she said.

'It really is, isn't it? And I get a lot of audience feedback. On my socials mainly, but emails too.'

With a sinking heart, Kat pursued her line of enquiry. 'I suppose it's all just members of the public. I hear true crime's a popular genre these days.'

He shook his head. Re-seated his glasses again. She wanted to scream at him to take them to an optician and get the hinges tightened. Either that or invest in some decent skincare products and degrease his nose.

'Elaine Forshaw's a listener.' He nodded, clearly enjoying himself. 'That's right, you heard me correctly. The Hertfordshire Police and Crime Commissioner. Amazing, huh?'

Tom was Elaine's nephew. Ethan made a podcast she listened to. Was Kat the only person in Middlehampton who didn't have the PCC's ear?

'Listen, Ethan, be careful around Callum Michie. You know who he is. He's only using you to get to the person we have in custody.'

'Oh, you mean Laura Paxton?'

Crap! The decision to break a pretty big rule, and give Callum Laura's name, had backfired spectacularly. If she had any chance of clearing her name and returning to official duties free of the taint of corruption, she had to be cleaner than clean. Now, here she was, discussing an open homicide investigation with a bloody podcaster.

'I can't say. But if you know which family Callum's a part of then you know you're on the fringes of some very dodgy activities. Don't let him suck you in.'

'If you came on the show, I wouldn't have to, Kat.'

If she went on the show, Linda would tear her a new one.

'Sorry, Ethan, no.'

He frowned. Then he huffed in a short, tight breath. His fists had bunched. Christ, was he going to attack her? Surely not in public, in front of multiple witnesses?

He took a step back. Kat relaxed fractionally.

'I get it. The important, or should I say *self*-important DS is much too busy to talk to the little people. Well, let me tell you something, Kat. One of these days I will be too big to ignore. You'll be *begging* me to have you on. And we'll just have to see whether I grant your request, won't we?'

Kat could only stare. What the hell? His lightning-fast flips between what he presumably thought was mild flirting to get an interview to almost delusional posturing was beyond her understanding.

While she struggled for a response that didn't include telling him where to stick his podcast, he wheeled away from her and marched off towards a coffee shop, his broad-beamed rear swaying from side to side.

She turned away to find the swans had stuck around to watch the show.

'I could almost believe Ethan did it to get my attention,' she said.

The swans hissed at her.

That's your best idea, is it? they seemed to be saying.

She arrived back at the station to be told Will had organised a press conference.

Chapter Twenty-Six

Kat stood at the back of the room Will Paxton had blagged from the council to hold an unofficial press conference.

With journalists, charity workers and assorted off-duty police officers filling the room, it felt hot and airless. The fact that the radiators were on and the venerable sash windows had all been painted shut long ago did not help.

Kat scanned the room. Recognised a few friendly faces. Dawn Jacobson, the editor of the *Echo*, must have felt Kat's gaze on her. She turned her head and smiled. Kat wondered if she knew about the corruption charge hanging over her. She smiled back. The effort cost her.

Two women flanked Will. Kat recognised one, a female DC from Hampton Hill. The other, presumably, was his lawyer.

Will leaned towards the narrow black wand mic.

'Er, hello, everyone, and thank you for coming. My name is Will Paxton. When I normally attend press conferences it's in my professional role as a detective constable. Some of you may even recognise me. But today I am here in a very personal capacity. That of a shocked husband. On Monday, for reasons we are still trying to understand, my wife, Laura, confessed to the murder of a woman named Alanna Michie. But she can't have—'

He grabbed for his water glass, almost knocking it over but for the quick thinking of his solicitor, who reached out and steadied the tumbler.

'I'm sorry. But Laura couldn't have murdered Alanna. They were friends. We' – he turned left and right to take in his outriders – 'can only think that someone forced Laura to make this confession. Maybe they're blackmailing her or . . . I don't know . . .' He ran a hand over his hair. 'Maybe they're threatening me somehow because of my role as a police officer. So I want to make this appeal. Please, if you know anything about this tragic and senseless killing, and especially if you've heard anyone talking about having committed it, or you've seen something on social media, get in touch with the police. If you don't want to do this, for your own reasons, please call Crimestoppers.'

He turned to his lawyer, who introduced herself as Stephanie Hendricks, and took over. 'My client would like to extend his condolences to the Michie family, especially Alanna's grieving husband, Callum.'

While Stephanie was speaking, Kat rescanned the room. Leaning against the opposite wall, in the shadow of a much taller and wider man, was Callum himself. His face was twisted, as if he'd bitten into an unripe plum. Or, let's face it, as if he'd just been widowed out of the blue. Christ only knew how he was feeling. Gangster or not, he'd obviously loved his wife.

Stephanie had just asked for questions.

Dawn Jacobson got in first, her powerful voice cutting through the sudden hubbub. 'Will, obviously we all feel for you, but can you tell us why you're so sure that your wife is innocent? After all, she has confessed and, from what I understand, forensic evidence does link her to the crime scene.'

He nodded. 'Like many people, and I'm so glad that the stigma about it has largely gone, Laura has mental health issues.

Depression, anxiety, feelings of worthlessness. She would have valued Alanna's friendship. It was fairly recent, which makes it all the more incomprehensible that she would do anything, anything at all, to jeopardise that. I mean, she hardly even wanted to have an argument about which coffee shop to go to, let alone anything as heinous as to actually—'

He stopped, reached for a tissue, pushed it against his eyes.

Stephanie laid a comforting hand on his arm. 'I think what Will is trying to say is that Laura had absolutely no motive to harm Alanna. I would also add that from a strictly physical perspective, the two women were very different in physique. Laura is slightly built. For the ladies in the room, a size six. Alanna, though by no means overweight, was tall for a woman, at five feet eight and a half, and possessed of an admirably athletic build. A very normal and indeed fit size twelve. Try and picture the scene.'

As Stephanie pointed out the inconsistencies in the police account of the murder, various journalists frowned as they made notes or held their recorders and phones aloft. Kat was impressed with the lawyer. She'd sown a few seeds of doubt in their minds.

After taking a few more questions, Stephanie ended the press conference by thanking the journalists and reiterating both the reward and her own contact details.

Kat turned to go and pushed through the door leading into the corridor. She hadn't got far when a commotion had her turning back.

Will had emerged into the corridor only to be confronted by Callum Michie, who was flanked by a couple of heavies in black bomber jackets. Shaved heads, tats, gold hoops in their ears. For God's sake, why not just get name badges printed up reading, *Lose teeth now. Ask me how.*

Kat hung back, despite her instinct to go and help a fellow officer. Will squared his shoulders. Walked up to Michie.

'I'm sorry for your loss.'

Michie bared small teeth. Like a rat's. 'Yeah, I just bet you are. So if it wasn't your missus who did it, who was it, then?'

Will spread his hands wide. 'I don't know. All I know is it couldn't have been Laura.'

Michie's lip curled back further. Behind him, the two goons flexed their biceps and rolled their shoulders.

'You don't *know*? Pretty poor coming from a detective.' Michie took a step closer. Will backed up until his shoulder blades hit the wall. '*Your* wife confessed. And from what I hear, her DNA is all over the murder weapon. So unless you give me somebody else, she's the one who killed *my* wife. And that does not' – he poked Will hard in the centre of his chest – 'sit well with me, DC Paxton. No, it does not sit well with me at all. Looks like there might be another widower in Middlehampton before long.'

Michie turned away and nodded to his men. 'Come on, we're out of here.'

'That better not be a threat, Michie,' Will called after him.

Michie slowed. Stopped. Turned.

'Oh, it's not a *threat*, DC Paxton.'

Then he left, flanked by thirty-odd stone of prime Hertfordshire beef on the hoof.

He'd left the punchline unsaid, but Kat could hear it echoing through the town hall corridors as if had been broadcast over the tannoy.

It's a prediction.

Time was running out.

Laura was already on remand. If she was convicted, it would be a long sentence. Maybe decades, if she didn't express remorse. And every day she was inside she'd be in danger from one of Callum Michie's thugs.

Kat just couldn't let that happen.

Chapter Twenty-Seven

As Kat walked up the steps to Hampton Hill police station, her phone rang. It was her friend and teammate Jess Beckett. Jess's son Alfie played on the same football team as Riley.

'I just saw the news on Facebook. Is it true? Laura Paxton's been arrested for murder?'

'I'm afraid so.'

'But she can't have! God bless her, she's a fierce wing attack, but a murderer?'

'I arrested her myself, Jess. At the crime scene.'

'But you don't think she did it, do you?'

'Look, I can't really talk about it. Not now. And I'm about to talk to Will again.'

'My God, he must be in bits.'

'He is.'

'But you're going to find out who really did it, aren't you? You have to.'

'I'm doing everything I can to solve it, Jess, that's all I can say. Look, I have to go. I'll catch you later, OK?'

Kat showed the Hampton Hill receptionist her badge. 'I'm here to see DC Paxton.'

Five minutes later, Will was leading her up to CID. He stopped off at a small kitchen to make them both a coffee before taking her to a quiet corner furnished with an L-shaped seating unit in grey suede and a low coffee table.

'What's this about, DS Ballantyne?'

She smiled. 'Please, call me Kat.'

He shrugged, a jittery rearrangement of his muscles that suggested a man surviving on black coffee, takeaways and adrenaline rather than sleep, routine and home-cooked food.

'OK, what's this about . . . Kat?'

'I was at your press conference.'

'Yeah, I saw you. What did you think?'

She nodded. 'Was it hard? I saw you going for your water a couple of times.'

'Bloody hard. I hate doing these things at the best of times, but when it's so personal, you know? I just hope I sounded OK.'

Kat swallowed a mouthful of coffee. A drip entered her airway, sending her spluttering and coughing until tears sprang to her eyes.

'Sorry,' she croaked. 'Went down the wrong way. Look, Will, I know you think Laura's innocent and—'

He lunged forward, glaring at Kat with red-rimmed eyes. 'I don't *think* my wife is innocent, Kat. I *know* she is. This isn't just another murder case. This is personal.'

'It's personal to me, too, Will. Laura's my friend. But holding press conferences? You're not helping her. You have to stay out of it. Let *us* handle the investigation.'

Will spread his hands wide. His face twisted. He looked in physical pain.

'What am I supposed to do, then? I can't just do nothing while Laura gets sent down for life for a murder I—' He heaved in a shuddering breath. 'Sorry, *we* both know she didn't commit. She won't let me get her a lawyer. She won't even talk to me. I'm going out of my mind here, Kat.'

He didn't look good, it was true. The taut muscles round his eyes gave him the wild look of a drug addict going cold turkey.

'Well, she's agreed to a legal aid solicitor so that's something, I guess. Can I come round tonight, after work?'

He frowned. 'To mine?'

'Yes. I thought maybe I could have a look at Laura's things. Has she got a laptop?'

'Yes, but I don't see how that will help.'

'No? Maybe whoever persuaded her to confess has been emailing her.'

'Don't you think I've already looked through her emails? I know I'm only a DC in general CID but I can just about remember how to do basic detective work.'

'Sorry, Will. Of course you have.'

He shook his head. Then all the fight left him like he was a fast-deflating balloon. 'No, I'm sorry. You're trying to help. I'm not getting much sleep.' He sighed, a pitiful sound that seemed to expel every last whisper of air in his lungs. 'What time do you want to come round?'

'Eight?'

'Whenever. I'll be there.'

Kat got up to go.

He stood as she walked to the door. 'Anything I can do to help, you let me know. Even if it's through backchannels. Here.' He passed her his card on which he'd written his personal mobile phone number.

'Thanks, Will. But you know you can't be involved in the investigation.'

'What? She's my wife! In case you'd forgotten.'

'No, I haven't forgotten. But that's the whole point. I'm worried that when we find the real culprit, their brief is going to have a field day, pointing to your involvement as problematic given your

123

obvious conflict of interest. You're personally involved already as the husband of the perpetrator—'

'*Alleged* perpetrator.'

She nodded.

'—so there's no way you can take any kind of role in the investigation.'

He closed his hand over hers, squeezing her fingers tightly around his card. 'Keep it anyway. Please. I'm begging you. Have you spoken to her?'

'Not since she was transferred to Bronzefield.'

At the mention of the prison, Will swallowed convulsively as if fighting nausea. 'They'll eat her alive in there, Kat. Please do something.'

As Kat drove home, she reflected that Will wasn't the only detective with a conflict of interest.

Chapter Twenty-Eight

Kat arrived home at just after 6.30 p.m. She hadn't heard from Liv and was starting to think maybe she'd had to stay on the farm to bring the cows in or pluck the chickens or whatever you did with them. Odd that she hadn't called to cancel, though.

As she opened the front door, the smell of tomato sauce rich with garlic flooded her nostrils.

'Mmm, something smells good,' she called out.

In the kitchen she was surprised to see Riley at the stove, a blue-and-white-striped apron tied round his waist. Van sat at the table, reading the *Echo*, a bottle of Moretti lager at his elbow.

Riley turned his head as she bent to kiss her husband.

'Hi, Mum. Liv's teaching me how to cook.'

A wine bottle clinked from behind the door. Kat whirled to come face to face with Liv. She was holding a bottle of white wine and unscrewing the cap. She smiled, displaying slightly crooked teeth.

'Hi, Thelma. Glass of vino?'

'I thought you'd had to take a rain check,' Kat said, hugging Liv tightly and almost being suffocated by the return pressure.

'Don't be daft! I just had a couple of things to wrap up. Took me a bit longer to get away than I thought. Oh, and Riley and I went food shopping, didn't we?'

Liv sloshed wine into a glass and handed it to Kat. She glanced the rim off Liv's and took a grateful swallow. Then remembered she'd be driving over to Will's house later and put it aside. She opened a bottle of fizzy water and filled a tall tumbler instead.

'So, chef, what's on the menu?' Kat said to Riley.

'Spaghetti alla Riley.'

'Sounds amazing. What's in it?'

Riley peered into the steaming saucepan he was stirring with a long-handled wooden spoon.

'Onions. Garlic. A lot of garlic,' he said with an over-the-shoulder grin. 'Tomato puree. Tomatoes. Fresh, not tinned. Bacon. And . . . uh, what was it again, Liv?'

'Fresh basil.'

'Yes!' Riley exclaimed, pointing the sauce-covered spoon at Van and sending a few drops splattering on to the *Echo*. 'Oops! Sorry. Fresh basil. Torn, not chopped. It bruises, otherwise.'

Kat nodded in appreciation. 'I'm impressed. I thought you preferred Dad's recipe: mince and tinned toms?'

Riley nodded as he went back to stirring, before lifting a spoon-ful of sauce to his lips and sipping cautiously. 'Mmm. Yes, but Liv said I ought to broaden my horizons and I should do it the proper way. This recipe's off TikTok.'

'Which is even more amazing,' Kat said, catching Liv's sly wink and nodding. 'I thought it was all cat videos or K-pop.'

Riley shook his head as if to say, *Adults. What are they like?*

The pasta was delicious and all three adults went to increasingly silly lengths to praise their thirteen-year-old chef.

'You should sell the recipe.'

'You should video yourself cooking it for TikTok.'

'Make a batch and sell it at school.'

'Make a massive batch and sell it on the internet.'

'Buy a food cart.'

'Start your own restaurant!'

'Enough!' Riley finally said – though Kat could see how much he was enjoying their admittedly over-the-top compliments.

After wolfing down his pasta, Riley departed for his room, throwing over his shoulder a cheery 'Chef doesn't have to clear up. Laters!'

Once the dishwasher was loaded, Van announced he was going to watch the Eels on television. Kat knew what he was really doing. Giving her and Liv some space. She loved him all the more for it.

'So-o-o,' Liv said, once they were seated across from each other at the table. 'Who's got it in for you and doesn't mind spending fifty grand to do it?'

'The only person I know with that kind of money is my dear old dad, and he's flat-out denied it to my face.'

'Yeah, but he's a bit of a lying bastard.' Liv took a sip of wine. Regarded Kat over the rim of the glass. 'No offence.'

'None taken.'

'You believe him?'

'He seemed to be genuinely shocked. I've interviewed plenty of liars and I honestly don't think he sent me the money.'

'Well, who did then? I mean how many people do you know with a grudge against you and a spare fifty grand?'

'That's just it. Nobody. I can't think of anyone who'd want me off the force that badly. I mean, I'd like to think I'm a good homicide investigator—'

'You're a *brilliant* homicide investigator, whatever Mutt-calf says on his stupid little podcast.'

Kat smiled. 'I'll take that. But in any case, literally, if I was off the force there'd just be another DS behind me to pick up where I left off.' She frowned. 'Why did you bring up Mutt-calf?'

Liv threw her hands up.

'Have you even *heard* that arsehole? He's just released a new episode of his stupid podcast. He was interviewing this detective, Will Paxton? The one whose wife confessed to that murder. Anyway, Mutt-calf started going on about how you're not doing your job properly. That was bad enough, but then he said he loved you!'

'He used those exact words, Liv? He didn't say he respected me?'

'No! Hold on, I'm literally going to play it for you.'

Liv fiddled with her phone and held it up. Ethan's voice emerged tinnily from the speaker.

'*I totally respect Kat.*' There! She'd been right. Liv was overreacting. Typical Liv. '*I love how she always puts a hundred and ten per cent into solving her cases. You could even say I love her.*'

'See?' Liv said, eyes flashing with that old, sparky fire that promised one kind of trouble or another. 'Anyway, I sent in a message telling him he's out of line and what a brilliant detective you are.'

Kat stared at the phone lying between them. He'd deny it, but Ethan Metcalfe harboured a grudge against her. Not for anything she'd done, but for what she hadn't. She'd never reciprocated his feelings. Never allowed him to get close. She'd blocked his every attempt to get her on his bloody podcast. And from what she could gather from Liv and Riley, he veered wildly from praising her to calling her professional judgement into question.

She pointed at the phone. 'I wonder if it's him.'

Liv frowned. 'If what's him?'

'The money. I wonder if Mutt-calf sent it.'

'Has he got that kind of cash?'

'I don't know. Look, forget it. It was a stupid idea.'

'No! It's not stupid at all. Look at the facts. He's been wanking his tiny little dick over you ever since we were at school. Now he's got that stupid podcast, which he mainly seems to use as a platform for dissing you over your cases, even though you solve them all.

You told me before he got in your face when you were hunting that serial killer. Your sidekick, what was his name?'

'Tom.'

'Tom had to hit him, didn't he?'

'Yeah, but Ethan's—' She stopped.

'Ethan's what?'

Kat recalled her meeting with Ethan on the riverbank. His behaviour fell short of the legal definition for stalking. But he'd shown a few worrying signs since she'd joined MCU. Including devoting more of his podcasts than she thought was healthy to her particular cases. But if he was announcing to his twenty-three thousand listeners he loved her, that was escalating things big-time.

'I was going to say he's harmless, but I'm not so sure. Do you really think he hates me enough to want to get me fired?'

'I'm not sure he hates you at all. Knowing him, he's probably got some crappy little fantasy about how he saves you and you give him a thank-you blow job before agreeing to move in with him and wash his crusty pants.'

'Eww! Liv, please!'

Liv released another salty cackle.

'Just saying. He's an incel, yes? A saddo in his back bedroom with all that computer kit. I bet he'd have no trouble hacking your bank account or whatever happened.'

'But fifty grand, Liv. Would he really have that kind of cash lying around?'

'I don't know. But maybe I should do a little digging for you?'

Kat wanted to say yes straight away. To recruit her mate on to Team Kat. But Ethan did seem a little unstable – recently, perhaps, even more than usual. She couldn't bear the thought of putting Liv in danger. Not after everything that had happened between them.

'You messaged him, right?'

'Not with my real name. I told him what a dick he was for not believing in you.'

'Maybe you could message him again. He told me he's got twenty-three thousand listeners. He could be getting a load of advertising money. Say you're looking for a job as an intern or something.'

Liv nodded, then winked. 'He won't stand a chance.'

'You've got to be really careful. If you end up meeting him, do it somewhere really public.'

'Listen, I could put Mutt-calf down with one hand tied behind my back.' Liv flexed her right arm, displaying an impressively defined bicep. 'Sixteen years of working on a farm, mate. Does wonders for you.'

'And you'd better disguise yourself. I don't want him recognising you. Not when he was around when you were . . . you know . . .'

Liv grinned crookedly. 'Murdered?'

'Yeah, that.'

'Mutt-calf only had eyes for you. Anyway, as far as he's concerned, I'm dead.'

'Please, Liv. Just in case.'

'Fine. I'll get a wig and some sunnies. Maybe undo a couple of buttons. Men can't focus on anything else if you show a bit of boob.'

Smiling in wry acknowledgement, Kat nodded. 'Then, yes. Do it.'

Kat left Liv searching for Ethan on Instagram. It was time to see Will Paxton again. Although she was nervous about the meeting, having Liv on her side and actively trying to track the money made her feel better than she'd been managing since Carve-up first dropped the bomb.

Maybe she was going to survive after all.

Chapter Twenty-Nine

The Will Paxton who opened the door to Kat just after 8.00 p.m. looked even worse than the one she'd spoken to earlier that day at Hampton Lane nick. His eyes were bloodshot, and as she squeezed past him in the narrow hallway she caught a strong smell of alcohol on his breath.

'How are you feeling?' she asked.

He slumped into an armchair and scrubbed at his cheeks with his palms. Reached for an uncapped bottle of Scotch and poured a generous measure into a glass at his elbow. Tipped the bottle towards Kat, eyebrows raised in mute enquiry. She shook her head.

'You know how burglary victims always say they feel? Even when the little scrotes have only taken replaceable stuff?'

Kat nodded as he took a big swig from the tumbler. They always used the exact same word. 'Violated.'

'Like that, only a thousand times worse. It's like somebody broke into my life and smashed it to pieces while I was asleep. You have to find out who made her confess, Kat. She won't last in Bronzefield. At the very least she ought to be out on bail.'

'You know they won't allow that, Will. Not when the charge is murder.'

He lurched forward and planted his hands on the glass-topped coffee table. His gaze was unfocused and she wondered how much he'd had to drink before she arrived.

'My wife is not a murderer!'

It wasn't a shout. More of a protest, his voice loud and cracking.

'That's why I'm here,' she said. 'Has Laura got somewhere she keeps personal stuff? Does she have any hobbies?'

He shrugged. 'She doesn't really go in for hobbies. She reads, plays netball, but that's about it.'

'Does she ever work from home? Is there a desk I could look at?'

'Sometimes she does little plans of activities to do with the children at school. It's all in the spare room. Upstairs.'

He'd sagged back into the chair and she had to prompt him.

'Can you show me?'

Sighing, he pushing himself up on his elbows and got to his feet. Every movement seemed to cost him in physical strength and emotional energy. She followed him out of the sitting room and up the stairs.

Looking round the small back bedroom, Kat realised she really didn't know that much about her teammate. And this neat if cramped space didn't reveal a great deal, either. No little knick-knacks on the desk, which was a functional pale pine number Kat recognised from a trip to the big IKEA in Wembley. No pictures on the wall, just a meticulously inscribed wipe-clean monthly calendar with red, orange, green and black circular magnets dotted across the days and, presumably, confirming to some system of Laura's.

The nearest thing to a clue as to her personality was a slab of weathered wood hung on a loop of hairy string, on which were painted a few of those motivational quotes that seemed to be every-where these days.

Live in the moment.

Be grateful.

Accept your life.

She turned and smiled at Will. 'She's so neat. I wish my workspace was so tidy.'

'It's part of her condition,' he said in a flat voice.

He'd alluded to Laura's mental health issues before. Maybe now was the time to ask him what he meant.

'Her condition?' she prompted.

'Anxiety, depression. She's a bit OCD, too.'

Kat nodded. 'Is she on any medication?'

He shook his head. 'We don't believe in all that stuff. Jesus, you go to the doctor and before you've even said how you feel they're fobbing you off with a prescription for antidepressants. It's just medicating the human condition.'

'Forgive me then, Will, and I'm honestly not prying, but how does she manage her mental health issues? I mean, those are quite serious things to deal with.' He frowned and Kat hurried to correct any wrong impression she'd caused. 'Obviously, it's entirely her choice about using medication. I do understand, honestly.'

'Well, she exercises regularly. I make sure of that. Walking mainly, and she plays netball, as you know. Mindfulness. Breathing. I suggested she go to a counsellor, but she was dead set against it.'

'Any idea why?'

He hesitated. Chewed his lower lip. 'I know how you'll take this, but she was embarrassed. Said she didn't like to think of herself as someone who needs therapy.'

'Look, Will, first of all, I'm not here to judge Laura—'

'—just to arrest her for murder.' He thumped the side of his fist against the wall. 'Sorry, sorry. I shouldn't have said that. It's the stress.'

'I understand. But what I was going to say was, if she *had* been having therapy, I might be able to talk to the therapist and get an insight into what might have driven her to confess to me like she did.'

'Oh. Well, yeah, that would have been nice, but . . .' He trailed off, seemingly exhausted by having to maintain his half of the conversation.

There didn't seem to be any point in staying. Will seemed a defeated man, leaning against the wall and picking at a loose thread on his jumper cuff. Kat thanked him and left.

On the drive back, the same questions chased themselves round and round in her head, like Smokey and Lois playing madly in the long grass.

Who had really killed Alanna Michie? Why? And how had they managed to coerce Laura into confessing?

Oh, and that other career-shredding enquiry.

Who sent me fifty bloody grand?

Because, despite having set Liv on Mutt-calf like a Rottweiler after a rabbit, deep down she couldn't really see him spending that much cash on what he had to know was a doomed cause.

Chapter Thirty

In a dimly lit room over a pub in Cooper's Field, Callum Michie was addressing a group of hard-faced men. One or two might technically be considered honest citizens. But only because, so far, they'd not been convicted of anything.

Callum raised the baseball bat he'd taken from under the bar. Frank hadn't been keen on this new direction, but in the end, Callum had won him over with a simple choice. 'You give me your blessing, Uncle Frank, or I'll do it anyway.'

'This is a bad idea, Cal. I told Kat Ballantyne she had a week.'

Callum had shrugged. 'No. This happens now.'

He tapped the bat on the whiteboard behind him, dead centre on an A4 colour photo of a pale-faced woman staring out with a blank expression.

'This woman is Laura Paxton. She killed Alanna. I want her dead. As of right now, she's on remand in Bronzefield. That's only an hour's drive from here. I want anyone with a mate inside, anyone with a tame screw in their pocket, anyone with any contacts there *at all*, to get going on this.'

'How are we going to do that, Cal?' someone piped up from the back.

He scowled. 'Get her on to the hospital wing. Something serious enough to have her transferred to MGH. Do her inside. Hang her with her own sheets and make it look like she topped herself. Poison her porridge. Jesus! Do I have to go in there myself? There's twenty grand and a year at a nice little Airbnb down in Marbella till it all blows over, for the bloke who gets it done and can prove it.'

'I heard the filth don't think it was her at all,' Dutch Alf – handy with a blade – called out.

'Makes no difference.' Callum shrugged. 'If it wasn't her, then find out who it was and do them instead. Either way, it's a life for a life, OK?'

At the back, Isaac Handy was staring intently at his fingers, which were currently busy rolling a joint composed of his own weed and a sprinkling of crushed ecstasy tablet.

Isaac nodded along to show the bad guys at the front he was paying attention.

Chapter Thirty-One

After another broken night, Kat slid out of bed at 5.45 a.m. Showered, cleaned her teeth and snatched a hasty breakfast, then took Smokey down to the farm for a walk. Clouds obscured the rising sun and it was still grey and dim as they reached the field known to the locals as The Gallops.

She unclipped him and smiled as he yelped with delight and raced off into the field, flushing out a couple of fat brown birds she thought might be partridges. If only suspects were as easy to drive into the open.

As the birds clapped up into the air, she peered into the distance. Even in the slowly lightening morning, there could be no doubt about the owner of the frizz of snow-white hair approaching from an intersecting path.

As Smokey and Lois, Barrie's black-and-white lurcher streaked off together, Barrie raised a hand in greeting.

'Morning, Skip,' the ex-cop said with a smile. 'There are larks still asleep, you know.'

'Trouble sleeping.'

He grunted. 'Tell me about it.'

He offered her a crumpled white paper bag.

She smiled and shook her head. 'Allsorts for *breakfast?*'

He raised his bushy white eyebrows and took a pink, white and black sweet from the bag, and chewed reflectively.

'Never too early for liquorice, Skip.'

'You're addicted. Maybe there's an AA group you could attend. Allsorts Anonymous.'

He grinned. 'Not bad.' A wink. 'For you.'

'Cheeky bastard!'

They walked on, matching their pace, as the dogs barked and cut wide swathes through the clover and long grass.

'Case interfering with your sleep, Skip?'

'A woman confesses to murdering her friend. Calls me from the crime scene. Refuses legal assistance. But I don't think she did it.'

'With you so far.' Then Barrie's fluffy white eyebrows elevated. 'Wait. This is about Alanna Michie, isn't it? Dangerous family to cross.'

Kat nodded. 'Exactly. Which is why I need to know who the real killer is. Why they murdered Alanna. And why they picked Laura to take the fall.'

'Any forensics?'

Kat nodded. 'Yes, and they all point to Laura.'

'Motive?'

'She claims she thought Alanna was having an affair with her husband.'

'You don't believe her.'

'The husband denies it.'

Barrie snorted. 'They tend to, in my limited experience.'

Kat let out a deep sigh. She hadn't told Barrie the whole truth about her insomnia. Yes, at 2.15 a.m. and 4.29 a.m., the case had woken her. But at 1.01 a.m., 3.00 a.m. and 5.43 a.m., it had been the mind-paralysing anxiety about the fifty grand.

He squinted down at her.

'You all right, Skip?'

'What? Yeah. I'm fine.'

He tightened his lips into a line as if he were trying not to blurt out a secret. Her intuition was spot on, it turned out.

'Listen, this is none of my business, but I was having a beer with an old mate at the weekend. And, well, he mentioned that the hyenas were sniffing around you. Something about some money?'

He'd phrased it as a question, but of course he knew. Copshops were like colanders when it came to gossip. Did she open up to him or not? They were friends. And he'd been job, so he understood every aspect of the life. Not just thief-taking, but the relentless paperwork, the snafus, the boredom, the fear of violence from suspects, and, yes, the pervasive stink of dirty cops.

She knew his views on the subject of corruption. She couldn't bear the thought that he'd turn away from her in her hour of need. Then Riley's words came back to her. *You're like the best cop in the whole of Middlehampton. Probably England.* And Van's. *You've done nothing wrong. You're innocent until proven guilty.*

They believed in her. But they were family.

'It's just a misunderstanding, Barrie, really. Nothing to worry about.'

He favoured her with a long, searching look. Then turned his head to whistle for Lois.

Chapter Thirty-Two

At her desk a couple of hours later, Kat shook her head. Nothing about this case made sense. She knew she was missing something, but she couldn't see what. Or even the *pathway* to the what.

The killer was forensically aware. It didn't mean all that much these days. Since the massive success of the *CSI* franchise on TV, even the dimmest villain knew the basics. Didn't stop the idiots from leaving prints, DNA and clothing fibres all over the place, mind.

But this guy wasn't just forensically *aware*. He'd actually put that knowledge into meticulous *practice*. Who would be that focused? Kat's mind reeled as she tried to hold on to the spinning matrix of possibilities that kept expanding as she thought about it. A smart villain? A villain with OCD? Or just a murderer determined to get away with that most heinous of crimes by cleaning up after himself? She shook her head, irritated with herself. Nobody could clean every single trace of themselves away. It wasn't possible.

No, but in an apparently open-and-shut case, resources would be directed elsewhere. Searches would be minimal, evidence collection rudimentary, forensic analysis pared back to the basics. After all, they had their perpetrator in cuffs well inside the golden hour.

She'd been *following* the evidence, but she ought to have been *examining* it.

Ten minutes later she was back at her desk, having descended into the basement to visit the Exhibits Room. In front of her was a translucent plastic box labelled with the details of the crime scene at the Michies' house on Chamberlayne Avenue.

She lifted off the lid and placed it to one side, then rummaged carefully among the individually bagged exhibits. The lipstick Laura had used to mark Alanna's forehead. A bagged hair that matched Laura's on length and colour. And the murder weapon itself. A man's tie in forest green, with diagonal stripes of gold and purple every couple of inches and a dark red stain Darcy had confirmed was red wine.

Donning nitrile gloves first, Kat slit the red chain-of-custody tape with a box cutter. The CSIs had done their job properly, cutting the tie free at the back of Alanna's neck, leaving the front intact. Not that it would tell anyone anything. This was no complex nautical knot that might narrow their search down to experienced sailors. Just the first half of a granny knot: a simple over-and-under twist.

She turned it over in her hands, examining the white label on the reverse. The manufacturer's name, Arthur Kennedy & Son, was prominent above the curlicued script reading *Pure Silk*.

On the widest part of the tie, creased now from being scrunched in the murderer's fist, was a crest above the initials MGC. The crest consisted of a shield bearing a white castle above two intertwined snakes. Kat shook her head as she peered closer. No, not snakes. Eels. Middlehampton FC's nickname. But then it would be M*F*C.

She frowned, staring at the ceiling. Then smiled, shaking her head. Maybe if she'd been a male copper, she'd have got it immediately. Middlehampton *Golf* Club. Of course! Carve-up would have an identical tie. She googled the club to be sure. The logo matched.

She held the tie up to the light, hoping to spot a hair or stray fibre one of the CSIs might have missed. Nothing.

No! Not nothing. Because in the light from her desk lamp she could make out initials woven into the broad green stripe above the club crest. She'd missed it at first because the thread was the same shade of green as the stripe in the tie. CM.

Her heart sank. Callum Michie. Laura's story was now more solid, not less. She'd arrived empty-handed, maybe intending just to have it out with Alanna. Then she'd seen the tie on the coat rack, just as she'd said. She'd snapped and used it to strangle her friend.

Or was it that simple? CM *could* be Callum Michie. But it could be all sorts of other people, too. Which other members of Middlehampton Golf Club had those initials?

The answer hit her like a train. There was one CM in particular who she knew only too well.

Colin Morton.

Her father.

He'd denied being the source of the fifty thousand. But now, here he was, reappearing in the murder investigation.

Kat felt clammy and cold, despite the warm day outside.

What if her father had committed murder – maybe even *planned* to commit murder – and then framed her with a corruption charge to get her out of the way? It was exactly the kind of devious ploy she could imagine him cooking up. And who did Colin Morton have in his pocket? None other than Stuart Carver. Her line manager and the man who'd had prior notice of the fifty K in the first place.

No wonder he was unhappy about her taking part in the Michie murder case.

Carve-up approached, at pace. She just had time to cover the evidence bag with some papers.

He looked down at her desk and sneered. 'Messy desk, messy mind, DS Ballantyne. Anyway, I'm off to HQ. All Hertfordshire DIs have been invited by the Chief Con. It's an all-day thing. I expect you to follow my orders and stay here. You look at cold cases, and if Tom needs some admin doing, I'll OK that, too. Yes?'

Rejoicing internally, Kat maintained a straight face. 'Absolutely. Yes, boss.'

Frowning, Carve-up turned away, straightening his suit lapels and weaving between the close-packed desks on his way out.

Breathing shallowly to avoid the stink of his aftershave, Kat went to the window. Carve-up eased his scarlet Alfa Romeo out of its parking space before executing a showy sliding turn on to Union Street.

She fished out her own car keys and went downstairs.

Chapter Thirty-Three

Middlehampton Golf Club occupied a picturesque plot of land to the west of the town. Rolling grassy hills and clumps of artfully planted broad-leaved trees. The narrow road off the A41 led to a pair of open wrought-iron gates, adorned with the club's double-eel crest and mounted between short curving brick walls.

Walking into the clubhouse, her feet sank into marshmallow-soft carpet. Woven into its green and gold fibres was the club crest. Fresh cut flowers in waist-high glass vases flooded Kat's nostrils with the scent of honey and peaches.

She approached the reception desk. A young woman with blonde hair swept up into a chignon raised her eyes from her keyboard and smiled. She still wore braces. Eighteen? Nineteen?

'Welcome to Middlehampton Golf Club. My name's Amelia. How can I help you?'

Kat held out her police ID. 'Hi, Amelia. Do you have such a thing as a membership secretary?'

Amelia seemed unfazed by Kat's ID and request. Her smile widened. Light from the electric chandelier overhead glinted off the silver wires on her front teeth.

'That would be Christopher. Were you looking to join? I know we have memberships available at the moment.'

She was well trained, Kat gave her that. It seemed a shame to interrupt her.

'Netball's my game, I'm afraid. But I would like to speak to Christopher, if he's available.'

Amelia's smile morphed into a conspiratorial grin. 'That's OK. You look a lot cooler than the average lady member. I can call him for you?'

'Please,' Kat said, delighted to be thought cool by a girl in her late teens.

Two minutes later, a white-painted door on the far side of the room opened. A tall, slim man in his forties with the confident aura of a top salesman emerged.

'DS Ballantyne? Welcome to Middlehampton Golf Club,' he said as he arrived in front of Kat and shook her hand briskly. 'Won't you come this way?' He called over his shoulder. 'Amelia? Tea for two, there's a good girl.'

Stiffening at the tone he used on the young receptionist, Kat turned back to her and smiled. 'Not on my account, thank you, Amelia. It's just a quick visit.'

In his office, her host gestured to an upright, tapestry-upholstered guest chair and plopped himself down into the more expensive-looking reclining number behind the desk.

'You'll be looking to join. Smart career move for an aspiring detective sergeant. As well as a healthy lifestyle choice, obviously. Lot of senior officers play here. Who knows, you might find yourself in a four with the Chief Constable of Hertfordshire.'

The positive effect of his natural good looks and confident manner had evaporated the moment he'd launched into his sales spiel, not giving Kat a chance to speak. He'd patronised her as easily as he had the young girl on reception.

'I'm investigating the murder of a young woman who was strangled with one of your club ties,' she said. As he opened his mouth, she continued, leaving him gaping. 'I need an up-to-date list of your members, please.'

He ran a hand through shiny but sparse sandy hair.

'Murdered? Who?'

'Her name was Alanna Michie.'

'But it can't have been one of our members. They're entrepreneurs, army officers, politicians . . .' His tongue flicked over his top lip. 'I mean, half of Middlehampton FC belong!'

She felt a moment of sympathy for his naive idea about the sort of person who could – or couldn't – commit murder. But only a moment.

'At this point, all I know is that the murder weapon was a Middlehampton Golf Club tie.'

He sat back in his chair and swiped a hand over his mouth.

'Oh, thank God. That's it, then, isn't it? It's not a member at all. Someone must have stolen one of our ties.' He leaned forward, dropped his voice to a low murmur. 'Probably one of the staff. A groundskeeper, maybe, or a caddie. A cleaner! I can give you a list of all their names.'

'That would be helpful, too.' A beat. 'Along with a list of your members, please.'

His features settled into a sly, defensive cast. Forehead wrinkled. Lips pulled to one side. She knew what was coming.

'Well, about that. I mean, I'm not sure whether you're aware, Detective Sergeant, but there are rules. Privacy and so on. You'll need a warrant, I'm afraid.' He leaned back. Smiled. 'I'm sorry you've had a wasted trip. Do come back when you have the necessary paperwork and I'll be happy to help.'

Kat had been expecting him to refuse, but it was still a knock-back. However, she wasn't done yet.

'Is Callum Michie a member?'

He shrugged. 'I couldn't say. We have over five hundred.'

'No, of course not. So, how does a member go about acquiring a club tie?'

'We keep a number in stock. Once their membership has been approved by the committee, and they've paid their joining fee and first year's membership fee, they can just come and see me and buy one.'

'Do you offer a personalisation service?'

She knew they did. But she was interested in how he'd answer. Honestly, as it turned out.

'Up to three initials. Gold or green thread.' He ran his own tie through thumb and forefinger. 'Thirty pounds plus VAT.'

'Do you keep a record of who's ordered one?'

'It's on the database. "CT" for club tie and "M" for monogrammed.'

'Is there any way someone other than the member could get hold of the tie after it's been embroidered?'

His eyes widened. 'You think someone might have picked the lock and stolen a monogrammed tie. Of course! So it *could* have been one of the staff?'

'It could have been anyone, Christopher. It could have been you.' A thought struck her. 'What's your surname?'

'Miller, why?'

Her pulse kicked up a little. 'No reason. Just curious. Goes with the job, I'm afraid.'

She reassessed the man sitting across the desk from her. Six foot. Athletic build. Broad shoulders. Long, strong fingers, square nails neatly manicured. Good-looking, in a public-school sort of way.

If Kat's doorbell rang and she opened the front door to see Christopher Miller standing there, smiling his plausible salesman's smile, she thought she'd probably invite him in if he offered her a half-decent reason. Like being the membership secretary at Van's golf club.

'And there's really no way you can let me have a look at your membership records?' she asked. 'It is a murder investigation, after all.'

He barely managed to hide the sneer. 'Like I said, DS Ballantyne. There are rules. Come back with a warrant. Until then, my hands are tied.'

She rose to her feet.

'Please don't get up,' she said, not sensing he was about to do any such thing.

She closed his office door behind her and wandered back to the reception desk.

'Did you get what you needed?' Amelia asked.

Kat smiled and shook her head. 'Sadly not. Your Mr Miller is a stickler for the rules.'

Amelia looked left and right, then inclined her head. Kat leaned across the blond-wood riser.

'Not when it comes to the female staff,' she murmured. 'He's a bit handsy.'

Kat shook her head. 'Worth complaining about?'

Amelia barked out a short sharp laugh, then covered her mouth. Whether from embarrassment about the noise, or her braces, Kat couldn't tell.

'I'd be collecting my P45 the same day. It's like a bloody cult in here. They all back each other up. The pay's OK, but you don't half earn it.'

'Sounds a bit like the police,' Kat said with a wry smile. 'Listen, Amelia, what I was asking Christopher about, it wasn't really that much. I just need to know which of your members have the initials CM and have also bought a monogrammed club tie. You couldn't—'

Amelia smiled broadly, exposing those pretty bejewelled braces again. So her earlier embarrassment had been about making too much noise.

'Give me a minute. I can do it from here.' She tilted her head sideways, towards Miller's office. 'He doesn't need to know.'

Amelia's varnished nails clicked on the keyboard.

'I'm just searching the database . . . there we are! Three. Shall I print you off a report?'

'That would be great, thanks.'

A printer beneath the reception desk hummed, and shortly, Kat held a sheet of warm A4 paper in her hand, still slightly curled from the rollers.

She scanned the three lines of text.

Michie, Callum

Miller, Christopher

Morton, Colin

The column headed 'CT' – 'club tie' – bore a tick against each man's name. Another column, then, in the column headed 'M' for 'monogrammed', another three ticks.

She had her suspects. Her guts squirmed as she read the third name.

Oh, Dad, what have you done?

Chapter Thirty-Four

Kat drove home. She needed to talk to Liv about the money. With every passing day, every passing *hour*, her downfall at the hands of Carve-up and his 3C-ACU buddy DI Senior was creeping closer.

She found Liv in the kitchen, reading the *Echo*.

'Fancy a coffee?'

Liv nodded. 'Sure. How's your morning going?'

'On the case, good. I've got some promising leads. How about you? Any joy with Ethan?'

Liv snorted. 'Please don't put the words "joy" and "Ethan" together in one sentence.'

'Have you, though?'

Liv adopted a passable American accent. Kat thought it might be Californian.

'Is that the actual Ethan Metcalf? Oh my God, I just love your podcast. My name's Tiffany? Tiffany Taylor? I'm studying new media here at Middlehampton University, and I am so *so* trying to land an internship? But, ya know, I'm twenty-nine and it's kinda hard to get folks to take me seriously? I think it's because I did some lingerie modelling? Back when I lived in LA?'

Kat shook her head. 'Please tell me you didn't really go in with that?'

Liv answered in a half-decent impression of Ethan. 'Maybe I could help you out, Tiffany. And don't worry about the modelling. Not everybody in Britain is uptight about sex. I think it's cool.'

Kat shuddered. 'You're right. He really is a creep.'

'I'm meeting him.'

'What? When?'

'Tomorrow. Don't suppose you've got a push-up bra, have you?'

Kat rolled her eyes. Every now and then Van would get it into his head that having sex while she was trussed up like a turkey would be a turn-on. She'd go along with it a couple of times and then suggest if he liked it so much maybe he should try wrangling himself into a suspender belt before getting down to it.

'What do you think?'

'You have!' Liv said, grinning. 'Let me guess, Van bought it for you.'

'What size are you?' Kat countered.

'Thirty-four B,' Liv said.

'Close enough. Poor old Mutt-calf won't know what hit him.'

Kat found Tom in the kitchen stirring granules of lumpy instant coffee into a mug of boiling water.

'Hey, Tomski. So, listen. I got the tie used to strangle Alanna out of evidence. It's got a crest and a monogram. Nobody picked it up before, probably because we were all so focused on Laura's confession. The crest is for Middlehampton Golf Club and the initials are CM. So I paid a visit to the club. You've played up there, haven't you? Didn't you say Carve-up took you there your first week?'

Tom looked at her askance. 'He did, but so what? Nothing against the rules about playing golf with your boss.'

'No, of course not. Although technically *I'm* still your boss.'

'Yeah, but technically, you shouldn't even be involved in this case. So technically, I'm *your* boss.'

There it was again. That niggling feeling Kat kept getting that she wasn't a hundred per cent sure where Tom's loyalties lay. No time for that now. They had a murderer to catch. Never mind a corruption charge to defeat.

She placed the sheet of computer paper on Tom's desk. Jabbed the point of her index finger on it.

'Three members of Middlehampton Golf Club have the initials CM. The same initials I found on the tie the killer used to strangle Alanna Michie. And before you say anything, yes, number three is my dad.'

'Jesus. You don't think . . . ?'

'That my dad's a murderer?' The tip of Kat's tongue touched the roof of her mouth. Then she stilled it before the 'no' could emerge. *Could* her dad be a murderer?

She'd always thought of him as a crooked businessman. Not a great look, but not uncommon in Middlehampton – or any big town, come to that. But still streets away, literally, from being a cold-blooded killer.

But then, how much did she really know about him? Until recently, not that he'd had a child with another woman, Tasha Starling, a former business partner. She'd died, along with her husband, in a light plane crash. An accident, he'd told her.

Out of nowhere, a horrifying suspicion flashed into her detective's mind. The number-two motive for murder after sexual jealousy: money. What if Tasha had found out about his dodgy dealings and backed out of their arrangement? Maybe even threatened to go to the police? He would never allow that to happen.

How hard was it to sabotage a light plane? Kat had no idea and no time to consider the question further. Queasily, she shoved the thought down and returned to Tom, who was looking at her strangely.

'Earth calling Kat.'

'Sorry, Tom. Lost focus there for a second.'

'I just asked you what possible motive he could have to murder Alanna Michie?'

'He could have been sleeping with her.'

'He's old enough to be her dad!'

Kat merely raised her eyebrows.

'I know, I know. When did that ever count for anything? And you did tell me he . . .' Tom stared into the remaining milk foam in his coffee cup. 'Well, that he fathered a child before with a mistress. He's got form.'

'So compare him to what we know about the killer,' she said, even as she struggled with the notion that she was a killer's child, wanting to see how Tom put the puzzle pieces together.

Tom coughed nervously. 'One, we know he's had at least one affair before. Two, he's the right gender for the murderer. Three, he's physically strong enough to have overpowered Alanna.'

Kat couldn't hold back any longer, even though adding more points caused her stomach to clench with anxiety.

'Four, he owns a tie that matches the murder weapon.'

A fifth point surfaced from the murky swirl of suspicions in her brain: it also gave him a powerful motive to have Kat sidelined with a corruption investigation. The money had appeared in her account before Alanna's murder. But maybe he'd been planning it all along.

'We should pull them all in,' she said. 'They've all got CM-monogrammed club ties. Now, in an ideal world, one of them won't be able to produce his tie. We can get the lab on to the one we've got in evidence, and we'll find their DNA on it.'

'But if it comes back with Callum Michie's DNA on it, all that'll prove is that Laura's telling the truth,' Tom said. 'She found his tie in his house and used it to kill his wife.'

'Not necessarily. Because it all looked so cut and dried, nobody's done anything with the tie. Nothing! Carve-up told Darcy she couldn't test it for DNA yet, remember? If it's got Callum's DNA on it, fine, it's his. But what if it's got his skin cells on it, too? At the ends, I mean. Embedded. That will show he pulled it tight round Alanna's neck.'

Tom's dark eyebrows drew together, creating a deep furrow directly above the bridge of his nose.

'I don't want to be picky, Kat, but that's a pretty big if. And his lawyer would surely just argue that the epithelials got there when he was tying it.'

'No, Tomski. I've looked at it. The ends are really twisted and scrunched up. Permanently creased. Nobody ties a tie like that. It's basically ruined. So if his epithelials are in amongst the fibres, it would show he was grabbing it tight like a garotte.' She looked him in the eye. He was finding it hard to meet her gaze. She sighed. 'You think I'm reaching, don't you?'

'I think, as lead investigator, we have a new lead we need to pursue. I'll get them all in.'

They left the kitchen agreeing Kat would sit in on the interviews but, as before, Tom would lead.

Chapter Thirty-Five

Rather than the usual stink of body odour and tobacco smoke – or, more frequently these days, vape flavours that ranged from sweet to cloying – interview room 2 was perfumed by two expensive scents. One from Callum Michie; the other from his quietly but stylishly dressed lawyer.

Kat didn't believe in auras. Or, for that matter, angels, ghosts or coincidences. But had she been so minded, she'd think Callum Michie's aura would be the colour of a nuclear explosion. A white-hot core haloed in screaming scarlet, tinged with black. A human fireball radiating so much anger it was palpable.

His glare could have cut through a steel-lined bank-vault door faster than a thermic lance. Unhappily for Kat, it was currently focused on her.

In contrast, his lawyer appeared to have her own inbuilt air-conditioning system. Beth Sharpe's aura would have been a cool ice blue or maybe a pale sage green. With an expensive name, like a Farrow & Ball paint colour. Tundra, maybe. Or Glacier. She clicked the button on a slim gold ballpoint with an angular bird-boned thumb, offered Kat a smile that hardly reached the corners of her lips, and waited.

'Thanks for coming in, Callum,' Tom began.

'It's Mr Michie to you, son.'

Tom blushed. 'Oh. Right. I apologise. Mr Michie, you are here voluntarily, and you can leave at any point. I do need to remind you that you are being interviewed in connection with the murder of your wife, Alanna Michie.'

As Tom recited the rest of the official caution, Kat was concentrating on Callum's facial muscles. Looking for anything that might suggest they were interviewing a murderer and not a grieving husband. After all, the statistics said it was likely to be him.

He gave nothing away, breathing steadily, if noisily, through his nose.

Tom cleared his throat. 'Mr Michie, can I ask where you were between midnight and 10.00 a.m. on Monday, 20th May?'

'Why are you asking me this? I thought you had the murderer in custody.'

Kat had been expecting this. Had told Tom as much. Callum was going on the offensive from the start.

'We have a person in custody who confessed to your wife's murder. But evidence has come to light that throws doubt on the veracity of that confession.' Kat kept her face immobile as Tom slipped into using the stuffy official language. *Veracity!* Who used words like that outside copshops and courtrooms?

She asked the question again, in simpler language. 'I don't think she did it, Callum. So I'd like to ask you again for your whereabouts on the date and times DC Gray just gave you.'

'Abroad.'

'Where?'

'Spain.'

'Specifically?'

He bared his teeth. 'Specifically, it's none of your business.'

Beth leaned sideways, just a fraction, and murmured behind her hand. Callum huffed in a breath, nodded. Presumably taking the mild telling-off his lawyer had just given him. That seemed sensible to Kat. After all, why pay for the best criminal defence solicitor in Middlehampton if you weren't going to take her advice?

Professionally, she'd have preferred him to lose his cool completely. Emotional interviewees often revealed more than they'd ever intended to before taking their seat opposite a homicide detective.

Kat nodded, consulted her notes. It was just a delaying tactic, to let Callum build up a head of steam again. 'I appreciate this must be stressful for you, Callum. I do, really. You've just lost your wife and I am truly sorry for that. But all I'm trying to do here' – she glanced at Beth and smiled slightly – 'all *we're* trying to do here, *all of us*, is eliminate you from our enquiries. And the simplest way for that to happen is for you to have a solid alibi. Isn't it?' she couldn't resist adding, given this was by no means his first rodeo. 'So, can you tell us whereabouts in Spain you were on Monday for the stated period of time?'

'Marbella,' he growled.

This time Kat did manage to resist temptation. Her head, rather than shaking, remained as steady as the uniformed PC standing guard in a corner. Marbella? Of *course* it would be Marbella. Capital of the Costa del Crime. And still, after all these years, a favoured hangout of ex-pat British villains.

'Business or pleasure?' Tom asked, leaning forward, clearly anxious to maintain the idea he was in control.

'The purpose of Mr Michie's visit to Spain is irrelevant, Detective Constable,' Beth said, pinning Tom with a beady gaze. 'You asked my client for an alibi. He has given you one. He was, as the Latin has it, elsewhere.'

'Can anyone confirm your presence in Marbella?' Tom asked.

Anyone without a criminal record of their own, Kat wanted to add.

Callum clamped his lips. He turned to his solicitor. Wordlessly, she unzipped a slim burgundy leather portfolio and withdrew a transparent plastic wallet, A4-size. Taking her time, she slid the Ziploc fastener all the way along the closure and withdrew a navy-blue booklet gold-blocked with the UK's royal coat of arms. She laid it on the table and placed two small rectangles of paper printed with small black text beside it.

'That is Mr Michie's passport.' A maroon fingernail stabbed the document and pushed it a few inches closer to Tom and Kat. 'And those' – two stabs, like a bird of prey's talons trapping a small rodent – 'are his boarding cards from the outward and return flights. As you can see, Mr Michie entered Spain via Malaga airport on Friday 17th May, having travelled on British Airways flight BA 0446, which departed Terminal Five at 11.27 a.m. and arrived in Malaga at 3.11 p.m. local time. He arrived back in the UK on Monday, 20th May, having travelled on Swissair flight LX 318, which, after a transfer, departed Zurich at 10.30 a.m., bang on time – very efficient, those Swiss – and arrived in Heathrow at 11.24 a.m. Actually, one minute ahead of schedule,' she added with a smile as friendly as a box-cutter slicing paper. 'We can also provide credit card receipts confirming Mr Michie's presence in Spain during the time you have specified. Phone records will show you calling him at 1.31 p.m. on Monday 20th. Between his landing and accepting your call, he was visible, no doubt, on a great many CCTV and ANPR cameras at the airport, its amenities and car parks, and his journey home.'

As alibis went, Kat thought it was right up there.

'Thank you,' Tom managed, his eyes skittering over the page of evidence that Callum Michie hadn't murdered his wife. 'I'm sorry to have to raise this painful subject with you, Mr Michie, but, as you know, your wife was strangled with a tie. We now know that this tie was in fact a Middlehampton Golf Club tie. It was also monogrammed with the initials CM. Do you own such a tie?'

Callum folded his arms across his chest. 'No.'

Kat drew her head back. This was not the answer she'd been expecting.

Tom looked nervously at Kat before asking, 'Are you sure?'

'Of course I'm bloody sure! I think I'd know if I owned an MGC monogrammed tie, don't you?'

Tom withdrew a sheet of paper from his file, with Callum's name highlighted in grey. Kat had photocopied the printout from the club, having masked off Christopher Miller's and Colin Morton's names.

'According to the club's records, of which this is a part,' Tom said, 'you *did* buy a monogrammed tie.'

Callum shook his head. 'I *ordered* a tie. I only joined last month. There's a thirty-day wait for the monogramming service. I haven't got it yet. Check with the club, or the manufacturer or whoever makes the bloody things.'

'Perhaps we can change the subject, Callum,' Kat said, leaning forward. 'Can you think of anyone who might have wanted to hurt Alanna? Did she have any enemies?'

Callum frowned as he thought. This time she did catch a tell. A brief sliding of the eyes off to one side. Was he going to clam up or would he share whatever he knew?

'We were at a nightclub a couple of weeks ago. The Pumphouse on King Street.'

Kat nodded. 'I know it.'

'It was late. Early, actually. Maybe 2.00 or 3.00 a.m., I'm not sure. This woman started yelling at Alanna, calling her a slut and whatever. Then she said, "I'll choke you with your own stockings, you slag."'

Kat made a note, her pulse picking up. Threats to kill, even when made in the heat of the moment, under the influence of alcohol or drugs, were still that. Threats. To kill. You had to treat them seriously.

'Do you know this woman's name?'

'Yeah, I know it. Denise Luck. She's married to Peter Luck. I'm guessing you've heard of him?'

Kat nodded. What cop in Middlehampton hadn't heard of Peter 'Bad' Luck? A violent man who'd served time for armed robbery and arson – among other, equally reprehensible crimes. This was a lead, but it would need handling with kid gloves. Inside chain mail ones.

'We'll look into it. Anyone else spring to mind?'

'I'd have thought Bad Luck's missus was enough, wouldn't you?'

'We have to be thorough, Callum, that's all.'

'Well, no, in that case. Alanna was lovely. Maybe she fell out with friends from time to time, but only in normal ways like everybody does. Not so one of them would want to murder her.'

On a subtle signal from Kat, Tom drew the interview to a close, switched off the recorder and thanked Callum for coming in.

'Private word?' Callum asked Kat as Beth and Tom moved towards the door.

Outside, she saw Callum was hanging back, letting Beth Sharpe leave before him.

'Catch you later,' she murmured to Tom.

Callum folded his arms.

'All that?' he said. 'The make-nice cooperating with your investigation? Answering DC Dimwit's questions? That was for Beth's benefit. But you're running out of time. If it wasn't Laura Paxton, then you'd better find out who really killed my wife. And when you do, you'd better get them into protective custody fast. I meant what I said when I spoke to you before. There's going to be justice for Alanna. Proper Old Testament justice. Strutt family justice.'

Then he left her there, inhaling the mingled remnants of his aftershave and Beth Sharpe's perfume.

She sighed.

Denise Luck probably wouldn't remember their first and only previous encounter. But Kat did. A vicious fight outside a nightclub that went from nought to GBH in about five seconds flat. PC Ballantyne had sustained a split lip and lost her bowler cap in the melee, during which she'd attempted to arrest Denise.

'Attempted' being the operative word.

Kat wondered whether the woman she'd last seen sprinting down London Road, barefoot, spike-heeled shoes swinging wildly from her bruised right hand, would remember her.

She hoped not.

Chapter Thirty-Six

Kat approached the front door of Peter and Denise Luck's semi-detached house, trying to ignore her galloping pulse.

Taking a steadying breath, she thought she understood how the Christians must have felt before a Roman legionary prodded them into the arena for a tête-à-tête with a lion. Why had she volunteered to check out the lead just because Tom was busy on the Hartsbury murder? Why couldn't she obey orders? Just for once?

Cooper's Field wasn't the roughest neighbourhood in Middlehampton. But you'd rarely see a lone copper. Certainly not on foot. Most preferred to travel double-crewed in a marked car. And even then, they'd likely as not be checking in the vehicle for some bodywork repairs at the end of their shift.

Next door, a huge low-riding white American convertible sat, like a barge stranded at high tide. Its many chromed parts glinted in the sun. A bumper sticker on the back read, *How's my driving? Call 1-800-FU.*

Kat straightened the lapels of her M&S jacket, wishing it was made of Kevlar with ceramic inserts instead of a wearable, easy-care, cotton-viscose mix perfect for work-to-weekend.

'Copper, are you? You've got balls coming here!' a high-pitched voice called from behind her.

She turned. The voice belonged to a grubby-faced cherub astride a BMX bike, one trainer-clad foot planted on the pavement, the other resting on the pedal. Twelve, maybe thirteen. Riley's age. What appeared to be a roll-up – or as she caught a whiff of its sweet-scented smoke, a joint – dangled from his lower lip. All in all, quite the image. A pint-sized James Dean.

'So have you, smoking that in front of me,' she retorted.

'Go on then, arrest me,' he said, holding his hands out, wrists together. 'I dare you.'

'Some other time. Maybe when you're a grown-up, eh?'

He curled his lip. The effect would have been cool, but it resulted in him almost losing the joint. He had to fumble it to stop it falling to the ground.

Turning away from him, and there being no bell she could see, she gave a good hard rap on the glass panel.

A splash of pink appeared behind the pane of swirling frosted glass. Blonde hair. Dark blobs for eyes and mouth.

The door opened.

The rail-thin woman confronting Kat radiated hostility. Ropy forearms blue with old tattoos folded across her bust. Eyes spidery with mascara and narrowed to slits. Frosty pink lips set in a line like a razor slash.

'We don't talk to the filth.'

'Is it that obvious?'

Denise looked Kat up and down. 'Cheap suit. Sensible heels. No make-up. Ponytail. Might as well wear a sign round your neck.' She peered at Kat. Maybe she needed glasses. 'I know you, don't I?'

Kat swallowed her nerves down. 'I used to patrol the Field back when I was in uniform.'

Denise sniffed. 'And look at you now. All spick and span in your "My First Detective" outfit.'

It was a good line. But more to the point, Denise hadn't slammed the door in her face, had she? This was all part of the ritual. Opening moves that had to be observed before moving to principal business.

Kat produced her ID. 'I'm Detective Sergeant Katherine Ballantyne. I was hoping to have a few words.' She glanced over her shoulder at the BMX rider, whose eyes were out on stalks. 'Inside?'

Denise looked over Kat's shoulder. 'Piss off, Tommy Green, or your mum'll hear how you've been spying on Leanne Weller through her bedroom window.'

The cherub's pristine wings fluttered to the ground, revealing pointed red leathery numbers instead. With a scowl, he pedalled off, cackling as he swerved in front of a white van, which braked sharply, horn blaring.

'What's this about?' she asked Kat. A buying signal of sorts.

'The murder of Alanna Michie.'

Denise blinked. Wordlessly, she turned and walked back into the hall.

'Tea?' Denise asked once the two women were facing each other in the immaculate kitchen.

'Yes, please.'

Denise filled the kettle. 'Don't think this is me getting all cosy. My mum raised me to always offer guests something to drink. That's all this is.'

'Well, it's appreciated all the same. My mum's the same, though you're more likely to get a stiff G&T than a cuppa.'

Denise sniffed. 'That you thinking we're building rapport, is it? Do they teach you that at police school, or wherever you lot learn the art of piggery?'

Kat had to suppress a smile. Denise's jibes sounded just as forced as the rookie cop Kat had been, reciting the official caution while dodging Denise's swinging fists. There was an edge of fear beneath the bravado. And why shouldn't there be? The grapevine would have told her exactly why Kat had turned up on her quarry-tiled front doorstep.

Tea poured. Bags squeezed. Milk added. Sugar refused. Now, the two women sat facing each other across the glass-topped dining table. No chessboard needed. Both could see the layout of the pieces.

Kat made her opening move. 'How well did you know Alanna?'

'I didn't.'

'But your paths crossed?'

'I cross paths with lots of people.'

'A witness reports you and her having an argument in The Pumphouse two weeks ago. Early morning. You said, and I'm quoting here, "I'll choke you with your own stockings, you slag." Can you tell me what the argument was about?'

Denise shrugged her narrow shoulders. Took a sip of tea. Buying time. Or unconcerned.

'She was giving Peter a good look down her cleavage. I told her to put them away. We've all got them and hers aren't even real.'

'Weren't. She's dead, Denise.'

'Aren't, weren't . . . She won't be flashing them at anyone again, will she?'

'Except the pathologist. Look, Denise, this is serious. You were seen threatening to strangle Alanna Michie two weeks before she was murdered in the same way, so I really think—'

'Do I look like I care how she was murdered? The woman was a slag. I stand by that. And before you ask, let me save you the trouble. I didn't kill her. Give me the date and time you need.'

'Between midnight and 10.00 a.m., Monday morning.'

'In bed with Pete, then breakfast here. Then a mani-pedi at Body Beautiful on North Street till just before 11.00 a.m. My nail tech was a lovely little Thai girl called Sarocha. Evans, if you can believe it. Must have married a Welsh bloke, or else her mum did. Coffee with a mate, Louise Lenneghan, at the Costa on the High Street. The big one. I'll give you her number, she'll confirm it. We were there until about 12.30 p.m., then I went shopping. Plenty of CCTV all over the place.' She leaned back and took a swig of her tea, then plonked the mug back down on the table with a loud and unpleasant clank. 'Try picking holes in that. See where it gets you.'

Kat shook her head. 'There's no need. I believe you, Denise. In all honesty, I just had to come to eliminate you. I'd have been failing in my job otherwise.'

Denise snorted, but she gave Kat an appraising look. 'So you don't think the Paxton woman did it.'

'We're just tying up any loose ends before it goes to court.'

Denise's overplucked eyebrows lifted towards her hairline. 'You don't play poker, do you?'

'No.'

'Don't bother starting. You'd lose everything. Was that all? Or did you want to interview Pete as well, see if he has a grudge against Callum Michie?'

'Does he?'

Denise lifted her chin and tilted her head to one side, closing her eyes to reveal lids sparkling with metallic powder.

'That's his car outside. You can ask him yourself.'

Kat swallowed. Great. She was about to come face to face with one of Middlehampton's most notorious and violent villains. A man who'd once broken a copper's jaw during a routine traffic stop.

The key scraped in the door. It opened and then closed again. Footsteps. Kat turned in her chair, which had its back to the kitchen door. Stay sitting or look more authoritative by standing? No time to think. She remained in her chair. Hoped it looked more like she and Denise were already friends.

Peter Luck didn't so much enter the kitchen as invade it.

It wasn't just his physical size. Although at six-five and at least fifteen, sinewy, muscular stone, it was impressive. It was the malevolent energy he radiated. His dark eyes bored into Kat's like pokers pulled from a brazier.

'Who's this, Den?'

'Mr Luck, my name is —' Kat began.

'I didn't ask you,' he growled. 'I asked my wife.'

'Take it easy, Pete,' Denise said. 'She's a DS. Katherine Ballantyne. Came to ask me about an alibi for that tart Alanna Michie's murder.'

He walked close behind Kat's chair and placed hard hands on the back of it, and leaned down close enough for her to smell him. Leather, sweat.

She forced herself to relax, even though her pulse was throbbing in her ears.

'Why?'

'Why, what?'

Now he squatted behind her and reached around each side of her chair to put his hands on the table, caging her inside arms that had cradled sawn-off shotguns, twisted enemies' heads to breaking point, shoved explosives against vault doors.

'I strongly advise you not to play games with me,' he murmured.

Kat took a breath, not liking the fluttery sensation as the air passed her vocal cords.

'As I told Denise, I am conducting a thorough investigation. Even with a confession, there are inconsistencies I need to clarify.'

'Like what?'

'I can't disclose that to you.'

Kat desperately wanted to wipe her forehead. But she didn't trust her hand not to shake. If this was a game, it was the kind that could very easily end with the board flying skywards, the pieces raining down like hail and the losing player making the intimate acquaintance of the tiled floor.

Peter Luck's breathing was loud in her left ear. Then it stopped altogether.

One, two, three . . .

He laughed. Brutally loudly in the silence. She flinched.

'You've got bottle. I'll give you that.'

He stood, shaking his head, and rounded the table to kiss Denise. Then reached down and took a mouthful of tea from her mug.

Kat felt as though her bladder might let go. She clamped her thighs together.

'Does that mean you're not going to throw me out bodily?'

Still chuckling, Peter Luck sat heavily beside Denise. 'Shall I tell you what I think? I think you don't like this Paxton woman for Alanna Michie's murder. Confession or not, she's the wrong sex, for a start. Women don't strangle. Or they don't other women anyway. Kids, maybe, but those slags are just sickos, aren't they? What was she even doing mixing with the likes of Alanna? That's what I'd be asking. I mean, a cop's wife and a member of the Strutt family? That's a bit odd, wouldn't you say?'

Kat nodded. He was right. She'd been looking at the wrong things. And it had taken an armed robber to show her.

'Any other tips?' she asked, smiling to show she appreciated the irony of this conversation.

Apparently so did Peter Luck. 'This must be a first,' he said. 'The filth asking Bad Luck for help solving a case. So, it's a bloke. He's killed Alanna Michie because, what? She owed him money? Unlikely. She was married into the family. They've got cash stashed away all over the shop.'

'An affair gone sour?'

He shrugged. 'Could be. But what kind of bloke has an affair with Callum Michie's missus? He'd have to have balls like watermelons. Bloke like Callum finds out you've been slipping it to his wife, he's not going to be keying your Audi or calling you out in the pub. You'd get a nice little visit at 3.00 a.m. from a couple of his blokes and a one-way trip to the gravel pits over in Sheepton.'

Denise rose from her chair. 'You want a tea, love?'

'Go on, then.'

She glanced at Kat. 'Got time for another?'

'Please.'

Kat felt some of the tension leaving her shoulders. And the urge to pee had vanished. Having Peter and Denise Luck if not on her side then at least willing to talk without threatening violence was a good thing. Not just for this case, either. Kat had always believed in cultivating relationships with all of Middlehampton's residents, on both sides of the fence.

'Maybe it's her old man,' Denise said over her shoulder.

'A cop?' Peter scoffed. 'I mean, we all know there's some seriously bent coppers out there, but murder? That's a stretch.'

Denise brought three mugs of tea back to the table.

'Why did she?' This was aimed at Kat. 'Confess, I mean?'

'I don't know.' Kat shook her head. 'It's the other half of the mystery. Who murdered Alanna Michie and how did they get Laura Paxton to put her hand up?'

'I knew this bloke once, back when we lived in Watford,' Peter said, blowing across the surface of his tea. 'He had beef with this guy who was inside. Proper serious. So he confessed to a string of burglaries to get himself put away. Took him a while and some string-pulling, but eventually he got transferred to Long Lartin, too. Next night, the bloke he didn't like "hanged himself"' – air quotes – 'in his cell.'

169

'Come on, Pete!' Denise said. 'You're not seriously suggesting this Paxton woman wanted to get inside so she could off some rival from her crochet class or whatever?'

'No. But maybe she had some other reason.'

'I'm working on the assumption she was coerced,' Kat said. 'The murderer threatened her or maybe her husband.'

'Why pick her, though?' Denise asked.

'They knew she and Alanna were friends?'

'But that makes her a worse candidate, not a better one. They'd have been better off picking someone who hated her. And before you say it, I never hated the woman, I just thought she was a tart.' She shot a meaningful look at her husband.

Peter held his hands up. 'Let's not get into all that again, Den. I told you it didn't mean nothing. We'd all had a few.'

Something about the way Denise talked about Alanna set Kat's senses tingling. 'Denise, was there anything else about Alanna that makes you call her a tart? I mean, showing a bit of cleavage in a nightclub isn't exactly front-page news, is it?'

'There were rumours that she was cheating on Callum.'

'Don't suppose these rumours included a name?'

She shook her head. 'Sorry.'

Kat mulled this over. If Alanna Michie *was* having an affair, then Callum would have a motive. Alibi notwithstanding, he'd be back in the frame. After all, as Peter had said, men like Callum Michie could always call on a couple of men who'd do his bidding.

Up to and including murder.

Chapter Thirty-Seven

After leaving the Lucks, Kat drove over to her father's office in South Lane, Middlehampton's business district.

She emerged from the whisper-quiet lift doors on the floor occupied by Morton Land and pushed through the double doors into the reception area, where her dad's PA, Suzanne 'Suzy' Watkins, acted as gatekeeper. As a little girl visiting her dad's office, Kat would shyly accept a sweet from a big jar Suzy kept behind her desk.

'Is he in?'

'Yes, but he's got a meeting in ten minutes, so you'll have to be quick.'

'You might want to reschedule it,' Kat said, heading in to her father's office without knocking, leaving Suzy frowning with irritation. *Tough.*

Colin Morton looked up from the papers spread out over his desk, an aircraft-carrier-sized workspace fashioned from aluminium and toughened glass. Smiled.

'Kitty-Kat, to what do I owe the pleasure?'

'Please don't call me that, Dad. You know I hate it.'

Maybe he picked up the purpose of her visit from her tight expression. At any rate, his smile faded.

'Or is pleasure off the agenda this afternoon?'

Thinking of her dad as crooked had long been the norm. But now she felt as much adrenaline in her system as when she'd ventured inside Peter and Denise Luck's pebble-dashed citadel. He had a tie that matched the murder weapon. And, as Tom had said, he had form as an adulterer. Once again, the question swirled: how well did she really know him?

The smell of his Aramis aftershave was overpowering. She felt suddenly nervous.

'I need you to come down to the station with me. To be interviewed under caution.' She swallowed. Felt like a little girl again. 'You would have the right to legal representation and the interview would be entirely voluntary. You'd be free to leave at any time.'

With each successive sentence, her heart rate increased by a few more beats per minute. Now it was charging along as though she were about to host a press conference. He regarded her silently for a few seconds. Then he sighed. He capped the chunky red and gold fountain pen in his right hand and placed it on top of the papers he'd just been scrutinising.

'I need to call my lawyer. Can I meet you there?'

She blinked twice, bewildered at his docility. She'd expected a lot more to-ing and fro-ing before he'd agree.

'You're not going to give me some spiel about your meeting? Make me sweat first?'

He shook his head as he picked up his phone. 'I know my younger daughter. And I know that look. What would be the point?' He peered at the phone screen. Tapped it and brought it to his ear. 'Half an hour?'

'Fine. Just so you know, it won't be me conducting the interview.'

He shrugged. 'Probably for the best. Wouldn't want you caught sulking on tape, would we?' He held up a hand; his gaze went out of focus. 'Donald? I need you.'

Leaving him to make the arrangements with his solicitor, she left, smiling a goodbye at Suzy, who was on a call of her own. Before her dad arrived at Jubilee Place, she wanted to have a chat with Tom and Leah about handling the interview.

Because it wasn't just the conflict of interest that was making her sweat. So far she'd hidden the level of her involvement in the case from both Carve-up and Linda. But bringing her dad right into its heart?

She'd be under scrutiny like never before. This was going to take her closer than ever to the line she'd never ever dreamed she'd be in danger of crossing.

Chapter Thirty-Eight

Kat watched her two DCs from the 'wrong' side of the one-way glass. She felt frustrated not to be in there instead of Leah. But given the interviewee was her dad, even she could see that any evidence gained in such a situation would be tainted. Not to mention her own dubious standing as a detective on active cases.

Facing Tom and Leah were Colin Morton and his seventy-something lawyer. In the brief pre-interview meeting, Kat had warned Tom that Donald McIntyre was a cross between a legal super-computer and a spitting cobra.

Noted, he'd responded drily.

He glanced over at the mirror. She told herself he'd be fine.

As the more experienced DC, Leah would be taking the lead. Tom had surprised both female detectives in the meeting ahead of the interview by saying as much.

As she waited for Leah to conduct the business with the recorder and recite the caution, Kat watched her dad. He was smiling, hands folded loosely in his lap. It was weird. Even the innocent looked nervous when being interviewed in a police station. She couldn't blame them. But her dad seemed utterly unconcerned. A gambler with an ace up his sleeve.

Leah opened her file. 'Thank you for coming in, Mr Morton, we'll try not to keep you,' she began. 'Hello again, Donald.'

This courteous opening was also part of the plan. Trying to undercut any status-posturing Colin might indulge in: *Do you know who/how busy I am?* The greeting to his lawyer was an on-the-spot improvisation. Kat awarded Leah the first point.

McIntyre stretched his lips a little wider. Possibly readying his fangs to project twin streams of venom at Leah's eyes.

'Do you have a question for my client, DC Hooper?' he hissed.

'Indeed, I do. Mr Morton, do you own a Middlehampton Golf Club tie?'

'Yes.'

'And is that tie monogrammed with your initials?'

'Guilty as charged.'

'Is that a yes?'

'Sorry. Yes, I do own such a tie.'

Leah produced the wine-stained tie in a transparent plastic evidence bag.

'Could you take a look at this tie please, Mr Morton.'

Kat watched her dad pick up the bag and turn it in the light from the overhead fluorescent tube. He brought it close to his eyes.

'Sorry, really could have done with my reading glasses. If I'd known . . .' He smiled as he trailed off.

Something about the way he was handling the bag – almost playfully – made Kat worried. This was a bust. He wouldn't have come in quite so meek and mild if he'd been the killer. It was all for show. He was enjoying himself.

He turned to his solicitor. 'Why don't you take a look, Donald? I'd like your opinion.'

As he spoke, he dipped a hand into his trouser pocket. It emerged clutching a glossy red cylinder. Kat's eyes widened. A lipstick? What the hell was he playing at?

Before either Tom or Leah could object, Colin had the object in his right hand and was levering out a shiny silver blade with his thumbnail. A Swiss Army knife. Which he was angling towards the tape-sealed top of the evidence bag.

'No! What are you *doing*? Stop!' Leah shouted. 'You'll break the chain of custody.'

Kat's dad dropped the bag as if it contained a tarantula. His eyes widened and he covered his open mouth with his palm. The whole thing came off as stagy to Kat.

For some peculiar reason of his own – *To rile you, dummy!* – her dad was engaged in nothing more than play-acting.

'I am *so* sorry, DC Hooper,' he said, closing the knife and slipping it back into his pocket. 'Of course. How stupid of me. I apologise.'

Leah snatched the bag off the table, checked the tape was intact then held it out towards Colin.

'Can you see the monogram? CM. Those are your initials, yes?'

'No.'

Leah frowned, glanced at Tom.

'Your name *is* Colin Morton,' Leah said. 'Therefore, C and M *are* your initials.'

'I'm sorry. Again,' he said. 'Those are *two* of my initials. My name, my *full* name, is Colin *Alexander* Morton. And as for my club tie . . .' He turned to McIntyre. 'Donald, would you mind?'

Now Kat saw it. The corner of the ace peeping shyly from her dad's snowy shirt cuff.

The lawyer nodded solemnly. Although Kat still caught a flicker of a smile – and, she thought, the forked tip of his tongue. From his briefcase, he produced a long, narrow brown envelope. He pulled the flap open and tipped it up over his other hand.

Into his waiting palm slithered a green, purple and gold tie. He picked it up, examined it briefly, then turned it to face Leah and Tom.

'This is Mr Morton's monogrammed Middlehampton Golf Club tie. As you will see – yes, DC Gray, do, please, come closer

– it bears his initials. All *three* of them. C, A . . . and M,' he finished triumphantly before handing Leah the tie.

'The third initial cost an extra seven-fifty, but why not, eh?' Colin Morton added.

Leah gave the tie the most cursory of glances before handing it to Tom. Tom checked it then handed it back to the lawyer. Kat thought that when it came to strangling people with ties, she was beginning to understand how the killer might have felt.

'My client can produce a receipt, and we can furnish you with the name and number of the managing director of Arthur Kennedy & Son. He will confirm that Mr Morton has just this one monogrammed tie. My client has instructed me to say that you are welcome to take his tie into evidence. You should test it thoroughly. I am confident the only DNA you will find belongs to my client, either from hair, sweat or epithelials.' McIntyre grinned evilly at Tom, before switching his reptilian gaze to the one-way glass. 'I gather you're a recent recruit, DC Gray. In case you're unfamiliar with the term I just used, "epithelials" simply means skin cells.'

Kat caught Leah shooting Tom a warning glance, but she was too late.

'Of course I know what it means!' Tom snapped. Rounding on Morton, unable to help himself, he raised his voice. 'You know what, Colin? Money? Status? Power? They're not a get-out-of-jail-free card. Not in Middlehampton, not anywhere. Nobody is above the law. You've been wasting our time. Which, as I'm sure your expensive lawyer knows, even if you don't, is an offence.'

Kat's heart sank. Tom had allowed her dad to get under his skin. He was inexperienced, but even so, it was a rookie error. Literally.

Rather than reacting, Colin turned towards his lawyer. 'I don't know about you, Donald, but to me, that sounded rather like a threat.'

McIntyre nodded and made a precise little note on his legal pad.

Kat could tell Tom was already bitterly regretting his outburst. His mouth had turned down and he was staring at the tabletop as if he could burn a hole through it and disappear.

'You know, Tom, this is such a cliché,' her dad said, 'but I do, occasionally, play golf with your boss.'

'What you get up to socially with DI Carver has no bearing on this investigation,' Tom shot back. Bravely, Kat thought.

Colin frowned and shook his head. 'You misunderstand me, Tom. I didn't mean Stuart, though of course we do play together regularly. No, I mean the *big* boss. The Chief Constable of Hertfordshire Constabulary. Ingrid Young? You probably haven't met her. Very bright lady. And a demon with a driver. Plays off an eight handicap. I'll tell her we met next time we're teeing off together. I'm sure she'll be fascinated.'

Kat sat back, shaking her head. At the moment the lawyer had produced the three-initial tie, she'd seen what had happened. They'd been played. Colin Morton had known in advance that he'd be shown a monogrammed tie.

Tom been lured into a trap and then lost his temper when the two older men had sprung it. Yelling like that was unprofessional, but she didn't think her dad, or his lawyer, would make a complaint. For Colin Morton this was just a bit of sport. He'd probably been looking forward to it ever since she'd asked him to come in.

She blamed herself. She should have warned Tom that her dad would try to wind him up. But there was something else between the older and younger man. Something her dad had exploited to goad Tom into that wild flash of anger.

The door opened behind her. The change in air pressure sucked air from the corridor into the room, bringing with it the overpowering stink of Carve-up's aftershave.

Chapter Thirty-Nine

Kat started guiltily. But then steadied herself. She wasn't taking part in the investigation.

Carve-up stood just behind her right shoulder. 'I suppose I can forgive you showing an interest,' he murmured right into her ear. 'Might be the last murder investigation you ever get to see close up, after all. How's it going in there?'

And with a flash of unwelcome insight, for which no degree in criminology was necessary, she knew who'd tipped her dad off about the tie.

She spun round and leapt to her feet, unwilling to cede height advantage to Carve-up.

'You *told* him, didn't you,' she demanded. 'That's why he brought his tie in.'

He sneered. 'Don't be stupid, DS Ballantyne. Why would I tell him about the monogram?'

She smiled mirthlessly. Carve-up was cunning. But he wasn't smart.

'How did you know I meant the monogram, Stuart? As far as I can recall, we haven't discussed it.'

His eyes bulged in panic. 'I, er . . . I . . . I know you took a tie into evidence. I just assumed it was monogrammed. But obviously I would never share that with a potential suspect.' He regained some of his usual swagger. 'In fact, DS Ballantyne, I resent your insinuation that I would tip off someone as to the direction of an interview. An interview you shouldn't even be watching.'

Kat turned away. *She* knew he'd done it. That was enough.

'Of course. Maybe he just *guessed* he'd need to bring in his own monogrammed tie. Now please be quiet. They're just finishing up.'

Kat returned her attention to the glass. The lawyer was closing his leather portfolio.

'Will there be anything else? My client had to cancel a meeting to attend this interview. He does, passionately, believe in helping the police, but he is also a very busy man.'

'No,' Leah said. 'That's everything. Thank you for coming in, Mr Morton. You've been very helpful.'

'Don't you want my alibi, DC Hooper?' He smiled at Tom. 'Tom, you've not said anything for a while. Don't you want to check it?'

'For the record only, then, Mr Morton—'

'Colin, please.'

'Colin . . . can you tell us your whereabouts on Monday morning?'

'Yes. I was with my wife until 7.30 a.m. when I left for work. I arrived at my office at 8.00 a.m. and I was in meetings until noon. My PA Suzanne Watkins can confirm the details.' A beat. 'If you feel that's necessary.'

Kat shook her head. More fun and games.

Leah reached over and switched off the interview recorder before stalking out of the room. Rather than getting up, her dad stayed in his chair, nodding to the lawyer, who left a few seconds after Leah.

Kat frowned. What the hell was going on?

Her dad leaned towards Tom and spoke in a low voice. 'I've been impressed with your progress so far, young Tom. I can see you going all the way. *If* you play your cards right. But I have to say . . .'

He rubbed the tip of his nose. 'It would be a shame if certain *unfortunate* facts were to come to light about you. I can't imagine your career would be quite so stellar after that, can you?'

Tom swallowed. Kat could see his Adam's apple bob up and down in his throat. He paled. Looked as though he might throw up. Then a pink blush crept over his neck and up on to his jaw.

Now Colin Morton did stand. He rounded the table and patted Tom on the shoulder before leaving.

Kat stared in at Tom. He looked sick. But why? What had her dad meant about 'certain unfortunate facts'? Was this the lever he'd jammed under Tom's self-control before upending it?

He'd spoken earlier about Tom's words sounding like a threat. But Tom had merely been stating the law. Whereas what *he'd* just said was the genuine article. She needed to talk to Tom about it. Urgently.

Behind her, Carve-up left the room, tutting.

Kat waited for Tom outside the door to the interview room.

'Well, that could have gone better,' he said.

Kat inclined her head towards the observation room. Tom followed her in, his cheeks aflame. To find that he had a welcoming committee.

Leah sat there, her face like thunder.

'What the actual f—' she started. Then clamped her lips. Breathed in loudly through her nose and tried again. 'Learn that at university, did you, Tom? What were you *thinking*? We'll be lucky not to find ourselves having to explain to Linda why a helpful witness was intimidated in an interview.'

'Look, Leah, Kat, I . . . I'm sorry, OK? He just got under my skin. I know it was unprofessional.'

Kat puffed out her cheeks. 'These things happen, Tomski. We've all lost it in an interview at some time or other.'

Leah looked outraged. Eyes wide, fists bunched on her hips, she stared at Kat. 'No, we haven't!'

'What *did* happen in there, Tomski?' Kat asked. 'And what did my dad mean about "certain unfortunate events"?'

He blinked.

Leah was staring at him, brow furrowed.

'I can't tell you here,' he said. 'Can we go out for a quick drink?'

She checked her watch and nodded. If he couldn't bring himself to tell her inside the station, it must be something bad. She led the way to a nearby boozer.

The Queen's Head was quiet, and Kat found them a table in a dark corner. She bought a round of drinks: lime and soda for her and Leah, a Coke for Tom.

He took a quick sip and coughed. Wiped his mouth. Shot each of them a quick glance then looked down at the table and started speaking in a low monotone.

'It happened at Durham. My final year. We'd just come out of our last exam. We were so happy, you know? Like, all that hard work was over and we had a few precious weeks of carefree life before the results came through and we'd all know how we'd done.

'Some of us shared a couple of bottles of champagne by the river. Janis – she was my girlfriend at the time – and I went off for a drink together. Not one of the student bars, a proper pub. The Angel Inn. You didn't get many students in there. It was more of a locals' place. Bikers, heavy-metal types, ex-miners, you know? Just regular people. It was supposedly off-limits to us, but really it was perfectly friendly if you went in for a quiet pint and didn't spend your evening waving your college scarf around and talking about postmodernism. Only this time . . .'

Tom closed his eyes. Screwed them tight and winced. Kat wanted to reach out and touch his shoulder; he looked in such pain.

'Tell us, Tomski,' she murmured. 'It can't be that bad.'

But it was.

Chapter Forty

The story Tom told Kat and Leah sounded like a bad dream. But one Kat had witnessed as a copper more than once.

'One of the bikers came over to us. He wasn't one of those sad middle-aged men who buy a Harley instead of getting a weave. He looked like the real thing. Wiry. Bony, really. Covered in ink. Sharp cheekbones. And he had this wild look in his eyes. Like he might bite you if you annoyed him.

'He said he wanted to buy Janis a drink. But when she refused, he kept pushing, you know? Pretending to be offended. But really, he was just showing us we were in the wrong place. It was his territory, and we had no right to be there.

'He said she ought to be more friendly, seeing as she was an immigrant.' He smiled crookedly for a second. 'Janis was Texan. Anyway, I said, stupidly, she wasn't an immigrant, she was an international student, and it was like he'd been waiting for me to say something.

'He turned to his mates and made this big show of how I was disrespecting him. He mimicked her accent and then . . .' Tom took another swallow of his Coke, scrubbed at his eyes, which were glistening in the pub's lights. 'And then he said she had to give him a kiss to, as he put it, "repair the damage your sissy little boyfriend just did to international relations". I told him to back off. That's when it kicked off. He swung a punch at me. Janis screamed.'

'Oh my God, Tomski,' Kat said. 'How bad was it?'

He shook his head. 'No, that's just it. He didn't connect. I'd joined the university boxing club my first week. My dad taught me when I was being bullied at school. I found out I was good at it and I started boxing competitively on my sixteenth birthday.'

Kat could see now where the story was going, but she knew Tom had to tell it his own way and in his own time.

'Go on, Tomski.'

'I slipped the punch. And' – he inhaled raggedly – 'I counter-punched. It wasn't a hard shot, but I caught him right on the point of his jaw. He just dropped.'

'Then what, Tomski?' Leah asked, her glass suspended halfway to her lips.

'We just ran for it. Janis stopped a cab on Crossgate.' A smile flitted over his mouth and was gone. 'You could have heard the whistle in Newcastle. Anyway, the police came round the next day. A DS and a DC. They asked if they could come in. We all sat around the kitchen table. I knew it had to be about the fight. The DS told me the biker died at 3.05 a.m. that morning. She said they thought he was just suffering from a concussion, but he had a blood clot on his brain.'

Tom wiped a hand over his forehead, which was greasy with sweat. His face was pale.

Kat couldn't bear to see him in such pain. And his brutal honesty was stirring powerful feelings of guilt inside her. Not just for not fully trusting him about the corruption charge, but for using him to keep her involved in the murder investigation.

She touched his elbow lightly.

'You don't have to do this, Tomski. Whatever happened, you survived it and you're here now. And you're leading a murder investigation. You're a good cop and a good person.'

'Am I, Kat?' he snapped. 'Am I really? I killed a man. They say it only takes one punch and they're right.'

'What did they do, Tomski?' Leah asked, leaning forward and speaking in a low voice.

'What do you think they did? They arrested me on suspicion of murder. I thought that was it. My life was over before it had even begun. One minute I was having a drink with this beautiful Texan redhead who I was getting ready to tell I loved her. Then I was sitting in the back of a marked Mondeo being driven to Durham police station.'

He wiped his eyes on a handkerchief he'd drawn from his trouser pocket.

'In the end they didn't charge me with anything at all. Not even GBH.'

'Self-defence?' Leah asked.

He sniffed. 'Yeah. There were a dozen witnesses who saw him throw the first punch. He was well known to the police. Had a string of convictions for violent offences. It turned out he had a family history of blood clots. The doctors said it might have happened anyway, even without the fight.'

'Jesus, Tomski, that must've been terrible,' Leah said. 'Did it come up in vetting when you applied to the force?'

He nodded again. 'I told them everything. But I had supporting statements from the DS who arrested me, the Durham coroner, the pathologist who conducted the autopsy. It wasn't my fault. I was never charged. No record, no problem,' he finished, aiming for a smile Kat could see cost him a lot of effort. 'And as you know, Elaine Forshaw's my aunt, which helped iron out a few wrinkles.'

Leah frowned at this. Kat thought she knew why. Fast-track kid getting strings pulled for him again. Then something Tom had said early on came back to her now.

'You said when you first joined MCU, your relationship with Janis ended after a fight. I thought you meant a boyfriend-girlfriend fight, but you didn't, did you?'

'After they let me go, we went out for a drink. But something had changed. She said even though they hadn't charged me, she couldn't see herself with someone who'd caused another person's death.'

'But you didn't!' Leah burst out. 'That was the whole point. Anyway, he was the aggressor, not you.'

Tom smiled sadly. 'Which is what I told her, but it didn't do any good. Maybe it was her *fahn* legal *mahnd*, but that was it. She went back to Texas, and I never saw her again.'

'Is that why you don't drink?' Kat asked him.

He nodded. Sipped his Coke. 'I never want to risk being out of control again. I hadn't had much, but maybe if I'd been sober, I'd have tried talking my way out of it instead of reacting the way I did.'

Kat shrugged. 'Don't be too hard on yourself, Tomski. Maybe you would, and maybe you wouldn't. But maybe he would've pulled a knife. Or been high on meth. Or his mates might have joined in. You did what felt right in the heat of the moment, and obviously the police agreed. It was proportionate and reasonable in the circumstances.'

'I know, Kat. And I wish I *could* just let it go. But sometimes at night, when I close my eyes, I still see those weird blue eyes of his.'

'Hey,' she said softly, 'dry *your* eyes or people will think me and Leah are putting the screws on you.'

As jokes went, it was a lame one, but it did the trick. He smiled and blew his nose. Cleared his throat and turned to Leah. 'Bet you think I'm even more of a fake copper now?'

She grinned. 'Jubilee Place's very own nepo-baby.'

Kat relaxed. It was going to be all right. Tom had got his secret out into the open and nobody – else – had died.

Except. There was still her dad's thinly veiled threat in the interview room. Did *he* know? She wouldn't put it past him. And her anxiety as she considered the extent of his reach – and potential lawbreaking – ticked up another uncomfortable notch.

It sped up further as she considered her own complete lack of honesty on a third issue. Liv's continuing presence, not just among the living, but right here, in the heart of Middlehampton.

How would Tom – how would everyone – react, if they found out, and knew that Kat was concealing the fact? Hell, she was concealing Liv herself, in her own home.

Chapter Forty-One

Last night, he'd been able to sleep for the first time since Alanna's murder.

Maybe it was putting the contract out on Laura Paxton two days ago. Finally he felt he was in control. That bitch would be dead inside the week, he was sure of it. Then Alanna would be avenged and he could start at least trying to rebuild his life.

Callum looked at his watch. *Damn!* He was late for the family meeting.

The doorbell rang. Twice. Then whoever it was hammered a fist against the door.

For God's sake! Frank had actually come over to drag him there in person. Like he didn't trust him or something. Frank thought he had to keep Callum on a tighter leash than everyone else. Well, that would all change. When he'd dealt with Laura Paxton, people would see that Callum was a man who got things done.

He strode down the hallway, pausing to stare down at the spot where they'd found Alanna, before squaring his shoulders and pulling the front door open, ready to have it out with Frank there and then if that's what it took.

Only it wasn't Frank at all.

The guy was dressed in bulky black clothes like a night-club bouncer and was rocking a seventies look. Bushy moustache-and-beard combo. Long wavy brown hair. Tinted aviator sunglasses. Something about the bloke was familiar. But Callum couldn't place him.

He readied to push the guy away and slam the heavy door in his face. And if that didn't work, well, a good solid right cross probably would.

'It's about your wife's murder. I want to help you get justice for Alanna. Can I come in?'

That was a surprise. Blinking, Callum stepped back.

'Justice?'

'I heard there was twenty K for anyone who gets rid of the Paxton bitch.'

'Who told you that?'

The bloke snorted. 'Common knowledge, Mr Michie. Word travels fast when there's that kind of cash in play. You going to invite me in or what?'

Callum frowned. The guy sounded serious, and he obviously had contacts. Looked like he could handle himself, too. Maybe he was a pro hitter.

What the hell.

'Come on, then. I'm supposed to be at a meeting, but as it's about this anyway, we can talk first.' He turned to lead him into the kitchen. 'You want a coffee?'

Chapter Forty-Two

Frank checked his watch. Shook his head.

Everyone else had made the effort to get there on time. So where the hell was Callum? His nephew could normally be relied on to be punctual.

He rang Callum. Voicemail. Left a message: 'You're late.'

He turned to Raymond, resplendent today in a light wool suit. Chestnut threaded with burnt-orange windowpane checks, and a pair of brown and white co-respondent shoes.

'You heard from him this morning?'

Raymond shook his head, setting his short dreadlocks swinging. 'Not in a while, Frank. You want me to go rouse the boy?'

Frank shook his head. 'You stay here. I'll go.'

As the others began checking their phones, Frank left the Hope and Anchor and climbed into his black Jaguar XJ. He loved the big saloon with its wraparound luxury. The only car equally at home ferrying politicians around and men like himself. Red box in the boot or a sawn-off twelve-gauge, made no difference. The Jag was for people who knew what it meant to have arrived.

Unlike Callum bloody Michie, who had ideas above his station.

Callum clearly thought Frank couldn't see the naked ambition that burned in his eyes brighter than the blast from a shotgun cartridge on a pitch-black night. But Frank had been running his various enterprises, and enforcing their territory the old-fashioned way, when Callum was still nicking other kids' pocket money.

He turned into Chamberlayne Avenue, drove three hundred yards down the leafy cul-de-sac and parked on the street. Callum's BMW was on the drive. Shaking his head, Frank crunched over the gravel and stuck out his finger to ring the doorbell.

Nothing.

He pounded the side of his fist against the door.

Nothing.

Frank got his phone out. Pulled up 'Recents' and called Callum again.

Chapter Forty-Three

Tom had just returned from the golf club with Christopher Miller.

Miller had agreed to be interviewed under caution once Tom had outlined the alternative. Arrest.

Kat hadn't even needed to ask if she could sit in this time. They'd agreed between them she would. In fact, Tom had gone one further, surprising Kat.

'Do you mind doing it on your own, Kat? Stuart's got me under the cosh on the Hartsbury murder, too. I've got really behind on my policy books.'

'You're sure?'

'You'd be doing me a favour.'

'What about Carve-up? He'll go ballistic if he finds out.'

'Then we'd better make sure he doesn't,' Tom said, winking.

And now she was sitting opposite Christopher Miller, who'd opted to be interviewed without a solicitor.

Once the preliminaries were out of the way and the recorder was running, Kat looked across the cheap table at Miller. Here was another of the men who comprised the three leading suspects in Alanna Michie's murder.

'So, Christopher, as you know already, you are here to answer questions about the murder of Alanna Michie.'

'Yes, and I've been thinking about that. Didn't I read in the *Echo* that someone had confessed? A woman, at that.' He tilted his head to one side and smiled slyly. '*Why* are you investigating? I'd have thought it was all wrapped up with a pretty pink bow.'

'A woman is lying dead in a refrigerated drawer at Middlehampton General Hospital, Mr Miller,' she said patiently. 'She was strangled with a monogrammed tie from *your* golf club. There's really nothing pretty about it.'

Miller flushed. 'No, of course not. I'm sorry. Just a little nervous.'

She pushed on, softening her tone. Keeping Miller off balance.

'Of course. I understand. Police stations can be daunting places.' She rolled her eyes. 'Just ask one of our new recruits. And to answer your question, I'm just making sure of a few details that are puzzling me. Did you know Alanna Michie?'

'Pardon?'

'I was just wondering whether you knew Alanna.'

His gaze flitted off to one side. 'I didn't *know* Mrs Michie.'

'That sounds like you'd met, at least.'

'Her husband joined last month. We had a ladies' day a week after his membership was approved. Mrs Michie attended. She was very, what shall we say? Pleasant.'

Kat leaned back a little. Letting Christopher's weak-tea word hang in the air between them. The kind of women who married into crime families like the Strutts could be described in all kinds of ways, but not, she thought, pleasant. Feisty? Often. Strong? Most of them. Forceful? Definitely. Fiery-eyed dragons with a look that could cut you as deep as a butcher's knife? Occasionally. Denise Luck being a prime example.

'Did you speak?'

'I think we may have exchanged a few words. I was on hand to ensure things ran smoothly.'

'Did you find her attractive?'

'Pardon?'

There. That evasive word again. There was nothing wrong with his hearing. And it was hardly an offensive question. People did it when they needed time to think.

'Did you think she was attractive? *I* thought she was. I just wanted to get your take. You're a man, after all.'

He ran a hand over his hair, hooking that wayward lock back into place.

'Well, I suppose so. You know, they were *all* very nicely turned out. Hair, make-up, dresses. Look, what exactly are you driving at, DS Ballantyne? I didn't do anything wrong, you know.'

'I'm not driving at anything, Christopher. I'm trying to build a picture of Alanna Michie's last few days on Earth before she was brutally murdered. You were one of the people who met her during that period.'

He folded his arms. 'Yes, but so were dozens of other people. Hundreds, probably. Other club members. Work colleagues, shop assistants . . . all sorts.'

'Indeed. But not with the initials CM and not with a mono-grammed tie from the golf club of which you're the membership secretary. I see you have *your* tie on.'

He looked down and ran his fingers across the glossy silk surface.

'All the male staff do. It's club policy. Maintains the brand image.'

'I can't see your initials, though.'

He held out the broad strip of fabric and inspected it as if doubting her. Looked back at her, grey eyes hooded.

'No.'

Interesting. His talkativeness had deserted him.

'But you *do* have a monogrammed tie, yes? Can you tell me where it is?'

He narrowed his eyes. 'How do you know that? I told you I wouldn't share our records with you without a warrant.'

It was a feeble counterattack. To use Tom's phrase, she slipped the punch.

'I was just chatting to a couple of your members outside. I think one of them must have told me. So, where is it, Christopher?'

The silence stretched out between them. She stared into his eyes. Was it all about to end? Or would he simply swing back into that affable persona and tell her he'd got egg on his tie and it was at the dry cleaner's?

'I lost it.'

Kat made a note. 'Lost it where?' she asked, without looking up.

'I know how this looks. But I didn't kill Alanna.'

Now Kat did raise her eyes to lock on to his. Because after steadfastly referring to her as 'Mrs Michie', under stress he'd switched to using her first name.

'I'm not suggesting you did. I'm just asking what happened to your monogrammed tie. You said you lost it and I'd like to know where, that's all.'

'It was at a dinner.'

'Go on.'

'Now and again a group of us get together for a bit of a boys' night out. We have a couple of drinks first, then go to a nice restaurant. You probably do the same with your colleagues, I imagine, don't you?'

Sweat had beaded on his upper lip, and he brushed it away with his forefinger. A vein was pulsing at his right temple. He was hiding something.

'You were wearing your tie, I take it?'

'Yes.'

Kat frowned. 'So how did you lose it? Was it hot? Did you take it off?'

'It got red wine spilled on it. Clumsy bugger – sorry, *chap* – knocked my glass over while reaching for the bottle. Splashed it everywhere. I did take it off. I was going to try and rinse it with water from the jug.'

Kat stared at him levelly. He'd just admitted to owning the murder weapon, and he didn't seem to realise it. 'I'm with you so far, but I still don't see how you could lose it altogether.'

'I don't either! Look, honestly? I'd had a fair bit to drink. Few G&Ts beforehand, doubles, another at the restaurant and then wine, obviously. Couple of brandies afterwards with the cigars. My memory's hazy. But the next morning I realised I didn't have it. And as it was basically ruined, I decided to order another one. I just haven't had a moment to deal with it. In the meantime, I'm wearing a plain one.' He ran his thumb and forefinger down the tie, straightening it on his chest, which was moving up and down rapidly. His eyes widened. 'Wait! You're not suggesting it was *my* tie that the killer used, are you?'

'We have a tie in evidence that has the initials CM embroidered on to it. It also is stained with red wine. That does sound like yours, Christopher.'

Christopher's wasn't the only pulse that had recently jacked up. Kat's was bumping uncomfortably in her throat.

He was physically strong, agitated and, if she was right, a violent murderer. And she was alone with him in an unmonitored interview room.

Tread carefully, Kat.

196

Chapter Forty-Four

Frank swore as Callum's phone went to voicemail.

This time he didn't bother leaving a message. It looked weak, apart from anything else.

Maybe Callum wasn't in. Maybe he'd gone for a walk. The poor sod was still grieving, after all.

Frank went round the back of the house, getting tangled in a thick clump of overgrown roses, swearing as thorns pierced his trousers and scratched his legs. Freed from their spiny clutches, he peered in through the kitchen's side window. No sign of Callum, although a bowl with a spoon in it sat on the worktop beside an open box of cornflakes.

At the front door again, Frank crouched down and opened the letterbox. Peered inside. Nothing. He thought he'd try rousing his nephew on the phone one more time. After that, he'd give it up as a bad job and rejoin the rest of the family at the Hope, Callum's absence now an item of Any Other Business.

And then he experienced a strangely dislocating sensation. Two phones were ringing simultaneously. One, with a muted burr directly into his left ear. The other, in his right. Callum's ringtone, an irritating snatch of rap that drove Frank crazy whenever it went off in a meeting.

Callum's phone was inside the house.

Frank got to his feet and hammered on the door.

'Callum! You in there? It's Frank. You all right, mate?'

In the silence, Frank thought he heard a door opening somewhere to the rear of the property. Deciding against another fight with the roses, he looked around for something heavy in the front garden. He grabbed a white-painted rock with the house number picked out in black and hurled it with all his might at the bay window.

Fearing the worst, he cleared the jagged fangs of broken glass clinging to the window frame with a stick and laid his jacket over the sill.

Once inside, he ran from the sitting room into the hall, searching desperately for his nephew.

Chapter Forty-Five

Kat moved her chair back a little.

'Just now, you called the murder victim "Alanna".'

Christopher frowned. 'That was her name. You said it yourself.'

'Yes, but up to that point, you'd been calling her "Mrs Michie".' Kat leaned forward. 'Listen, Christopher, if there's something you need to get off your chest, just tell me. You'll feel better. What did you *really* think of Alanna Michie?'

He looked at his hands, which were clamped together tightly.

'I know how this will make me look,' he murmured.

'How *what* will make you look?'

'I fancied her, OK? At the ladies' day I noticed she was on her own and I went over to make conversation. That's when I realised. She was stunning. And she started flirting with me.' He spread his arms wide. 'I'm only human, DS Ballantyne.'

'So you flirted back?'

'Yes, I flirted back. You would have too.' He blushed again. 'I mean, if you were me. But it was harmless. At least I thought it was, but I couldn't get her out of my head.'

'Let's take a breath, Christopher. How about we establish a basic timeline? Can we do that?'

He scragged his fingers back and forth through his hair and smoothed the ruffled waves flat again. 'We can do that. Yes.'

'Good. So, when was the ladies' day?'

'Last Wednesday.'

'The 15th, yes?'

'Yes.'

'And when was your boys' night out?'

'Saturday.' He drew in a quick breath. 'The 18th.'

'Which was when your tie went missing. And Alanna was murdered on Monday 20th.'

His head had begun shaking during this process. Kat had seen it before. As pieces began to line up in a clear picture, culprits would go into denial. Disputing provable facts. Objecting to physical evidence. Asking for lawyers.

'I didn't murder her. Take my DNA. It'll prove it.'

He tipped his head up and snapped his mouth open wide, showing his back teeth. Free of fillings. A man who looked after himself.

'Close your mouth, Christopher,' Kat said.

He complied, wiping a little spit from his bottom lip. 'Do it now. I insist. You've got DNA already, right? From the crime scene. They always do. So take mine and compare them and then you'll know it wasn't me.'

Was his demand that of an innocent man, confident he hadn't done anything wrong and willing to be sampled to prove it? Or that of a cold, calculating killer who knew he hadn't left any DNA at the scene for a comparison?

'Wait here,' she said.

She returned with a swab kit, and after rubbing it firmly around the insides of both cheeks, she sealed it into an evidence bag.

'Let's go back to this boys' night. Who else was there?'

He rubbed his cheek. 'Gary Arrowsmith. Paul Davies. Darren Taylor. Look, there were quite a few of us. Perhaps it would be better if I emailed you the list, when I've had a chance to think clearly.'

Kat smiled thinly. 'Take your time.'

'Well, let's see.' He looked up at the stained ceiling tiles. 'Sean Steele. Mike Gibson. Ernie Worsdale. Steve Parsons. Oh! One of your colleagues. Stuart Carver, with a friend. God, he's such a bad boy! Sorry, inappropriate.'

'Can you remember this friend's name?'

'Sorry, no. You have to understand, DS Ballantyne, it was a big group. I mean, we're talking twenty-five blokes. We usually take over the whole place, or at least a big private room if the restaurant has one. I usually just book a big table and then we all rock up. You know?'

Kat did know. Cop dinners could often be the same. Maybe not twenty-five, but certainly ten or fifteen.

She nodded. 'Maybe you could send me that list when you've remembered everyone who was there.'

'Of course. No problem.'

'Just one more question, Christopher. Where were you on Monday morning?'

He frowned. 'At work.'

'From what time?'

'Nine-ish?'

'How about before then?'

'At home.'

'Can anyone corroborate that?' She glanced at his wedding ring. 'Mrs Miller, perhaps?'

'Sal's away this week. She's cabin crew with BA. Long-haul.'

'I see.'

He checked his watch. 'Was there anything else? Only I am sort of absent from work, you know? Plenty to do back at the club.'

Now came the moment of truth. Did she let him go or arrest him? His alibi was shaky at best. Time of death was sufficiently flexible that he could easily have killed Alanna Michie before turning up for work.

And the business with the DNA was just a distraction. The murderer had left no trace of himself at the crime scene apart from the murder weapon. Which, at the moment, looked as though it belonged to Christopher Miller.

But there was a huge problem with the picture.

Why would a murderer forensically aware enough not to leave a single print, blood spot or hair strand behind him use his own tie as the murder weapon *and then not take it away with him*?

It looked more as though someone was trying to frame Christopher Miller for Alanna Michie's murder. Presumably the same person who'd found a way to induce Laura Paxton to confess to the crime.

Kat stared into Christopher Miller's grey eyes, searching for a sign that here was a wrong 'un. Saw nothing. Counted to three.

'Thanks for coming in, Christopher. You're free to go.'

With the room to herself, Kat swore quietly, then began reading over her notes from the interview.

In the 'Guilty' column, she was able to add a few big plus-points.

Christopher Miller's tie looked almost certain to be the murder weapon. He had no alibi worth the name.

And he'd admitted to at the very least a flirtation with the victim. It wasn't exactly motive, but it pointed at motive. He'd tried to take things too far. She'd rejected him. Enraged at a mere woman deciding whether he could have his way or not, he'd lashed out and then strangled her.

The story about losing his tie felt like little more than a convenient fiction. How on earth could she find a way to corroborate it?

But in the 'Innocent' column, points stacked up, too.

He'd volunteered his DNA.

He had at least provided *some* kind of alibi, even if it was partial.

And he'd answered every single one of Kat's questions. If he couldn't remember twenty-five names from a drunken dinner – well, he wouldn't be the first.

Not to mention the fact that she'd so far found no connection between Christopher Miller and Laura Paxton. Or, for that matter, her father or Callum Michie.

She leaned back and rolled her head on her neck, feeling as well as hearing the vertebrae crackle and pop like a bloody bowl of cereal.

Suddenly the stink of the interview room was too much. Wrinkling her nose, she pushed her chair back and got to her feet.

Her phone rang.

When she saw the name of the person calling her, she hurried out and answered as she was marching across MCU towards the exit.

Chapter Forty-Six

Kat spoke as she pushed through the doors and into the stairwell.

'What's up, Frank?'

Kat took the stairs two at a time, wanting to be outside of the precincts of Jubilee Place before engaging in the meat of a conversation with a known felon. She wasn't to get her wish.

Frank was talking in short, tight sentences. He sounded like he was under enormous stress. Like a man holding up a collapsing roof. Keeping it together. Just.

'Callum's dead . . . murdered. I'm at his place now . . . with the body. Got here ten minutes ago. You need to get yourself over here, Kat. Someone's taking aim at my family . . . and I don't like it.'

She didn't even think about the consequences of leaving the station on official police business. If Carve-up wanted to make something of it, she'd go right over his head. Straight to Linda. He was on the verge of obstructing a criminal investigation himself and she was sure in her gut he knew more than he was admitting to about the money in her account. Kat reached the ground floor and took the left turn that led towards the car park.

'Stay there, don't touch anything. I'll be there in ten. And Frank? I'm sorry for your loss.'

She signed out a car this time, needing the blues and twos. As usual, the effect on Middlehampton's motorists had her cursing inside sixty seconds. Rather than pulling over or just speeding ahead until they could find somewhere safe to do so, they hauled their grey boxes on to pavements, stopped halfway across junctions, blocking her route, or just continued ambling along at twenty-five, oblivious to the car bearing down on them with a pretty electric-blue dashboard ornament.

As such, it was closer to twelve minutes than ten when she turned into Chamberlayne Avenue. She passed a long, sleek, stealthy black Jaguar she assumed was Frank Strutt's, parked on the road, then spun the wheel over and scrunched to a halt beside a BMW on the Michies' gravel drive. *Except it's not theirs any more, is it? Because they're both dead*, she thought incongruously as she got out. Weird, how homicide work took you sometimes.

Frank was standing in the open front door.

'Heard you arrive,' he said, stony-faced. 'He's in the kitchen.'

Callum lay face up between the island and the cooker. Eyes bulging horribly, a trickle of blood winding its way from the corner of his mouth and down to the floor. A livid bruise darkened his neck, which was dented in by a couple of inches as if someone had stamped on it.

Kat crouched beside the body. Felt under his jaw. Leaned down and brought her face within a few millimetres of Callum's nostrils. No pulse. None expected. No cooling breath agitating the fine hairs on her cheek.

'I think I heard him.'

She looked up at Frank. 'Callum?'

He shook his head. 'The guy that killed him. I was out the front, had my ear to the letterbox. I heard Cal's phone ringing as I called it, then I heard the back door go. He must only just have done it when I arrived. Christ!' He smacked his palm down on the marble-topped island. 'If I'd got here a few minutes earlier, I could have saved his life.'

Kat stood. Faced Frank. Gangster or not, the man had just lost a second family member inside a few days.

'Listen to me, Frank. You are not to blame for Callum's death. The only person who is, is the man who murdered him. Now, I need to make some calls. Can you wait for me outside?'

With Frank gone, Kat called Jack Beale, Darcy Clements and the response team dispatcher. While she waited for the troops to arrive, she squatted by the corpse.

'So, what happened to you, Callum?'

She wasn't a pathologist, and was wise enough not to leap to conclusions. But she was still certain she knew three things about Callum Michie's death.

One, manner of death. Homicide. More than that: murder.

Two: cause of death. Strangulation: the dark purple bruise across his oddly deformed throat spoke eloquently to that.

Three: time of death. Around 10.45 a.m.

The formal identification of the victim was also complete.

All they needed was the identity of the man who'd murdered him. And Kat knew something else, too. When they caught Callum's killer, they'd catch Alanna's as well.

She was about to get to her feet when something on Callum's neck caught her eye.

She leaned closer. Just visible on the skin above his shirt collar was a small red mark with a darker edge. At first, she thought it was a cigarette burn. Using a pen, she pushed the collar down. Three centimetres below the mark was its twin. No. Not cigarette burns. These particular injuries came from the metal contact points of a stun gun. He'd been incapacitated by fifty thousand volts and then choked out.

She went outside. Frank was puffing on a vape in the front garden. Clouds of cherry-scented vapour issued from his mouth. She half expected to see flames, too.

'I'm truly, *truly* sorry, Frank. Can you tell me exactly what you saw and heard when you arrived? Were there any cars out the front? Anyone acting oddly on the street?'

He turned his head away and exhaled another billowing lungful of sweet-smelling vapour into the air.

'He was supposed to be at a meeting at the Hope. To discuss what we were doing about Alanna, which is pretty bloody ironic. He was late so I called him. Went straight to voicemail. I came over here. Tried him again. Nothing. Went round the side. Scratched myself up on a bloody rosebush. Look.' He pointed at a torn trouser leg. 'Ruined these. So I looked through the letterbox and called him again. That's when I heard his phone ringing. I put the window in and climbed over. Found him in the kitchen.'

'And when did you hear the back door going?'

'I don't know. When I was calling him the last time, I think.'

'We'll need you to come down to the station to make a formal statement.'

'Whatever.'

'He'll have left a trace behind, Frank. They always do. And I think it has to be linked to Alanna's murder.'

'Oh, you worked that out, did you? Well, I can see why you got promoted!' he shouted. Then immediately flushed. 'Sorry, Kat. Uncalled for. I apologise. It's just—'

'A shock. I know. Look, the response team will be here in a few minutes. Maybe just wait in your car. That is your Jag I saw, isn't it?'

He nodded.

'Call whoever you need to. But Frank, let us handle this. Please?'

His answer was eloquent. A long, hard, silent stare. He stalked off, back towards his hearse-like Jaguar.

Kat stared after him.

Great. The Strutts had been hot to trot on a revenge killing when it was Alanna, an incomer, who'd been murdered. But now one of their own was down. This was going to get ugly. Fast. She needed a result before the Strutts went on the warpath.

Except . . .

She ran to catch up with him.

He whirled round. 'What?'

'You know what this means, right?'

'It means someone's coming for members of my family. And I need to stop them.'

'No! It means it can't have been Laura Paxton. She's on remand at Bronzefield. And if she didn't kill Callum, she didn't kill Alanna.'

He shrugged. 'Maybe. But somebody did. And he's going to pay.'

Sirens.

She looked over Frank's muscular shoulder. Blue lights. A marked car roaring down Chamberlayne Avenue.

The whole circus of death was rolling into town for the second time that week. And this time, no way was she going to let Carve-up prevent her from cracking the ringmaster's whip.

Whatever game he was playing, whatever devious moves he was trying to pull, it was over. This was her case now. Whatever happened with the corruption investigation, she was going to nail Alanna's killer.

Chapter Forty-Seven

Kat's phone rang as she was driving back to Jubilee Place.

She stabbed the Accept Call button on the hands-free kit. Her pulse jumped upwards, and it had nothing to do with the black-and-white cat that streaked across the road in front of her, causing her to swerve.

'Hi, Iris. I hope this is good news.'

'Oh, it is definitely good news. I am one step away from solving this little puzzle you set me.'

Kat's belly squirmed. She felt panicky. 'Good' for Iris might easily mean exactly what she'd just said. Solving a puzzle. She was that kind of person. Whereas, for Kat, it needed to mean: *The money's clean. It came from a long-lost great aunt who left it to you in her will.* Or something similar.

'Can you explain? In simple non-accountant words, please.'

'I'll try. But it is, actually, very complicated. So, where shall we start? Are you familiar with offshore trusts?'

'Honestly? No.'

'Really? I thought you would be. Well, basically, the money came from a sort of, how shall I put it? A *nest* of interconnected financial entities. All based in tax havens. Panama. Delaware. Guernsey. Anguilla. It's not the most sophisticated arrangement

I've ever worked on, but it's doing a reasonable job of hiding the beneficial owner.'

'Sorry, Iris, you're losing me. Beneficial owner?'

'The ultimate owner of the money. I'm in touch with a colleague in the Bahamas. Guy by the name of Enrique. I won't have his answer until tomorrow morning. But then I'll know. And, obviously, as soon as I know, you'll know, too. Well, not precisely as soon as I know. I'll have to call you, unless you're telepathic. You're not, are you?'

'No, Iris. Although sometimes I wish I was. It would make my job a hell of a lot easier.'

'Hmm. I suppose it would. Although you could probably find something a lot better paid. Like being a bond trader.'

Kat indicated for the turn into Crown Street. Jubilee Place loomed overhead.

'Listen, Iris, you're a star but I have to go. You'll call me tomorrow, yes?'

'Yes. I just said that, didn't I?'

A nest of interconnected financial entities? Did that sound like the sort of scheme Ethan Metcalfe could cook up? Kat had no idea. But maybe she and Liv had been guilty of writing him off as a loser, when all along he was capable of so much more than his podcast. Maybe this was it. They were going to trace the money back to him and she'd be free.

She parked behind Jubilee Place, excited at the prospect of slamming the door on the looming corruption charge, and called Liv from the car, eager to find out how her lingerie-assisted sting with Ethan had gone.

'How did your date with Mutt-calf go, *Tiffany*?'

Liv snickered. 'Poor sod was no match for my boobs and your push-up bra. I did have a wig on, but if he managed to make eye contact once in the whole time I must have missed it.'

'Did you find anything out? Is he good for the money?'

'Good for it? Oh, I think we can safely say he's good for it. This is it, Kat. We've got him.'

Kat's pulse skipped along. 'Go on, then. Don't keep me in suspense.'

'Right, for a start, he owns his house outright. His mum died a couple of years ago and he inherited it. I did a bit of digging on Rightmove. It's worth half a million, easy. So he could have taken out a loan. But that's not all. You're not going to believe this, but he made this app for podcasters. And he sold it to some software company for one-point-five million quid. He practically got an erection telling me about the deal. So he's loaded, and he's got some kind of grudge against you because you won't put out for him.'

Kat smiled broadly. Her spirits were soaring. 'Liv, this is amazing!'

'You want me to put the screws on him, Thelma? Show him how I hold horses steady for gelding?'

'Oh my God, you don't, do you?'

Liv cackled. 'Nah. Vet does it all under local anaesthetic. Had you going though, didn't I?'

'You did, but it's a no, anyway. Sit tight. I need to think how to handle him.'

'You're the boss.'

Smiling, and feeling more relaxed than she had for what felt like a month instead of less than a week, Kat headed for the third floor and Linda's office. Between Iris and Liv, she was sure she was almost off the hook about the money. Liv hadn't pinned the money on Ethan, but it was a better lead than anything Kat had come up with so far.

She knocked on Linda's door and went in.

To her dismay, Carve-up was sitting facing Linda. She caught the tail end of his sentence. It included the words '. . . don't want Anti-Corruption crawling all over my department'.

'Nor do I, Stuart,' Kat said, gesturing towards the second visitor chair and being nodded into it by Linda. 'And I'm confident that I'll have the information I need to put everyone's minds at rest by tomorrow morning.'

'You'd better, DS Ballantyne,' Carve-up said, oblivious to Linda's pursed lips as he belittled Kat. 'You're running out of time.'

'Let's keep it civil, please,' Linda said, rapping her desk with the end of a biro. 'At least while you're in my office. That sounds positive, Kat. I hope we'll be able to draw a line under this.'

'Literally. I just heard from the forensic accountant who's looking into it for me.'

'Interesting that you can afford one. They're not cheap,' Carve-up said.

'She's a friend. She reckons she only needs another half a day.'

He either couldn't or wouldn't disguise the expression of disgust twisting his face.

'Was that all you came to bother Linda with, DS Ballantyne?' he asked. 'Because we're right in the middle of something.'

'What was it, Kat?' Linda asked, laying emphasis on Kat's first name as a rebuke to the clueless DI in front of her.

'Callum Michie was murdered just before 10.45 a.m. Strangled with some kind of weapon. I've just come from the house and—'

'What the hell, DS Ballantyne!' Carver interrupted. 'How many more times? I ordered you to work on cold cases. Out of the goodness of my heart, and respect for a colleague, I agreed you could provide limited admin support for Tom, and now you're tearing off trying to muscle in on yet another case. What is wrong with you?'

Kat simply ignored him. Turned to Linda. 'It has to be the same man that murdered Alanna. This clears Laura Paxton. I think I can solve this one, Ma-Linda, but I can't do it by creeping around pretending I'm helping Tom with' – she glared at Carve-up – '*admin*. Please can you put me back on active duty? I'm so close.'

Linda opened her mouth to speak, but Carve-up beat her to it.

'Bloody hell, DS Ballantyne! Time, manner *and* cause of death. And so specific, too. Jack Beale tell you all that, did he?'

Kat stared at her line manager. Was there really no end to the man's arrogance?

'No, I found that out for myself. *Stu.*'

'Well, forgive me, but as a lowly DI, I always thought we were trained not to jump to conclusions. Maybe he committed suicide out of grief for the lovely Alanna. Maybe he hanged himself. And as to the time of death, you ought to know by now that we can *never* put an exact time on it. A window of six to eight hours wouldn't be unreasonable.'

Despite the fact they were discussing a murder, Kat couldn't help enjoying the put-down she was about to deliver.

'I know he was murdered because he was tasered first. Unless you think people routinely shock themselves unconscious with a stun gun before killing themselves? But if that's not enough for you, there was no ligature round his neck. What I *did* see was a long, straight, livid bruise and a depression thicker than my finger over his trachea. I'd say his assailant used a metal rod or something out of a tool box, like a long-bladed screwdriver. Probably crushed his windpipe while constricting his carotid arteries. Forensics will tell me that. Finally, as to time of death, the person who found him confirmed that they heard the attacker making his getaway.'

'Who was the unlucky bystander?' Linda asked, as Carve-up scowled at Kat. She ignored him. Again. She could afford to.

'Frank Strutt.'

Linda's eyes flash-bulbed. 'Jesus wept! This just gets better and better.'

'I told him to keep a lid on the family. They were hot to take revenge on Laura Paxton. I have no idea whether he's going to play ball.'

'And you think that's wise, do you, DS Ballantyne?' Carve-up said. 'Cosying up to known criminals? In case you'd forgotten, you're a police officer and it's a police officer's duty—'

'Oh, for Pete's sake, put a sock in it, Stuart!' Linda erupted. He rocked back in his chair. 'I'll tell you what a police officer's duty is – and, for the record, it's got eff all to do with making sure the numbers on a bloody spreadsheet add up. It's to try and stop the assorted toerags, wrong 'uns and general psychopathic looney-tunes from spreading mayhem and misery wherever the fancy takes them. Kat's a bloody good detective and, despite enormous provocation from you, has kept it together. So, yes, Kat, as of right this second, you are back on active duty and leading this investigation. Stuart, if one word comes out of your mouth, I'll see you running cycling proficiency tests at Middlehampton Academy before the day's out. Clear?'

Scowling and breathing heavily through flared nostrils, Carve-up managed the briefest of nods.

Inwardly rejoicing, Kat said, 'I could really do with some budget.'

Linda nodded decisively. 'Ten grand. Spend it wisely. I'm down to the sticky stuff at the bottom of the pot till the end of the quarter. But, Kat, you're almost out of time. I've got The Undertaker on my back over this one. He wants to know why we're fannying around – my words, not his – keeping the investigation live when we've a suspect in custody. I'm bargaining with him for days and having to settle for hours, so you need to wrap this one up pronto, yes?'

Kat nodded. 'Yes, Ma—' and clamped her lips before she used her unofficial nickname for her boss and handed Carve-up fresh ammunition. She got to her feet.

'Hang on a minute, DS Ballantyne.' Stuart was leaning towards her, gripping the arms of his chair. 'Before you go charging off looking for some kind of gangland assassin, we've already got a suspect in custody for the murder of Alanna Michie. Now her old man's been done in, aren't you missing the obvious conclusion?'

Well, this was going to be good. Kat sat back. Caught Linda's eye. A single raised eyebrow spoke volumes.

'What do you mean?'

'Isn't it obvious? She's working with an accomplice. For some reason she's got this grudge against the Michies. She does the wife, gets cold feet or is seized by remorse or whatever, and dobs herself in. But it's too late to stop her partner. He goes after the husband. Keeps his end of the bargain.'

It was inventive, she gave him that. As in something out of a 1940s pulp novel.

Before Kat could reply, Linda exploded. 'Oh, for God's sake! Do you even *hear* yourself? From what I gather, Laura Paxton is a meek little thing. A copper's wife who works as a . . .' She looked at Kat for the detail, which she was happy to supply.

'. . . as a teaching assistant in an infants' school.'

Linda continued, eyes blazing at her hapless subordinate. 'Stuart, do you *really* believe, as a *senior* detective, that this woman, who spends her daylight hours wiping four-year-olds' noses and singing about the wheels on the bloody bus, leads a double life where she mixes with hitmen and cooks up double-murder plots?'

He opened his mouth to speak. Unwisely, in Kat's opinion. She was going to enjoy this.

Linda glared at Carve-up. 'You interrupted me a minute ago, Stuart, and I let it pass. But you should know it pissed me off royally. So the next thing to come out of your mouth better be, "Sorry, Linda, what was I thinking? Of *course* Laura Paxton doesn't have a criminal accomplice."'

Carve-up shut his mouth with a *clop* as his back teeth met.

'I meant it, DI Carver,' Linda said.

He frowned. Then he scowled. 'Sorry, Linda, what was I thinking? Of *course* Laura Paxton doesn't have a criminal accomplice.'

Kat got up. 'I have to go. Thanks, Linda.'

'One more thing, Kat. If the Strutts *are* on the warpath, it might be better to leave Laura Paxton where she is. Just for the moment. If we let her out, we'll have to arrange round-the-clock protective custody and I really don't have the money. OK with you?'

'For now, yes. But we're keeping an innocent woman behind bars.'

'Better behind bars than inside a box,' Linda said with a wry smile.

Closing the office door behind her, Kat nodded with satisfaction. Her hunch had been right all along. Laura Paxton was no more guilty of murder than Kat was.

Tom came over. 'All right? You look like the cat who got the cream.' A beat. 'Pun intended.'

'Oh, Tomski. More than you know. Come on, let's find Leah. We've got work to do.'

'What's happening?'

'I'm out of the long grass. At least as far as this investigation goes. Linda just put me in charge.' She hesitated. 'Oh, God, Tomski. I'm sorry. I know Carve-up gave it to you, but—'

He smiled. 'It's fine. Really. I was floundering, I don't mind admitting it. Look, am I ambitious? Yes, of course. But you and Leah, well, you've shown me I've got a lot to learn. And, well, how you reacted in the pub yesterday when I told you what happened. It, uh, it meant a lot.'

Kat patted him on the shoulder. 'Steady there, Bambi. No more waterworks, OK? You'll set me off and you really don't want to see what I look like when I'm crying.'

He grinned. 'Messy?'

She nodded. 'Messy.'

Back at her own desk she called Jack Beale, asking when she could expect his report on Callum Michie.

'Going to be a while, Kat. I've had an initial look at the body but the full PM's going to have to wait. I'm up to my ears in it at the moment. Fatal traffic accident on the London Road yesterday.'

'I really need that report, Jack.'

'Yes, and I really need a thirty-hour day. Sorry, Kat, not going to happen. Now, you'll have to excuse me but I have work to do.'

The line went dead.

'And I haven't?' she asked the air in front of her, before heading out on her first officially sanctioned bit of police business since Linda had benched her on Monday.

Chapter Forty-Eight

Kat found Jack Beale in his office adjoining the mortuary. He'd rolled his sleeves up and was bent over his keyboard, muttering to himself as his fingers flashed over the keys.

She leaned past him, trying to avoid staring at his rather lovely forearms, and placed a white paper bag and a takeaway cup by his right elbow.

He turned, frowning in irritation, then smiled when he saw who'd brought him a treat.

'Kat! This is unexpected. What's in the bag?'

'Kulicha. I bought them from the Kurdish cafe on North Street. Hatî. You said you were friends with John and Zerya. I asked her what your favourites were.'

Jack spread open the bag and took out a little brown and cream pastry spiral. He popped it into his mouth whole and closed his eyes.

'Take one,' he mumbled, offering her the bag.

The pinwheel of buttery pastry and date paste melted against her tongue. She swallowed and then nudged the cup towards him.

'Latte. Extra shot.'

He took a swig, then grinned up at her. 'And now you've wormed your way into my heart via my stomach, I reschedule everything and autopsy Callum Michie for you, is that it?'

She smiled. 'Do I have to have a reason for bringing a valued colleague a treat?'

'Sorry, Kat. Of course not.' Shaking his head and tutting to himself, he bent over his keyboard again. 'Well, thanks for the kulicha. See you around.'

Kat's jaw dropped. 'Really?'

Jack laughed. 'Got you! Look, I really don't have time for the PM, but I can give you the stuff I know you want. Will that do?'

'Go on, then,' she said. 'Before I take your cakes away.'

He grabbed the bag and moved it to the far side of the desk.

'Callum Michie was throttled. The murderer used a weapon of some kind. Not a ligature this time. More like a rod. I took some pictures. I'll email them to you. Whoever it was, they used enough force to crush his windpipe. It could have been a woman, but outside of a courtroom, I'm going to say it was a man.'

'Anything else?'

'I retrieved a fragment of material from the crush injury when I examined the body in situ. Darcy Clements has it now. I assume it was originally part of the weapon used to kill him.'

Kat left Jack to his sweetmeats and coffee and returned to MCU. There, she called in on Darcy.

'Did you get the sample Jack sent over?'

Darcy held up an evidence bag containing an inch-high, red-capped debris pot.

Kat squinted at the pot, but through the crinkled bag she couldn't see anything.

'You're going to have to tell me, Darce.'

'I'll need to send it off to a lab, but under my magnifier it looks like some kind of foam.'

'When will you know what it is for sure?'

'Might take a week, since I believe you've no real budget.'

Kat grinned. Pleased to be able to give Darcy her good news.

'Aha! Well, there, Mrs Clements – and rarely for you – you're wrong.'

Darcy looked at Kat askance. 'Me? The CSI Supremo? Wrong?'

'Only slightly. And there's no way you could have known, so you can keep your dignity. Linda just okayed me for ten grand. So let's get it on a quick turnaround if we need to. Did you get anything else from the crime scene?'

'You know what, Kat? I did. I got exactly the same as I did the last time I visited that house. Which is to say, precisely nothing. No fingerprints. No hairs. No fibres. No footprints. No cigarette butts, chewing gum wrappers or lottery tickets. No blood, no saliva, no semen. To say our guy is forensically aware would be an insult to forensically aware killers everywhere.'

Kat had to smile, despite the disappointment Darcy's words caused her. 'Come on, Darce, don't hedge. Tell me what you really think.'

Darcy laughed. 'You're looking at a guy wearing a noddy suit. A hazmat suit he bought off eBay. Or maybe something home-made. From a plastic shower curtain, maybe. If he's dressed normally, then his clothes are brand new and man-made fibre. He's probably wearing gloves and he's taped up his wrists, ankles and waist.'

'A pro, then? We're looking at a hitman.'

'That's your department, not mine. But my guess? When you catch him, it won't be some weed-smoking numpty with leisure-centre booties over his Nikes. You need to be ready. He's going to be fast, he's going to be strong, and he's not going to go easily.'

Back at her desk, Kat downloaded the images Jack had emailed over.

The fifth colour picture on her monitor looked like an abstract painting: overlapping splodges of green, yellow and a deep plum red. Jack had added a scarlet circle around a portion of the image where the discolouration was interrupted by a thin line of pale skin running across the bruise. According to the scale at the foot of the picture, the line was half a millimetre across.

Kat frowned. If the weapon was a rod or, as she'd speculated earlier, a long screwdriver, or even a specialist rolling pin, the bruise would be continuous. So what would cause that odd little gap?

Chapter Forty-Nine

While she scrutinised the post-mortem images, Kat's phone rang. She glanced at the screen.

'Hi, Isaac. To what do I owe the pleasure?'

'What? Oh, right, pleasure. Funny. Yeah, OK.'

He sounded stoned. It was part of the problem of having Isaac as a snout. He came up with good intel, but half the time he was high on his own supply and you had to double-check everything he told you. So far he hadn't tried to claim a bank blag was the work of the white rabbit, though, so she was inclined to cut him some slack.

'What is it, Isaac?'

'Can we meet?'

'I don't have a lot of time today, to be honest. I'm a bit busy.'

'Yeah, but I heard something today about Callum Michie. Maybe I also heard something else.'

'Oh, yes?'

'Yes. So?'

'Fine. Where?'

'I've got a new place. The cafe upstairs in M&S.'

'You're joking.'

'I'm not. Nobody I know would ever go in there. Plus they do this amazing chocolate fudge cake. Maybe you could . . .'

'If it's good information, I'll buy you a cappuccino and a slice of cake. Plus the usual.'

Ten minutes later, surrounded by elderly ladies and retired couples, she sat opposite Isaac. Between them, two cups of coffee and a wedge of chocolate cake slathered in squidgy icing and so dark it was almost black. Isaac took a huge bite and groaned, eyes closed.

'I heard Callum Michie's been cooled,' he mumbled.

'He's dead, certainly.'

'Exactly. Well, day before yesterday, right? I was in the Hope. At a meeting. Callum was offering twenty grand and a year in Marbella, all expenses paid, to anyone who'd cool – I mean who'd kill Laura Paxton. You know, in revenge.'

This was interesting. So Callum had gone against his uncle's wishes and declared open season on the person he saw as his wife's murderer. Maybe the real killer had got wind of it, decided to get his retaliation in first. With Callum dead, anyone looking for a fat paycheque and a year in the sun would have melted away.

Kat slid a twenty across the table, where it disappeared into Isaac's tracksuit top. 'Thanks, Isaac. How's your mum doing? Still having chemo?'

He nodded as he scooped up a smear of fudge icing with his fingertip and sucked it clean. 'One more session to go. Then it's radiotherapy, so there's loads to be positive about.'

He went for a smile, but it failed to stick. Swallowed hard so that the sharp lump of his Adam's apple jumped in his throat. He pushed the heel of his hand into his eye.

'Hey, Isaac, don't cry.' Kat reached across the table and closed her hand over his other forearm. 'Lots of people survive cancer nowadays. It's not like how it used to be. Your mum's a fighter, I'll bet.'

He sniffed. 'Yeah, but what'll I do if she doesn't make it? She's all I've got, Kat.'

'She'll be fine. And you will be, too.'

Kat left him at the table to finish his coffee. Wishing she felt as confident about the case as she'd just sounded to Isaac.

Chapter Fifty

Kat arrived home to an empty house. Apart from a scruffy, sooty-grey cairn terrier so pleased to see his mistress his claws skidded on the hall floor as he careered out of the kitchen to greet her.

'Hello?' she called out as she stooped to scratch Smokey under the chin.

No answer. She frowned before she remembered Riley's football team were playing away. An evening game against a school in Hemel Hempstead. Van had taken him. Liv must've gone too.

She straightened and wandered into the kitchen, where she opened the fridge and pulled out a bottle of Pinot Grigio. After pouring a generous glassful, she placed the glass on the countertop. She looked down at Smokey. He was sitting in front her, wagging his little tail so vigorously it was taking his rump with it.

'I swept the floor at the weekend, Smokes, but it's very kind of you. You want a walk?'

At the mere suggestion of a walk, Smokey sprang into action, racing to the front door where his lead hung on a brass coat hook Kat had screwed to the frame.

Smiling, and shaking her head, Kat took a quick sip of her wine then put the glass in the fridge.

As they walked round Stocks Green, Kat turned her mind to the case. Correction. *Cases*. The Michies' murders and her own imminent suspension. Which, if Iris was to be trusted, she could avert at the eleventh hour. Maybe she'd call Iris later.

Kat let out a sigh so loud an oncoming dog-walker smiled as he approached. A middle-aged man in a beige zip-up jacket and red trousers.

'Cheer up, love, it can't be all that bad.'

She walked on, offering him the tightest of smiles.

'There you are,' he said, unwisely. 'A smile costs nothing, doesn't it?'

'That's not what the aesthetic dentist on the High Street says,' she retorted, sending him scuttling off, head bent.

Back at home, she made herself a quick supper – spaghetti, butter, lots of black pepper and finely grated parmesan – and ate it with the rest of her now thoroughly chilled glass of wine while reading case papers.

She pulled open the dishwasher, hoping Van would have emptied it so she could stick her supper things straight in, but it was 'full of clean', as they put it. Sighing, she started transferring everything to its rightful place in a cupboard or drawer. He was a great husband and a brilliant dad, but one thing Ivan Ballantyne would apparently never master was the simple routine required to make the dishwasher their servant, not their master.

She poured more wine, took it through into the sitting room and called Iris.

'Hi, Kat. I expect you're calling me about the offshore trust.'

'I am. And I know you said you'd get back to me tomorrow, but I was hoping – and I know it's pointless – but I was really hoping somehow your contact in Bermuda—'

'Enrique lives in the Bahamas. I don't know anybody in Bermuda.'

'Sorry, sorry. You did tell me. It's just this is stressing me out, Iris. I'm drinking too much cheap white wine and it's not calming me down. In fact all it's doing is giving me hangovers when I ought to be at my sharpest.'

'Do you have a problem with alcohol? I believe a lot of police officers become psychologically dependent, if not actually addicted.'

Kat laughed. 'I don't *think* so.'

'Good. Because alcohol is a poison. That's why I don't drink. Although I probably eat too many M&Ms than are good for me. I wonder if I'm addicted to *them*. Do you think I could be?'

'I think it's highly unlikely. But if you are, at least the worst you have to worry about is your waistline. And maybe your teeth.' Kat glanced at the rest of her wine. Pushed the glass away. 'So?'

'So, what?'

'Have you heard back from Enrique?'

'No. As I said earlier today, he's calling me tomorrow. When I will call you with the good news.'

'You mean that the fifty K won't have come from a criminal enterprise?'

'How would I know that? It might have. I meant the good news that I will have solved the mystery of where it *did* come from.'

As an answer, it was less than satisfying.

Kat had long since removed the case files of Liv's apparent murder at the hands of the Origami Killer from their back bedroom. But she still used it as a home office. She went there now, closing the door behind her.

She stared out at the garden, dimly lit by a waxing moon. A worried-looking woman stared back in at her.

'Where did it come from?' she asked her reflection.

If the mute on the other side of the glass could speak, she'd have answered, *It's either your dad, Ethan, or as you just asked Iris, a criminal enterprise.*

But her dad was steadfastly denying it, Diana had been no help, and she couldn't ask Iris to start all over again looking at Morton Land. A favour could only be stretched so far.

Surely it couldn't be Ethan. Even if he did have the money, would he really want to risk the blowback when he was discovered as the source? Maybe it was from an OCG after all.

And then, like cars rear-ending each other's bumpers in a multiple shunt, a whole set of causes and effects rebounded forward in a chain.

Frank Strutt ran an OCG. *Crunch.* A copper's wife confessed to murdering Frank's niece. *Crunch.* Callum Michie put out a bounty on her head. *Crunch.* Callum himself was murdered. *Crunch.* Frank Strutt had access to plenty of ready cash. *Crunch.* Frank was so dissatisfied with her progress on the case he—

No, no, wait. The money had appeared before Laura confessed to killing Alanna. So bang went Frank's motive for getting Kat into trouble.

Unless.

Unless what, the window-woman asked silently.

'Unless he wants me gone for some other reason.'

But why? They maintained cordial if cool relations. And a man like Frank was far too savvy to ever get his hands dirty on a murder. He had men willing to do the wet work for him. And at least one layer of men who'd give *those* men their orders. She'd never tried to frame him – or anyone, come to that.

Despite what Diana clearly thought, and Riley had hinted at, there were plenty of honest coppers around. And DS Kat Ballantyne was one of them.

The trouble was, she was having the devil's own job proving it.

Chapter Fifty-One

Later that night, as Kat sat beside Van in bed, scanning case reports while he read a crime novel, he turned to her.

'You OK?'

'Yeah, fine. Why?'

'You've barely spoken a word to me since I got in.'

'Yes I have! I asked you how the game went.'

'You asked *Riley* how it went. Do you remember the score?'

'Of course I do. It was . . .' Kat stared at the ceiling, racking her brain as she replayed the chat earlier. Riley had been smiling. Triumphantly, in fact. They must have won. She tugged on her earlobes as she screwed her eyes shut. Snapped them open again. 'Two-one to us.'

'Impressive.'

'Told you.'

'And wrong. Three-two. Two-all with five minutes left to play. Although Riley did score the winner.'

'Oh God, Van. I'm sorry. It's just this bloody money. I spoke to Iris earlier and she's confident she'll know where it came from tomorrow. Trouble is, what if it's from some dodgy source? I'll be finished. Carve-up will call his weasely little mate from 3C-ACU and I'll be under the microscope for weeks. I might be suspended. Or even lose my job.'

Tears leaked from the corners of her eyes. She'd been doing a reasonable job of holding it all together for the past week, but with the crunch-point looming, her emotional tank had run dry. Suddenly she was crying properly, while Van pulled her into a hug.

'Hey, hey. It's not as bad as that. Come on, darling, you know you're innocent, don't you?'

'Yes, but—'

'Nuh-uh. No "yes, but". You've done nothing wrong. You're innocent until proven guilty. So you've got nothing to worry about, have you?'

'But that's the trouble, Van, I have! For a start, getting investigated by Anti-Corruption is like catching leprosy. Nobody wants to come near you in case they get infected. And what if they *do* find something? I mean, not that I'm on the take. But what if they do?'

Van turned to face her and put his hands on her shoulders. Frowned. 'Blimey, you're a bit tight, aren't you? These muscles feel like rock. Right. On your tummy. I'll give you a massage.'

Kat smiled at him. 'You mean it?'

'Now,' he said. 'Come on, get that T-shirt off. I can't do a proper job otherwise.'

'This isn't you trying to get into my knickers, is it?'

'Would you *like* me to try to get into your knickers?'

She shucked off her baggy grey T-shirt and slithered down the bed. Rolled on to her front.

'Get me nice and relaxed and then we'll talk about it,' she said into the pillow.

Moments later, Van was working his thumbs into her shoulders, making her groan with pain as the knotted muscles protested. Perhaps a nice relaxing marital shag was just what she needed after all.

Could Frank Strutt have sent the fifty K? In advance? Maybe he'd been planning to murder Alanna and Callum all along. He knew she was a dogged detective and likely to be involved in the case. So he'd poisoned the well in advance, hoping she'd be confined to quarters or suspended. And it had almost worked, hadn't it?

Then he'd also have to have had information he could use to coerce Laura Paxton into confessing. Compromising information was Frank's stock-in-trade. But how could he have got to Laura? She tried to figure out something even halfway plausible. But it was so hard, and Van was really digging into her knotty muscles.

She opened her eyes. Blinked. Van's side of the bed was empty. Frowning, she looked at the clock.

It was 6.59 a.m.

The green digits clicked over to 7.00 a.m. As the Radio 1 breakfast news burst from the little speaker, she smelled toast. Van came into the bedroom bearing a tray.

'You're awake! I thought we were going to have to resuscitate you.'

'I fell asleep,' she said, pulling herself upright and plumping the pillows against the bedhead as he placed the breakfast tray on her lap.

'That's one way of putting it. Another would be that you entered a comatose state about three seconds after I started massaging your shoulders last night. You didn't even snore.'

Her eyes flash-bulbed. 'I *never* snore! *You're* the one who snores.'

Van climbed in beside her.

'Drink your tea, stinky!'

Kat took a quick sip and a bite of the toast. Then she lifted the tray off her legs and twisted round so she could put it on the floor.

'I don't have to be up for another fifteen minutes,' she said with a grin. 'So if you're quick . . .'

Chapter Fifty-Two

Kat had just logged on to her PC when her personal phone rang.

She checked the number and swallowed hard, her stomach suddenly fizzing with nerves.

'Hi, Iris.' Kat's tremulous voice was barely a whisper above the thumping of her heart. She tried again. 'Iris! Hi. Did Enrique find the source of the money?'

'Well, it's very odd. He was on his way to a meeting with one of the bank staff when a car ran him off the road. It was quite a bad crash apparently. Enrique thinks it was deliberate.'

A wave of cold flashed across Kat's skin, raising goosebumps.

'He's OK, though, Iris? I mean, he survived?'

'He called me from Princess Margaret Hospital in Nassau. A concussion and cuts and bruises apparently. But yes, he survived. You may have to wait a little longer though.'

Kat's soaring hopes crashed to earth like a pigeon hitting an office-block window. As the feathers spiralled down around her, she tried to put a brave face on it. Iris was sensitive to what she perceived as criticism.

'Then I'll just have to wait. Please tell him I'm sorry.'

'Why? You didn't hit him.'

Kat had to smile. 'Then how about you tell him I hope he's not in too much pain?'

'Yes. I think that sounds a lot better. I *will* call you, Kat. That's a promise.'

Kat replaced the receiver with a shaking hand. Minutes before Enrique was about to wrap up his work, somebody had tried to kill him. That's what it sounded like to her. Whoever had sent the money must have been tipped off that someone was snooping into their financial affairs. Christ! Their reach stretched all the way to the Bahamas.

A shadowy monster – fear personified – placed clammy fingers on the back of her neck and whispered right into her ear. *If they'd do that, they might come after you. Or your family.*

Carve-up spoke from right behind her.

'Bad news, DS Ballantyne?' She turned. He was looking down at her with a smug expression on his face. 'That your tame forensic accountant, was it? Didn't sound like she'd got very far. Pity. Looks like you're well and truly screwed, doesn't it?'

She stood, not willing to give any kind of advantage to her hated line manager – physical, moral or procedural. And wondering, as she took in his wider-then-usual smirk, whether he knew about the attempt on Enrique's life. Whether he'd even engineered it.

'Let's get this straight, Stu,' she murmured, so only he could hear. 'If I *do* end up having 3C-ACU combing through my life, I'm going to make sure I cooperate fully with their investigation. I'll tell them *everything*. All my suspicions about where the money came from. *Who* might have known about it. *How* they knew about it. And *why* they might want to see me off the force. You know, people with dodgy pasts and even dodgier presents.'

He bared his teeth. The feral expression of a cornered dog. He was playing a dangerous game. After all, Kat knew all about his exploits back when he was a DC. He and two colleagues who'd called themselves the Three Musketeers had been extorting sex workers. She didn't have much evidence of Carve-up's wrongdoing beyond a single witness's testimony. But as Carve-up himself knew only too well, once you started flinging mud around, some of it always stuck.

And as she looked at him, she experienced a profound realignment of her feelings towards him. Up to this moment, she'd seen him as a pain in the arse. A smug, sexist, suited-and-booted pain in the arse. Maybe on the take from her dad – and others. But that was all.

Now, she wasn't so sure. Had he graduated from threatening prostitutes to taking bungs, to arranging hits for an OCG? Had he received orders to neutralise *her*? She fought to suppress the sudden shudder that rippled through her like a cold wind.

Meanwhile, Carve-up affected an insouciant 'I don't care' expression. All shrugged shoulders and raised eyebrows.

'Wild accusations, DS Ballantyne. If you've got some hard evidence – you know, like fifty K in *my* bank account – have at it. Otherwise, I suggest you focus on salvaging what's left of your career. I hear they're short of PCSOs downstairs.'

He spun on the heel of his Gucci loafer and headed for his office, leaving Kat with an uncomfortable thought. If she *was* found guilty of accepting bribes, even the role of police community support officer would be denied her.

She called Van, trying to breathe slowly and not give in to the terror threatening to overwhelm her.

'Hey. Everything all right?' he asked.

'Yeah. Yeah. Good. Look, Van, have you noticed anything strange at home?'

'Strange? What do you mean?'

'Oh, nothing. Just maybe, I don't know, someone loitering about in the street? Maybe someone you've not seen before? Watching the house?'

'No. Listen, darling, what is this? You sound terrible.'

'It's nothing. But listen, can you collect Riley after school?'

'Why? He usually makes his own way home.'

'Please.'

'Look, Kat, tell me what's going on. You're starting to worry me.'

What could she say? How could she tell Van what was scaring her without sounding like she was losing it? Nothing for it but to dive in.

'Someone tried to kill the guy in the Bahamas Iris is using to track down the money,' she blurted. 'I think . . . I'm worried they'll come after us, too.'

'Kat, is this a joke? Because I have to tell you, it's not very funny.'

'It's not a joke, Van.'

'What did the Bahamian police say?'

'I don't know. I don't think he reported it.'

'So how do you know it was deliberate?'

'Enrique told Iris he thought it was.'

'But he didn't think it was serious enough to call the cops.'

'I don't know, do I? Maybe they're too busy to bother with that kind of thing.'

'Look, Kat. Don't take this the wrong way, but isn't it a bit of a stretch to go from a hit-and-run in the Bahamas to me searching for, what, masked intruders in the back garden? I mean, come on, love, don't you think you're maybe overreacting?'

Van's laid-back attitude had been one of the things that had first attracted her all those years ago when they'd met as backpackers in Thailand. Now she could have screamed.

'Please, Van. Collect him from school. Just this once. I should know about the money tomorrow and then we'll see where we stand, OK? Maybe there's an innocent explanation after all.'

Van sighed loudly. 'I can't make a habit of it. Riley will probably give me a weapons-grade eye roll as it is.'

'Thanks,' she said, thinking that if all her husband had to contend with was a Riley Ballantyne Special, it would be a good day.

Chapter Fifty-Three

Kat sat at her desk, head cradled in her palms. Imagined Enrique, head swaddled in bandages, hooked up to a bunch of beeping machines in a Nassau hospital.

A wave of cold rolled over her. If someone wanted him dead, then lying immobile in a hospital bed made him a soft target. They might return for a second try. She had to do something.

Two minutes later she was listening to the phone ring in a hospital reception area four thousand miles away.

A double-click. Then a brisk voice answered. 'Princess Margaret Hospital, Pauline speaking. How may I direct your call today?'

Kat took a deep breath. 'Hello, Pauline. My name is Detective Sergeant Kat Ballantyne. I'm calling from Middlehampton police station in Hertfordshire, England.'

Kat explained who she was interested in, and after some audible keyboard gymnastics, Pauline came back on the line and confirmed that Enrique D'Oliveira was a patient. Brought in with a suspected concussion after a car accident. Scheduled to be discharged in four hours.

Kat thanked her and placed her next call. To Central police station on East Street. She repeated her introduction, and after stressing the urgent nature of her call, was connected to the station superintendent, Tamera Ledard.

'What can I do for you, Detective Sergeant?' Ledard asked. 'I have to say, it's not every day I get a call from a British homicide detective.'

Kat felt bad about bending the truth but dived in anyway. 'I'm investigating two linked murders, and I suspect somebody based in the Bahamas made an attempt on the life of someone I need to talk to. His name is Enrique D'Oliveira and he's being treated at Princess Margaret Hospital.'

Kat had prepared supporting material to back up her request for Enrique's protection. Didn't need it.

'And you need us to guarantee his safety until after your interview?'

'I think once he's spoken to an associate of mine, the risk will have passed. It's just twenty-four hours.'

'Leave it with me. I am a firm believer in interforce cooperation. Some of my male colleagues can be a little too proud about maintaining their independence. But we women know how the world works, eh, DS Ballantyne?'

'We do. So you'll send someone?'

'I'll supervise it personally. Get me out from behind my desk. Too much paperwork these days. For you, too?'

'Always.'

'I must go then. But rest assured, Mr D'Oliveira will come to no further harm.'

Kat replaced the handset.

Her mobile pinged with the sound of an incoming email from one of her priority contacts.

She glanced at the screen. NDNAD.

'Tomski!' she called out without looking up. 'Come and see this. We've finally got the DNA results from Alanna Michie.'

She looked up. Tom was nowhere in sight.

Leah called from across the office. 'He went out for a coffee. Can I see?'

Kat beckoned her over.

As Kat read the email from NDNAD, her jaw dropped. This was a turn-up for the books.

Leah looked sideways at her, a crooked grin on her face. 'I bet you're going to enjoy *that* particular conversation, aren't you?'

Kat's belly was squirming with anxiety as she digested the implications of the forensics. Someone she'd been close to dismissing had suddenly jumped right to the top of her suspect list.

She glanced over at Carve-up's office. There he was, hunched over his PC. Doing his metrics. She was about to give him some news that would really put a kink in his day.

But a quick trip to the pub first.

Chapter Fifty-Four

Entering the Hope and Anchor out of the spring sunshine, Kat's eyes initially struggled to see anything at all in the gloom.

Gradually, as her pupils adjusted, the pub lightened. Frank Strutt was behind the bar, polishing a whisky tumbler on a red-and-white bar cloth.

A murmur rippled around the Victorian boozer as its denizens scoped out the newcomer, recognised her, then went back to their drinks. Quieter than before. More watchful.

Kat didn't blame them. She'd arrested some, questioned others, seen a couple sent down.

She supposed there *might* be a punter or two who had no idea of the pub's reputation and just fancied a pint and a pickled egg. But they'd have to be a hardy breed to take in the gloomy interior and the scowls of its tattooed, muscled, shifty patrons, and think that, yes, this was *absolutely* the sort of place where they'd feel comfortable whiling away half an hour doing *The Times* crossword.

She crossed the room to the bar. Palms sweaty, heart over-revving like when she pushed her Golf too hard.

'Hi, Frank. Can I have a word, please?'

He carried on screwing the cloth into the tumbler, regarding her from beneath lowered brows. In truth, Frank Strutt did not look best pleased to see her.

'I hope this is to tell me you've arrested the person who murdered my niece and nephew.'

'We're—'

'—pursuing a number of promising lines of enquiry. Right.'

It might have been the stress of the looming 3C-ACU deadline. Or just that she was getting heartily sick of men finishing her sentences for her during this investigation. Either way she fixed Frank with a gimlet gaze and dropped her voice to a warning growl.

'As it happens, Frank, that's *exactly* what I'm doing. And one of them concerns *you*. We can do this out here if you like. But I think you're going to want to hear what I have to say somewhere private.'

He favoured her with a long, searching look. But Kat was beyond feeling threatened. She just stared back.

Frank tipped his head towards the far end of the bar. The closest he'd permit himself to an admission of defeat.

The back room reeked of stale beer and cigarette smoke. Clearly nobody had found the balls to tell the pub's landlord smoking was no longer permitted on licensed premises. Wisely, in Kat's opinion.

They faced each other across a battered table with a heavily scarred top. Generations of booted feet had kicked, scuffed or rubbed off most of the black paint from its cast-iron base.

'Well?' Frank said, folding his arms so that his biceps pushed out against the thin white cotton of his shirt.

How would the heavily built gangster sitting opposite her react to the question she was about to ask? Not with violence; that wasn't her concern. Frank was far too canny for that. He'd never attack a cop. Not unless he was sure he could get away with it.

Plus, as Tom had once observed, Frank and Kat had a relationship based on mutual, if grudging, respect. She'd walked up to the line, maybe even scuffed it a little with her toe. But she hadn't crossed it. Didn't need to. Given what she knew, and Frank Strutt didn't.

She took a breath. *Out with it, Kat.* 'Were you sleeping with Alanna?'

Frank reared back. Then he jabbed a sausage-like finger at her. 'You've got a nerve, coming in here and accusing me of something like that.'

'Is that a no, then?' she countered.

'Of course it's a no! What do you think I am? She was half my age for a start.'

'Not necessarily a barrier though, is it, Frank? Alanna was twenty-two. Well past the age of consent. Plenty of Hollywood power couples with that sort of age gap.'

'Yeah, but this is Middlehampton, isn't it? And I'm hardly Michael Douglas or Harrison Ford, am I?'

She tilted her head to one side. 'Maybe with some good lighting and a touch of concealer.'

'Funny,' he grunted. 'Was that it? Only I've got a pub to run. And in case you'd forgotten, two funerals to organise.'

'If you don't want to tell me, I'll get to it,' she said. 'We recovered DNA from semen in Alanna's vagina, and it's a match for yours. And I mean a direct, one hundred per cent match. We also found a chemical called polydimethylsiloxane. It's a lubricant used on condoms. I'm guessing you were being careful, but it split.' She shrugged, suddenly accessing a well of confidence she'd not known she possessed. 'It happens, so I'm told.'

The silence thickened, as if the air was once again full of the now-banned cigarette smoke that had tinted the Hope's pressed-tin ceilings caramel.

'Bloody DNA.' He shrugged. Rearranged his weight on the hard chair. Clasped his thick-fingered hands in front of him. 'Yes, I slept with Alanna. We were at a party and we'd had a few. Cal was coked off his head, picking fights, throwing drinks, and she wasn't happy about it. Crying, screaming, the works. We went upstairs to

241

find somewhere quiet for a chat and one thing led to another. She was a lovely-looking girl. You going to judge me for that?'

Kat shook her head. 'Not my department.'

'I didn't murder her, since that's obviously going to be your next question. Why would I? I just told you we went to bed. Plus you've got to be working on the assumption that whoever killed Alanna killed Callum, too.'

'I am, Frank, and that's the problem. You see, by your own admission, you were at the crime scene as he was being killed. You're a big bloke. I can easily see you overpowering Callum and strangling him.'

'But why would I? He was my bloody nephew, for God's sake!'

Could he really not see it? Was he *that* obtuse? He was a man. Of course he was.

Kat set him straight. 'You were shagging his wife. Maybe Alanna got a fit of the guilts and said she was going to tell Callum. So you killed her to stop her, but Callum already knew. Threatened to kill you so you got your retaliation in first. Calling it in to make yourself look innocent's an old trick. Either way, we've got the oldest motive for murder in the world.'

As she laid these facts out, her stomach clenched. Maybe Frank wouldn't attack her inside his own pub. But that left a world of possibilities outside its four walls. She swallowed down her anxiety. *Too late now, Kat.*

He shook his head. 'It wasn't me.'

'Where were you when Alanna was murdered?'

He blinked. Frowned. Then his eyes brightened. 'That was Monday morning, right? I was with Sue. The whole time. Ask her. Phone her now.'

'I'll get round to that. But you know as well as I do, Frank, a wife's alibi isn't exactly what a lawyer would call compelling evidence of innocence. And not being rude' – she tiptoed up to the line again, and this time stuck one whole foot over it – 'but when the wife in question is Sue Strutt, well, let's just say a jury mightn't place too much store by it, either.'

She was standing nose to nose with the caged fighting dog that lived inside Frank Strutt. He rarely let it out, preferring to have others go on the offensive for him. But, when cornered, Frank Strutt was more than capable of inflicting a nasty bite of his own. There were pages and pages in a folder in the basement of Jubilee Place, and the corresponding file on the Police National Computer, testifying to that fact.

He was breathing heavily, presumably thinking along the same lines.

'As I think I just told you,' he grated, 'before you insulted my wife. I didn't do it.'

She eyeballed him. 'Talking of insulting your wife, does Sue know, Frank?'

'Is that a threat?'

'It's a question.'

He tightened his right fist until the knuckles cracked.

'Well, then, Kat, the answer is no,' he said in a slow, eerily calm voice. 'And it would be better for everyone if it stayed that way. What happened between me and Alanna was private.'

His stare frightened her. She imagined dark warehouses out in the sticks. Dank, cold places smelling of stale piss and the overwhelming odour of fear. Cable ties. Blades. Car batteries. Screams. The crunch and scuff of spades in the county's heavy clay soil. The splash and thump as a body wrapped in heavy-duty black binbags dropped down on to the watery floor of the hole.

Some of her bravado deserted her. But not all.

'You had sex with a woman who ended up murdered less than two days later. It's not going to stay private very long if I find out you did it.'

'And as I think I already told you, I *didn't* do it.'

She stared at him. Hard.

'Well then, who did, Frank? Because right now, you're looking good for both murders. I mean, we've got your DNA on one victim and we know you were there again yesterday. I bet we can find your DNA on Callum's body if we look hard enough.'

'Of course you bloody will!' he burst out. 'I checked his pulse. I knelt beside his body.'

'So convince me otherwise. Come on, Frank, you must have a theory of your own as to who killed them.'

He rubbed his hand over his eyes. Pulled it down over his unshaven cheek with a rasp.

'Until Cal was killed, I thought it might have been him. The boy had a temper. You were half right. I thought she'd told him and *he* killed her out of jealousy.'

'But you didn't come to us.'

'Would you expect me to?'

It was a good question. People like the Strutts tended to work to their own definition of the rule of law. Basically, an eye for an eye, a tooth for a tooth, a beating for a beating, *and if you're shagging my uncle, God help you.*

'What were you going to do, then?'

'Not sure. I mean, she was dead, wasn't she? How would it help me or mine to see Cal banged up for murder? Maybe I would've outplaced him somewhere far away. Spain, Croatia, Germany? But matters were taken out of my hands, weren't they?'

'They were, and you know I'm genuinely sorry, Frank. And for asking you these questions.'

'It's OK. I get it. Like they say in *The Godfather*, "It's just business."'

'Just so long as you know that if my business finds any other evidence pointing at you, Frank, it's going to be you in the dock, not Callum.'

She left the Hope on legs she had to force to walk without wobbling. She was unconvinced of Frank's guilt. But equally unsure of his innocence.

Chapter Fifty-Five

After leaving Frank Strutt at the Hope, Kat found she could no longer ignore the pangs of hunger stabbing her insides. The nagging fears over the looming anti-corruption investigation had stifled her appetite more effectively than an early morning post-mortem, but her body was crying out for some energy.

She darted into a convenience store on Union Street to be faced with the last two items in the chiller cabinet: a huge, dry-looking Cornish pasty and a pallid tuna mayo sandwich on white bread. Tuna, then.

Kat headed back into the office, trying to dislodge a slimy lump of mushy white bread and tuna mixture sticking to the roof of her mouth. On the way up to MCU she dropped into Forensics. Darcy informed her the fleck of material Jack had tweezed out of the wound was hard-wearing plastic foam used in thousands of domestic and industrial applications. A bust, in other words.

Kat squeezed her eyes shut and tugged on both earlobes. Nothing about this case made any sense. She called over to Tom and Leah who were talking, heads bowed towards each other, at Leah's desk.

'Hey, you two, case review. Tom, can you get some coffees and meet us in the little conference room?'

'Little' was the word. Rumour had it, someone had once tried to swing a cat in the airless little cuboid. Apparently, they broke their elbow on the backswing and the moggy walked.

Kat took a cautious sip of the inky brew Tom placed in her hand.

'So, what we've got is two murders that *have* to be linked. Almost certainly the same perpetrator. But, as far as I can see, no reason whatsoever for them both to be killed like that. We've got one potential suspect in Frank Strutt. But he's got an alibi, and honestly, I don't see it. I don't *sense* it. And whoever I *do* identify as a suspect also has to have a connection to Laura Paxton *and* something on her that would persuade her to take the fall.'

'If this was a crime of passion, then why not kill Callum and Alanna together?' Tom asked. He jumped in on his own question. 'Except that wouldn't work with the method of killing, would it? Callum's hardly going to stand there while some enraged lover strangles his wife.'

'That seems unlikely,' Leah deadpanned. 'But then, why the gap, if he intended to murder them both?'

Kat shook her head. 'My gut's telling me he didn't. I think, yes, Alanna was a calculated act. But Callum was only targeted after he started making these threats to kill Laura Paxton or whoever had coerced her into confessing.'

Tom's eyes widened. 'Maybe that was a blind. Making it *look* like he wanted her dead, when he really wanted her convicted.'

Kat nodded. 'Agreed.'

'And you're still *sure* it wasn't her?' Leah said.

Kat screwed her face up. 'There are too many points where her testimony is contradicted either by the physical evidence or the MO. She claims she did it because Alanna was having an affair with her husband, but the DNA pointed right back at Frank.'

'So maybe it's him after all,' Leah said.

'If Callum had committed some act of treason against the family, maybe Frank would have had him bumped off,' Kat said. 'But to do it himself? At Callum's? It's not the way the Strutts work. Not that we've ever pinned anything serious on Frank, but he'd take Callum out to Ashridge Forest, or the gravel pits over in Sheepton.'

Kat frowned and placed a hand over her stomach, which had just churned unpleasantly. As soon as her mind stopped focusing on the insoluble puzzle of the Michies' murders, it immediately snapped over to the looming threat from 3C-ACU. When was Iris going to call? Could Kat find a way to confront Ethan? It had got to the point where she would almost have been happy to hear that the money had come from Albanian heroin dealers. At least she'd know.

Leah was frowning. 'Are you all right, Kat? You look pale.'

Kat nodded. Although her stomach performed a complicated move beneath her diaphragm as she was about to speak. She burped. A wave of nausea rushed over her. 'Can you excuse me? I have to go and be sick.'

She left the airless cubicle at a run, made it to the ladies with seconds to spare and threw up into one of the toilets. Undigested tuna floated in the water. After splashing cold water over her face and rinsing out her acid-tasting mouth, she stared at herself in the mirror.

'You're not stuck. You're just regrouping. Now think. How do we solve murder cases?'

And in that moment, Kat saw the obvious question she'd so far not asked. She hurried back to the conference room and her two concerned-looking DCs.

'Sorry about that. That'll teach me to buy my lunch from a shop that proudly displays a three-star food hygiene rating.'

'I think the canteen only has two,' Tom said. 'Anyway, while you were out, I was thinking about something you said to me on my first day in MCU.'

'"Never call me guv"?'

'"The simple answer is usually the right one." Like, don't look for a serial killer till you've eliminated the husband.'

Kat had to smile. 'Exactly, Tomski! So, tell me how that applies here.'

Tom straightened as he always did when he sensed a test being put before him. Kat caught Leah's eye; smiled. Just a little.

'OK. So, the very first thing in *this* case was that Alanna Michie was strangled. You got a call from a woman, a friend, actually, who confessed to her murder.'

Kat nodded. 'Go on.'

'So if we're certain it *wasn't* her, we should interview her again and push her on why she'd confess to a murder she didn't commit.'

Kat turned to Leah. 'You've just called me to confess to a murder you didn't commit. Why?'

Leah shrugged. Relaxed, where Tom was eager to please. 'Either someone was making a credible threat against my family, or I wanted to be inside.'

'And why would you want to be inside?'

'Either to get *to* someone or get away *from* someone.' Leah paused. 'Maybe her husband's abusive.'

'Pretty big step to confess to murder,' Kat said, sure she was on to something now. 'Why not just go to a women's refuge?'

'He's a detective. Maybe Laura was frightened he'd just find her and charm his way in or something,' Tom said.

Kat shrugged. 'I might go and talk to him.'

'Probably best to be subtle, boss,' Leah said. 'Last thing you want is a grieving husband filing a complaint against you for accusing him of beating her up.'

At that point, Kat thought she'd probably settle for rubbing a colleague up the wrong way if it yielded even a smidgeon of a lead.

Linda was pushing her hard to solve the case before Detective Superintendent Deerfield pulled the plug. If Kat failed, Laura Paxton would sink deeper into the justice system, while Kat herself would return to other duties, other cases. Assuming, that was, that she could clear her name over the fifty thousand.

Her stomach rolled over again and for a moment she thought she'd have to return to the ladies.

She checked her phone in case somehow she'd missed Iris's call. Nothing.

She called Liv, just in case she'd gone back to Ethan and 'persuaded' him to confess to sending the money. Yes, because life was always that simple.

'Hi, this is Liv. Leave a message.'

Don't let me drown, mate! Kat wanted to scream.

Chapter Fifty-Six

Kat jumped as her phone rang in her hand. But it wasn't Liv. And it wasn't Iris. It was Polly, one of the receptionists.

'I've got some phone messages for you, Kat. I think you need to see them for yourself,' she added cryptically.

Entering the public reception, Kat nodded a greeting to Polly.

'You all right, Kat?' the older woman asked.

Kat grimaced. 'Ate an out-of-date sandwich for lunch and it made a break for freedom.'

Polly pulled a face. 'I'm afraid I've got something else that won't agree with you.' She held up a sheaf of phone message slips. 'Sorry, but he made me take them down verbatim. These were as good as I could manage. He sounds a bit of a saddo, if you ask me.'

Kat took the bundle of slips from Polly's outstretched hand.

'Nice nails, by the way.'

'Thank you! I got them done at that new place by the Butter Cross. The colour's called Caught in the Nude. Chance would be a fine thing!' she added with a cackle.

Grinning, Kat turned away, scanning the top message slip. As she read the caller's name, the smile slid off her face.

From: Ethan Metcalfe.

Msg: Kat, call me. Urgently. You have my number.

Anxiety stirred in her gut. Maybe Liv really had gone back to put the screws on Ethan. But despite her bravado, she was still a slender woman. Whereas Ethan, though doughy, was a strongly built man.

She texted Liv.

You OK?

What if Ethan had kidnapped Liv? He'd have her phone, too. She sent a second message with a trap.

Thelma! Text me!

But Liv was Louise, not Thelma. She could tell Ethan and he'd text back the wrong nickname.

Kat flipped through the rest of the messages. Six in all.

From: Ethan Metcalfe.

Msg: Please call me, Kat. It relates to the Michie murders.

From: Ethan Metcalfe.

Msg: Kat, you have to return my call. I have a theory you need to hear.

From: Ethan Metcalfe.

Msg: Kat, I'm not prepared to accept no for an answer.

From: Ethan Metcalfe.

Msg: I insist you call me back, Kat. This is critical to the case. I need to speak to you today.

From: Ethan Metcalfe.

Msg: Kat, what have I done wrong? You can come on the show. Whatever you want. Just return my call. Please. I'm begging you.

From: Ethan Metcalfe.

Msg: I'm not going to call again, Kat. If you won't talk to me, I'll just have to talk to you.

Jesus! Ethan was certainly starting to sound a lot like a stalker. In fact he was starting to sound positively deranged. Maybe Liv was right about him. Maybe he really was the one behind the money.

A flicker of fear ran through her. Should she be worried? Was he actually a threat? No. No way was she going to allow a creep like Ethan Metcalfe to get inside her head. He was a sad little man with an unhealthy obsession with murder and an even unhealthier obsession with her. Plus, right now? She didn't really have the headroom to entertain a third major problem.

On the positive side, at least he'd kept his word. After the seventh call, he'd clearly given up. But where was Liv?

Her phone pinged. A text popped up on her home screen.

WTF? I'm Louise! I'm fine. Trying to dig into Mutt-calf's finances online. Nothing yet.

Breathing easier, Kat arrived at her desk to find a Post-it stuck to her monitor. All thoughts of Ethan fled her mind.

Linda O wants to see you urgently. Leah.

Leah had doodled a worried-face emoji beneath the brief message.

So this was it. Linda was going to pull the plug on the investigation. Laura Paxton would stand trial for murder and, unless she changed her story, be sent down for life.

Annie shot Kat a look she found hard to interpret as she knocked and entered Linda's office. Concern mixed with sympathy. Maybe a dash of *tread carefully, she's not in the best of moods*?

Clearly this wasn't good news.

It wasn't. Not by a long chalk.

Linda's face, unlike her PA's, bore a look all too easy to decode. A bigger dog had just shown his teeth.

'Sit down, Kat, and let me finish without interrupting, please.' She sighed heavily. 'I've just got off the phone with The Undertaker. He's changed his mind, or he's had it changed for him: he's told me to close the case. We've got a suspect in custody who sounds like she'll plead guilty to the murder charge on Alanna Michie. So we get a result without having to devote days to court appearances, paperwork and all the rest.'

Kat shook her head. Probably also an unwise decision, but she couldn't stop herself.

'No, Linda! I mean, ma'am. Please. You *can't* shut me down. I'm so close. I've got a new line of enquiry and it's only' – she checked her watch – '3.25 p.m. Can't you at least give me until the end of the day?'

Linda looked sceptical. 'What's this LOE then?'

'Frank Strutt was sleeping with Alanna Michie. I confronted him with DNA evidence and he admitted it. That gives him motive.'

Linda wrinkled her nose. 'Alibi?'

'Sue.'

'No surprise there, then. But there was no other physical evidence at the crime scene, was there? Hairs, fibres, prints?'

'No.'

'What about Callum Michie? You like Frank for that one, too?'

'Frank was there. Called it in from the house. His DNA'll be on the corpse, too.' Kat wanted to stop there, desperate to keep hold of the case for a little longer. But as she looked the Head of Crime in the eye, honesty got the better of her. 'He says he checked Callum's pulse, which could explain it. But it *has* to be the same killer, and if he did Alanna, then that means he did Callum, too.'

Linda held up both hands. 'Hold on, just a second. You're getting ahead of yourself. It's *likely* to be the same killer, but as we don't have any forensics apart from Frank's DNA, we can't say for sure. It could be a terrible coincidence. And also, "*if* he did Alanna"? That's a pretty big if, Kat. And I think you know it. So, let me ask you. Do you like him for it? For either murder?'

Yes! was what Kat wanted to scream. *Yes! I do. So let me keep going just a few more days.*

But how could she? When deep down in her copper's gut – that place where, however many times you repeated another of your mentor's sayings, *Follow the evidence, Kat,* the truth often resided – she felt nothing.

It wasn't Frank.

Oh, he was guilty of all kinds of heinous crimes, both recorded on his docket and unrecorded – because he'd never been caught for them, much less charged, tried and convicted. But of the murders of his nephew and his wife? No. Frank was clean. She'd bet her career on it. Bad choice of sentiment. Maybe that was what was at stake.

'Kat?' Linda prompted.

'Honestly? No.'

'Right, then. Go and talk to the CPS. Get the wheels in motion to have Laura Paxton formally charged with Alanna Michie's murder and get a date set for initial committal proceedings at the magistrates' court.'

Kat felt the ground she was standing on slipping beneath her feet. About to pitch her into a moral abyss where she collaborated with government lawyers to send an innocent woman to prison. It was time for a final desperate throw of the dice.

'You just asked me if I liked Frank for the murders. And I honestly told you I didn't. On that basis, you want to see Laura tried for murder. Now ask me if I like *her* for Alanna's.'

Linda sighed. Ran fingers through her hair. 'You're going to give me an ulcer, you know that, don't you, Kat?' She paused. 'Do you like Laura Paxton for Alanna Michie's murder?'

'No, I don't,' Kat shot back almost before the final word had left Linda's lips. 'So if you're willing to send her for trial based on my opinion of Frank, you ought to be equally willing not to, given what I think about *her*.'

Did it hold up as a logical argument? Kat was so blinded by her passion she wasn't sure if she'd expressed her point clearly. Or had she just condemned Laura with her own muddled syntax?

Linda eyed her with a look, half sceptical, half intrigued. A big cat faced with a dummy deer carcass concealing a wildlife photographer's video camera in its belly.

'I didn't know we had a philosopher in MCU,' she said, finally. 'What are you saying?'

'Give me another week.'

Linda's response was eloquent. All the more so for being entirely silent. She merely raised her eyebrows.

'Five days, then,' Kat said quickly.

'Not a chance. David Deerfield will crucify me. And in case you've forgotten, there's also the small matter of an upcoming 3C-ACU investigation. Unless you can explain how fifty grand mysteriously found its way into your bank account. Blow that and you won't be investigating anything except firms of local solicitors. Any news there, by the way? Because I really can't afford to lose you. No way will I get the money for a replacement.'

Kat shook her head, tasting tuna at the back of her throat and suddenly feeling sick again. 'Not yet. But I should have something by the end of the day.'

'Bloody hell, girl, you're taking this to the wire, aren't you? What's the hold-up?'

Kat explained about Iris's pursuit of the beneficial owner of the offshore trust in the Bahamas, and the unfortunate Enrique's brush with death.

'It's going to be all right, boss.'

'You don't sound that sure.'

Kat sighed. 'I didn't do anything! I'm innocent. Like Laura is. I know I don't have the evidence yet but neither of us deserves this!'

Linda's face softened and she shook her head. 'I must need my head examining. I'll call David and explain you're on the point of making an arrest. I'll say I want to avoid a miscarriage of justice. With all the flak the force is catching in the media, I can spin it as a win. David's very PR-conscious: I think he'll buy it. You can have till 3.00 p.m. on Monday. Clear it by then or Laura goes up before the beak.'

Kat opened her mouth. 'Best offer, Kat. Take it or leave it.'

'I'll take it,' Kat said meekly. 'Thanks, Ma-Linda.'

Linda smiled. 'Go on. Get out of here and catch me a murderer.'

Kat leapt from her chair and marched back to her desk at double-speed. She had no time to lose. She called Van. Told him she'd be late home. Or possibly not home at all. Then she texted Riley.

Probs going to be super-busy until Monday. Might not see you much. Love you. xx

She didn't expect a reply straight away. He'd be in lessons and the college had a strict 'No phones during the school day' policy. Broken regularly during breaks, but largely adhered to during lessons. But it made her feel better.

Next, she called Iris. Heart racing, she waited for her to answer. Had Superintendent Ledard kept Enrique safe in his hospital bed? Safe enough to reveal to Iris whatever he'd found out? Or was he even now lying dead, some vital drip dangling from a stand, disconnected prematurely from a now lifeless arm?

'Hello, Kat. I expect you want to know about the money?'

Kat swallowed hard against a surge of nausea.

'Please tell me you've got good news, Iris,' she whispered.

'Kat, I have good news. Enrique sent me everything about twenty minutes ago. He also said to thank you for the police protection. I've just been reading it through and making a few cross-checks, but I'm satisfied we've solved the mystery. I have the identity of the beneficial owner of the offshore trust.'

Kat's stomach was fizzing with excitement. She felt like laughing, or possibly crying. Or maybe both at once. Was it Ethan after all?

'Oh my God. You star! So?'

As Iris revealed the name of Kat's mystery benefactor, dark curtains swung shut across her vision. Her head seemed to topple forward off her neck.

Ignoring the vertigo leaving her feeling like she was on the deck of a storm-tossed ship, Kat asked Iris to repeat herself.

As Iris spoke, Kat's mind whirled. The implications of what Iris had uncovered were profoundly shocking.

'Are you there, Kat? Hello?'

'Sorry, yes, I'm still here. Look, Iris, I can't thank you enough. You've literally saved my career, but I really have to go. Can we meet up soon for dinner and a few wines? My treat.' She heaved in a breath. 'In fact, let me get us tickets to the ABBA show in London.'

'Yes, I'd like that very much. Both of those things. Oh, and I've emailed you a sworn affidavit confirming every detail of the paper trail. It's beyond the burden of proof for any employment tribunal or disciplinary panel to exonerate you. I'll see you soon, then, Kat. Bye.'

Iris hung up.

Kat pushed her chair back and hung her head between her knees.

She unclenched her jaw. Her teeth were painful from grinding them together as Iris had spoken. The anger coursing round her system like poison was making her light-headed. There'd be a reckoning for this. But it would have to wait.

She called HMP Bronzefield and made arrangements to visit Laura later that evening.

'Highly irregular' was how the tutting assistant governor put it.

'I'm trying to prevent a miscarriage of justice,' was how Kat put it. 'So you can either agree to my request right now or we'll take it to the Home Office.'

That seemed to do the trick.

Now for a conversation that would make asking Frank Strutt if he'd been shagging his niece-in-law look like a fireside chat.

Chapter Fifty-Seven

She headed out. She could think about the best approach on her way over to Hampton Lane copshop. Assuming Will was there. But if he was her man, she didn't want to tip him off by phoning first.

As Kat approached her car, a sudden movement off to her left made her jump. She whirled round to find Ethan Metcalfe striding towards her. He looked unwell. Pasty-faced – or was that his normal complexion? – dark circles under his eyes. Pale lips he appeared to be gnawing. He carried a large bunch of crimson roses, wrapped in black tissue paper.

He came to a stop no more than a foot away from her. His eyes, magnified by his gold wire-framed glasses, were wild, staring. He looked seriously short of sleep. Her pulse kicked up a notch.

What he did next took her completely by surprise. He knelt in front of her. For one ludicrous moment she thought he was going to propose. Instead, he pushed the flowers up at her.

'Peace offering?'

She shook her head. 'No thanks, Ethan. I don't want them. And for God's sake, get off your knees. You look ridiculous. What I *do* want is for you to stop calling me at work. Do you know you left seven messages for me? That's really inappropriate.'

'Inappropriate! I am your greatest fan. I am *literally* an online advocate for you. Look, I know all about the 3C-ACU investigation.

It's totally bogus, of course, but you need all the help you can get right now. And I can help you, Kat. I really can.' His voice took on a whiny tone she didn't like. 'Why won't you let me help you?'

What could she say?

Because you're a creep?

Because I'm a detective and you're a podcaster?

Because I'm worried you're stalking me?

His eyes narrowed and his top lip curled back from his scummy teeth. Her stomach turned.

'You don't like me, do you, Kat?' he asked, flinging the flowers to one side, where they hit the windscreen of a white Ford Mondeo and bounced on to the bonnet, shedding blood-red petals that slithered to the ground.

'It's not about liking you, Ethan. It's about being a professional. Now, if you'll excuse me, I have to go.'

She turned away, but he grabbed her shoulder.

She whirled round, hands up, ready to push him off or punch him. But he backed away, hands held up in surrender. 'Sorry, sorry, sorry – that was bad – uncalled for – I respect you, Kat – I respect all women – shouldn't have invaded your personal space.'

The words came out in a stream, and he wasn't making eye contact as he spoke.

'That's right, you shouldn't,' she snapped, looking over his shoulder but finding the car park empty apart from the two of them. 'That was assault, Ethan. I could arrest you right here. Is that what you want? To spend the night in the cells?'

'No, of course not,' he muttered. 'It's just, why can't you see how much I want to help you? We'd be so good together. A team! Yes, it would be unorthodox, but think of our advantages over the criminals. You know, you with your official police access and detective skills, me with my journalistic instincts and IT skills.'

261

Wow. Ethan had really lost it. She took another step towards her car, getting her keys out and sliding them between her knuckles.

'Ethan, this is real life. Not a podcast. Not some Netflix crime show. People are being murdered and it's my job to catch the killers. Which is what you're stopping me from doing. I'm asking you—' She stopped herself, gripped the keys tighter. 'No, you know what? I am *telling* you to get out of my way and leave this car park, which is a restricted area. Stop leaving messages for me. And stop referring to me on your stupid bloody podcast. I'm not interested in it, or you. Just leave me alone!'

Shaking, she turned away from him and thumbed the Golf's key fob. As she climbed in, Ethan shouted at her.

'You only care about people after they're dead! What's wrong with you?'

Breathing too fast, and not liking it, she put the Golf into gear and hit the throttle. The car lurched backwards. Swearing, she slammed the brakes on. The car stalled. After restarting the engine and this time selecting first gear, she pulled away.

As she drove past Ethan, she resolutely refused to look in his direction. But in her rear-view mirror she could just discern him standing alone among the cars, his arms raised from his sides as if crucified.

Maybe she should talk to someone in Response and Patrol about him. Make sure he didn't get inside the precincts of Jubilee Place again. She texted Liv and told her to watch out for Mutt-calf hanging round the house. The last thing she wanted was Ethan laying siege to her home. Or worse, conducting some half-arsed stake-out and spotting Liv without her disguise.

Forcing her thoughts away from Ethan, she started running through possible ways to open up the conversation with Will Paxton.

As she pulled into the car park at Hampton Lane, she thought she'd found an angle that might just work.

She locked the car and headed for the front desk.

Kat introduced herself to the civilian receptionist, who said she'd try DC Paxton's number for her.

While she waited, a couple of uniforms passed behind her, one in a smart black turban and sleek beard, bitching about how you couldn't hold on to anything in a cop shop unless you locked it away. 'More tea leaves in here than the Typhoo factory,' he said to her with a wink, clocking her police lanyard.

'He's gone home for the day, DS Ballantyne,' the receptionist said. She dropped her voice. 'To be honest, he's been doing that all week. Leaving early. Stress. You know, what with Laura being arrested and everything? I think it's broken him. He looks permanently on the verge of tears, poor lamb.'

Kat thanked her, storing away this new piece of information. Would an abuser really be 'broken' if his wife was in prison? Bolshy, maybe, eager to have her back. But on the verge of tears?

Could be an act, cynical Kat said.

Let's see for ourselves, realist Kat replied.

Chapter Fifty-Eight

Will showed Kat into the sitting room. It smelled unaired, musty. A can of Heineken stood on a side table beside the same armchair he'd been slumped in the last time she'd called round.

'How are you holding up?' she asked.

'How do you think? They're going to charge her any day now. Then that's it. She's gone from me. I mean, Christ, Kat! She's going to plead guilty. The defence brief will try to offer mitigation, talk about her mental health, but that's the trouble,' he said, rubbing at eyes already red-raw. 'Because we didn't believe in drugs or therapy, there's no evidence. The prosecution'll say it's all an act to get leniency. She's looking at twenty-five years, easy. How's she going to cope? You know her, you know what's she's like.'

Kat nodded. The receptionist's words came back to her. *Poor lamb.* Was she about to commit a huge mistake? Too late for second thoughts now.

'Will, I've been thinking how you and I can get Laura out of Bronzefield. And I think that her mental health does actually hold the clue. But to do that, I'm going to have to ask you some difficult questions. Now, I need you to hear me out and not take them personally. Can you do that for me?'

He scrubbed a hand over his stubbled chin. Took a swig from the can.

'Ask away. My life's already coming apart, I think I can handle some intrusive questions.'

'Thank you. I've been wondering whether Laura might have some sort of inferiority complex, or maybe it's persecution or a need to be punished. I'm not a psychologist.' She smiled. But his dark eyes remained as flat and expressionless as a dead fish's. 'But has she ever suggested that she thinks you're, I don't know quite how to put this . . .'

'Spit it out, Kat. Has she suggested I'm what?'

'Abusive?'

'Abusive.' His voice was as flat as the dead-eyed stare he'd just given her.

'Yes. I'm wondering whether – in her mind, obviously – she thinks she'd be safer in prison.'

He leaned forward. 'From me, you mean?'

'Yes.'

'You think I'm *abusing* her?'

'I'm asking whether you think she might *believe* that. Because of her issues.'

He leaned back again, took a long pull on his beer.

'Look, Kat. I appreciate what you're trying to do for Laura. Really, I do. But do you have any idea what it's like being married to someone with needs like Laura's?'

'I don't, Will, no.'

'Well, I do. She wasn't like it at first. It was perfect for a year or so. Then these behaviours, they just sort of crept up on me. She started refusing to go out. Said she'd be happier staying in. She'd go to bed and not get out for days. Not shower, anything. I tried to talk to her. Find out what was wrong, but she just used to ignore me, or even shout at me.' He sniffed loudly, and knuckled his eyes. 'Once, I was loading the dishwasher and she yelled at me because I wasn't following her system. I tried to do it how she wanted but she started screaming and then she picked up a skillet and hit me with it.'

Kat tried to picture her petite friend lashing out with a heavy bit of cast-iron cookware. How well did she really know Laura, after all? Nobody in this dammed case was who they appeared to be. Did that go for Laura, too?

'I'm sorry.'

He brushed her apology away with a sweep of his hand. 'Look, I admit I'm not the perfect husband. I'm a cop, after all. You know what the job demands of you. Late nights, early mornings. Working on the weekend. I try my best, but honestly, sometimes I'm just glad to be out of the house for a bit. You know, going to the pub after work when I should go straight home to Laura?'

Kat nodded, thinking of her earlier call with Van. And her text to Riley. He still hadn't replied. Was he angry? Or, worse, not even bothered?

'And you don't think there's anything you've done that she might have misconstrued as abuse? Nothing that would have led her to confess to a murder she didn't commit?'

'I shook her just the once. I'm not proud of it. But she was just totally unresponsive. Catatonic. I'd cooked her a meal. Healthy, you know? Lots of fresh veg, organic sockeye salmon with butter and fresh dill. I'd read this book and it said good nutrition is vital for mental health. She just left it to go cold. When I asked her if she wanted me to cut it up for her, she screamed at me and lashed out. The whole lot went flying.' He shrugged. 'Told me I knew what she liked and if I was a good husband, if I really loved her, I'd know that. I'm afraid I lost it. Grabbed her by the shoulders. I shouted. I'm not proud of it. But it was like shaking a rag doll. She went limp. I just left her to it. Went out and got drunk.'

He could be lying, of course. Abusers were extremely clever at concealing their activities. But she had to admit to herself, his story did fit the facts.

And now she was wondering whether she'd been wrong about Laura all along. If Will was telling the truth, then Laura had brained him with a saucepan for not loading the dishwasher correctly. Lashed out over the plate of home-cooked food. It all sounded pretty controlling. Could she have been wrong about her friend all along? Behind the meek little mouse who sang 'The Wheels on the Bus' for a job, was there an unpredictable and violent control freak?

She thanked Will for his time and left him to his Heineken and his TV.

It was 5.15 p.m. Time to leave for the meeting she'd booked with Carve-up and DI Senior.

Savage pleasure and adrenaline coursed through her as she drove back towards Jubilee Place, making her foot tremble on the throttle.

Chapter Fifty-Nine

No doubt sensing he was about to 'take the win', Carve-up had really gone to town.

He'd laid on a cafetière of what smelled like freshly brewed coffee and put a plate of biscuits beside it. Red and gold foil, segments of pale and cocoa-brown shortbread, rippled chocolate coatings: he'd been out specially. She spotted the purple box in the wastepaper basket. Waitrose. No doubt he thought he could be magnanimous in victory.

For the meeting, Carve-up had installed a digital interview recorder on the credenza beside his desk.

He was trying – not very hard it seemed – to suppress the trademark smirk that kept creeping over his lips. Kat might almost feel sorry for him. He'd placed DI Senior beside him, so that the two men appeared to be a mini judging panel.

Fine by her.

'Close the door behind you,' he said.

Unnecessarily in her opinion. Although, given what she was about to do, she was sorry he hadn't instructed her to leave it open – the better to display her final humiliation to the rest of the department.

'Shall I be mother?' he asked in a mincing tone as he poured coffee for DI Senior. 'Milk?'

'Not for me.'

'Sugar?'

'No, thank you.'

Of course. Anti-Corruption types were all the same. Didn't like to show any signs of weakness such as enjoying sweetened coffee.

He poured one for himself, and then another for Kat. He picked up the plain white china milk jug and tilted it decorously towards Kat's mug.

'Kat?'

Unbelievable. Only now that he imagined she was about to confess to wrongdoing did he have the decency to use her name. She shook her head.

'Help yourself to biscuits, everyone.'

Carver nudged the plate of temptations closer to Senior's right hand. He shook his head. Kat imagined jamming one of the thickly coated treats up Carve-up's nose.

'Right then,' Carve-up said, actually rubbing his hands together. 'Let's get this over with. I'm recording this interview so we all have access to a single source of audio verification. You, DS Ballantyne, will definitely want a copy for your disciplinary hearing. So, earlier, you led me to believe that you accepted you had run out of time and had no wish to drag proceedings out to the bitter end. Hence why you called this meeting with DI Senior and myself.' He leaned back, and ran his thumb and finger over his peacock-blue silk tie. 'Why don't you tell us everything? Sooner it's out in the open, sooner we can all move on, eh? No need to make this any more painful than it has to be.'

Kat nodded. She strove to keep a straight face as she spoke in a faltering voice. 'I totally agree, Stuart. First of all, I want to say that I now appreciate just how much of a stain police corruption is. Not just on Hertfordshire Constabulary, but on the service as a whole, and wider society.'

She glanced across the desk. Carve-up was a much better actor than she was. Nodding along, his face grim. Senior looked like a vampire eyeing up a virgin as the last rays of the sun disappeared behind a nearby mountain.

'Continue,' Carve-up said.

Kat nodded. Essayed a gulp. Somewhat stagy, she thought, but to judge from his gloating expression Carve-up bought it.

'Taking money, whether a few pounds, or fifty thousand, from an organised crime group or even an individual wrongdoer, is obviously completely and utterly inappropriate . . .'

She'd chosen this word carefully. Carve-up snapped up the bait.

'It's more than "inappropriate", DS Ballantyne. It's criminal.'

Kat nodded. Even ventured a little lip wobble. 'Which is why I am happy to confirm that the money that appeared in my current account a week ago was a gift. Wholly unexpected, but a gift nonetheless. From my father, Colin Morton. You play golf with him, I believe, DI Carver.'

A muscular spasm afflicted Carver's entire face. His goateed jaw worked as though a mouthful of expensive fillet steak had turned out to contain a lump of gristle. His eyes flicked left and right.

Beside him, Senior made a note.

'You can't possibly know that,' Carve-up said. 'It was a Swiss account. Numbered.'

Kat held up a printed-out copy of Iris's email. She passed it to Senior.

'The document I have just handed to DI Senior is a sworn affidavit from Iris Hart. Iris is a chartered accountant. She is also an accredited Home Office forensic accountant. She is very happy to provide 3C-ACU with a list of her credentials. They include working on numerous fraud cases for forces including Hertfordshire Constabulary since 2012.

'Although, for reasons known only to himself, my father decided to route the money via the aforementioned Swiss bank account and a series of offshore trusts, Ms Hart has definitively identified him as the ultimate beneficial owner.' She swallowed. What she was about to say wasn't a lie. She had no evidence to the contrary. But it still felt like biting into a rotten apple. 'My father runs a property business in Middlehampton named Morton Land. The firm's accounts are audited every year. All corporation and other taxes are paid in full and on time.'

Next she quoted from 3C-ACU's own regulations.

'You might recognise this next statement, DI Senior,' she said with a smile before reciting the text she had committed to memory.

'"A gift from a parent to a child or vice versa cannot be construed on its face as a corrupt payment unless there is *prima facie* evidence of the monies being used to procure commercial, financial or other advantage. For this charge to be considered, there must be, as a minimum, a) an identifiable trail of money flowing from donor to recipient and b) a reciprocal flow of valuable and confidential information from recipient to donor *that would not otherwise be available to the donor.*" Which there isn't.' She glared at Carve-up, whose face had curdled. 'Or not between my father and *me*, at any rate.'

Carve-up reacted to this as if stung by a wasp. 'What's that supposed to mean?'

'Nothing, Stu. I was just denying to DI Senior that I supplied confidential information to my father. Why?'

Trapped, Carve-up switched tracks.

'If it really was him, why didn't he come forward straight away to clear your name?'

'I don't know. It's something I plan to ask him myself. Along with why he went to such lengths to disguise the source of the money.' She turned to Senior while picturing her dad with a

Taser's barbs stuck into his chest. 'My father has a peculiar sense of humour.'

Senior folded the document and slid it into an inside pocket. He turned to Carve-up.

'Anything to add, DI Carver?' He waited. Carve-up appeared paralysed. Kat had seen statues with more life in them.

'*I* have something to add,' Kat said.

Senior nodded. Then his mouth did something odd, the lips twisting out of shape as if he were in pain. After a couple of baffled seconds, Kat realised he was smiling.

'Go ahead, DS Ballantyne.'

'I believe someone told DI Carver that the money was going to appear in my bank account before the transfer took place, and its source. A communication he chose not to disclose at the time. He knew an awful lot of detail about the Swiss account and so on. That has to be worth a look, don't you think?'

And with that, she rose from the visitor chair, leaned across the desk, ignoring Carve-up, and shook DI Senior's hand.

'It's been a pleasure.'

Resisting the urge to give the door a Riley Ballantyne special, she left it wide open and strolled back to her desk.

Chapter Sixty

With enough time to pop home before setting out for HMP Bronzefield to see Laura Paxton, Kat drove to Stocks Green.

On the way, she considered what to do next about her father.

When Iris had said it couldn't be a corrupt payment because it came from her father, Kat had kept her lips tight shut. How much, and yet how little, Iris knew about her father's business dealings.

But when Kat had asked him, he'd flatly denied it. And she'd believed him. Stupid woman! Well, that was the last time she'd allow him to get away with telling lies. First that dreadful revelation about Jo, her half-sister – murdered before Kat could even say 'Hey, sis.' And now this.

But why? Why would her dad work so hard to conceal a huge payment into her account? The answer was so obvious, her nausea resurfaced and for a moment she thought she'd have to pull over to vomit. She heaved in a breath, and another, and another. Her head swam, but the nausea passed.

She had proof. Her own father had set her up for an anti-corruption investigation. Worse still, he'd tipped off Carve-up. But why? What possible reason could he have for trying to get her kicked off the force?

Molly's voice came back to her. Uttering the short sentence Kat herself had quoted to Tom.

The simple reason is usually the right one.

So, why *would* a businessman whose only crime was greasing a few palms want to remove a homicide cop from her job?

Because . . .

She gripped the wheel tighter as the answer swam into focus before her eyes like a ghastly head-up display.

. . . it wasn't his only crime.

Chapter Sixty-One

Kat couldn't remember the rest of the drive. She'd negotiated roundabouts, traffic lights, the various left and right turns she needed to make to arrive home, on autopilot. Instead, her mind was consumed with a single horrifying thought that spun round and around like a never-ending fairground ride from which she couldn't emerge.

The only people frightened of murder detectives were murderers.

Not thirty minutes earlier, she'd been imagining a row about the money. A vicious, recriminatory row involving screamed accusations and blustering denials, demands for the truth and flimsy excuses involving bad-taste practical jokes. A row that would have shattered their precarious relationship for ever.

But now?

Now she was frightened to have that confrontation. Because spreading out at its base, like a rotten root ready to topple the whole family tree, was a dark, ugly suspicion. Colin Morton had done something dreadful and he was worried his daughter was going to dig it up.

'No!' she shouted as she turned off the ignition. 'Not tonight, Dad. You're not screwing up this moment for me.'

She left the car resolved to wall off the suspicion blooming inside her like a toxic black fungus. Maybe she was wrong. Maybe there would prove to be an innocent explanation. Maybe she was just being paranoid.

Yeah, right. And maybe Carve-up would have applied for a transfer to Aberdeen by the morning.

'Hello!' she called out as she dumped her bag inside the front door. 'Anybody home?'

'Hi, Mum,' Riley called back. His voice cracked again, as it was doing more frequently these days to his annoyance and, despite their love for him, Kat's and Van's amusement. Hidden amusement, but still.

She found her son at the kitchen table, bent over a maths textbook. Liv was smoking in the garden. She spotted Kat and waved.

'Dad around?'

'He took Smokey out for a walk. Said he'd be back later.'

She bent and kissed the top of his head. He twitched her off, tutting. She wanted to tell Van, but in person, not over the phone.

'What's the homework?' she asked, putting the kettle on.

'Algebra. I mean, what even is the *point* of algebra? Why not just use actual numbers? It's not as if anyone needs algebra in the real world, is it? Like, I'm hardly likely to go into a shop and say, "Oh, hi, can I get a-minus-b apples," am I?'

'To be fair, you're hardly likely to go into a shop and buy any apples at all.'

'That's not the point and you know it! God! You're so lame.'

'Sorry, darling. Been a trying day.'

He slapped his pen down on the workbook. 'Caught your murderer yet?'

'Nope.'

'Found out where the money came from yet?'

'I have, actually.'

He grinned. 'Who?'

She smiled back, though the effort cost her. 'You were right all along. Grandpa.'

'Seriously?'

'Seriously.'

'But you said he didn't.'

'Maybe it was Grandpa's idea of a joke.'

Riley pulled his mouth to one side. Scratched the top of his head with his pen.

'How much was it again?'

'Fifty thousand pounds.'

He grinned wolfishly. No, he looked too innocent. Maybe wolf-*cub*-ishly.

'Can I have some?'

'No!'

'Why not?'

'Because it's still fishy, that's why.'

'*Fishy*,' he repeated in a tone that suggested anyone who looked a fifty-K gift horse in the mouth needed their head examining.

'As a fish pie with extra fish.'

He rolled his eyes.

She ruffled his hair and left him to his homework, then went outside to join Liv, who was sitting on the swing set.

'So, I found out who sent the money. And it wasn't Ethan. It was my dad all along.'

Liv's eyes widened. 'I *told* you! The lying bastard! What the hell was he thinking? You said you could have been sacked. Charged with corruption. We should go over there together. Tell him what a total dick he's been.'

'We really shouldn't.'

'Well, you need to sort him out, then. This is serious.'

'Er, hello? I did, just, manage to work that out by myself.'

Liv bit her lip. 'So, what *are* you going to do?'

'I don't know. I need to pick the right moment. You said it yourself. He can't be trusted.'

'I said he was a lying bastard.'

'Exactly. So I can't just barge into his office. He'll just stonewall me or say it was all a mistake.'

Kat stared at the trees beyond the back fence. Oh, it was a mistake, all right. One she'd make him pay for. But with the truth this time.

Chapter Sixty-Two

HMP Bronzefield was a privately operated prison. Kat noted that the company behind it was the same one that ran the canteen at Jubilee Place. Wondered whether the prisoners got better food than the cops did.

In full sun, the administration block might have been a public library. Terracotta facings and gold-coloured brickwork. Although the red-and-white-striped barrier pole and guardhouse did under-cut the impression somewhat.

It still might have passed for a council building or even student accommodation. She glanced up at the narrow windows. No rows of empty vodka bottles or Post-its spelling out anti-tuition-fee slo-gans, however.

After passing through the various levels of security, she was finally greeted by a bespectacled young woman wearing a colourful batik headscarf.

'I'm Chidimma, Laura's peer worker.'

Kat followed her down a corridor lined with artworks created by prisoners. One picture caught Kat's eye: a stark image, in radi-ant, over-saturated reds, greens and yellows, of a woman's face. She looked past the viewer as if unconcerned, or maybe angry, at being observed. Her face radiated sadness, although she wasn't crying.

The image stuck out amid the paintings and collages of landscapes, wildlife and scenes of family life.

Chidimma led her into a room that reminded Kat of the 'friendly' interview room at Jubilee Place. A new-looking sofa upholstered in nubbly brown fabric; a matching armchair. A blond wood coffee table on which rested a box of tissues and a stripy-leaved plant in a pot. Plastic, Kat noted.

'If you'll wait here, DS Ballantyne, I'll fetch Laura.'

A few minutes later, Chidimma was back, accompanied by Laura Paxton in a baggy grey T-shirt and lilac jogging bottoms. A pair of fluffy pink slippers completed the outfit.

'How are you coping?' Kat asked once they were alone.

Laura shrugged. She avoided making eye contact. 'It's all right, I suppose. Food's pretty manky.'

Her voice was a monotone. She didn't so much sit as sag into the armchair's squishy cushions.

'Any trouble from the other prisoners, you being a copper's wife?'

Laura shook her head. 'None. It's because I'm a murderer. You get respect for that.'

Kat had met cocky murderers before. Both pre- and post-conviction. You could see the thrill it gave them. All she saw in Laura's eyes was a sort of overwhelming tiredness. Like she was resigned to her fate. No bravado. No swagger.

Was this the face of a domestic monster who'd tried to brain her poor, long-suffering husband with a Le Creuset? She couldn't see it, however hard she looked.

Either way, Laura had given Kat the opening she needed. And it had come almost before she was ready. But she had her questions prepared, so all she had to do was ask them.

'Laura, that's why I'm here. You see, I know you *didn't* murder Alanna. And maybe you haven't heard this, but since you've been on remand here, Callum Michie has also been murdered. I believe by the same person. That seals the deal, really, doesn't it? Why don't you tell me what's going on? Why you confessed to a murder you didn't commit? Who are you covering for?'

Laura's eyes flickered into life. Her lips tightened and her fingers crawled together in her lap and began twining around each other. 'Why are you doing this to me? I *did* commit it! I strangled her and I wrote that word on her forehead with her lipstick. You found my DNA on it, right? And on the tie?'

Laura didn't sound angry. To Kat, her friend sounded frightened. Desperate.

'Yes, we did. And normally that would be enough for me. But nothing about it makes any sense. Not your stated motive for killing her. Not the method. Not the lack of injuries you would surely have sustained as Alanna fought for her life. We've discussed all this.'

Laura had been shaking her head as Kat talked. 'No, you're wrong. It *was* me. Why won't you *believe* me? You *have* to believe me!'

'I don't believe you because it isn't true. Listen to me, Laura. Here's what must have happened for your story to be true. You strangled your friend to death. That took between five and ten minutes. Apart from a brief time when she might have been unconscious or winded, she would have been struggling. Thrashing around. Clawing, kicking, scratching, doing whatever ever she could, desperate to stay alive.

'At no point during that awful, interminable period of time, as the life force gradually left your friend, did you stop. You carried on with that act of extreme violence that female murderers, even from the most broken and abused backgrounds, never use except occasionally on children, yanking that tie so tight it cut into her throat, until she was dead.

281

'And after she was dead, with her lifeless corpse contorted on the floor in front of you, perhaps even lying back against you, you went up to her bedroom, selected a lipstick and scrawled an insult on her skin.

'But then, out of nowhere, after behaving basically like a psychopath, *now* you felt guilty? *Now* you felt remorse? You expect me to believe that, after all that brutality, *now* you came to your senses and called me to confess? I'm sorry, Laura, it doesn't wash for me, and I don't think it will wash in court. I think your barrister will make the same points I'm making. They'll argue that you're being coerced or that you confessed while the balance of your mind was disturbed. I think, once the judge has studied the evidence, they'll agree, and dismiss the case. They're not going to want to jail an innocent woman.'

This was a lie. Kat was sure that, given the court backlogs and the insane pressure on everyone from clerks to barristers to judges, cops to jurors to solicitors, they'd be happy to 'take the win', as Carve-up would put it.

Laura's reaction startled her. She leaned forward so suddenly Kat reared back in surprise.

'No! They have to find me guilty! They have to! I *need* to be in prison. I can't go back.'

'Why?' Kat asked softly. 'Why can't you go back, Laura? Back to what?'

Laura's gaze flattened out again. She slumped into the armchair. Her face, animated as if by electricity a moment ago, resumed its saggy muscle tone.

'Nothing. I murdered her. I should be punished.'

'Will says you struggle with your mental health. Is that right?'

The beginnings of a wry smile twitched across Laura's lips.

'He said that?'

'Yes.'

'Well, I must then, mustn't I?'

Kat found her answer interesting. It was the sort of response Riley would give. A huge verbal shrug. A surrender to superior force. A tone that said, *I didn't do it but you're not going to believe me, so fine, whatever you say, can I go now?* Did Laura see Will as the one holding all the cards? The sane one? The one who tried his best but was never good enough? Or was it simpler than that? Did she genuinely feel he had superior force on his side?

Kat smiled at Laura.

'How do you struggle, Laura? What specifically is wrong with you?'

Laura shrugged. Her gaze skated off to one side. She was buying time. Kat had seen it many times before in other, less cosy interview rooms than this one.

'The usual.'

'Sorry, Laura, what do you mean by that?'

'Anxiety? Depression? Eating disorders?'

'I'm really sorry. But I'm puzzled. When we've played netball together, you've always seemed pretty happy. Out there on the court, or in the changing rooms. Maybe not the life and soul of the party, but you know, basically OK.'

Laura barked out a sardonic laugh. 'Maybe I'm just good at hiding things.'

Kat studied her. Yes, maybe she was.

'Will said you don't take any medication for it. Can you tell me why?'

Laura was nibbling at her lower lip. As Kat watched, she nipped a loose piece of skin between her teeth and peeled it free. Scarlet blood beaded. Laura winced and plucked a tissue from the box to staunch the bleeding.

'I tried, but the side effects were bad. I got vomiting and diarrhoea, headaches, insomnia. I flushed them down the toilet.'

Kat retrieved a phrase Will had used. 'So it wasn't because you don't believe in medicating the human condition?'

Laura snorted. 'What? No! That sounds like some kind of wellness crap from an Instagram influencer.'

Interesting. 'Ever try therapy? Lots of people swear by it.'

Laura swallowed. Her gaze flitted away from Kat like a trapped songbird caught inside a house. As Kat sat, perfectly still, waiting for an answer, Laura seemed to retreat into herself. Her arms crossed in front of her body, hugging around her narrow rib cage. She looked off to one side, turning her whole head away from Kat. It was as if she hoped she could make herself invisible.

Laura shook her head. 'Therapy can't cure my problems. I'm tired. I'd like to go now, if it's all the same to you.'

Kat was desperate to get through to this somehow *absent* woman sitting in front of her. Her body language alone spoke eloquently to her state of mind. The woman was terrified. One last try.

'Laura, does Will bully you? Does he hit you? Is that why you confessed to Alanna's murder? Made up that story about his affair? To get away from him?'

'No! We love each other!' Laura started crying. 'I want to go. Please. You can't *make* me answer your questions.'

Chidimma got to her feet, her expression one of barely suppressed anger. 'Laura, my love, do you want me to take you back now?'

'Yes, please,' she said, getting unsteadily to her feet.

Alone in the room, Kat swore in frustration. She knew Laura was lying but she couldn't prove it, and nor could she force her to open up about the killer's identity. Maybe she was telling the truth after all. Maybe Frank Strutt had found a way to put pressure on her. God knew, he had enough experience.

She got to her feet. She'd just have to find another way to the truth.

On the drive home, the realisation that she was free of 3C-ACU hit her again. Kat smiled and tapped out a little drumroll on the Golf's steering wheel. So the day hadn't been a total bust. Maybe they'd go out for family dinner on the weekend to celebrate.

She also had the delightful problem of what to do with the money. For now it could stay where she'd put it, transferred over from her current account into her deposit account. With interest rates creeping up, she might even earn enough to pay for the family's pizzas.

Sliding the key into the front door at 10.15 p.m., she heard laughter.

Riley's hee-hawing adolescent squeaks and pops as his poor overstressed vocal cords tried to find a comfortable register. Van's deeper snorts. And, interweaving with both male voices, Liv's unmistakable shriek.

Chapter Sixty-Three

Frowning, yet also intrigued, Kat went into the kitchen to find her two boys seated at the table with Liv, who caught her eye and rolled her own clownishly.

'I was just telling Van and Riley about the risks of milking with cold hands.'

Kat leaned over and kissed Van. Riley shied away as she neared him. As clear a piece of body language as she'd ever encountered in an interview.

Don't touch me. Not cool.

'Glass of wine, darling?' Van got up from his chair. 'We've had a couple already, I'm afraid.'

'That would be lovely,' she said, tightly. 'Riley, bit late for you to be up, isn't it?'

His face darkened. 'Dad said it was OK. It's Saturday tomorrow. And I *am* thirteen now.'

'Well, I'm thirty-four *and* your mum, and *I* think it's time you were in bed.'

'Oh, let Ri stay up a little bit longer,' Liv said. 'He's got loads of great stories about the college. Do you remember how stuck-up we always thought they were?' She turned to Riley. '*You're* all right, obvs.'

Liv and Riley fist-bumped.

Kat felt cornered. It made her unaccountably angry with her friend and her husband. While she'd been out working, driving down to Bronzefield and back on a Friday night, they'd been larking it up. Drinking wine and swapping apparently *hilarious* tales about school and Liv's efforts as a bloody milkmaid.

'Can I, Mum. Please? Just till eleven?'

Kat checked her watch. 'Half ten.'

Riley batted his eyelashes at her and made puppy-dog eyes. 'Ten forty-five?'

'Or you can scoot off now. Your choice.'

'Ten thirty works for me.' He turned to Liv. 'Does it work for you?'

'I guess it'll have to. The boss has spoken.'

And then she winked. She actually bloody winked at Riley.

Kat took a slug of the wine. Felt the alcohol hit her stomach and then, seconds later, her bloodstream. Rather than relaxing her, it opened the locked gate behind which she'd been corralling her emotions.

Any day now Laura was going to be tried and sentenced to life. Safe from prosecution, the real killer could have her silenced behind the grim forbidding walls of whichever Victorian hellhole they sent her to, closing the loop altogether. All this, plus the shocking revelation about her dad, and Kat's growing suspicions about his motives.

Her temper burst its banks.

'I can see how much fun you three seem to be having, but I'm trying to prevent my friend being sentenced to life for a murder she didn't commit, so forgive me if I'm a little tetchy.'

At once, the mood changed. Liv leapt to her feet, staggering slightly. Kat wondered how much wine she'd had. She rounded the table and took Kat by the shoulders, staring deep into her eyes. 'Oh my God, I'm so sorry, Thelma. What's going on?'

Kat slid her eyes in Riley's direction. Shot Liv a meaningful look. But Riley caught it anyway. Now that the air had well and truly gone out of the balloon, he seemed not to care about his just-negotiated bedtime extension.

'Night, Dad; night, Mum. Night, Liv.' He paused at the door. 'You're mum's coolest friend. Like, by miles.'

Kat sat in Riley's chair. Drank some more wine. Sighed.

'Sorry to come in like a thunderstorm on a bank holiday. But I'm really up against it on this case. I've got until 3.00 p.m. on Monday, then it's going to the CPS.'

'Where were you just now, love?' Van asked, covering her right hand with his left.

'HMP Bronzefield. But before we get into that, ask me how the rest of my day went?'

Van grinned. He knew what had to be coming. But, bless him, he played along. 'How was the rest of your day, darling?'

She clapped her hands together. 'It was epic! Iris came through. I thought maybe Liv or Riley would've told you.'

Van shook his head. 'Please say it wasn't your dad.'

'Yes, it bloody was!' Kat drained her glass and went to fetch another cold bottle from the fridge. 'After denying it to my face as well. He had this whole nest of companies set up. The trail ended up in the Bahamas in an offshore trust with one C bloody Morton Esquire as the sole beneficial owner.'

Van looked thunderous. 'Why the hell would he do that to you?'

The air went out of Kat's balloon too. She'd been trying to sustain at least the semblance of a good mood after being exonerated. But it was like someone scared of flying reaching their holiday destination. Sure, you could enjoy yourself, order a cocktail, sit by the pool with a trashy novel, eat in nice restaurants. But there was still the return flight. And boy was it bumpy.

She entered the clear-air turbulence of her own anger.

'Because he's a lying, manipulative bastard who—'

She stopped herself. Accusing her dad of some unspecified murder probably wasn't a wise course of action.

'Who what?' Van prompted.

She gulped some wine down. 'Who for reasons I intend to find out, decided to completely bloody betray me. I mean, he went out of his way to make me look corrupt, hiding the money trail halfway round the world and' – another gulp – 'it looks like someone tried to kill Iris's contact in the Bahamas.'

Van blanched, sending his pale Scottish complexion into a very pasty place indeed.

'You're not suggesting your dad had something to do with it?'

Kat spread her arms wide. 'Honestly, I don't know what I'm suggesting.'

'I wouldn't put it past him.' This was Liv, who was glaring at Van. 'He's a creep. Always so smug about his money, even though it's obvious how he makes it.' She turned to Kat. 'Sorry, mate, but he never liked me, and I guess the feeling rubbed off.'

Kat shook her head, sighed out a shuddering breath. 'It's fine. I honestly don't know what to think. But the money came from an account he controls, and he denied it to my face more than once. Why would he do that, Van? Why would he try to get me kicked off the force?'

Poor Van. She could see he was struggling to process all this. As she was herself. Up till two seconds ago, the worst her husband had thought of his father-in-law was that he was a bit dodgy. Now she was expecting him to concede the man might be a murderer.

'I don't know, darling,' he said finally. 'And you're sure it was him who sent it?'

'Iris told me he's the beneficial owner of the account.'

'And nobody else could have, I don't know, hacked into it?'

'It's an offshore bank account, Van, not Gmail.'

He held his hands up in surrender. 'I'm just struggling with this, that's all.'

'Sorry, sorry,' she said, rounding the table to hug him. 'Me, too. I need to talk to him.'

'You need to *arrest* him,' Liv interjected. 'Get him in one of those windowless rooms with the tape recorder and the wonky chair.'

Kat grinned. 'And shine the desk lamp in his face.'

Liv's mouth quirked upwards as she smacked a fist into an open palm. 'Soften him up a little first.'

It was too much. She and Kat dissolved into laughter. Van shook his head.

'So that's it,' he said, accepting a refill from Liv. 'You're off the hook?'

'Yep.' Kat held her own glass out for a top-up. 'Had a meeting with Carve-up and the 3C-ACU hyena this afternoon. Even managed to drop Carve-up in it at the end. I'm a free woman.'

She heaved a huge sigh, shaking off the stress that had been clamped over her shoulders like a kitbag full of riot gear.

Van half rose from his chair and leaned across the table to kiss her.

'Well done, darling. I hope he looked suitably chastened.'

Kat wrinkled her nose. 'Carve-up? Chastened? It's not in his repertoire of facial expressions. He looked like a sheepdog caught gnawing on a lamb bone. Anyway, I'm sorry for snapping. Apart from the business with my dad and the money, today has not been my finest.'

'It's fine. But I am going to leave you two with the wine. I've had too much already,' he said, getting to his feet.

'Lightweight,' she said, kissing him.

Alone with Liv, Kat sipped her wine.

'I don't know how I'm going to get through to her, Liv. She's clearly hiding something, but I can't get her to open up. I started thinking maybe her husband's an abuser. I asked her but she said no. She just sits there passively, while I try everything I can to persuade her she'd be better off talking to me. She just withdraws into herself. It's almost like she's trying to make herself disappear. You know? Become invisible. No eye contact, no animation, nothing.'

As Kat described Laura Paxton's attitude, Liv's eyebrows drew together.

'I've got a friend on the farm,' she said in a quiet, thoughtful tone. 'Her name's Connie. She arrived six months ago with her daughter in tow. Audrey's eight. You could have been describing Connie just then. Can you guess why she came to join us?'

Kat didn't have to think too hard or too long.

'To escape her husband?'

Liv nodded. 'Bastard. Women get that whipped-dog look after a couple of years of control. They just try to vanish. They learn that anything they do – *everything* they do – is going to be picked apart, criticised. They're punished for it, or demeaned and belittled some more. In the end, they just give up. Connie looked haunted for three months. Even now, she hides when anyone comes to the farm. Audrey's a bit better but she still gets this frightened, watchful look. You know? Like a mouse when there's a cat around.'

Kat shook her head. 'I just told you I asked her whether her husband's abusive, but she flat-out denied it. Said she loves him, and he loves her. And it does fit with what he's told me.' She frowned as a memory bubbled up: Kat comforting a woman with a fresh black eye who'd insisted she'd walked into a door. 'She *could* be lying, but if she is, she's the best I've ever come across.'

Liv shook her head vigorously. 'There were girls like Connie who ended up in Shirley House, too.' Liv was referring to the children's home where she'd lived until turning eighteen. 'They'd been abused to the point they thought they deserved it. I used to tell them they should've hit back, or run away, but they couldn't imagine doing it.' She banged a fist down on the table. 'God, it used to make me so angry. Still does. They were beautiful, innocent, sweet girls, and those men just turned them into something less, you know? Like half-people.'

Kat nodded. Because it all made sense now.

Chapter Sixty-Four

Kat was up early on Saturday.

No alarm clock needed. Her brain pulsed and throbbed beneath the thin bones of her temples. She'd stayed up far too late with Liv, drinking more wine and setting the world to rights.

First things, first: a couple of paracetamol. Then maybe some fresh air would soothe her pounding head.

After walking Smokey, she made toast and coffee.

Liv appeared in the kitchen doorway. Dressed and with her rucksack dangling by its strap from her hand.

'Morning, lovely.' She yawned. 'I need to head back to the farm.'

Kat experienced a pang of sadness. Despite the brief blow-up the previous night, she'd loved having Liv around.

'Oh. OK. Got time for a coffee before you leave?'

'God, yes. And I'll have *that*!' she said, snatching the slice of toast out of Kat's hand and taking a bite. She came closer. 'I've loved this, you know, Kat. Seeing you, meeting Van and Riley. It's been fun. And it was so cool helping you get the info out of Muttcalf. We're going to see each other more often, now, aren't we?'

Kat smiled. 'Of course we are! And it was really great, you having my back like that. Like old times.'

'Always and for ever,' they said in unison.

◆ ◆ ◆

Once Liv had left, waving frantically out of the car window, Kat drove over to Chamberlayne Avenue. For now, she'd decided to leave Laura's reasons for confessing alone and return to the business of evidence.

The previous day, Tom had reviewed every bit of CCTV footage he'd been able to find from the street on the morning of Callum Michie's murder. And had come up with nothing.

But Kat had dug deeper. Reviewed the door-to-door spreadsheet. And found a couple of houses where they'd not been able to speak to the householder. One in particular had caught her eye.

Number 15. Right next door to the Michies.

The note read, *Nobody home. Call back.* Which, so far, nobody had done.

Arriving in the tree-lined avenue, she pulled up outside the neighbour's property behind a sleek blue sportscar, and walked up the short gravel drive. A white transit van bearing the name of a building firm occupied the parking spot in front of the house. The discordant shriek of an angle grinder at the rear of the property had her massaging her temples.

She rang the doorbell. A regular push-button model. No inbuilt camera. Scanned the eaves. Couldn't see any tell-tale boxes or discreet white plastic housings, although there was an alarm bearing a well-known Middlehampton security firm's logo. She waited, hopes fading.

The door was opened by a man in his forties, stylishly rumpled in a navy linen jacket, white shirt and faded jeans. Bare feet. Nice-looking.

'Can I help you?' he asked with a smile, rubbing a stubbled chin bisected by a raw-looking scratch.

Kat produced her warrant card and introduced herself.

'Are you Mr Robinson?'

'That's right. Matt.'

He held out his hand and they shook.

'I'm investigating the murder of your neighbours.'

'Yes, I—' He frowned. 'Wait. Neighbours, plural? You don't mean—'

'I'm afraid Mr Michie has also been murdered. Yesterday morning.'

'Jesus! I got home really late last night. I've been away on business. I thought the crime scene tape was still there from Alanna. This is awful. Is it some kind of vendetta?'

'Why would you say that?'

Robinson frowned. 'Well, you know, a married couple both murdered within a week of each other. That looks suspicious, wouldn't you say?'

'*All* murders look suspicious, Mr Robinson, that's rather the point.'

He looked crestfallen. Kat winced as the angle grinder shrieked against something hard and metallic.

'Sorry. Not your fault. Let me start again. When my colleagues were conducting their door-to-door enquiries after Mr Michie was murdered, you weren't in.'

'That's right. Like I said, I was away on business. Portugal. I'm a location scout for the movies. I do a lot of work on thrillers. Maybe that's why my mind went to the idea of a vendetta.'

She looked at his chin. 'How did you get the scratch?'

He touched it with a fingertip. Winced. 'Nasty thornbush half-way up a hillside in the Algarve.'

'You might want to put some Savlon on it. It looks infected.'

He shrugged. 'I probably should. I don't look after myself properly. Not since the divorce.' He offered a self-deprecating smile. 'Sorry, probably too much information.'

'Can I ask, Matt, do you have any security cameras on your property? We're trying to find anyone who might have inadvertently captured the killer on video.'

He shook his head. 'None on the house, I'm afraid—'

'Oh, well, it was worth a shot. Sorry to have wasted your time.'

He held a hand up. 'Hold on, Detective Sergeant. I said there are none on the *house*. But my car has them. It's a Tesla Model S.'

'Is that the one parked on the road?'

'Usually it's on the drive, but I need to keep it clear for James and his lads.' He nodded at the builder's van. 'Teslas have this feature called Sentry Mode. If it's enabled, they start recording when anyone gets too close. It's all-round vision, too.'

Kat felt it, then. A flame of excitement flicker into life. 'And is *yours* enabled?'

'It is, yes. In fact, I got an alert yesterday as I was getting off the plane. Some guy got a little close. Basically knelt down right behind it. Do you want to see? The footage is on my laptop. Come in. I can make some coffee.' He smiled. 'You look like you could use a cup.'

Five minutes later, perched on a chrome barstool with a red leather top, Kat was sipping a mug of freshly made coffee from a bean-to-cup machine in Robinson's impressively high-tech kitchen.

While he set up his laptop, she checked out the room. He was clearly a keen cook. Expensive-looking kitchen knives were ranged along a magnetic strip to the left of the hob, jars of varicoloured pasta clustered against a pillar, and a long thin marble rolling pin sat in a wooden cradle on the glittering grey granite work surface.

Her pulse picked up. Here she was, talking to a man, while drinking his delicious coffee, who lived next door to the two murder victims. He was tall, fit. Kat stared at the rolling pin. Long. Narrow. Cylindrical. Wondered if it had a groove or even an imperfection around its circumference.

She was seized with a sudden desire to take a swab from the just-healed wound on his face. Edged away from him, just a little, under the pretext of making herself more comfortable on the stool.

'It's popular with golfers, isn't it? The Algarve?' she asked casually.

'It's fantastic! I'd have loved to fit a few rounds in, but work, you know?'

'You play, then?'

'After a fashion.'

Her pulse sped up.

'Do you belong to the club here? MGC?'

'It's full of ghastly salesmen and overweight business types, but yeah, I do. Why?'

She shrugged. 'No reason. Do you socialise much with the other members?'

'Maybe the odd dinner if the restaurant's nice.'

She nodded. 'Kind of like the police. Sometimes, if we've just closed a case, we have these dinners. They can get really messy, you know? Wine splashing everywhere. Suits getting ruined. I swear the dry cleaner's on Union Street is only in business because of us. Yours are probably a lot more civilised.'

He nodded. Not smiling. He pointed at the satin-finished silver MacBook.

'Here we go.'

On the screen, footage from Robinson's car's 360-degree cameras from the previous morning spooled along at impressively high resolution.

Kat advanced the video until the timestamp read 10.15 a.m. Then she sped through at four times the normal speed.

'There!' Robinson said from beside her as a dark figure flashed in and out of shot.

She rewound and this time played the footage of the intruder at half speed. The figure, a man dressed in black, was in shot for fifteen seconds.

He approached the car from the rear, heading in the direction of the Michies' house. Then he stopped, crouched down and took something from his pocket. A short black tube. A collapsible baton? It could be.

Her suspicions of a moment ago vanished as she peered at the screen.

The man's long-billed black baseball cap obscured his face. She caught a glimpse of a moustache.

'It's annoying, isn't it?' Robinson murmured from beside her. 'If only he'd take it off.'

'Annoying' would just about cover it, Kat thought, willing the mystery man to push the cap back to scratch his head. Was that long hair emerging at the back? It was hard to tell. His build was bulky, although to Kat it looked more like the result of thick clothing than the guy's physique.

And then, he stood up. As he did so, he turned towards the car and presented his face, in glorious, full-colour HD video, to the camera. Kat hit the pause button.

She stared open-mouthed at the image. She recognised him. Even through the obvious disguise.

The shock was physical. Her stomach lurched as if she were on a rollercoaster.

Police corruption manifested itself in various forms, from taking money from criminals to perverting the course of justice. But murder? That was a first for her.

Mind you, Carve-up had made the jokey remark in front of her and Linda that scumbags like Callum Michie were hardly a great loss to society.

She swallowed. 'Can you send it to me?'

'Have you got an iPhone?'

'Yes.'

'I'll AirDrop it to you.'

With the footage safe on her phone, Kat headed home to collect a couple of items, then drove to HMP Bronzefield.

Chapter Sixty-Five

At the prison, a guard – whip-thin, bored expression – led Kat to a pale door marked *Recreation*.

'She's in there.'

Kat went in. Laura was facing the window. She started. Spun round, lower lip trembling.

'I've got nothing to say to you.'

Kat shrugged. 'I can't force you, can I? But it was quite a long drive, so shall we have a cup of coffee? Look, I brought some nice stuff from home.'

She took a flask out of her bag along with a packet of Mr Kipling's Bramley apple pies.

Minutes later, they were both drinking the coffee she'd made with hot milk before setting off.

'It's good,' Laura said.

'Have a pie, too.'

'Thank you.'

'Listen, Laura, since I came to see you yesterday, I've found something out about Callum Michie's murder. I think it really changes things. Come and sit beside me.'

She took her phone out, synced it to her MacBook and pressed play on Matt Robinson's video.

Hip to hip, the two women sat facing the laptop. But as the figure in black emerged into frame for the first time, Kat switched her attention to Laura, alert to her reactions.

Laura's cheek twitched and she let out a breathy gasp. Little by little, the blood drained from her face, accentuating the greyness everyone called 'prison pallor'. As the figure on screen removed the black cylinder from his trouser pocket, she started shaking her head.

'No, please, no,' she moaned in a childlike voice. 'I don't want to see this.'

'Keep watching, Laura, please.' Kat strove to keep her tone neutral. The last thing she wanted to do was bully this fragile, vulnerable woman. 'Just another few seconds.'

The figure – the killer – straightened. And revealed himself.

Chapter Sixty-Six

Laura emitted a deeply unsettling sound as she watched her husband on the video. Somewhere between a moan of the purest agony and a cry. She covered her mouth with both hands, one on top of the other.

Kat put a comforting arm around the other woman's heaving shoulders.

'I think we both know what this means, don't we, Laura? It means Will murdered Callum Michie. I'm guessing because he found out Callum had put a price on your head. Will couldn't allow that to happen because he wanted you back with him, under control. That's right, isn't it?'

'No.' She pulled her lower lip back in between her teeth, and started biting. 'I don't know.'

'I think you do. But let me tell you what *I* know. I know that the chances of Alanna and Callum Michie both being murdered by strangulation, by two different strangers, within a week of each other, in their own home, are close to zero. In fact, scratch that. They *are* zero. Now, with that video, I have enough evidence to go straight from here to your house and arrest Will on suspicion of murder. But I need your help, Laura. You see, on its own, the video evidence is enough for an *arrest*, but I'm just not sure it's enough for a *conviction*.'

'What do you mean?'

'I mean, if I can't find the murder weapon, then Will could just say, "Well, I was there, but I was just out for a walk. The object I'm taking out of my pocket in the video is a torch." Or he could claim it was a cigar tube, a collapsible walking pole . . . almost anything. Even if we *can* prove it's a baton, his lawyer could easily explain it away. Will's a serving police officer, after all.'

'What would happen then?'

Kat shrugged, hating herself for this very necessary piece of play-acting, but sure that in the end it would help both her and Laura Paxton.

'I'd apply to have his detention increased but his lawyer would argue against it, and my inspector would probably order Will's release.'

'So he'd be basically free?'

'I'm afraid so, yes.'

Kat paused. She'd thought of various approaches to this next question. The question that might solve two brutal murders and save an innocent woman in the process. None had seemed quite right as she'd tried them out in the car on the drive down.

'Tell me honestly, Laura,' she began, letting her insights guide her words. 'How would you feel if Will was released without charge?'

Laura's mouth worked. Tears rolled freely down her cheeks. Without appearing to notice, she reached for a tissue and began shredding it methodically, rolling each torn fragment into a tiny white worm that she let fall from her fingers on to the wooden table.

Kat waited, keeping her breathing steady and slow. The ticking of the white-faced wall clock filled the room. She watched as the slender red second hand completed a full circuit.

Through the sprung base of the sofa, she could feel Laura trembling violently. Her nostrils tingled with the rank smell of fear, an odour every copper who'd ever conducted an interview with a suspect learned to distinguish.

'Laura, you can tell me,' she said, into the silence. 'I know you're frightened of him. I don't know exactly what he's done to you, what he *does* to you. I do know you thought confessing to Alanna's murder would mean you'd escaped him. But it's not right to sacrifice your life like this. There are other ways to keep yourself safe. Ways I can help with. As a Crown witness in a double-murder trial you would be eligible for police protection.'

Laura whirled round.

'Yes, but for how long, hey? A week, a month? And what would happen when the money ran out? I'm basically a sitting duck. He could just serve his sentence and come for me once he gets out.'

She clapped a hand over her mouth.

But it was too late. She'd just admitted she knew Will was the killer. And why she'd confessed in the first place.

Kat pressed her advantage home. 'You could enter the witness protection scheme. We'd make sure he could never find you.'

Laura was still shaking her head. But there was less energy to the metronomic movement than there had been just a few minutes ago.

'You don't know that. Will's a detective. He could find me.'

'Not if you give me a full statement, Laura. Not if you tell me what you know. I think Will is guilty of not one but two premeditated murders. The fact that he's a serving police officer is what the courts call an aggravating factor. I doubt he'd see the outside world for at least twenty-five years. Are you really going to pass up this opportunity to get away from him?'

Laura inhaled deeply. 'I can't. I'm sorry.'

Kat desperately wanted to bring Laura round. But every appeal she'd made to her friend's own self-interest had so far failed. Laura was seemingly determined to go down for Alanna's murder. Perhaps she was calculating on staying inside for life. And in the women's estate, where Will would never be able to reach her.

As the seconds ticked by, she saw one, final approach that might work.

'Tell me how you met Alanna,' she said.

Laura looked round at her. Surprise showing in her eyes.

'It was after netball. I was late finishing getting changed. I stopped for a cup of tea in the cafe and she was there. She had a latte, I remember. The place was full so I asked if I could share her table. She said yes and so I sat. She asked me what I was doing there and when I said playing netball she laughed and said she thought that was just for schoolkids. We just got talking after that. I got the impression she was a bit lonely, like me. So we agreed to meet in town for a coffee. It just went on from there.'

'You liked her.'

Laura smiled. 'She was so different to me. Glamorous. Lovely clothes. She said her husband was a businessman, but I got the impression she meant something a bit, you know, dodgy. I didn't mind. *She* was my friend, not Callum.'

'Did she ever come round to yours?'

Laura shook her head immediately. 'That wouldn't have been . . . appropriate. But she invited me to hers. So lovely. And that kitchen . . .'

'You got to know each other quite well.'

Laura nodded. 'After a while she gave me a spare key. Asked me if I'd go round and water her houseplants when she and Callum went away.'

'Is that how you got in after Will killed her?'

Laura's head bobbed. 'Y—'

She gasped then covered her mouth again. Stared down at the table, now speckled with tissue fragments. She smiled sadly.

'You're good, Kat, do you know that? Better than Will,' she added in a low voice. 'They said at his last performance review he needed to improve his interviewing skills. Apparently, he talks more than he listens. He was so mad.' She paused and looked away, somewhere far from the prison. Rubbed her right arm, high, where a T-shirt sleeve would cover a bruise. 'That was not a good night.'

'He murdered your friend, Laura. I think it's time you tell me what happened. Time he faced justice for what he did to Alanna.'

'And Callum,' Laura said, nodding.

'Tell me.'

Kat set her phone recording and laid it on the table. Raised her eyebrows in a mute appeal for permission. Laura nodded again. Inhaled a deep but steady breath.

Chapter Sixty-Seven

Laura looked away from Kat, focusing on a distant place only she seemed able to see.

'It was early Monday morning. Will started going on about how I was getting too friendly with Alanna. He said she wasn't the right sort of person for a police officer's wife to be hanging around with. You know, because of who she was married to. I said we were just friends. Will got really angry. I can always tell because his breathing goes really still. He doesn't shout or anything. But he gets this watchful look. Like he's, I don't know, like some kind of wild animal creeping up on its prey.'

'Did he hit you? Is that where you got the bruise on your forehead from?'

'That was unusual for him. Mostly he likes to hit me where the bruises don't show, you know?'

Kat knew only too well. She'd read enough medical reports on abused women's injuries. Breasts, bellies, kidneys and upper thighs were their abusers' favourite targets. Her heart filled with pity – and anger – as Laura began filling in the details of the cruelties Will had inflicted on her.

'What happened next?' she asked softly.

'He told me to go and stand in the spare bedroom, facing the wall. I wasn't to come out until he called for me. I heard him moving around the house. Cupboards opening, stuff like that. Then he went out. He slammed the front door.'

'And what did you do?'

Laura looked round, surprised. 'I waited like he told me, of course! Sometimes he likes to trick me. He'll go out then sneak back in. He caught me once, back in the kitchen, making myself a cup of tea.' She shuddered, touched her belly. 'I didn't make the same mistake again.'

'How long do you think he was gone for?'

'About an hour. He called me down and he made me stand in front of him. He said, "You don't need to worry about your so-called friend Alanna Michie any more. You won't be having any further contact with that slag." And I said, "What do you mean?" or something like that. He said, "I killed her."'

'Those were his exact words?'

Laura frowned. Closed her eyes. 'No. He said, "I've *just* killed her." I think I screamed. He slapped me. Then he said nobody would ever trace it back to him because he'd set up someone to take the fall for it.'

Kat saw it clearly. At the golf club dinner, Will had seen his chance when Christopher Miller had got wine on his tie. Maybe he'd even spilled it himself in order to steal it. *My bad, mate. Here, take it off. I'll get it dry-cleaned for you.*

'Then what?' Kat said gently.

'I was crying. He told me to stop it or he'd really give me something to cry about. And then I said I didn't believe him. I was out of my mind, Kat. I would never have stood up to him otherwise. I said he was lying. Alanna was alive. So he told me to go and take a look for myself. Held his hand out. He had Alanna's spare key in it.'

Kat saw it, then. How the rest of that morning had played out for Laura. But she needed to have it on record in Laura's own words.

'What did you do?'

'I took the spare key, and I drove to her house. I let myself in and I saw her lying there, her face all distorted and horrible. I broke down. But then, out of nowhere, I saw a way out. If I confessed to the murder, I'd be locked up for life. I'd be free of him.'

'You weren't worried he'd find a way to get in to see you?'

'No. He might be a cop, but they can't force you to see visitors.'

'And there really was no other way out you could see?'

Laura shook her head. 'If I'd stayed, he'd have killed me in the end. It's what they do, isn't it? Recently he's been hitting me more, and doing worse things.' A fat tear rolled down her cheek. 'Sexual things. So I wrote that word on Alanna's forehead and I used the lipstick. Then I pulled really hard on the tie. You know, so I'd get my DNA all over it.'

'And you wrote "cow" because you couldn't bear to use anything stronger. She was dead and you didn't want to insult her memory.'

Laura nodded. 'I hated myself for doing it, but I thought poor Alanna was already dead and maybe she'd understand.'

'Why do it at all, though?'

'Will's always explaining how you get these cranks who confess to every murder. How the police keep a detail back to screen them out. I was the only one who knew about the lipstick. You'd have to believe that I'd killed her.'

'I see.'

Kat wanted to tell her that calling from the scene of a murder and confessing was good enough for an arrest at least, but she held back. It didn't matter. Not now anyway. Maybe Will's lawyers would try to make something of it. But that was looking too far ahead.

First, there was a certain police officer she had to see.

After reassuring Laura everything would be all right, and inwardly praying she was telling the truth, she left her at the prison. As Linda had said, Bronzefield was still the safest place for her.

For now.

Chapter Sixty-Eight

She was waiting for him outside his house.

She'd called him repeatedly since getting home from seeing Laura at Bronzefield, leaving message after message. He'd finally answered late that night. He'd been 'away with the lads'. Refused to talk on the phone, merely saying he'd see her at his house at 6.30 p.m. the following day.

So now she sat in her Golf and waited, staking out Carve-up's boxy, post-divorce terrace house like he was a third-division villain. After the way he'd worked with her dad to have her booted off the job she loved, she hated him more than ever. But she needed him. Chain of command.

His scarlet Alfa Romeo finally entered the cul-de-sac at 6.41 p.m.

Kat jumped out and went to stand at the end of his weed-punctured concrete drive while he pulled off the road. He scowled at her through the windscreen.

'It's Sunday,' was all he said when he climbed out. 'Do we really have to talk shop at the weekend?'

Kat breathed in. Held it for a count of three. Let it out again. Hoped she could trust herself to speak without shouting.

'If you'd returned one of my calls yesterday, Stuart, we could have done this then.'

He smirked. 'Track day up at Silverstone, wasn't it? Bunch of us DIs went up. No offence, DS Ballantyne, but I'm hardly going to interrupt a day like that to talk to you, am I?'

'And today?'

He shrugged and went to the back of the car. Hefted a bag of golf clubs out of the boot.

'Inter-force golf tournament. See previous answer.'

'I'm sorry I interrupted your fun. Can we go inside?'

He grunted as he lifted the rattling bag of clubs on to his shoulder.

'Come on, then.'

He made no offer of coffee, which suited Kat fine. Straight down to business.

'I've solved the Michie case,' she said.

'Which one?'

'Both of them. It's Will Paxton. He did Alanna *and* Callum. I've got him on CCTV outside Callum's on the morning of his murder, dressed all in black with a really shonky disguise, taking a weapon of some sort out of his pocket. Plus Laura Paxton's changed her story. She now says Will told her he killed Alanna.'

His eyes widened and he smiled. He actually smiled. 'You're joking.'

She felt like slapping the smirk clean off. 'No joke, Stuart. This is the real thing. I want to arrest him.'

'I hope you're one hundred per cent sure about this,' he said. 'Because of all the things I could be doing today, listening to you make a case for an arrest of a brother officer, a detective no less, is pretty low down on my list.'

'It's him. Laura told me what really happened.'

'And you're certain she can be trusted?' He twirled a finger at his temple. 'I heard she had mental health issues.'

'Ever hear of coercive control? He's been abusing her. Sounds like he might have been raping her, too. She told me she was terrified he'd kill her, so she confessed to Alanna's murder to get away from him.'

'Why should we believe her? Maybe he does knock her about a bit. But if anything that gives her more of a motive to commit murder and get herself sent away.'

Kat stared at her boss. Was he serious? Despite all the evidence pointing away from Laura, *that* was his response? Of course it was. Corrupt *and* stupid.

'She's gone on record, Stu. She explained what happened, how and why. It's enough for an arrest. And I want the full works. He's a violent man with access to weapons. He's a fight risk and probably a flight risk, too. I want uniforms and a firearms team in support.'

Carve-up's expression changed. His initial surprise now gave way to a look she'd seen many times before. A calculating expression as he weighed up not the facts, but the costs and benefits to him personally of making a decision.

'Well, of course I hear what you're saying, DS Ballantyne. And I can imagine how, to a female detective, this story about coercive control would sound really compelling, but you have to see the bigger picture. You see, what we have here, as I think I may have mentioned at the start of the week, is a slam dunk. We have a suspect whose DNA is all over the victim. She literally called you from the primary crime scene, and until, what, you coach her into changing her story so now *she's* the victim, she sticks to it like crap to a blanket. *I'm guilty, I done it,*' he keened in a grating, high-pitched voice he presumably thought sounded like Laura Paxton in distress. 'As I've been trying to tell you, take the win, DI Ballantyne. It's right in front of you. This can go to trial, she pleads guilty, gets sent down, and you, me, MCU, we all get a gold star on our sticker charts and a big green checkmark on the monthly clearances spreadsheet. Move on.'

As Carve-up had been talking, Kat felt her temper rising. Her heart was crashing against her ribs like it wanted to escape and help her beat the DI to death in his own kitchen.

'Stuart Carver, you are literally the stupidest, most arrogant, lazy, arse-licking, *pathetic* excuse for a DI I have ever met. No! That I've ever even *heard* of.' She held up a hand as he opened his mouth to interrupt. 'Do you actually believe the torrent of weapons-grade rubbish that just came out of your mouth? I mean, do you? I've just set out a totally solid case, with evidence, for a full-fat arrest and you *dare* to accuse me of coaching the witness? I'd laugh if this wasn't so unbelievable.'

He flushed. 'Now, just you wait a minute, DS Ballantyne.'

'No! *You* wait a minute, DI Carver. Will Paxton is guilty of two murders. He is also employing typical methods of increasingly violent coercive control against his wife, frightening her to the point she would rather spend the rest of her life in prison than risk spending another day in her marriage to him. I want to arrest him at 6.00 a.m. tomorrow morning and I want support. Either you agree and sort it for me or I go to Linda and ask her.'

He regarded her through narrowed eyes for a few seconds. Then he gave in. Raised his hands in surrender. That shrewd look was back.

'Look, I'm sorry, OK? I was out of line. I'd just got home after a long drive and I wasn't really in work mode, if you know what I mean? You say you like Will Paxton for it? Fine. Leave everything to me. I'll sort a firearms team, backup, the whole shebang. Go in hot and heavy and bring the creep in.'

Kat frowned, wrong-footed. 'That's it? You're changing your mind?'

313

He smiled affably. 'You'd rather I stuck to my guns? I mean that was quite the little speech, Kat. If we'd been in the office, I'd probably have to write you up, but I can see how emotionally invested you are in this dreadful business, so I'm going to give you a free pass this time. Just don't make a habit of it. Everybody at work knows we don't exactly see eye to eye without you tearing me a new one in the middle of the office.'

Heart still cantering along, Kat was having trouble suppressing the trembling in her leg muscles. 'I want the team to meet me for a briefing at 5.00 a.m.'

He nodded. 'Whatever you say.' Time for a quick trademark smirk. 'Guv.'

Shaking her head, she excused herself and left him there, filling the kettle.

Chapter Sixty-Nine

Despite the adrenaline running through her veins like high-octane petrol, Kat had to suppress a yawn before addressing the small group of officers in front of her.

'I want this to go smoothly. We have intel that places the suspect at the target address. Will Paxton is violent, and as a police officer he has access to any weapon you'd find in the armoury. That means anything from a Taser to a bloody machine gun. The AFOs go in first. Get him down and immobilised. Incapacitated only if absolutely necessary. When it's secure, I'll come in with Tom and make the formal arrest.'

In front of her, Tom was nodding and making notes. She saw his hand was shaking and offered him a quick encouraging smile.

Carve-up, surprisingly, had insisted on attending and stood at the back, leaning against the wall, sipping from a brushed aluminium travel mug.

Once questions had been dealt with, Kat nodded. 'Let's go. I'll see you all at the suspect's house.'

She took Tom and descended to the garage, where the metallic grey Volvo saloon she'd booked out was waiting for them.

'Ready for this, Tomski?'

'As I'll ever be.' He scratched his nose. 'Do you really think there's a chance he'll have a firearm?'

'I don't know, mate, I really hope not. Anyway, by the time we go in, he'll be surrounded by Middlehampton's finest AFOs pointing their big-boy guns at him.'

As she pulled out on to Crown Street, she watched the support vehicles follow her out of the car park. Eight officers ought to be plenty. She'd not performed an arrest with authorised firearms officers before. The thought of actual gunfire had her sweating, despite the coolness of the Volvo's interior.

Her thoughts drifted to the upcoming interview with Will Paxton. He'd have a lawyer with him, of course. No copper would ever consent to be interviewed without one, even for a traffic offence, let alone two murders.

As she rehearsed approaches and strategies, she drove on autopilot, making the correct turns to bring her to the Paxtons' house while leaving her conscious mind free to focus on securing the second confession of the case. This one genuine. It would be hard – but not, she thought, impossible.

'Where's the van?'

She snapped back into the present.

'What's that, Tomski?'

Tom was looking over his shoulder. 'The support van. It's not there any more.'

'It must have been caught at the lights on London Road.'

Tom wrinkled his nose. 'Why didn't he just put his siren on and blow through?'

He had a point. It was imperative they all arrive together. If Will spotted anything out of the ordinary, say he was up for a pee or an early morning cuppa, he could panic. Put two and two together and make trouble.

Kat called the chief AFO on her radio. But all she got was a brief spurt of static.

'Mine's out of charge. Tom, try yours.'

They were early at the address. She made the last but one left turn and pulled over as Tom tried to raise the support van.

'Nothing. Mine's dead, too. I'm sorry, Kat. I could have sworn I left it on charge on Friday.'

Kat shook her head. 'Not your fault. Happens all the time. I'll call Carve-up. See if he knows what's happened.'

Carve-up's phone went straight to voicemail.

'Crap!'

She pocketed her phone again.

Now what?

Chapter Seventy

By his calculation, it would take her no more than fifteen minutes to reach the Paxtons' house. He waited for twelve minutes then called the firearms chief.

'Tony? It's Stuart Carver here. Look, there's been a change of plan. We've got credible intel the suspect's not at that address. He's in the wind. Abort, OK? Come back for a bacon roll and a brew. We'll go through our options later, once DS Ballantyne's back in the office. Sorry for the early start. I'll call off the response team, too.'

Smiling to himself, he sat back in his leather executive chair. Then he picked up his phone again.

'Thought you might like to know our mutual problem's about to run into a spot of bother. Very high chance we won't have to worry about her after today.'

He hung up. Whistling to himself, he went down to the canteen. All that talk of bacon rolls was making him hungry.

Chapter Seventy-One

'Have you got a baton with you?' Kat asked.

'I didn't think I'd need one. I thought the AFOs would have him trussed up like a turkey before we even got inside.'

'Yeah, me too. OK, not to worry. There ought to be at least one in the boot. And we've got the element of surprise.'

'You're not saying we go in anyway, are you?'

'That's exactly what I'm saying, Tomski. Right now is probably our best bet to arrest this sod. He'll be full of sleep. Probably in his jammies. Soon as he opens the door you give him a nice hard shove – in fact, trip him, too. I'll come in right behind you. We're both screaming "Armed police! Armed police!" He'll be too disorientated to notice we haven't got guns. We get the cuffs on him and then, bang, it's done. Into the back and he's in the custody suite in time for me to treat you to breakfast.'

Tom looked doubtful. 'You said he had access to firearms.'

'Yes, I did. And it's possible. But realistically, I don't think he's going to come to the door brandishing a Heckler & Koch, is he?'

'He might. He knows he's committed two murders. He's a cop. Who else is going to be knocking on his door this early in the morning?'

Tom had a point. She had to concede that.

'Change of approach, then. I ring the doorbell. When he opens the door I smile and say I've got an exciting new development. Proof that Laura couldn't have murdered Alanna. I'll say we've got credible evidence Callum did it in a fit of jealousy.'

'So who killed Callum?'

'A friend of Alanna's from before they were married. No! An ex. A *violent* ex who just got out of prison.'

'Why are you coming round so early in the morning, though? Why not wait till a more civilised hour, or even go and see him at work?'

'It couldn't wait. I've been working round the clock to free Laura. I thought he'd want to hear it as soon as I had it.'

'That works.'

'Let's do this.'

They exited the car together. Kat rounded the back to open the boot. And swore. Nothing but zig-zagging sweeps of light and dark grey carpet where a vacuum cleaner had swept the liner.

Tom looked over her shoulder. 'Oh.'

'It's fine,' Kat said. 'We're this close. And the plan's sound. We won't need them.'

Tom nodded slowly. 'Boss?'

'Yes, Tomski?'

'Don't take this the wrong way, because I am absolutely not trying to be sexist here. But if it gets, you know, *kinetic* in there, will you let me put him down for you to cuff him?'

'That's very sweet of you. Yes, if it does get' – she winked, despite the roiling in her gut – '"kinetic", I hereby authorise you to use reasonable and proportionate force to subdue him. Now, ready?'

Tom went for a smile. 'As I'll ever be.'

As they walked across the road and up to the Paxtons' house, Kat tried to visualise the next few minutes. Striving to anticipate Will Paxton's reaction.

Would he fight? Run? Come meekly? In the end, as they reached the front door, she decided she'd just rely on her training, and her partner.

She rang the doorbell. Her breathing was pretty steady, but her pulse was racing.

It didn't matter. It would all be over soon.

Chapter Seventy-Two

The door opened.

Smiling, despite the effort it cost her, Kat took a half step back, a tiny signal that she wasn't a threat.

They'd caught him in the middle of his shave. The lower half of Will Paxton's face was white with peaks and swirls of foam. A stark pink strip stood out from his left cheekbone to the edge of his jaw.

His eyebrows shot up. The effect would have been comical if not for the fact they were about to arrest a violent, controlling man who'd committed two murders in the last seven days.

'Kat! What brings you here so early in the morning? I'm not even dressed.'

His eyes slid past her to Tom. Narrowed. She had to start talking, fast, before he became suspicious.

'I've got some news about Laura, Will. It's really good. I've got a solid lead on Alanna Michie's murderer. I think it could be her ex. He's just been released from prison. Eight years for aggravated assault. Looks like he did Callum, too. Can we come in?'

He nodded. His shoulders dropped.

'Yeah, of course. So when did you hear about this ex, then?' he asked as he let them in.

Kat nodded for Tom to follow her, passing a leather bag of golf clubs propped against the wall at the foot of the stairs.

'Just now, actually. I've been working insane hours to get Laura cleared.'

He led them into the neatly furnished sitting room. 'And you brought your bagman, I see?'

'Part of his training.'

'Ah, I thought he looked like a Bambi. How are you liking it working homicides, Tom?'

Tom smiled and stepped forward. Kat looked down. His fists were clenching and unclenching reflexively. She glanced at Will. He'd seen the twitchy movements, too.

Tom drew in a breath. 'Will Paxton, I am arresting you—'

Paxton lashed out at Kat, catching her a glancing blow on her cheekbone.

'Slag!' he screamed at her as she staggered back.

Before he could hit her again, Tom leapt between them and grabbed Paxton by the biceps.

'That's enough, you bastard!' he shouted.

Snarling, Paxton headbutted Tom and then shoved him hard in the chest with both hands. Arms windmilling, Tom stepped back in a vain attempt to regain his balance, but Paxton sliced a foot out and round, tripping him and sending him flying backwards.

He smashed down on to the coffee table. The glass shattered with a loud crack and Tom went through the metal frame before landing in a twisted heap inside the rectangle of welded steel.

Paxton dashed for the door. Kat was torn. She ought to go after him but Tom's face was white and he was clutching his right thigh. Bright red blood was welling around his fingers.

'Tomski!'

'I'm fine. Go get him, boss.'

'You're not. You're bleeding. We need help.'

'I'm fine!' he yelled. 'For a minute or two. Go, GO!'

Torn between her burning need to arrest Paxton and concern for her injured partner, Kat was paralysed.

Then everything turned white and pain ripped through her head, blinding her for a second. She staggered sideways. As she fell against the sofa she saw Paxton advancing on her, a large-headed golf club gripped in both hands.

As he reached her, she managed to roll sideways, off the cushions and on to the floor. Her ears were ringing, and dark spots kept blossoming in the periphery of her vision, but she managed to stand up and took a step back. She held both her hands up, palms outwards.

'You don't want to do this, Will. I'm a police officer, like you.'

'A bent one, from what I hear,' he sneered, breathing heavily through his mouth. 'I'd offer you a bribe but from the sounds of it you've got more money than you know what to do with.'

He shifted his grip and swung the heavy-headed club at her. She reared back and the chunk of highly polished steel whistled harmlessly past the tip of her nose. Then Paxton grabbed her by the shoulders and whirled her round. Before she could react, the shaft of the club was dragged tight against her throat. Paxton yanked her back against him, so close she could smell the soapy shaving foam on his cheeks.

'I've done it twice, I think I can manage another two,' he hissed right into her ear, then he wrenched back on the club, pulling the steel shaft hard into the soft flesh of her neck. 'Then we'll have to make it look like you and Bambi over there had a fight.'

Her pulse was throbbing painfully in her ears. She knew she only had seconds left before she blacked out. Was this how Alanna had felt? How Callum had?

Her unarmed defensive tactics course was a long time ago now, but there was one lesson she'd always remembered, because it involved cunning, not brute force.

Go with your attacker, not against him, the UDT instructor had told them. *He's not expecting it and the shift in weight unbalances him.*

She leaned into Will and drove her heels into the carpet, back-pedalling against him as hard as she could.

It worked.

The pressure on her neck eased, then disappeared altogether as he lost his balance and fell behind her, tripping over Tom's outstretched legs as his grip on the club slipped.

He crashed down among the shards of glass from the shattered coffee table.

'Bitch!' he screamed.

Coughing, wheezing, eyes streaming, her head agonisingly painful, Kat looked around for something she could use as a weapon. Her eyes fell on a pine bookcase. And a gold and silver metallic object about ten inches tall.

She grabbed it and whirled round to face Paxton, who had just got to his knees. He was swearing constantly, a stream of violent, pornographic language as the sharp slivers of glass tore through his pyjama trousers and lacerated his knees.

'I'll kill you, you c—'

The rest of the word was drowned out as, with a yell, Kat swung her improvised club and connected solidly with the left side of his head. Will Paxton's eyes rolled upwards until all that was showing were the whites. He keeled over sideways, thankfully away from Tom, coming to lie in a heap among fragments of smoked glass.

'Tomski!' she gasped. 'Are you OK?'

'Yeah,' he said tightly. 'Gonna need a few stitches, I think. Cuff him, Kat, for Christ's sake, before he comes round.'

Kat pulled her handcuffs out and snapped them around Paxton's wrists after dragging them behind him. For good measure, she took Tom's pair and cuffed Paxton to the frame of the ruined coffee table.

'Boss?'

Tom's voice sounded odd. Faint, somehow, as if he'd exhaled all the air in his lungs first.

'Yeah, Tom?' she said as she reached into her pocket for her phone.

'I think you need to get that ambo over here fast.'

Then his eyes closed, and his hands fell away from his thigh. Scarlet blood hosed from the wound.

'Oh my God! Tomski!'

Kat dropped her phone and drove her fist against Tom's thigh. The shard must have pierced an artery. Her hand was immediately soaked in blood.

'Tourniquet,' she hissed. 'Tourniquet.'

She dragged the belt out from Tom's trousers and threaded it around the top of his thigh, right into the crease of his groin. After feeding the free end through the buckle she yanked it as tight as she could manage, gritting her teeth as she pulled it tighter still.

With the buckle secure, she gingerly let go of the free end. It held, but blood was still flowing out of the wound, and there was a foot-wide pool beneath Tom's leg. His face was deathly pale, and behind his closed eyelids, she could see fluttering movement.

Now she called 999.

'I'm a police officer.' She gave them her collar number. 'I have another officer down.' You weren't meant to say the injured party was a cop. Supposedly it could cause the ambo crew to take unnecessary risks getting to the scene. Nobody she knew – cops or paramedics – cared. 'He's bleeding badly from a wound in his thigh. He's unconscious and unresponsive. Please, hurry,' she added.

She reeled off the address and hung up.

She ran into the kitchen and came back with a couple of tea towels, which she folded into a thick pad. She jammed it over the wound and then, for the next five minutes, maintained the pressure while she waited for the ambulance.

When the paramedics arrived and broke the front door down with a splintering crash, she was almost in a trance, murmuring the same words over and over again to Tom's immobile form.

'Stay with me, Tomski. Stay with me.'

She looked up into the brown eyes of the female paramedic.

'Rosemah, it's Tomski. He's lost a lot of blood.'

'I know, Kat, but it's going to be all right,' the short, efficient woman said. 'Can you sit there for me, my love? We'll take it from here. Ryan's taking care of him.'

Kat let Rosemah help her up and place her on the sofa. Groaning, Will Paxton raised his head off the floor.

Kat spoke in a low, even voice. 'Will Paxton, I am arresting you on suspicion of the murders of Alanna Michie and Callum Michie. And on suspicion of the attempted murder of DC Tom Gray. You do not have to say anything, but it may harm your defence if you do not mention, when questioned, something you later rely on in court. Anything you do say may be given in evidence. Do you understand what I have just said to you?'

He nodded.

'Say it!'

'Yes! I understand.'

He lay his head down on the carpet and closed his eyes.

Kat watched as Ryan and Rosemah manoeuvred Tom's limp body on to a stretcher.

'Look after him,' she said. 'Tell him I'll be up to see him as soon as I can.'

Tom's blood had soaked into the carpet and spread out to where the object she'd used to disable Will Paxton lay on its side.

The tiny metal golfer's head lay half submerged in the glistening red carpet pile.

Chapter Seventy-Three

Finally, backup from Jubilee Place arrived.

Will Paxton was fully conscious by this time, although Kat had warned him that if he moved a muscle or uttered a single word, she'd use the golf trophy on him a second time.

Once he'd been removed from the property and taken to Jubilee Pace in a marked car, she pulled on a pair of gloves and covered her shoes in booties and started an initial search. She was looking for one thing in particular.

Upstairs, she opened the door to a small bedroom furnished as a home office.

The room was bare apart from a desk and office chair. In a wire in-tray was a pile of identical sheets of paper. They looked like the type of forms that regulated every aspect of police life. Red and grey boxes containing headings in all caps.

They were headed *PERMISSION REQUEST*.

She picked up the top sheet.

Under the heading *REQUESTED ACTIVITY*, someone – Laura, Kat assumed – had written in a soft feminine hand: *Play netball. Wednesday, March 20th, 2024. From 7.00 p.m. to 10.00 p.m.*

Another heading read *PEOPLE INVOLVED*. Laura had written the names of the Malbec Mafia team, including Kat's.

Across the whole thing, at a forty-five-degree angle, an official-looking stamp had been applied. In red ink, it said, simply, *APPROVED*. A scrawled but legible signature across the stamp showed that Will Paxton had given his wife permission to play a game of netball with her friends.

Kat flicked through the rest of the sheets. Among the 'requests' were shopping trips, visits to see Laura's parents and doctor's appointments. She was just about to throw them down in disgust when a sheet caught her eye. Laura had asked for permission to have coffee with Alanna Michie the week before she was murdered. This piece of paper bore a different stamp, applied so heavily the red ink had smeared.

DENIED

Suddenly, Kat was filled with a violent rage. She wanted to drive back to Jubilee Place and, in an old-school, 1970s manner, take Paxton into a dim, stinking, concrete stairwell out of view of any cameras and shove him down it.

Swallowing down the emotion, so strong it left a sour, metallic taste at the back of her throat, she continued her search.

In the second drawer down, resting on top of a pile of computer paper, lay a collapsed ASP-21 extendible baton. She nodded with grim satisfaction. The idiot had kept it.

Somewhere in the baton's telescopic sections, she knew Darcy Clements would find skin cells belonging to Callum Michie, maybe even flecks of blood or saliva. If they were lucky, Paxton would have left his own DNA on it, too. She remembered the fleck of foam Darcy had recovered from Callum's neck wound. The padding of the baton's handle. Paxton must have grazed Callum's throat with it as he strangled him to death.

◆ ◆ ◆

After checking in with Julia Myles, the custody sergeant, Kat went in search of Tony Kaminski, the chief AFO. She found him down at the range, where he was watching a posse of new recruits shoot 9mm pistols.

The air was full of the acrid stink of burnt propellant. She sneezed violently.

'What the hell just happened, Tony?' she demanded, hands on hips.

He looked surprised. 'What do you mean?'

'One minute you're there, the next we're on our own. Tom and I nearly got killed this morning,' she said, massaging her throat. 'It was only because I smacked Paxton with his own golf trophy that I'm here at all.'

Tony's brow, a roll of muscle over a thick ridge of bone, lowered still further. He ran a hand over his shaved skull, which gleamed in the overhead lights.

'You went ahead with the arrest?'

'Yes, we went ahead with it! What did you *think* we were going to do?'

'Carver stood us down. Said he'd got credible intel the suspect was on his toes.'

Kat's mouth dropped open. This was incredible. Carve-up had just escalated so far beyond his usual petty acts of bullying or patronising name-calling.

'You're sure about that, Tony?'

'Yeah, I think my combat-addled memory can just about recall what a senior officer told me a couple of hours ago.'

Kat shook her head. Then she looked up into the six-footer's blue eyes. 'Sorry for shouting, mate. This wasn't on you.'

Over the racket of six Glock 17s being fired in unison, she left the range and went in search of Detective Inspector Stuart Carver. Not trusting herself to behave. Not caring, either.

She found him in his office. Where else?

'You bastard!' she shouted, not bothering to close the door.

The look on his face as his head jerked up was so transparent, he might as well have used one of Will Paxton's stamps to print *GUILTY* on his forehead.

'DS Ballantyne,' he choked out. 'You're back.'

Her heart was thumping, and her breath came in short gasps. She wanted to vault his desk and choke him with her bare hands.

'Surprised, are you? Yeah, I'm back. Tom isn't, though. He's up at the hospital with his femoral artery held together with his own belt and a couple of tea towels. He nearly died, Carver, and I'm going to see this comes back on you.'

'I don't know what you're talking about.'

Kat had heard a lot of lies in her career as a police officer. Some more convincing than others. This one lay at the very bottom of the entire, festering pile.

'You pulled Tony Kaminski's team off.'

'I did no such thing.'

'Don't lie to me. I just spoke to him. He confirmed it. He said you told him you had credible intel Paxton had fled. You stood him down, you bent bastard! Were you actually hoping Paxton would kill us? Because he very nearly did.'

Carve-up was shaking his head. He was trying to get himself worked up into a state of righteous indignation. But he was failing, badly, His pale cheeks were blotched with pink and he was having trouble meeting her gaze. Probably just as well; it would have burned his eyes right out of their sockets.

'A misunderstanding. I said go carefully because we had intel he was armed. He must have misheard me. The line was atrocious.'

And then Carve-up played a terrible card. 'It's his word against mine. I'm the ranking officer. Talk to whoever you like, you'll only make yourself look bad for botching the arrest. You should have aborted when you realised your support was gone.'

Kat sprang at him, holding back only at the very last moment. She leaned over his desk, hands planted, and glared down into Carve-up's shifting eyes.

'It was only gone because *you* called it back!' She jabbed a finger at him, wishing it was curled round the trigger of one of those Glocks in the basement. 'This isn't over.'

Then, on the verge of tears as she thought of Tom's pale face as Rosemah and Ryan had carried him out to the ambulance, she left for the hospital.

Chapter Seventy-Four

The doctor standing in front of Kat had a speck of blood just under her chin. A great deal more spattered the front of her green scrubs and the scuffed yellow Crocs on her feet.

Dark circles beneath her eyes spoke of a long shift at Middlehampton General's A&E department.

Kat couldn't process what she'd just been told.

'Sorry, Doctor. Can you say that again, please?'

The young woman sighed. 'He lost a lot of blood before he reached us. We had to give him eleven units. The surgery was successful in that we repaired the damage to the femoral artery. But he didn't come round from the anaesthetic.'

Kat staggered back. A high-pitched ringing blotted out the doctor's next words.

The exhausted-looking doctor spoke clearly as she repeated her previous sentence.

'I'm afraid he's in a coma.'

'But if you closed up the wound and gave him all that blood, why isn't he awake?'

'Look, I know you want to hear something hard-edged and scientific, but the truth is, we just don't know.' She drew the back of her hand across her forehead. 'Sometimes trauma patients just don't come round. Not immediately, anyway. The stress to their bodies is too much and the brain shuts down to protect itself.'

'But how long will it take before he *does* wake up?'

'I don't know. An hour? A day? A week? I hope it will be soon, but at this point all we can do is monitor his vitals and keep him on drips.'

A painful lump had formed in Kat's throat. Swallowing against it, she asked if she could see Tom.

He was in a side room in the intensive care ward. He looked so fragile, like a little boy in a bed too big for him. Tubes and wires snaked into and out of him, connected to monitors, drips and other devices whose functions Kat couldn't even guess at.

She sat beside him and reached for his right hand. The index finger was clamped by a turquoise plastic clip like a clothes peg.

'Oh, Tomski,' she whispered. 'I'm so sorry. Carve-up did this. He tried his best to have us killed. I don't know why. I should never have let you come in with me. I mean, neither of us should. I should have aborted. Waited for another chance when we *did* have backup.' She bent over and pressed her forehead to the back of his hand. 'Please don't die, Tomski,' she whispered, her throat tight. 'Please don't die.'

All around her, the machines went on with their job of trying to keep the young man alive. Their electronic chirrups the only sound apart from the wheezing hiss of the ventilator.

Chapter Seventy-Five

The interview room was the unfriendliest in Jubilee Place. Tiny, overwarm, filled with a rich stink of bodily emissions of which sweat and bad breath were the least offensive. The neon tube overhead plinked and flickered.

It had taken three hours for a duty solicitor to turn up to represent Will Paxton. Kat had used the time to order a full search of the Paxtons' property. Once that was underway, she'd called Linda Ockenden and set wheels in motion to have Laura released from Bronzefield and all charges against her dismissed. Laura would go and stay with her parents at first.

She also chased Christopher Miller for the list of members present at the dinner where he'd lost his monogrammed tie. A task that had got lost in the frantic activity leading up to Will Paxton's arrest. When it arrived via email, she was not surprised to find Will's name on it. Obviously he was the 'friend' Carve-up had invited.

She pushed her anxiety about Tom and her rage at Carve-up into a squashed-down package and locked it away inside her. She'd go back to the hospital later, but for now she had to talk to the man who'd put him there. She faced Paxton now, with his nervous-looking solicitor fiddling with a ballpoint pen. Beside her, Leah sat, giving Paxton a level stare.

Kat repeated the official caution, this time adding her own name to the list of Paxton's victims.

'Will, how would you react if I told you we have CCTV footage of you at the scene of Callum Michie's murder, dressed all in black, wearing a disguise and bringing out a police baton from your trouser pocket?' she asked.

Paxton blinked. She knew what she'd just said had caught him by surprise. 'No comment.'

'I expect you probably surveyed the road for security cameras, doorbell cams, all that,' Kat said. 'But you missed the neighbour's Tesla. They're pricey, but you do get a nice little feature called Sentry Mode, did you know that? It doesn't matter. They do, and Mr Robinson's Tesla Model S caught you, minutes before Callum Michie was murdered, looking like a Poundland ninja. I'll ask you again. How do you react to that?'

Paxton stared at her levelly. 'No comment.'

'I see. How would you react if I told you that we subsequently found a police baton, specifically an ASP-21, commonly known as an "extendo", in your home office?'

He shrugged. A tiny smile flickered across his lips. 'I'm a serving police officer.'

'Of course. Extendos aren't standard-issue equipment for DCs, though, are they?'

'No comment.'

'You didn't steal it from a response officer at Hampton Lane, then?'

His smile vanished. 'No comment.'

'You see, while I was waiting for you last Friday, I overheard a conversation between two response officers. One was complaining about his gear being stolen. A thought occurred to me and I went back and I found that officer. Then I asked our forensic coordinator to compare his reference prints on the system to some we found on the baton. They were an exact match. So, Will, would you care to explain to us how PC Singh's extendo ended up in your desk?'

Paxton yawned. It came off as stagy to Kat. 'No comment.'

Kat turned her head fractionally to Leah.

Leah leaned forward. 'Did you murder Alanna Michie?'

He glared at her. His lip curled. 'I'm entitled to be interviewed by an officer at least one rank higher than my own.'

'At a disciplinary hearing, which it looks likely you'll be facing as well as criminal charges, yes. But this is a regular police interview. So I'll ask you again. Did you murder Alanna Michie?'

'No.'

'Did you murder Callum Michie?'

'No.'

Kat took over in a seamless move they'd agreed beforehand once Leah had pressed Paxton on the two murders.

'Where were you last Monday morning, Will?'

'At work.'

'Sorry, I should have been more specific. Where were you before work?'

'At home?'

'I see. At home.'

'Yes.' He smirked. 'Laura will confirm it.'

'I very much doubt that, Will.'

'Laura's a good girl. She'll do what's right.'

'Let's leave Laura out of it, for now. How did you feel when Laura made friends with Alanna Michie?'

'No comment.'

'Really? Can you explain why there is a home-made form in the office in your house where Laura has requested permission to have coffee with Alanna Michie and you've stamped it *Denied*?'

'No comment.'

'You didn't approve of Alanna Michie.'

Perhaps feeling he ought to do something to earn his fee, the solicitor spoke for the first time. 'What's your question, DS Ballantyne?'

'Did you approve of Alanna Michie?'

His lip curled. He could control his words, but not his facial muscles.

'No.' A shadow of a smirk. 'Comment.'

'I imagine it must have made you very angry, Will. Laura, the wife of an up-and-coming detective constable, socialising with the missus of a known criminal. A member of the notorious Strutt family, no less. I mean, hardly likely to impress the brass when it came to your sergeant's board, was it?'

His jaw muscles were bunching and squirming beneath the skin of his cheeks – which, she was pleased to see, were still only half shaved.

'Alanna Michie was a . . . a bad choice of friend for Laura. I was only doing what was right. She could do better. I only want what's best for her.'

'Is that why you let her play netball? Because there were a better class of woman on the team?'

He shrugged. 'You're on it, aren't you? A fellow police officer. It was appropriate.'

Kat swallowed down a surge of nausea. This man in front of her, calmly discussing which people were suitable for his wife to associate with.

'Why did you attack DC Gray when he tried to arrest you?'

'No comment.'

'Why did you try to strangle me with a golf club?'

'No comment.'

'OK, Will. Let me lay this out for you. I am confident that the baton we found at your property was the weapon used to murder Callum Michie. We're waiting for lab results to come back but I am also confident Callum's DNA will be present. Juries love DNA, you know that. We may even find your prints on it unless you always handled it wearing gloves like you did in the Tesla video. We also have video footage placing you at the scene while clearly trying to disguise your identity. That's way beyond what I need to take this to the CPS. They'll authorise me to charge you with murder.

'We also have, though these will obviously be lesser charges, the fact that you attempted to murder both DC Gray and me a few hours ago at your property. And this time, you weren't even the slightest bit careful. You left your DNA and prints everywhere. Plus, you know, we're kind of witnesses? What my DI would call a "slam dunk" on that one.

'Now, you probably thought you'd been clever when it came to Alanna Michie's murder. You stole a monogrammed golf club tie from Christopher Miller and used it to strangle her, hoping to misdirect our investigation. And it's true Mr Miller has no alibi for that morning. But Mr Miller has direct recollection of losing the tie at a so-called boys' night out at which it turns out you were present. It's not perfect, but frankly, he makes a more compelling witness than you.

'On its own, though, that probably wouldn't be enough to charge you with Alanna's murder. But here's the thing, Will. Your wife, who you've been coercively controlling for I don't know how many years, assaulting her, raping her, has discovered somewhere deep down in her soul a spark of *courage*. Given the kind of man you are, I'd call it an enormous spark. She has told me exactly what transpired on the morning of Alanna Michie's murder. And she's prepared to testify to that effect in court.'

'NO!' he roared, causing the slightly built lawyer sitting next to him to flinch and jerk sideways. 'The stupid little bitch can't. I forbid it. I FORBID it!'

Rather than tensing, Kat relaxed. She had him. And they both knew it. He glared at her, hatred twisting his features.

'Your days of forbidding Laura to do anything are behind you. She's going into the witness box and she's going to tell the court how you confessed to the murder. So that's two murders and two attempteds.' Kat turned to Leah. 'What do you reckon, DC Hooper?'

'Sentence-wise, you mean?'

'Yeah. How long will DC Paxton be spending inside? I mean, he ought to know, what with the fact he's still, just, a DC. But maybe with all the stress of the last week he's forgotten.'

Leah wrinkled her nose. 'Well, him being a cop's an aggravating factor, of course. That's not going to sit well with the judge, is it? Got to be twenty-five, minimum. Could be longer. Maybe a whole-life tariff?'

Kat shook her head. 'Leah's right, Will. It really isn't going to sit well. It's not going to sit well at all. Especially if it's a female judge. I notice you have a bit of a problem with women. Looks like it's going to get worse. And let's not even start on what happens to police officers in prison. You'll be spending your sentence on Rule 45. Imagine that. The rest of your life locked up on the beast wing with a bunch of nonces, grasses and bent coppers. Always looking over your shoulder. Never able to relax. Not even able to have a shower unsupervised.'

'DS Ballantyne, you're harassing my client,' the solicitor piped up.

'Compared to what he's done to his wife, let alone the Michies, I'd say my "harassment" is pretty inoffensive. But fair enough,' she said calmly. She turned back to Paxton. 'Will, I want to give you another chance to admit to your crimes and have at least something your brief can offer the court in mitigation, so I'll ask you again. Did you murder Alanna Michie?'

'No comment.'

'And did you murder Callum Michie?'

'No comment.'

'Why did you attempt to murder myself and DC Gray?'

'No comment.'

'Have it your way. Interview terminated at 4.47 p.m.'

She turned off the recorder.

'See you in court,' she couldn't resist adding.

From the interview room, Kat went straight to see Linda Ockenden. The meeting did not go as well as she'd hoped.

Chapter Seventy-Six

After laying out the case that Carve-up had deliberately put her and Tom's lives in danger by calling off the AFOs, Kat sat back, expecting Linda to launch an immediate investigation into the DI's conduct. Instead, Linda hemmed and hawed before saying that DI Carver was right. It was one man's word against another's.

Had the call been recorded? Kat had to shake her head. Well then, where was the evidence? And Kat *could* have stood down on her own account. She'd been the officer in charge and she'd put both herself and her subordinate at risk. If anything, Kat ought to be thankful *she* wasn't facing a disciplinary hearing.

'But Ma-Linda! We could have been killed! Talk to Tony Kaminski. He'll back me up. Carve-up told him to stand down.'

Linda's eyes flashed dangerously. 'I think, as this is a meeting about a very serious accusation, you should show proper respect to your senior officer. As I said, if DI Carver denies standing the AFOs down, you have nothing. Maybe it *was* an honest mistake. They do happen.'

'*Nothing* that man does is honest! He's a bent copper and you know it,' Kat burst out, instantly regretting it.

Linda drew in a breath and let it out in a controlled hiss. 'I'm going to pretend I didn't hear that remark. You're understandably concerned about Tom and you've also just survived a violent attack

342

by a murder suspect. You're traumatised. I want you to go and see one of the psych team right now. Get some counselling sorted. Three sessions minimum. Then concentrate on the case against Will Paxton. Because, at the end of the day, Kat, you caught him. I know I wasn't initially supportive, and you were contending with that ACU weasel, but you stuck to your guns. I'm proud of you.'

'But—'

'That's all, Kat.' Her look darkened. 'I mean it. That will be all.'

Kat got to her feet. How was this even happening? Just when she'd thought Linda would side with her, she'd revealed herself as brass through and through. Taking Carve-up's version of events when it was as clear as day that he'd actively sought to put her and Tom in danger.

Despairing, she closed Linda's office door behind her.

Counselling sounded about right. First question, what the hell was she doing trying to bring killers to justice when the biggest villain was sitting in his own expensively furnished office, thirty yards away?

Chapter Seventy-Seven

The following few days were some of the most stressful of her career. Tom had still not come out of his coma. And she'd had to grind her teeth through her initial therapy session with a psychologist.

On Friday afternoon, Kat was sitting at Tom's bedside, telling her bagman about the week's events as the monitors beeped and the breathing pump hissed. Her phone vibrated in her pocket, making her jump. She glanced at the screen: a text from Leah.

> Just heard Will Paxton hanged himself last night. Cellmate found him. He wrote

Kat swallowed down a surge of rage and shock. No. This was not how it was supposed to happen.

Paxton should have had to face justice in court. Confronted with the evil acts he'd committed, towards Laura as well as the Michies. Before being found guilty by a jury and sent away for life.

Instead, he'd taken the coward's way out. And presumably left a self-pitying suicide note behind him.

But as her feelings threatened to overwhelm her, a second text arrived. Leah must've hit send too early.

GUILTY on his forehead in lippy. Remorse is a terrible thing, huh?

Remorse? One thing Kat knew about violent, controlling men like Will Paxton: they were incapable of feeling remorse. They thought if they wanted something, they should have it. People who didn't see the world their way were wrong, plain and simple.

And why did he have a cellmate? Surely, as a cop, he'd have been subject to the strictest interpretation of the Rule 45 regime. Something didn't add up.

She called the prison.

Where she learned he'd never been on Rule 45 in the first place.

After a three-hour round trip to HMP Woodhill, she parked a few hundred yards down from the Hope and Anchor and marched back towards Frank Strutt's pub.

Frank was sitting at a corner table, a mug of coffee at his left elbow. He was running through till rolls and jabbing numbers into a big-button calculator. A pair of black-framed reading glasses of the type one could purchase in any supermarket or branch of Boots perched on the end of his nose.

He looked up as she sat facing him. Smiled widely, exposing his teeth. The lion that got the zebra.

'Kat, this is unexpected. What can I do for you?' He held up the mug. 'Want one? I just made a pot. Kenyan. Notes of stone fruits and chocolate.'

'I'm good, thanks, Frank. Did you hear the news about Will Paxton?'

Frank's face was open, pleasant and, apparently, uncomprehending. 'News?'

'Apparently he hanged himself last night.'

'Did he?' Frank asked in a reasonable facsimile of surprise. 'Well, you can't expect me to say I'm sorry to hear it, Kat. Not after what he did to Callum and Alanna.'

'No. But the thing is, Frank, before he killed himself, he wrote the word "guilty" on his forehead using a lipstick.'

Frank shook his head. 'I believe that's called poetic justice.'

'Maybe. But Will Paxton didn't strike me as the poetic sort.'

'Prison changes a man.'

'Not in three days, it doesn't. And the letters were surprisingly even. The right way round, too. Neat trick, given he didn't have a mirror.'

Frank frowned as he prodded at the calculator. Adjusted his reading glasses and peered at Kat over the frames.

'What's your point?'

'My point is, I went over to HMP Woodhill before coming to see you. Talked to the governor. It's weird, because apparently the prison never received a Rule 45 note for Will Paxton, so he went into gen pop. Weirder still, his new cellmate Jack Haines, the guy who raised the alarm, only got moved into Will's cell last night. And when I checked who'd visited him, do you know whose name I found?'

'Surprise me.'

'One Raymond Jeavons-Hume.'

Frank shrugged, tightening the thin white cotton of his shirt tight around his cantaloupe-sized deltoids.

'Jack's a friend of the family. Got himself into a spot of trouble recently. Maybe Ray went in to tell him to keep his pecker up. No law against it, is there? Offering a friend a little moral support?'

'None at all. It's just quite a coincidence, isn't it? Your Mr Fixit goes and sees one of your guys. The next night he gets a new cell, sharing with the man who murdered two members of your family.

A man who by rights ought to have been segregated. And the next morning, said man is found hanged – that is to say, strangled – with a lipsticked word on his forehead.'

'You've lost me, Kat. What are you saying?'

Kat leaned closer and dropped her voice. 'I think you sent Raymond to deliver your order to kill Will Paxton in revenge for Alanna and Callum. And you pulled strings to have Jack Haines transferred into Will Paxton's cell to carry it out. You made sure he had a red lipstick and told him to write that word on Paxton's forehead. How am I doing?'

He favoured her with an appraising stare in which she thought she could see dire purpose.

'Sorry, Kat. You'll have to excuse me. I'm settling my accounts.'

And Frank went on totting up numbers on the chunky, almost toylike, calculator.

Outside the pub, Kat took a deep, steadying breath. Maybe it was time to re-evaluate her relationship with Frank Strutt. She had a sick feeling she'd been incredibly naive. Thinking that because she knew Frank of old, and he gave her the odd titbit of intel, there was some mutual trust and, as Tom had said, respect.

But maybe she was more like one of those little birds that perched inside a crocodile's mouth, picking scraps out of their teeth. The crocodile didn't snap its long, toothy jaws shut because of respect. It was because it found the bird useful.

And when the little bird had flown off somewhere else, the huge reptile, a predator since the dawn of time, went about its business. In this case, ordering a murder. A murder she ought to investigate.

She shook her head. What was the point? She could just imagine Carve-up's reaction. And Linda's for that matter. Paxton had killed himself. Out of remorse. The evidence was right there. Oh, she could point to Raymond Jeavons-Hume's visit. To the screw-up over the Rule 45 note. But what would it achieve? A shrug of the brass's shoulders and a mumbled, 'These things happen, Kat. Let it go.' Maybe even a suggestion that justice had been served.

But that wasn't how Kat saw it.

She turned the news over and over in her mind as she drove home. She had less than an hour before they were due at her parents' house for a long-delayed family dinner and a confrontation with another powerful man.

Chapter Seventy-Eight

Leaving Van to pay the cab driver, Kat climbed out on to the gravel outside her parents' mock-Tudor house on Gadelands, a leafy private road. Her heart was racing, despite the large glass of Pinot she'd necked before leaving.

A gold-plated replica of the statue of Eros at Piccadilly Circus stood on one leg in the middle of a grassy island, looking as if he'd stumbled there drunkenly during a particularly debauched party.

Kat turned to Van, who'd joined her on the front doorstep.

He touched her on the arm. 'Ready?'

'Said the hangman to the condemned woman.'

'It's not that bad,' he said with a grin as the door opened and a small, hairy ginger-and-white . . . thing . . . raced out, barking like a demented wind-up toy before baring tiny needle-like teeth at Kat. Yapping manically, the ferocious little dog darted towards her ankles, forcing her to retreat.

'Jesus! What the hell!' she yelled. 'Bugger off, you ratty little thing!'

Yelping, it scuttled back inside between her mum's ankles.

'What have you done to Sidney?' Sarah Morton demanded.

'The little bastard was going to bite me!'

Her mum shook her head. 'Impossible, darling. Sidney's far too timid; he wouldn't hurt a fly. You must have scared him. He's very sensitive to people's auras. I only got him yesterday. He's still finding his feet, poor little thing.' She turned away before Kat could frame a suitable response. 'Ivan, you look lovely. Is that new aftershave I smell?'

'Hi, Sarah,' Van said, leaning in to kiss the proffered cheek. 'Just my usual. Imperial Leather.'

She poked his chest. 'Oh, *you*! So funny. Come on, Daddy's just opened the champers.'

'Are we heading for the *lounge*, Mum?' Kat asked, deliberately using a word she knew would wind her up.

'We are in the *drawing room*, darling.' Sarah rolled her eyes at Van, as if hoping to enrol him in her despair at her younger daughter's lack of sophistication. 'Nobody says "lounge". It's so, so . . . *déclassé*. Isn't it, Diana?'

'Hi, Diana, Eamonn,' Kat said as the two couples met on the threshold.

As she took in her sister's clothes, two emotions vied inside Kat. The first, embarrassment at her own far more modest outfit. The second, resentment. Just because Diana spent more on a dress than Kat earned in a month didn't mean she was a better person. Yet standing there in an emerald-green cocktail frock that set off her red hair, with what had to be diamond earrings and a matching pendant at her throat, Diana looked undeniably gorgeous.

Her father was standing by the grand piano, talking earnestly to Nathan. Clearly about the family business, into which he had recently inducted his son.

Leaving Van in conversation with Eamonn about the football, Kat made her way across the room to a heavily made-up young woman inspecting some silver-framed family photos. Nathan's girlfriend Kristeena, presumably. She'd been left alone and that didn't seem fair.

Her mum intercepted her with a hand through her arm. 'Now Kat's finally arrived let's all go through to the dining room,' she trilled.

Kat was dismayed but not surprised to see that her mum had laid out handwritten place cards for everyone. She found herself sandwiched between Eamonn, who she quite liked, and her father, who, it was fair to say, she didn't.

Van was miles away, saying 'a thorn between two roses' to Diana and Nathan's girlfriend, who rewarded him with a squeeze of his bicep and an adoring look that would have ignited asbestos.

For the entire first course, smoked salmon wrapped around grilled asparagus, the conversation around the highly polished oak table flowed like the wine, which Colin poured frequently, and generously.

But as they began applying wooden-handled steak knives to eight perfectly cooked sirloins, Colin turned to Kat.

'Did you enjoy that, Kitty-Kat?' he murmured, before dipping a cube of rose-pink steak into a puddle of Colman's English mustard and popping it into his mouth.

'It was lovely. Though everyone's wee is going to smell later.'

He frowned, then swallowed. 'Not the asparagus. Your little bit of theatre at the police station. I mean, really, bringing me in for questioning. Do you *seriously* think I'm capable of murder?'

The morsel of sirloin in Kat's mouth contained a chunk of fat. She kept chewing, but the rubbery blob disgusted her. She panicked at the thought of it sliding down her throat. She snatched her napkin off her lap and spat it out.

'Well, do you?' he persisted, sawing angrily at the meat and removing another chunk.

She glared at him, the alcohol fighting a losing battle against the adrenaline now flooding her system. 'You know what, Dad? Given the right circumstances, I think *anyone's* capable of murder.

351

You, me, Mum, even Princess Diana over there. It just needs the right trigger.'

'Well, nobody pulled mine. And I resent being dragged away from my business to answer a bunch of stupid questions from a couple of wet-behind-the-ears DCs.'

Heart pounding, Kat slammed her cutlery down on to her plate. Everyone looked round.

'Right! First off, they're not wet behind the ears. Leah's an experienced detective and—'

'—Tom's a recent graduate with precisely zero understanding of the real world.'

Breathing heavily, and ignoring Van's warning glance, Kat kept going. *Nobody* got to insult her team. Least of all Colin Morton, with his gladhanding of councillors and dodgy business dealings – *and involvement in murder!* her subconscious screamed. *Especially* not when Tom was lying in a coma at MGH.

'Well, he understands the way *you* work, Dad,' she snapped. 'I told him all about where that mysterious payment came from. Because in case you hadn't heard . . .' She turned to the table at large, taking in their startled expressions. 'Oh, yes, everyone, you'll be pleased to hear I've been cleared of taking bribes. Because, guess what? The mystery benefactor who sent me fifty thousand quid from an offshore trust in the Bahamas in an attempt to send my career down the toilet was my dear old dad. Wasn't it, Dad? And oh my God!' She pressed her palms together. 'I never even *thanked* you.' She laid a hand on his arm. 'I'm giving it all to a women's refuge right here in town.'

Her breath coming in rapid, shallow gasps, Kat grabbed her dad's glass, hers being empty, and drained it. The room swam for a second, then settled. Across the table, Van's expression was as readable as a large-print book. *Well done! Now let's try to get out of this in one piece.*

352

Her father stared at her, mouth hanging open. A bright yellow blob of mustard spotted his chin.

In contrast, her mother's face bore an expression of animal ferocity. Eyes flashing. Nose wrinkled. Pale pink frosted lips drawn back from her teeth, on which Kat could see a fleck of lipstick on one canine.

'How *dare* you speak to your father like that! He would never do *anything* to hurt you. *Any* of you,' she added, swinging her wine glass round in a circle to encompass her three children. The action resulted in a sizeable quantity of Australian Shiraz-Cabernet sloshing on to the white damask tablecloth. 'Oh, Kitty-Kat! *Now* look what you've made me do! It's *ruined!*'

Kat got to her feet. 'You're drunk, Mum. And I'm sure you can bung it into the machine. Just turn the dial to "white wash". You know, like dad uses for his business deals.'

Sarah Morton was down but not out. She also stood, staggering slightly and grabbing Nathan's shoulder for support. She pointed a pink-nailed finger at Kat's heart like a spear.

'Your father is a property genius! All this?' Another wide-swinging hand, now mercifully free of a wine glass. 'That's Daddy's business acumen made flesh. Anyway,' she said, sitting back heavily in her chair, 'Suzy handles all the banking, not him. He's *far* too busy for all that boring financial stuff.'

In the ensuing silence, loud as a block of shoddily built flats being dynamited, Kat looked down at her father. He was glaring at her mum as if he wanted to kill her. Talk about finding the right trigger.

Kat resumed her own seat and turned to her father.

'Is that right, Dad?' she murmured. 'You get Suzy to do your dirty work, do you?'

'I'm not sure this is the appropriate forum for a discussion of that kind, Kitty-Kat.'

It was a decent enough attempt at a patronising put-down. And it might have worked, once. But not now.

She tipped her head to one side. 'No? You're probably right.' She put her knife and fork together and signalled with her eyes to Van that she wanted to go, then leaned closer. 'Maybe we should save it for an interview room, eh?'

Lips tightened into a thin line, he favoured her with a long, hard stare. But, beneath the scent of his Aramis aftershave, she detected another, instantly recognisable smell.

Fear.

Chapter Seventy-Nine

Halfway home, Kat turned to Van and asked him to drop her off at the hospital.

'I need to see Tom. I'll get a cab home. Don't wait up.'

Her badge got her a personal escort to Tom's room in the High Dependency Unit.

In the darkness, Tom's right cheek glowed a greenish-blue in the reflected light of the EEG screen. A steady once-a-second beep punctuated the silence, shifting in and out of phase with the asthmatic wheeze of the ventilator.

The room smelled of disinfectant.

Alone with her comatose bagman, she took his hand in hers, careful not to dislodge the pulse oximeter clipped over his index finger. She spoke quietly, barely audible over the wheeze and hum of the life-support machines.

'Oh, Tomski, I made allowances for my dad and now I think I've been blind to what was right in front of me. Carve-up's in his pocket. I always suspected it. But I never dreamed it went this deep. They tried to get me kicked off the force on a corruption charge, and when that didn't work they tried to set us up so Paxton would kill us. Why would he do that unless he's got some massive secret he's frightened I'm going to discover? I told him I'd leave him alone unless I discovered he'd murdered somebody. But what if he has?'

A giggle threatened to escape her lips. She imprisoned it behind clenched teeth. When she had herself under control again, she risked saying it out loud.

'I mean what if he literally killed someone? He's in construction. He could have buried the body in the foundations of some building he's put up right in the town centre. Like the bloody mafia.'

She shook her head.

'I'm getting ahead of myself. I know that, Tomski. The first question is, who really sent that money? Was it him? Or was Mum right? Did Suzy do it?' She squeezed his hand. 'You have to get better, Tomski. You have to wake up. I need you.'

The machines beeped. The ventilator heaved up and down.

And behind translucent lids in which tiny blue veins pulsed, Tom's eyes darted left and right, up and down, like trapped birds.

ACKNOWLEDGEMENTS

I want to thank you for buying this book. I hope you enjoyed it.

As an author is only part of the team of people who make a book the best it can be, this is my chance to thank the people on *my* team.

For sharing their knowledge and experience of The Job, former and current police officers Andy Booth, Ross Coombs, Jen Gibbons, Neil Lancaster, Sean Memory, Trevor Morgan, Olly Royston, Chris Saunby, Ty Tapper, Sarah Warner and Sam Yeo.

For their patience, professionalism and friendship, the fabulous publishing team at Thomas & Mercer led by Eoin Purcell and Sammia Hamer. My editors past and present, Jane Snelgrove, Jack Butler, Vic Haslam, Leodora Darlington and Kasim Mohammed; development editor Russel McLean; copy-editor Gemma Wain and proofreader Gill Harvey. Plus the wonderful marketing team, including Rebecca Hills, Jessica Sharples, Hatty Stiles and Nicole Wagner. And Dominic Forbes, who, once again, really smashed the brief with another awesome cover design.

The members of my Facebook Group, The Wolfe Pack, are an incredibly supportive and also helpful bunch of people. Thank you to them, also.

And for being an inspiration and source of love and laughter, and making it all worthwhile, my family: Jo, Rory and Jacob.

Andy Maslen
Salisbury, 2024

ABOUT THE AUTHOR

Photo © 2021, Kin Ho

Andy Maslen was born in Nottingham, England. After leaving university with a degree in psychology, he worked in business for thirty years as a copywriter, while also continuing to write poetry and short fiction. In his spare time, he plays blues and jazz guitar. He lives in Wiltshire.

Follow the Author on Amazon

If you enjoyed this book, follow Andy Maslen on Amazon to be notified when the author releases a new book!

To do this, please follow these instructions:

Desktop:

1) Search for the author's name on Amazon or in the Amazon App.
2) Click on the author's name to arrive on their Amazon page.
3) Click the 'Follow' button.

Mobile and Tablet:

1) Search for the author's name on Amazon or in the Amazon App.
2) Click on one of the author's books.
3) Click on the author's name to arrive on their Amazon page.
4) Click the "Follow" button.

Kindle eReader and Kindle App:

If you enjoyed this book on a Kindle eReader or in the Kindle App, you will find the author 'Follow' button after the last page.

Printed in Great Britain
by Amazon

46072026R00209